Inimicus

Inimicus

The 11th Percent Book 4

T.H. Morris

Dedication

This book is dedicated to Ariel Mathis, Donna Moore, and Melannie Johnson Savell, for helping me make it as crisp, clean, pristine, and sharp as humanly possible, and also dedicated to Matthew William Harrill, who took it through his world-famous Acid Test, and declared it worthy.

Acknowledgments

Man. The 11th Percent Series, Book Four. Number four. Can't believe that I'm here. And I thought that I was accomplished when I got the *first* book released. To think, there is more to come, but it's those present moments...those present victories...that we celebrate right now. That said, I would never ever say that I got this far by myself. The tight core of supporters that surrounded me from the beginning is still here. To my family-you're the best. I wouldn't be the man that I am now had I not been blood-bound with you, experiencing your tutelage, support, love, and camaraderie. You're irreplaceable, I mean that. My beautiful wife Candace still challenges, inspires, and motivates me to be a better man. She was my first fan from Minute One, and remains so to this day. Dzintra Sullivan, thank you for always being a great friend, supporter, and inspiration. I'm so glad that your own creative contributions are soaring to such heights! Patti Roberts of Paradox Book Designs is an icon in my eyes now. I swear, this woman has the ability to take one's mental vision out of their head, and turn it into a creative masterpiece. One of my favorite moments is when I give her the ideas and themes that the next book will convey, and she says, "Leave it with me." When she says that, I know she gets it, and I punch the air in victory every single time! Tiffany Wyke, Joe Compton, Jessica Wren, Amanda Hoey, Jon Lowery, Margot Robinson, Jared Mingia, Brenda Jarrett, Patrick Foster...where would I be without you guys? I can answer that...I don't even want to know. Cynthia D. Witherspoon, my informal sister and collaborator in the Chronicles from the Other

Side series, it's always a blessing to hear your ideas, create new lore and lit with you, and to have your support.

And the people that the book is dedicated to, Ariel Mathis, Melannie Johnson Savell, Donna Moore…you guys mean the world to me. Due to your assistance with this book, I will call you guys the chains on this bike that is Inimicus, because you kept things in motion. You are truly an amazing group of women, and an invaluable asset to this craft. And the final person the book is dedicated to…Matthew William Harrill, author extraordinaire and creator of The Acid Test. You're the best in the world, man. I thank you abundantly and genuinely for always being real and direct, yet informative and unswervingly helpful at every turn. I can honestly say that I am happy that my book and I took your Acid Test, and passed with flying colors! The list goes on and on…just like I said in Lifeblood, if I named everyone, it would be a book all by itself. So I will simply say thank you from the bottom of my heart and soul, and I could have never done these things without you. Trust and believe that.

Contents

1

The Crystal Diner

Jonah's dream started off odd enough, but then it got worse.

He was in a palatial bookstore, clad in a slate-grey button down, matching blazer, and his reading glasses. He had his own table, engulfed by books with eerily blue covers that all bore his pen name, J.J.A Rowe. The huddled patrons that surrounded him were gleeful, exuberant, and impatient. They all held books of their own, which all bore Jonah's pen name. The scene was absolutely perfect. As a matter of fact, if there were a word above "perfect," Jonah might say that the word didn't do the scene justice.

The problem was the fact that Jonah had had this dream before.

On a summer evening a couple years before, Jonah had experienced this same scene. He sat right here (even the attire was the same) amidst a sea of people who wanted their books to be autographed. The activity had been invigorating and fun, but then it was derailed by the appearance of a frightening figure that'd been dread-locked and pale. He gave Jonah harsh critiques and made no secret that he doubted Jonah's ability to handle some "coming storm." Then the scene worsened as black crows descended into the crowd outside, and the people became savages. It was as if the presence of the crows triggered primal and evil behaviors in the populace.

With that old scene still sharp in Jonah's mind, he scanned this new one for any variations. There didn't appear to be anything sinister here. There wasn't anything but mirth and marvel on every face that he saw. He even recognized some of the faces in the crowd: his best friends Terrence and Reena, Kendall Rayne, Reena's girlfriend and Jonah's former professor, Vera Haliday, Bobby Decessio, Liz Manville, and Malcolm Mercer. Even Royal Spader was there, deftly picking an oblivious patron's pocket. But the familiar faces did nothing to assuage Jonah's anxiety. In that previous dream, he'd witnessed his friends get trampled in the crowd.

Despite all of the activity and suspicion, one question nagged at his mind: How was he aware that he was in a dream? He knew that this was a dream. He had no doubts about it. The whole huddled masses thing was a sham, because he knew in the back of his mind that his writing career had yet to take off. That damnable writer's block hadn't faded, although Kendall's Creative Writing class did wonders for his confidence. But he pushed that thought away. It helped nothing at the moment.

"Okay," he said above the din, "what's going on?"

"About time," said an unfamiliar voice.

When the person spoke, all the people froze, as though someone hit a PAUSE button somewhere. Jonah rose and saw a new figure.

It was a black man whose clothing and demeanor were unlike anyone else's. With his severe haircut, dark brown jacket, black cargo pants, and black boots, Jonah thought that he resembled a modern-day cowboy, sans all the dust. But what wrecked the profile for Jonah were the bow and arrows, which were neatly strapped to the guy's back.

"I was wondering when you were going to ask that question," said the man quietly.

Jonah surveyed the new figure. "Um, you didn't happen to bring a gang of crows with you, did you?"

The man laughed. "No crows, Jonah. This isn't a reproduction of the dream you had all that time ago. I simply manufactured the setting because literary fame is where your heart is."

Jonah straightened. "Manufactured?"

"Yes," nodded the man. "Fashioning dreams is one of the attributes of Protector Guides."

"You're a Protector Guide?" Jonah narrowed his eyes. "And you guys can fashion dreams? Jonathan never did that."

The Protector Guide shrugged. "We all have free will, Jonah. That is just as true for Spirits as it is for physically living beings. But I enjoy fashioning dreams because the dream realm is more interwoven with the spiritual realm than you know."

"So why did you wait to reveal yourself?" asked Jonah.

"Because you had to verbally acknowledge that this was a dream," said the guide simply. "It was my dream, but this is your mind. Free will, remember?"

Jonah nodded, thankful to have finally encountered a Protector Guide that was concise. It was a welcome change. "So why did you do this? Why are you here?"

The guide's brown eyes darkened somewhat. "There are things that you need to see. Protectors can't interfere, but we can alert. Listen to me very carefully. You need to pay attention to every detail that you can, because this is a Spectral Event that cannot be repeated. My ethereal powers will be rather taxed, so when the Event blanks out, you will have seen all that I am able to show you. One more thing: fine-tune your senses. You are an ethereal human, after all. Focus on feelings. Not every living being on Earth and Astral Plane has to resort to noise from their mouths to communicate."

"Um, okay," said Jonah, eyeing the Protector Guide. "May I ask why? And who are you, by the way?"

The guide looked Jonah in the eye. "Things may very well be changing, Jonah. Upheaval. It would be unfair to be caught unawares. Now, activate your Spectral Sight. You will see the things that I'd like you to see."

"But what about these people you froze—?"

Jonah gestured to all the fans, but his voice trailed off when he realized that there wasn't a single soul in sight. He looked at the guide in alarm.

"I created them for a level of comfort," he explained, "although that didn't quite work the way I hoped. Now go into Spectral Sight. And to answer your other question, my name is Daniel."

"Alright then," said Jonah, who had no desire to dwell on the fact that he was taking all of this on faith. "Thanks for—whatever, Daniel."

"Don't bother committing my name to memory," warned Daniel.

"Why?" questioned Jonah as he took a deep breath and willed the actors to perform in his mind.

"Because you won't remember it when you wake," answered Daniel. "Plus things may be quite hazy."

"Wait, what?" said Jonah quickly, but now that his eyes were open and his Spectral Sight was activated, Daniel and the bookstore scene were gone.

Because of the inauspicious tone in Daniel's voice, Jonah didn't know what to expect. Dark spirits and spiritesses? Minions (if there were any left)? Someone hurting spirits from a Spectral standpoint?

But he didn't see any of those things. He saw a cozy diner that bore a bright white sign which identified the place as *The Crystal Diner- Where the Cooks Shine and the Food's Fine.*

Jonah frowned. Since when had his Spectral Sight revealed hole-in-the-wall diners? Was the place haunted or something?

Jonah noticed that a light rain dampened everything, but as he was in Spectral form (or dream form or whatever), it had no effect on him. That was good. He couldn't very well be all sleuth-like and whatnot if he had to focus on dryness.

As a slim, hooded patron entered the diner, Jonah tried to gauge the surroundings. The Crystal Diner was comfortably tucked between a Meineke and a BP gas station, both of which were closed. Factoring in the density of the night sky, Jonah surmised that it was very late. Must be one of those twenty-four-hour spots.

While Jonah still wondered why Daniel saw fit to show him a diner, someone edged into his line of sight. He wasn't hooded like the previous patron. He was a slim man with an angular face and hair the color of rust, which looked slick due to the increasing rain. He favored his left side as he moved to the diner, as though he'd recently been in a scuffle or the weather had aggravated arthritis. But that wasn't what caught Jonah's attention. He remembered what Daniel said about focusing on feelings. And gauging this guy's feelings wasn't troublesome at all. It was frightening how easy it was to do. Maybe it was because of Jonah's current dream form, but he was well aware of the man's emotions. And they unnerved him.

This man with the slight build and the hampered left side was evil. There was no other word for it. Pernicious, calculating waves just radiated off of him. It felt like he not only did evil things, but got enjoyment out of them.

The vibe was so strong that, even in this dream form, it made Jonah almost nauseous.

Jonah followed the man into the diner without hesitation. The place wasn't exactly buzzing, but he attributed that to the fact that it was nearly four in the morning, according to the clock near the restrooms. There were several customers in the place in addition to the slim, evil guy. A truck driver at a stool was digging into a plate of steak and eggs, which made Jonah shudder. The eggs seemed to be over easy, which he found disgusting. There was a man in a booth sipping at steaming coffee, and a woman seated in the rear, with her back to everyone. Jonah realized that this was the customer who walked in prior to the slim man and himself. She'd removed her hood, and her blond hair was in shambles around her face. Jonah couldn't make out her face due to the wet strands that obscured it, but he didn't need to. She was frustrated. There was no question.

"Mornin', sir!" said a jovial man from behind the counter. Jonah guessed that he must be the owner of the diner. He was a rosy-faced guy with curly hair and a rotund belly. He resembled what Santa might look like if he dyed his hair and decided to take a day job.

The man barely acknowledged the salutation and seated himself near the register. The owner, undaunted, moved toward him with a menu and a pitcher of water in tow.

"Y'know, you been coming here at this hour for 'bout two weeks," he said in a conversational sort of way, "and you never say much. Are you alright?"

The man gave a ghost of a nod, took the menu, and pointed to a platter that consisted of sausage, eggs, and grits. Jonah hoped with everything in him that the waiter would take the guy's order and just leave him be, but he wouldn't take the hint.

"Very good choice, sir!" he went on. "I'll have it out to you in no time! You'll have to forgive me, but I'm gonna keep working on you. Ma said kindness is always the best weapon!"

The slim man looked the owner in the eye, and Jonah gauged his intent with horror. But just then, the scene changed once more.

He now stood in a widely-shaped room. The place looked as if it had been quite a sight at one time, but had become dreary and derelict with age and passage of time. Dusty furniture lined one wall, and an ancient rug took up the entire floor. Jonah couldn't help but notice that every piece of furniture, every detail, and every object in the room seemed trained on one thing in the room: a handsome fireplace, unlit and barren. The wide chasm of darkness within must have been a stark contrast to the roaring flames which undoubtedly dominated it in days long since past.

Jonah walked to the window and looked outside, but he saw no identifying characteristics on account of the darkness of night and the pouring rain. He tried very hard to make out something outside before a sharp gust of wind brought his attention to the center of the room. A figure in dark clothing stepped out of nothingness and tossed a twig at the fireplace. Jonah's eyes narrowed. Twig portal meant Spirit Reaper.

The person pulled out a tiny flashlight, knelt at the fireplace, and moved a small tile to reveal a box. Placing the flashlight between their teeth, the person pulled out a handkerchief that had recently been saturated with blood. Jonah's eyes widened. What was going on here?

The figure in black wrung the handkerchief, and several droplets of blood dripped into the box, which appeared to be full of ashes. Apparently satisfied, the figure tossed the handkerchief aside, gathered some of the bloodied ashes and tossed them into the fireplace.

Flames rose instantly, mighty and high. Jonah jumped backward. What the hell had been in that blood? Gas?

He was also unnerved by three other things about this fire. The first was the fact that the flames seemed to expand and contract, like the fire was breathing. The second thing was that the flames, bright as they were, seemed tinged with blackness. The final—and most daunting—thing was the temperature. The room chilled when the flames burst forth. The fire burnt cold.

"*Transcendant, I desire your presence.*"

Jonah noticed that these words came across his mind, much in the same manner that Bast intimated her thoughts. He frowned; why would someone intimate thoughts to an icy fire?

For several seconds, nothing happened. Then the flames took on an even darker tinge, and the room's temperature dipped lower.

"*I am here.*"

Jonah was glad that he was in dream form, because he spat an involuntary exclamation that would have surely betrayed his presence if he'd been physical. Though the words were in intimated form—Jonah heard no voices—the feeling from them was venomous. It chilled the blood.

"*The implementation of the lambs' schemes has begun,*" intimated the figure in black. "*Just like you said.*"

The fire cackled for many moments. "*That is pleasing news.*"

The figure straightened somewhat. "*I will never disappoint you, Transcendent.*"

The fire breathed for a little while. "*Those are refreshing words, given recent events. We have had much to repair, thanks to the 49er's audacity.*"

The figure's head tilted slightly to the right. "*Transcendent, I was opposed to the 49er's involvement from the minute one. I've been itching to kill Jonah Rowe since he dared cross into your zone. It should have been me all along—*"

The flames rose to a frightening height, and had enough force to knock the figure in black flat on their back. Jonah could see that the fire pulsated with unmistakable rage. Despite the dark tinge, the fire shone with such brilliance that it was too much for Jonah's eyes, and he shielded them, though he could still see the flames through his eyelids. Movement prompted him to glance through his eyelashes, and he saw that the figure in black was no longer prone. The person now prostrated before the flames.

"*Forgive me, Transcendent, my words moved faster than my thoughts—*"

"*Never question me,*" intimated the flames, and Jonah could almost hear the growl that would have been present had the words been voiced. "*I had my reasons for using the vampire, as you very well know. Despite his mutinous blunder, he had some advantages nonetheless.*"

Jonah's eyes flew open at those words, though his pupils ached due to the brightness of his flames. What was this about the 49er? What mutiny? What blunder? And he had had some advantages? What had he done right?

"*Do you have it?*" intimated the flames.

The figure straightened with pride. "*I do, Transcendent.*"

The figure withdrew a corked vial from a pocket and placed it on the floor. It was full to the brim with what could only be blood.

"*Yes,*" intimated the flames. "*The other item as well. Place it here before me.*"

The figure obeyed, and Jonah was so shocked that he nearly fell backward.

The figure lowered down a thick card, which illustrated a sheathed sword and a closed eye.

The Inimicus card.

Jonah felt a chill that had nothing to do with the contradictory fire.

"*I got it seconds after the 49er threw it on the ground,*" intimated the figure. "*I had to wait for Rowe to leave the area, or he'd have seen me.*"

"*You have done well, Inimicus,*" intimated the flames. "*Now lower your hood. I tire of my own disciple wearing a disguise in my presence.*"

The figure began to lower the hood, but at that very moment, the scene began to blink and fade. Alarmed, Jonah realized that Daniel's power over this Spectral Event must be dissipating.

"NO!" he shouted out loud. "I need a few more seconds, Daniel! WAIT!"

But Jonah found himself shouting the last word to a sunlit ceiling. He'd awakened at last.

2

Spiritual vs. Physical

Jonah stayed prone on his bed, wide-eyed, winded, and disoriented.

That was one of the strangest dreams, visions, or whatever it was, that he'd had in his life, and that was saying something. It had been so jam-packed with details that he didn't even know where to begin, but when he tried to start, his brain seemed somewhat short-circuited. Some Protector Guide—at least he thought, because it was hard to re-call—had reconstructed a damnable dream he'd had once before, and then invited himself into it. He'd known everything about Jonah, but Jonah barely remembered a thing about him. If Jonah concentrated very hard, he could almost recall that the guide promised that he'd forget his name, and damn if he hadn't been right. Jonah couldn't even remember what the guy's name sounded like.

He closed his eyes tightly. The trick of only looking into his mind had assisted with rejoining mental puzzle pieces in the past, but it didn't seem like it would oblige him this particular morning. But he had to try something. The information seemed too important to let it slip away.

There had been a café—no—a diner. He couldn't remember the name of that, either. Some morning customers got an early start on feeding their faces, and there was also a portly, annoying waiter that pestered a guy who seemed... off.

Jonah frowned as he lay in the tangle of blankets. His memory got hazier by the second.

The scene shifted to some sort of room. Yeah. That was right. He'd been in a room where some person dripped blood in ashes and roused a cold fire. A cold fire that—spoke?

Did Jonah remember that right? No, he hadn't. The fire hadn't actually spoken. Jonah had seen words splashed across his mind. That cold fire and the hooded person intimated a conversation through thought. They hadn't spoken a single word.

He shook his head. Things were fading like trapped heat from a window in winter.

Stop trying to recall everything, he scolded himself. *Focus on the essentials.*

And there *were* essentials. That hooded person intimated something about "lambs" moving forward with some plan, and there had also been something about how they'd been itching to kill Jonah Rowe.

Itching to kill him.

Then Jonah remembered something with perfect clarity. It was the one recollection that no amount of hazy memory would deter.

The Inimicus card.

That word and that card prompted Jonah to pull himself from the bed and stand so as to allow blood to flow through his body in a simpler way.

Jonah remembered that the presence in the fire referred to that hooded person as Inimicus. That damned word again. Jonah had very little knowledge of it, but the bit that he did know was unnerving enough.

A few months ago, the 49er, a vampire who also happened to be one Creyton's most loyal followers once upon a time, had a fit of reckless ambition and attempted to take Creyton's place as Alpha. When it became clear that his plot would flop, he'd thrown a card on the ground that depicted an open eye, an exposed blade, and the term Scius. But Jonah witnessed the card transform into a new picture that showed a closed eye, a sheathed blade, and the term Inimicus.

Jonah's friend, and resident Latin expert, Malcolm Mercer told him that Scius and Inimicus were "gloved" cards in a mythological game. Scius was the obvious enemy, while Inimicus was the enemy you never saw coming. It was supposed to be a game, a myth… but this was the second time Jonah had seen the supposedly mythological term.

The presence in the flames identified that disguised figure as Inimicus. Who was that cloaked person? It had to be that guy from the diner. Who else could it have been?

The hooded figure made it clear that they wanted to kill Jonah, and that guy certainly looked capable of killing.

That jolly waiter hounded that man in an attempt to get him to show emotion. And then Jonah saw the cloaked figure drop blood into a box of ashes. That couldn't have been coincidental.

The one thing that Jonah couldn't understand was why the man bothered to disguise himself. He hadn't done so at the diner, so it seemed, at least to Jonah, to be a pointless triviality. It wasn't like he could know that someone in a dream state watched him walk into the place, could he?

A faint smack made Jonah jump and turn, but he shook his head. His wallet, which he'd perched on the bedside table the night before, had fallen and hit the floor. Jonah picked it up, and looked over some of the things within it: his driver's license, his check card, a faded picture of his grandmother, and an as-yet-unused blank check. It was the blank check of all things that pulled on Jonah's attention. Not the possibilities that it provided him, but its source, Turk Landry. That man was an appallingly opportunistic Eleventh Percenter who used his ethereality to pose as a psychic medium and made himself obscenely rich in the process. But the guy had one good quality: a remarkably sharp spiritual attunement.

Jonah made a wry face. Spiritual attunement was something he wished he had at this particular moment. He'd been so sharp in that dream-vision; connections made sense, shifts and transitions were like unthinking reflexes, and he'd gleaned so much just from people's feelings. For God sakes, he'd witnessed a mental conversation, and got every word. But that was a dream form. A spiritual form.

That was all well and good, for as long as the ride lasted. But now he was back in physical form.

The Protector Guide warned Jonah that he wouldn't remember his name and many other things when he woke up. He recalled that part just fine. It was almost as if the Guide had thrown Jonah a bone with a...Spectral Event? Yeah, that's what he'd called it. Thrown him a bone from a spiritual standpoint while conceding that his wakeful, third-dimensional mind would maintain all that he'd seen.

"Thanks for that," grumbled Jonah. "Whatever your name was."

If only Jonah had a way to remember as much information as he could before it disappeared like snowflakes in hell...

Something registered in Jonah's mind, and he looked out of the bedroom window. Despite looking, he didn't really see anything, because he only registered one thing in his mind. His writing.

It was interesting how Jonah only had this realization now. He's always been a writer, but was plagued with a deep writer's block that was lenient enough for him to write editorials and school assignments, but not enough for him to write full-fledged novels.

He shook his head so as to detach the negative. Those were concerns for another day. It wasn't like he wanted to write a novel at the moment. He just wanted to maintain important data.

The thought, however annoying, gave Jonah an idea. He grabbed a pen from the bedside table, open his notepad that he used for his grocery lists, and began to pace, racking his brain.

"Approach it like a story," he whispered to himself. "Like a story. Where does it start?"

He walked to the notepad, scribbled the words, "*It Starts,*" and resumed pacing.

It was indeed a challenge, because a great many of the memories had already slipped away.

"Come on, Jonah," he prodded himself, "no need to focus on the negative. The story started—in a dream! A manufactured dream!"

He wrote that bit down on the notepad and left it again.

"Okay...the dream...which led to...led to..."

He shrugged and jotted down the words, "*Led To.*"

"The next part's easy," he told himself. "The diner with the evil psycho."

Jonah recorded that.

"That was pretty quick right there," murmured Jonah. "The diner, which switched to the creepy room."

He wrote some more.

"Blood and ashes—immaterial. But that cold fire...with that presence..."

Jonah attention sharpened. He knew that presence in the fire. There was no point deluding himself. It was Creyton's presence in that fire.

But how could that be? Creyton got destroyed—again—that night in S.T.R! He should be on the Other Side!

Jonah forced himself to focus. As jarring as that realization was, he had to focus on the Spectral Event. Had to write down details before they disappeared.

Painstakingly, he filed the questions about Creyton's presence away, and wrote down, "*Cold fire with Creyton's presence.*"

"Okay, okay," he mused. "Creyton was—was pissed about the 49er trying to take his place. That also ticked off this Inimicus person, who is itching to kill me."

Jonah scribbled down the final notes. He couldn't recall anything else. When he got the last note out, though, he noticed something that made his eyes widen even more than they did when he realized that it was Creyton's presence in that cold fire.

His random jotting of notes had actually created a haphazard message. He had been so deep in thought that he hadn't even realized what he had done. He'd just yanked fragments from his mind and put them down on paper. It seemed that throughout his yanking, he'd subconsciously attempted to make connections that his eyes hadn't seen.

He had to get his reading glasses to figure out all that he had written. The stilted, broken words seemed useless when he wrote them down, but when he read it as a whole, it took on a brand new meaning.

The broken notes translated to:
It Starts
With a manufactured dream
led to
the diner with the psycho
switched to
creepy room
cold fire with Creyton's presence
49er's screwup
led to Inimicus
who wants to kill me

Jonah stared at the message. His own writing told him that the man in the diner, who had to have been Inimicus, planned to rectify the 49er's failure and come after him. He wanted to succeed where the 49er had failed with his Haunts, mind games, and vampire army.

But now Jonah had to revisit the thoughts that he'd filed away. How could Creyton be in that fire? Jonah knew for a fact that Creyton's essence, or whatever it had been, got snuffed out that night in S.T.R. when Jonah rescued Vera and used the nurse's healing endowment to attack him. As Creyton's disguise had been artificial and impure, his form exploded the minute such pure essence hit him. So how did he get into that fire, and make it burn cold?

And where did Inimicus come into play? Was Jonah right about that guy in the diner? Was he the sheathed blade on the card, the embedded enemy that Jonah would never see coming?

But if that was the case, then the dude at the diner would be in for a rude awakening. According to Malcolm, Inimicus was supposed to be an enemy that you'd never expect in a million lifetimes. Thanks to Jonah's dream encounter with the Protector Guide, he'd already seen the guy's face.

He had to make doubly sure that the guy's image was another memory that didn't fade. He'd have to call Reena so she could do a sketch image STAT. If he could remember the guy's face, a name wouldn't be necessary. Jonathan could help him fill out all the blank places. If this guy was in league with Creyton, Jonathan probably knew everything about him.

Jonah just had to remember his face.

His thoughts moved back to Creyton's essence in that fire. What was his goal? To use his tool for vengeance? To live vicariously through his lackey?

Jonah looked over the words on the notepad and snorted. This wasn't the first time a strange message had been encoded in his own writing, and, though he went through some truly dangerous crap, all had ended in a Creyton's vanquishing. And now he was a damn fire who gave telepathic orders to a secret spy who wasn't so secret anymore. With Jonathan and his friends on his side, plus the fact that the secret guy wasn't so secret anymore, he liked his odds. He just had to call Reena to get the face sketched out.

He reached for his phone when movement from another room made him push the morning's thoughts away. It wasn't the time or place for them; he was a guest in someone's home. This would be a good day, and there was no room for fear or suspicion.

He returned his gaze to the window when the inevitable knock came.

"You up, Jonah?" said a voice that accompanied the knock.

"Yeah, Nelson," replied Jonah.

"You decent?"

Jonah shook his head. "Dude, did you think I went to bed in a damn speedo, or something? Come on in!"

Nelson opened the door, laughing as he did so. "You can never be too careful, man! Have you been up long?"

"A little while." Jonah filed the thoughts further away. "Had an odd dream, and needed to gather my thoughts and whatnot." Hey, it was true enough.

Nelson shook his head. "You're friends with the Sybil from the TV show now. You think those weird dreams come from hanging with her?"

Jonah snorted. "I'm certain that's not it."

"Well hey," Nelson shrugged, "she is a pretty woman."

Jonah raised an eyebrow. "You'd better not let Tamara hear you callin' some other woman hot."

"She knows she's the only one for me," said Nelson dismissively. "But come on, dude! She's got breakfast ready."

Jonah nodded and followed his friend, not even bothering to register the fact that all remaining thoughts of the morning's dream slipped away from his head.

3

The Brand New Home and the Same Old Bitch

Jonah was still familiarizing himself with Nelson and Tamara's new layout, but he knew that it was a definite step-up, since they'd upgraded from his old apartment.

When Nelson and Tamara had gotten married, Jonah had subleased his apartment to them. He became a full-time resident at the Grannison-Morris estate and no longer needed it. They'd been very grateful for the place then, and were excited to start their lives together.

Now, a year later, they were still as happy as ever. But, as Nelson had told Jonah, the aspect of living in an apartment had gotten old relatively quickly for them. As such, they had moved into a small house still within city limits. It had the total package: more room and space, and no noisy neighbors or tenant meetings. Jonah loved their place. He'd been their guest for nearly three days now and was excited about the evening's festivities. Their housewarming party coincided with their one-year wedding anniversary.

Jonah had to laugh when he saw Nelson slink up behind Tamara at the stove and kiss the back of her neck. He'd known that Nelson had been smitten with the woman ever since he'd first laid eyes on her in that shoe store, and a year of her company had only intensified how he felt. Jonah suddenly got a strange feeling in his gut that he couldn't really place. Then, as if his brain decided to catch up with his gut feeling, he wondered if he'd ever have that kind of excitement and comfort with a woman.

Where the hell had that come from?

"Alright, alright," he muttered, more to distract himself from the awkward thoughts than anything else. "Enough of that. You have a guest present."

Nelson chuckled, and Tamara turned to gaze over at Jonah in mock defiance, which was no less alarming. Her vividly blue eyes blazed with every emotion, even the play ones.

"Don't tell us what we can or cannot do in our own house," she scolded. "If I wanted Nelson to take me, right here in this kitchen, I'd kick you out without a moment's hesitation."

Jonah laughed. Yeah, Tamara meant it as a joke, but a lot of truth was said in jest. "Duly noted, ma'am," he played along.

Tamara's eyes softened somewhat, and her smile returned. "Did you have a good birthday last week?"

"Oh yeah." Jonah waved his phone at them. "I'm still getting text messages from people now."

Nelson and Tamara seated themselves at the table with Jonah, where they began to eat bacon, eggs, and waffles.

"I guess it's safe to say that your mid-to-late twenties have been interesting, huh?" Nelson asked him.

Jonah used swallowing the eggs in his mouth to mask the look of awkwardness he pulled. "You have no idea," he replied. "So how's Essa, Langton, and Bane?"

Tamara snorted. Nelson rolled his eyes.

"Interesting, much like your twenties," he answered.

"Really?" Jonah doled out a bit more syrup on his waffles. "How so?"

"First off, Langton hasn't been doing very well, health-wise." The indifference in Nelson's voice was testament to how big of an asshole Jonah's former boss was. "He's been missing stretches at work, and his wife's at her wit's end. And on the days he's actually in the office, he's not even strong enough to harass us about work."

"Aww," said Jonah with as little emotion as Nelson. "Years of bad choices, bad dealings, and bad food tend to have that effect. So what has he done? Delegate things to Jessica?"

"Mmm hmm," said Tamara instantly.

Jonah snapped his attention to her, and then back to Nelson. "Seriously? Jessica Hale practically runs the office?"

"Pretty much," said Nelson, with a roll of his eyes. "It's given her a rather high opinion of herself, which is saying something, since she had one already. It's a joke, really; she hasn't even gotten an official promotion from her current position."

"Now that you mention it," said Jonah with a frown, "what *is* Jessica's position?"

"The same thing it was when you were there," answered Nelson.

Jonah raised an eyebrow. "I didn't know what it was then."

"Neither did the rest of us," Nelson deadpanned.

Jonah and Tamara got a nice laugh out of that one. He couldn't imagine Jessica in a position of power like that, because she already had enough clout as it was because she was so far up Langton's ass (or was it the other way around?).

"I hope Langton's health improves soon," said Nelson after the laughter, "if for no other reason than to depose Her Highness."

Jonah's mind wandered. He remembered Jessica all too well. She was about four years older than he was, but her level of maturity made those extra years immaterial. She'd made Jonah's life a living hell from the first day they'd met, as she always seemed to be more aware of his shortcomings, more so than anyone else's. But she had Langton wrapped around her little finger for a myriad of reasons, the most obvious being her keen memory for gossip and her trampy outfits.

"You can ask her all about her experiences atop the food chain, Jonah," scowled Tamara, "when you see her tonight at the party."

"I'm sorry," said Jonah stupidly, "but say what?"

"You heard that right." Nelson gripped his fork a little more tightly. "She is gonna be here tonight."

"But why?" demanded Jonah. "I understand why you guys felt the need to invite her to the wedding, but why will have her in your house?!"

"Two reasons," said Nelson with little inflection in his voice. "The first one is self-preservation. If I've invited so many co-workers without her being one of them, we both know that there will be things said. I enjoy my job, and have been there this long because I've learned how to navigate through B.S. like that. And the second one," for some reason, most of Nelson's indignation evaporated, "well—let's just say that there is something I want you to see. I want you to have a good dose of entertainment before you've gone back to your friends in Rome, N.C."

When the party began several hours later, things were so light-hearted and warm that Jonah didn't even think about Jessica. It was fun to converse with Nelson's dad and Tamara's sisters, as well as former colleagues that he liked back in his accounting days like Fredrick Park, Cheyenne Usher, and Clayton Tarr. One person that he was most pleasantly surprised to see was Mrs. Souther, the receptionist whom everyone loved.

"Jonah Rowe," she said in that motherly tone of voice that he'd grown accustomed to back in his accounting days, "you look so well. And boy, you are wasting away!"

Jonah shook his head. His physique had made marked improvements since Reena had aided him in his ability to eat toward his body type. He still was far from a comic book hero, which was completely fine.

"I wouldn't say that, ma'am," he told her in a rather sheepish tone. "But I'm grateful for the compliment just the same."

Mrs. Souther motioned Jonah away from the door, so he wouldn't get struck with it by new arrivals. Once they had space, she eyed him in a shrewd sort of way.

"I wonder," she said to him, "whether or not you have someone special that's keeping you in line."

Jonah stood there for a moment, and then laughed. That was why Mrs. Souther got him over to the side. It had nothing to do with the door; she was just being her usual self. As worrisome as it was, he found it highly amusing.

Mrs. Souther raised her eyebrows, inviting him to share. What the hell.

"Well, I'm nowhere near marriage, like Nelson and Tamara," he obliged, "but um—there is this woman…"

He paused there. How to describe Vera? He wasn't really sure how to do it.

Mrs. Souther barely noticed the hesitation. "So you *do* have a lady that you've taken a liking to," she said. "You're together?"

"Well, no—"

"Why not?" prodded Mrs. Souther.

"I—" Now the experience wasn't so amusing anymore. "I-I just want to be patient, I suppose."

Mrs. Souther shook her head. "You kids. Patience has its virtues, but sometimes, you've just got to jump!"

It took them getting that far into the conversation for Jonah's face to warm. "Well, how is your job going, ma'am?"

Mrs. Souther's eyes narrowed, but she smiled. She acknowledged the change of subject, but had the willingness to roll with it. He loved this woman. "I'm retiring in eight months, son," she said with the tiniest trace of wistfulness. "I'm past the September of my years, but I don't expect you to get that reference—"

"I do," said Jonah without hesitation.

Mrs. Souther raised her eyebrows, which prompted Jonah to shrug.

"Nana was a huge fan of Sinatra," he explained.

Mrs. Souther smiled and nodded. "Good taste! But anyway, yes. I'll be free to do what I want in a few months. Jessica's even got me training my replacement."

The smile fell from Jonah's face as he choked back a scathing comment. "Well, if anyone deserves the rest, it's you, ma'am," he said instead. "Despite that, I'm sure that your expertise and advice will be greatly missed—"

"Change is necessary, Rowe," said a familiar voice.

Jonah closed his eyes, and employed the deep breathing techniques that he learned from Felix Duscere. Mrs. Souther's hand, which was on Jonah's forearm, tightened somewhat. Acknowledging her, he gave her a brief nod, braced himself, and turned to Jessica.

She'd cut her strawberry blonde hair to a chin-length bob style, which would have been a nice touch on any other woman. But this was Jessica. The French-tipped nails? Constant. The snug blouse? Of course. And the black skirt that was about the length of one of Tamara's dish towels? Jonah didn't expect anything else.

The hair may be different, but it didn't matter. Jessica Hale was the same old bitch.

"Change is necessary and natural," she continued, regarding Jonah with the usual distaste. "You either adapt, or perish."

Jonah took a level breath. Mrs. Souther actually gave a smile, which would have amazed Jonah had he not known she'd dealt with false people for years.

"Very good to see you Jess," came Nelson's voice, and suddenly, he was there with them. He hadn't changed either; he could sense and diffuse tension just as well as he did in the old days.

Jessica turned her gaze to him. "Got a housewarming present for you, Nelson," she muttered. "Tam should love it. Tony!"

Jessica actually snapped her fingers, and Anthony Noble bumbled into the door.

Jonah gaped in shock. Anthony was another former colleague. He might have been tolerable if he hadn't worshiped Jessica. He would have done anything for her to notice him and give him the time of day. Apparently, he had finally gotten his wish.

But if Jonah judged things just based off of this interaction, it was the furthest thing from a dream come true.

"Where were you?" Jessica demanded.

"Oh sorry, Jess," he mumbled. "I was only taking a call on the porch—"

"Hang up the damn phone," she snapped. "We're at a party; why are you taking calls anyway? Give Nelson the present."

Anthony complied with Jessica within seconds. Jonah was surprised he didn't bow as he did so. He glanced over and noticed Jonah's presence.

"Oh hey, Rowe," he said. "How's—?"

"I'm going to mingle," interrupted Jessica. "Go busy yourself with—I don't know. Just do *something*. It's a party, after all."

"Right, sweetie," said Anthony sheepishly.

He moved in for a quick kiss, but Jessica ducked out of the way with scorn.

"Are you out of your mind?" she demanded. "It took me thirty-eight minutes to properly apply this makeup!"

"Right! Right." Anthony's response was so sycophantic that Jonah could have gagged. "So sorry, sweetie."

He shuffled off, and Jessica sneered after him.

"Nice house, Nelson," she said, despite the fact that she hadn't seen anything past the living room. "Now, if you'll excuse me. Rowe, Marguerite."

Jonah's blood rose to a boil. *Marguerite?* Did the skank have no more respect for Mrs. Souther than that?

Mrs. Souther swallowed, but she didn't say anything. She patted Jonah's arm with a smile, crossed the room, and immersed herself in conversation with Tamara's mom.

Jonah unclenched his fists. "My God," he grumbled to Nelson. "What I wouldn't give for her to not be a woman for just five minutes."

"I know, Jonah," said Nelson, who looked as if he didn't appreciate the way Jessica had addressed Mrs. Souther, either. "But she and Anthony have been together for about six months now. It was rather random, too; she practically ordered him to ask her out when we were leaving work one day. You'd have thought he'd flown to the moon."

Jonah looked over at Anthony's slavish form across the room. "Well, he fell back to earth pretty fast, didn't he? How can that idiot, in good conscience, allow her to treat him like that? You'd think he was a one-legged, mange-ridden dog."

Nelson looked at Jonah in all seriousness. "Jonah, don't you get it?"

Jonah stared at his friend blankly. "Get what?"

"There is someone for everyone," said Nelson. "So it figures that he is the perfect dog...for the perfect bitch."

Jonah burst out laughing. Even his anger with Jessica faded. It was fun. So much fun that nothing could quell it. Not Jessica, not Anthony—and not Creyton's presence in a fire with his psychotic servant.

4

Green Aura, Green Envy

After two more days with Nelson and Tamara, Jonah bade them good-bye and was back on the road to Rome. In days past, the aspect of the end of a vacation was a depressing one. These days, however, things were much better.

The trip took about three hours. Jonah enjoyed so many things about it: his friends, good food, dependable pets, and invaluable guidance, at least on most matters. The very first time Jonah had awakened there, he'd been bewildered, injured, and as ready to return to his "real" life as ever.

That was then.

Now the place itself was a familiar comfort and had more aspects of reality than the so-called "real" world. It was the best thing since his childhood home with Nana.

Had he truly been freaked out by the place at one time?

He turned onto the rocky drive that led to the estate, knowing exactly who he'd see when he reached the end. He was already prepared for the mirth and probable tackle.

He got out of his car and glanced to his left where the gardens were. As expected, Liz Manville was there, straw hat atop her head and filthy gloves on her hands. As happy as he was to see her, it was who usually accompanied her in her horticultural exploits that he was more interested in seeing.

But the person with Liz wasn't Vera. She was a little shorter than Liz and had a straw hat of her own that appeared to be more of a hindrance than a help because it kept sliding down her face and blocking her vision.

"Hey Jonah!" Liz removed her gloves and hugged him. "I was looking for a reason to take a break!"

"Hey Liz," grinned Jonah as he hugged her back. "I was curious as to why you had a new addition today."

Liz looked Jonah in the eye, not fooled at all. Jonah could have grimaced. At twenty, Liz might still be very young, but she had never been one to ignore the obvious.

"Vera is in her room, watching some play," she told him, "and this isn't some new addition. It's my sister. Nellaina!"

The younger Manville girl was so focused on what she was doing that she hadn't noticed she was working alone. Liz calling her name roused her from her preoccupation, and she gave Liz an annoyed look.

"How many times do I have to tell you to call me Nella?" she moaned. "It's not that—"

Then she finally noticed Jonah.

"Oh!" She scrambled to her feet, and tore off the straw hat, which revealed brown pigtails. "You're Jonah Rowe! Sorry I didn't notice you before!"

Jonah wasn't surprised that she hadn't noticed him, as that straw hat had been too big for her head. Jonah could see the family resemblance now that he saw Nella's face. She seemed almost as chipper and perky as Liz, but Nella's eyes were very dark, almost black. She had a rather chubby frame, and her welcoming grin included braces.

Jonah loved her already.

"It's quite alright," he told her. "How do you know me?"

"Liz talks about you all the time!" she answered. "You're a great hero!"

Jonah blinked, and glanced at Liz, who smiled and shrugged.

"Jonah, you've saved more than your fair share of hides since you've been here," she reminded him.

Jonah felt some of his embarrassment fade, and he smiled at Nella.

"I appreciate the praise," he said. "You're a Green Aura, too?"

Nella nodded, though some of the light left her face. "I'm not as good as Liz and Sandrine—that's our oldest sister," she said when Jonah frowned. "But Mom says time will take care of that."

"And practice," added Liz.

Nella looked so sad that Jonah pitied her.

"Look, Nella," he said in a bracing tone, "I'm the Blue Aura, and there are a bunch of things that I still haven't got figured out. Your sister is the best Green Aura I know. So I know that you will be great, too."

Nella's smile was radiant, and she ignored Liz's blush. "I wish *I* were a Blue Aura," she said longingly.

"No, you don't," said Jonah automatically, and he turned to leave them to their work. Nella grabbed his wrist.

"Wait!" She seemed struck with inspiration. "Could you help Liz and me with the tilling?"

Jonah frowned as he looked at the next sequence of rows. They were strewn with weeds, and looked tight-packed and tough. He'd tilled earth in the past, and it was backbreaking, tedious work that he didn't feel like doing at the moment. "Sorry, but I hadn't really planned on yard work— and you seem to be doing a kick-ass job already—"

"Oh, come on, Jonah," said Liz, making her voice a bit supplicating. "Surely, you'd do this favor for your favorite little sisters...?"

The look that they gave Jonah melted his heart. But it annoyed the hell out of him, just the same.

"You'd better be glad I love you, Lizzie," mumbled Jonah, ripping off his polo. "And since you're her sister, I guess I love you, too, Nella!"

Both young women squealed with delight. Jonah didn't share their enthusiasm, but at the same time, being the big brother who helped out his little sisters wasn't all that bad.

After some toiling, extensive elbow grease, and reconsideration of his decision, they were done. Liz and Nella were more than a little grateful, and both regarded Jonah as though he were the answer to their dreams.

"Thank you so much for that, Jonah!" said Liz. "You probably don't even know it yet, but you probably helped your own self out by doing this!"

"Really," said Jonah, who wiped his face for the umpteenth time. "How do you figure?"

"Horticultural therapy is invaluable to stress relief," said Nella. "Who knows what negative feelings you just released, just through good old-fashioned time in the dirt!"

Jonah looked at their sunny faces, and simply decided to humor them. He didn't have it in him to shoot down that theory. "I promise to keep that in mind. See you, Liz. Nice to meet you, Nella!"

He grabbed his bag from the car, and went inside. Now, he needed a shower, but there were two other people he wanted to see beforehand. He knew where to find at least one of them.

He reached the kitchen and was nearly knocked backward by the sound of seemingly unintelligible music. The lone figure standing near the sink turned, though Jonah didn't have the faintest clue how he'd heard him. Terrence nodded in his direction and gave a quick wave, brandishing a paring knife as he did so.

"WHAT'S UP, JONAH?" he bellowed. "HOW ARE YOU?"

"GOOD!" Jonah shouted back, hoping his ears wouldn't bleed. "JUST—WHAT IS THIS?"

Terrence turned off the music, which left a blaring silence. "What did you say?"

Jonah's ears remained rather raw from the recent pounding. "I said I'm good, and asked what that was."

Terrence looked at his half-prepared dish, which Jonah saw included some chicken. Then his eyes widened in comprehension. "Oh, you mean the music!" he said. "It's The Incline Down, my favorite alt-rock band!"

"The Incline Down?" repeated Jonah, pleased that his ears had re-acclimated to the lower decibel levels. "Can't say that I've ever heard of them."

"Not surprised," replied Terrence as he returned to the food. "They never compromised their music for increased radio play. They're better than half of the shit that's considered mainstream."

Jonah wouldn't have known either way. As he wasn't a fan of alt-rock, he couldn't tell one band from the next. "Right," was all he said.

"You're a mess, dude," observed Terrence, who looked Jonah over. "Did that happen on the road? Did you A/C go out, or something?"

"No, man," said Jonah. "I was helping out Liz and Nella in their garden. That's why I look like this."

"Damn," said Terrence. "Talk about backbreaking…you burned all that energy—you probably need to eat something. Luckily, you're just in time! I've got some lunch here you might be interested in."

Jonah looked into the bowl again, and his eyes widened. "Is that your chicken salad? The world-famous chicken salad?"

"Yep!" Terrence looked proud as all get-out, and Jonah could see a sense of accomplishment in his features that wasn't usually there. Despite everyone's endorsements, Terrence didn't feel like he had any real skill or profound talent, particularly as an Eleventh Percenter. He didn't even feel that way about cooking, which was second nature to him. "I fixed the kinks that were there last time!"

Jonah frowned. He hadn't recalled any kinks. "Come again?"

"There wasn't enough sea salt in the mayonnaise that I made last time," said Terrence with a shade of irritation. "But I rectified that."

Jonah raised an eyebrow. "You know, you have moments when you're just like Malcolm," he muttered. "This is perfect!"

"Much like your writing," said Terrence shrewdly. "Hey, Reena!"

Jonah turned, and sure enough, she was there. She'd just come from a run, which Jonah always found ironic, because speed wasn't an issue for her, due to her ethereality. She nodded to Terrence, and went to sink to wash her hands.

"Great to see you, Jonah," she told him. "Did Nelson and Tamara like the bamboo plant I got for them?"

"Loved it," laughed Jonah. "Tamara set it up near the entertainment center."

Reena beamed. "I saw you out there, working with Lizzie and Nella. Cool of you to help them like that, and I imagine the physicality was exhilarating."

Jonah frowned. "You saw us? Where were you?"

"I saw you from the woods."

"You were running in the woods?" Jonah demanded. "With all the thorns—brambles—undergrowth—"

"Exactly," said Reena. "Learning to avoid all of that really improves coordination."

Jonah shook his head. Reena Katoa, the Fanatic Eternal.

"How about coordinating yourself to a chair, and eating something?" suggested Terrence, who pushed a plate of chicken salad her way.

Reena took it without hesitation, which made Jonah grin. She normally ignored most of Terrence's cuisine, but Terrence's chicken salad was her guilty pleasure. She looked leery of the bread, though, but Terrence put her at ease.

"It's rice bread, Reena," he said. "And you know it's full of celery, and nothing dairy. Obviously, there is no garlic in it."

They all bowed their heads. Jonah knew that Terrence didn't like reliving his brief experience as a vampire from a few months ago. An aversion to all things garlic was a result of that.

Reena quelled the awkward moment by grabbing the sandwich and eating it with great relish. "This is perfect, Terrence," she said. "And that's coming from me."

More people ventured in, which was fine, because Terrence made plenty: Douglas Chandler and Spader were first, followed by Malcolm, Maxine, Benjamin, and Magdalena. Malcolm made inquiries behind Nelson and Tamara as well, because he, like Reena, had supplied a housewarming present in the form of wooden dinner trays.

"They adored those things," Jonah told him. "When I said a friend made them, they swore that I was lying. They thought they were imported."

Malcolm, who never really was too overt with his emotions, managed a smile, and went on his way.

Several other people spoke to Jonah over the lunch as well, such as Sherman, Akshara, Noah, and Drakeson, as well as Ben-Israel Larver. Jonah was still on the fence about the No. 2 Green Aura at the estate. He didn't hate him, but his rigidity and inflexible nature led to an infuriating disagreement nearly a year ago. But when Terrence had been attacked by the 49er, Ben-Israel was one of the first ones to respond. That elevated him several notches, but Jonah still wouldn't refer to him as a buddy or pal.

Liz and Nella finally vacated the garden, but this time they were accompanied by the person Jonah had expected to see when he drove up: Vera Haliday.

She'd been watching a play when he'd first shown up, but she must have caught up with Liz and Nella shortly thereafter, and worked up a bit of a sweat herself. Jonah watched her grab a banana to eat with her sandwich, as opposed to the chips that Terrence and Spader had. She pulled her hair down before she peeled it. Jonah shook his head. The woman was so carelessly and nonchalantly beautiful that it kind of pained him that she couldn't see it.

Vera must have felt Jonah's eyes on her, because she looked up at him from her food. She half-smiled at him, and then mouthed the words, *"We Can't Kill the Soprano."*

Jonah kept his face straight and nodded, hoping that this would work out well.

A few months, prior, he, Terrence, and Reena received blank checks from Turk Landry, a paranormal investigator who sought "atonement," but that was total bullshit. They'd discovered that he was an Eleventh Percenter who didn't wish to be exposed. They had decided to keep the checks because—well, fuck Turk Landry. Terrence used his to treat his entire family to a steak and lobster dinner at a swanky chop house in Charlotte, and Reena used hers on a three-week trip for herself and Kendall. But Jonah had been advised to wait.

He knew what he wanted to do with it, and that was to have a wonderful date with Vera. Once Vera made it clear that she was amenable to that, Reena warned Jonah that patience was his best bet.

"You can't blow it on some quickie get-together that you could do at any time," she'd told him. "Show her that you put some thought into it. It will be much appreciated."

So Jonah took Reena's advice, and asked Vera what she wanted to see. He'd learned quickly that his assumption of the movies was wrong.

"A play?" he'd said after her exuberant clarification. "So you didn't mean movie theater?"

"Of course I didn't mean the movies," had been Vera's response. "We can do that any old Saturday."

"But Vera," Jonah even tried to include supplication in his voice, "I'm not made for the theatre. Aren't most of those plays girly and stuck up?"

"Most of the prominent playwrights are men, Jonah." Vera hadn't been deterred in the slightest. "You will love it!"

So, with Jonah's trying as hard as humanly possible to keep his misgivings and opinions to himself, they'd discussed plays that might strike them. They'd narrowed it down to two, which were on the same night: *The Deferment of Change,* which involved a frontiersman trying desperately to maintain outdated values and business dealings with the Industrial Revolution on the horizon, and *We Can't Kill the Soprano,* which entailed a self-absorbed centerpiece of a musical troupe who had to choose between the path to superstardom, and remaining loyal to the situation that made her relevant in the first place. Jonah left the choice to Vera, and she'd just mouthed her decision to him. They would see the latter play Saturday night.

Once he'd nodded to Vera, he turned to Terrence. "When will Alvin and Bobby be back?"

"Thursday," responded Terrence as he made a third sandwich. "Dad and Mama really wanted them to visit their Aunt Monica, since they couldn't make her eighty-ninth birthday."

Jonah frowned. "If Bobby, Alvin, and everybody are there, then why are you not with them?"

Terrence made a face, which he salvaged with a huge bite. "She never accepted me as family," he said. "The bitch used to tell Bobby and Alvin that they did the family no favors when they brought me home with them."

Reena winced. "What did Ray and Sterling have to say about that?"

"They've hated her for as long as they've been in the world," grinned Terrence. "Dad and Mama don't appreciate her views of me, either, but they keep up the visits because the hell she'd raise if they didn't isn't worth the trouble."

Jonah sighed. He still had family in the world, but they were basically strangers to him, and based on the level of intelligence they'd exhibited—or lack thereof— throughout his life, they were better off that way. Terrence's family wanted to keep the familial linkages strong, but they got resistance for that from this old woman. Some people in some families just needed to get over themselves and catch a clue.

"It doesn't matter, truly," said Terrence. "I've got the best mom and dad, four, no, *five* brothers, and all my people here."

Jonah's regarded his best friend. The indifference in his voice seemed a little contrived. But he decided not to mention it, and clapped him on the arm.

"You're covered on all fronts," he told him. "But you can keep The Incline Down, though."

"Jonah, you do realize that what you just said is an oxymoron, right?" said Reena in her trademark authoritative tone. "If you're inclining, then you're not actually going down. That's a decline."

Jonah and Terrence looked at each other and snickered. The way they felt at that particular moment was what it felt like to be Reena. What it felt like to know something in the presence of an oblivious party. The look was not missed by Reena, who eyed them with more sternness.

"What's funny?" she questioned.

Terrence's grin didn't waver as he looked Reena in the face. "The Incline Down is a band, Reena."

Reena blinked, and a sheepish look invaded her features. "I knew that," she mumbled.

While Jonah was distracted by the fellowship of his friends, he hadn't forgotten that crazy dream. The scratch paper where he'd jotted the ominous thoughts down remained stashed in a notebook, and he hadn't told Jonathan anything. He hadn't told Terrence and Reena either. The words on the page were far-fetched and ludicrous, but the most annoying part was that most of the dream had slipped from his mind. His thoughts were inconclusive at best after he'd first had the dream at Nelson and Tamara's, but even those thoughts were gone now. The two things he remembered clearly were Creyton's cold fire and the hooded person.

Inimicus.

Part of him wanted to remember the rest of it. But another part of him wanted nothing to do with it. He didn't need those thoughts with his date coming up, and his new narrative class shortly after that.

Bobby and Alvin returned from their Aunt Monica's (which was in Kentucky) on Thursday. Neither Decessio brother was pleased that they had to go at all, so no one expected glowing stories. Terrence was happy to have them back, and Jonah was excited about their return to the fold as well.

But then something happened shortly after their return that made Jonah want to bash Bobby's head in.

Bobby returned to the weights to get his mind off the crappy visit to Kentucky. It had always been a ritual for them to train together, and despite a nagging discomfort in his mind, Jonah joined them on Saturday morning, hours before his date with Vera. Bobby was his usual intense, primal self, but Jonah had long since grown accustomed to that behavior. He was actually much more comfortable with weights now than he'd been when he'd first met them. By no means was he a specimen like Bobby, but the workouts no longer made him feel as though his muscles were ablaze.

They completed the workout without incident, but then Bobby, as zealous as ever, challenged them to do three barbell curls past failure. As a show of good faith, he pumped out three himself, no problem. Terrence did two, muttered, "Screw it," and stopped. Alvin flat-out refused. Jonah, who'd planned to do the same thing, was now under the gun. He completed one, fine. The second was tougher. The third was halfway up when Jonah felt what seemed like a flame in his left arm.

"Goddammit!" he snarled as he dropped the weight.

Alvin and Terrence gathered round, and Bobby went to find the nearest Green Aura he could find. Jonah knew why he bailed; it had been his idea to go past failure, but he was fine. Jonah had paid for Bobby's zeal, and now Bobby didn't want to look him in the eye.

Why did this have to happen today?

Jonah was so pissed off that he wanted to get one of his batons and injure Bobby's arm in retribution.

Bobby returned with Liz, which was a relief, because he could have run across by-the-book Ben-Israel. She happened to be spiritually endowed, so she splayed her fingers over Jonah's arm, and waited for her fingers to gleam green.

"Brachial sprain," she diagnosed with a furrowed brow. "A pretty rough one."

Jonah focused on Liz so as not to throw a bilious glare at Bobby. "Can you fix it?"

"Absolutely!" said Liz. "I can fix it with no issue! I can inject the area with a salve, and you'll be right as rain in about nineteen hours—"

"Nineteen hours?" shrieked Jonah. "Liz, I'm taking Vera to the theatre tonight, don't you remember?"

"Jonah, I don't doubt that Vera would want you at full strength—" began Liz, but she stopped when Jonah rose. It wasn't an act of intimidation, but one of supplication.

"No, Liz," he said. "I cannot reschedule this. Vera has her heart *set* on that play. I'm begging you. Please get my arm ready. Just go into your little black bag and give me some painkillers or—"

"Hell no," said Liz acidly. "No way I'm giving you any of those things. Here." She pulled a glass vial no larger than a perfume sample from her pocket, uncapped it, and held it in Jonah's face. Jonah looked at it in confusion. "Drink it," she ordered. "It'll quell the pain."

Jonah tossed it back with the hand of his good arm. It numbed the fire significantly.

"Now come with me," said Liz.

She led Jonah out of the weight room, but not before she threw a furious look at Bobby. All he could do was hang his head as Alvin and Terrence laughed.

Several hours later, Jonah was at the front door, car keys in his right hand while his left arm was slung snugly against his chest. Vera met him there, looking beautiful in a silvery shirt that showed more cleavage than she usually did, and a black skirt. She regarded him with just a trace of concern.

"Jonah, are you sure that you want to—?"

"Yes," said Jonah, steadfast and resolute. "Liz has got me fixed up good and proper."

"And you aren't in pain?" asked Vera.

"Nope." That was the truth. Liz was a godsend, just like her tonics. "I just feel a warm sensation, but Liz said that indicated that her solution was doing its job. I'm great. This night's gonna be perfect. I'm sure of it."

Vera grinned. "Alright, then. Let's do this!"

"Let's," said Jonah. "You're gorgeous, by the way."

Vera chuckled. "You flatter me. But you look great yourself."

The smile that Jonah gave her in return was a little forced. Not because he wasn't excited to do this with her, but because he still wanted to kill Bobby. If anything went wrong, it was his fault.

No. He wouldn't think that way. The night would be perfect.

Because he said so.

Jonah only drove with his right hand anyway, so the long drive was no problem. He'd thrown an extra cherry on top (an idea he'd gotten from his new friend Eva McRayne) with dinner reservations before the play. Vera hadn't seen that coming, and was pleasantly surprised. Batting a thousand so far.

They were seated near the back of the restaurant, which worked out well, because it meant they weren't in the thick of the waitresses and patron traffic. Jonah's only criticism was that the place wasn't brightly lit. It was almost like he'd need his reading glasses for more than just the menu.

"Jonah, this is awesome," complimented Vera. "The Maiden's Rose? I didn't even eat here when I lived in the city."

"Neither did I," said Jonah. "I passed this place a million times on my way to do the number crunching, but I was never willing to come in here alone."

"And yet, we could've gone anywhere, even someplace closer to the theatre," said Vera in a pensive tone. "I'm pleased, don't get me wrong. I was just curious as to why you chose it."

Jonah gave her a half-grin. "I thought it was nice illustration of your love of roses."

Vera opened her mouth slightly, and Jonah knew he'd scored more points. Still batting a thousand.

"So did you really get paid in roses when you first became a stage actress?" he asked her.

"Oh yeah," snorted Vera. "I didn't make that up. I played Guinevere a couple times when I was seventeen. The guy in charge gave me three dozen of them just for '*being the fairest.*'"

They laughed, but Vera sobered quickly.

"Of course," she ran her thumb along her jaw line, as if by reflex, "I didn't have the scars back then."

Jonah looked at her intently. "Are the ones on your jaw and your upper arm the only ones?"

T.H. Morris

Vera sipped some wine. "No. I have a few scars on my thighs, several on my back, and some on my stomach. One stretches from the top of my abdomen, just under my left breast, to the bottom of my torso. It's a good thing I didn't get any on my chest, else shirts like this would be designated *verboten*."

Jonah took a deep breath. "Are you willing to tell me how you got them now?"

If it had been anyone else, any other first date, he wouldn't have asked. He wouldn't have even breached the subject. But he and Vera were a different case. They'd first met under abnormal circumstances, been in physical life-threatening situations together, and had something in common with each other that no one else in the entire Maiden's Rose could boast. As selfish as it sounded, Jonah felt like he'd earned the right to know.

Evidently, Vera felt something similar. "I got 'em in a fight," she answered. "A big, nasty, fucked fight."

"With whom?" asked Jonah.

Vera sipped some more wine. "My older sister."

Jonah almost loosed an exclamation, but remembered that he was in pleasant company. He kept his voice down. "Why?"

Vera took a breath. It almost seemed as though she went to another place and time in her eyes. "Jonah, my sister was…born bad. Something was off about her; like her wiring at birth was out of whack, or somethin. She seemed to get some sick pleasure out of getting in trouble, all the damn time. She did any and everything you could possibly name. My mother was terminally ill—lung cancer. But she tried really hard to have a steel resolve so as to deal with my sister. And one night…it just reached a boiling point. I was twenty, my sister was twenty-five. She came in late one night after doing her usual God-knows-what, and Mom told her she was no longer welcome in our house. My sister actually tried to hit her. She actually tried to attack our cancer-ridden mother. I lost my shit."

Jonah felt his jaw muscles clench. He'd heard enough, but had to know the end. Vera obliged him.

"We started brawling, Jonah. It wasn't some bullshit, prissy-ass cat-fight; we were both out for blood. Mom was screaming, but I barely heard her. I don't know how long we fought, but it ended when I cracked a mug across my sister's back, and she shoved me through a glass coffee table. She escaped with only a bloody lip. A fucking *bloody lip.* I don't know where she is, but I have no doubts that she is still beautiful. Meanwhile, here I am, this mutilated, maimed mass of flesh."

Jonah frowned. He couldn't believe that Vera viewed herself so hor-ribly; if he had heard that description without seeing her, he'd have conjured up the grisliest, sickening picture imaginable. A picture that didn't match her at all.

"Vera, listen to me," he said, an imploring note in his voice. "You are beautiful. I don't see a mutilated mass of flesh, I see a woman went through something sick, and emerged stronger. Your scars didn't rob you of beauty. They simply mean that you are a fighter, and a survivor. How beautiful your sister might still be doesn't mean a damned thing. She probably has nothing on you, because every bit of you is beautiful. Face, body—all of it."

Vera raised an eyebrow. "And how long have you been noticing my body, Jonah?"

Jonah felt heat in his face, and Vera snorted.

"Kidding," she said. "But I hear you."

Jonah sighed. He was glad that they were back on the original sub-ject. "I'm not just saying it, either," he persisted. "I didn't just say it to elevate myself in your eyes."

Vera's right hand lay on the table near her plate. It would have been a perfect opportunity for him to clasp it in a reassuring sort of way. But he couldn't, thanks to his gimp left arm. Bobby was going to pay, in the worst way imaginable.

But then Vera placed her left hand over his right.

"You're already pretty high in my eyes, Jonah," she told him.

Those words lightened his mood considerably, and they finished their meal with conversation about the upcoming play.

Jonah sat through the first half of the play quite surprised. He had no idea that it would be so enjoyable. He'd created the driest experience imaginable in his mind, and there were probably theatre experiences that were like that, but *We Can't Kill the Soprano* wasn't like that.

Vera was deeply engrossed into it, and Jonah caught himself actually rooting for Drea Davenport, who was the titular soprano. Yes, she was a real bitch in some scenes, but over the course of things, she began to reveal herself as someone who actually gave a damn about something other than her career. When intermission arrived, Jonah felt like he'd been jarred from an actual movie. Vera noticed the jolt, and smiled hugely.

"And you were so sure that you wouldn't like this," she said.

Jonah kept his face mostly impassive. "Okay, fine. It's much more entertaining than I thought," he conceded. "Are plays usually like this?"

Vera gave that some thought. "More often than not," she said at last. "If the play has a message, you can usually enjoy it. Of course you have your shit ones here and there, but mostly, they're great."

Jonah shook his head. "Drea really got thrown for a loop after seeing the family she could have."

Vera smiled. "Those family units are a great benefit to many people. You never know what fits you."

"I don't doubt that," said Jonah. "My friend and his wife have been married a year, and they've been talking about having kids almost the whole time. They can *have* it."

Vera looked at Jonah thoughtfully. "Wouldn't you like to have kids somewhere down the line?"

Jonah half-smiled. Again, if this had been a first date with any other woman, he'd have freaked out and ran. But once again, he and Vera were a special case. "Actually, I don't really want children," he confessed. "I'm not insulting or shaming anyone who has children, or wants to have them. I just don't feel that's for me. I've always considered my art—the books, editorials, and things—to be my babies."

He hadn't actually told anyone that before, and he wondered what Vera would think about it. Interestingly, she nodded.

"It's funny that you feel like that," she said, "because I'm the same way. I want to be a prominent playwright; make original plays, put my own spin and spunk into old ones—that sort of thing. I, too, have always viewed my artistic contributions as the mark I leave in this world. I don't tell too many people that, because it's met with such resistance and objection. But other opinions don't matter a damn to me; I'm not going to change them, and they're not going to change me. But it's refreshing to be around someone who is on my wavelength. I almost feel like I should thank you, Jonah."

Jonah smiled. That was a relief.

It was at that moment that he and Vera realized, once again, that they'd locked fingers. She was situated next to his functioning arm, so it was easy enough to do. But neither of them was embarrassed. As a matter of fact, if this was the precedent they were setting, Jonah didn't think he'd mind. Vera sure as hell didn't seem to.

Over an hour and a half later, *We Can't Kill the Soprano* was over, and Jonah and Vera were on their way back to the estate, chatting animatedly—in Vera's case, at least— about what they'd seen. What began as a potential tedious experience turned out to be an awesome night. Even he couldn't have guessed that he'd done this well, even with one arm!

Then—

There was a loud pop, an audible expulsion of air, and the car dipped awkwardly at the back. They both knew what had happened, but given the current situation, it was no small issue.

"Jonah, did you just have a blowout?" asked Vera in disbelief.

Jonah cursed under his breath, and drove the car to the shoulder. He should have complimented the night's events after they'd gotten home. He just had to jump the gun. Damn.

"Is that what happened?" asked Vera again.

"Yeah," muttered Jonah. "Yeah, that's what happened."

"I can't change a damn tire!" said Vera.

"Vera, I would never ask you to do that!" said Jonah. "I can change the tire."

"Not with one arm, you won't," Vera shot back.

Oh. Shit. "Right."

Jonah stepped out of the car, flashlight in his good hand, and headed to the ruined tire. The blowout was on the back left. When he cast the light upon it, he made a sour face.

A nail. Of all the drivers, of all the nights, of all the cars, this damned nail had to ruin Jonah's tire.

"I ran over a nail," he told Vera. "Just let me call Triple A."

Vera did not look comforted. "Jonah, I really don't like this. It's pitch-black dark, we didn't get authorization from Jonathan to use the *Astralimes,* and we aren't exactly in civilization at the moment."

Jonah wasn't frightened by the dark or the sticks, though. He'd grown up in it. But he didn't want to belittle Vera's anxiety. "Don't worry. I'll call Triple A. We'll be up and running in no time. Besides, we're Elevenths. We aren't vulnerable or anything. Just relax in the car for the time being."

Vera lowered herself back into the car. Jonah pulled his phone out of his pocket and made to dial Triple A.

He didn't have a signal in the sticks.

Jonah choked on the swear word he wanted to say, lest Vera hear it. They were in the middle of nowhere, with no service. Jonah's incapacitated arm prevented him from doing the job, and, as Vera said, they weren't about to do an unauthorized *Astralimes.*

Had he just told Vera not to worry? Had he just done that?

Jonah screwed his eyes shut as he tried to figure out how to break the bad news to her. Then he saw headlights through his eyelids. He opened his eyes and was momentarily blinded. That was his own damn fault; if the lights shone that brightly through his eyelids, they were probably bright as all hell with them open. You live and you learn.

"Are you okay here? What's the matter?"

Jonah froze. That was a woman's voice. He tried hard to focus; those headlights were like miniature suns. But his eyes finally managed to adjust.

The voice belonged to a black woman, who was nearly eye-level with him. He noticed that she wore a leather vest and jeans, as well as baby-blue boots. Not exactly the outfit one would expect from someone perusing a country highway at night. What was she doing out here?

When Jonah's eyes completely adjusted, he could actually make out her face, which showed concern and curiosity.

"Hey, man," said the woman. "I asked if you're alright."

It was at that moment that Jonah realized that he hadn't actually answered her. "Yeah," he said. "I mean, no. We were heading from the city, see, and everything was fine till we hit a nail in the road. My phone has no service out here, so Triple A's out, and I can't change the tire because of my arm—"

The woman nodded before Jonah finished, grabbed a band from around her wrist, and tied up her hair. "I'll help you. Pop your trunk, and tell your friend there to get out of the car."

"No problem," said Jonah readily, and he neared the window. "Vera, step out of the car! We've got some help!"

Vera stepped out of the car once more, and turned to see their savior. Her expression was initially one of gratitude, but when she saw the woman, the friendliness fell from her face, and her eyes grew quite cold.

Jonah frowned. What was that about?

The lady didn't acknowledge Vera's expression, and went to work. Now Jonah wasn't leery that this woman was out here at this time of night. A passerby who knew how to apply a spare! He looked over at Vera, who would no doubt be grateful that they were no longer stranded, but she faced the woods with a scowl as dark as the night itself. Weird.

"Done," announced the woman, who removed Jonah's jack, and hoisted his punctured tire into his trunk. "Mind you, the spare could do with some extra air, too. Handle that when you get to where you're going, alright?"

"Of course!" Jonah was so full of gratitude that he didn't know what to do. Now he could get Vera home safely! "You are a lifesaver! Thank you so much!"

The woman waved a hand. "Just glad I could help."

"That you did," said Jonah. "What's your name, anyway?"

The lady shook her braided ringlets loose from the band, which she returned to her wrist. "Rheadne," she replied. "Rheadne Cage."

"Pleasure to meet you, Rheadne," said Jonah. "I'm Jonah, and this is—this is Vera."

Jonah almost placed a label on Vera that he didn't think either of them had established just yet. He certainly didn't want her to feel awkward or uncomfortable. He couldn't go wrong with calling her what her mother named her, could he?

"Pleasure, Jonah." Rheadne nodded at him. "Safe travels. Have a good night, Vera."

Vera barely acknowledged that, and lowered herself back into the car. Jonah followed suit.

"Can you believe our luck?" he said. "What were the odds *she'd* show up? That took no time at all! And Triple A would take—"

"Yes," said Vera in a bored tone. "Hooray. Awesome."

Jonah turned to her. "What's up?"

"Nothing." Vera gazed determinedly ahead. "Take us home."

"But I—"

"Home, Jonah. Now."

"Vera, what—?"

"I said nothing, Jonah. Now, will you drive?"

5

Work and School

"Oh, Jonah," Reena moaned. "You didn't."

They'd returned to the estate much later than antici-pated—obviously—and Vera left Jonah at the car without another word. Confused, he'd gotten some sleep, and sought out Terrence and Reena the next morning. He recounted the previous evening's details, from the Maiden's Rose to the tire. Terrence looked just as confused as Jonah felt, but Reena, who looked pained, made that remark.

"Didn't what?" he asked.

"Jonah, are you serious right now?" Reena looked at him in disbelief.

"Serious about what?" demanded Jonah.

Reena tossed her paintbrush to the side none too gently, and turned to face Jonah completely. "Did you really treat Vera like that? In front of a stranger? A *female* stranger, no less?"

Jonah glared at her. "I treated Vera just fine! I was the perfect gen-tleman!"

"The holy hell you were!" snapped Reena, which prompted Terrence to put some distance between himself and Jonah, so that he wouldn't share in the tirade. "Jonah, you know that Vera is self-conscious. She dislikes her weight, and her scars aren't just physical. She laid herself bare to you, and then you fawn over a stranger?"

"Reena, I didn't fawn over her—"

"Was she homely?"

"Hell no, she was beautiful as hell—"

"I rest my case." Reena's face was full of savage triumph.

Jonah's thoughts were a sirocco. Frustration, defensiveness, confusion played tug of war in his mind. Terrence came to his aid.

"Reena, you are being unreasonable," he snapped. "This lady, whoever she was, could very well have been apathetic to their plight. But she stopped and helped them out! What was Jonah supposed to do? Be terse and indifferent?"

"YES!" Reena shouted.

They both stepped back. Jonah didn't know why Reena was so riled; shouldn't *he* be the one going crazy?

"Jonah, you just said that this woman was beautiful as hell," said Reena. "You described her as a lifesaver. That was the very word you used. So during your introduction, you basically said, 'Beautiful Lifesaver, meet…*Vera.*'"

Jonah stared at her. "Reena, I didn't say it like that. You make it sound—"

"Exactly, Jonah," interrupted Reena once more. "You didn't hear yourself. But Vera and that woman did. With that one introduction, you said, '*You are a wonderful, magnificent lifesaver. And oh yeah, this is Vera.*'"

"Now hold on, Reena," began Jonah with heat, but Reena, unmoved by his rise, raised a hand.

"If I'm wrong, Jonah," her voice was quiet now, "then swear to me, and I mean put up your right hand, and swear to me, that you would've acted the exact same way if your savior had been a beer-bellied, toothless, ass-crack showing, tobacco-chewing man."

Jonah opened his mouth, and then closed it. Reena was right. If it had been a guy, he'd have said his thanks, and moved on. Instead, he'd been overly complimentary, and had done so in front of Vera.

Well, shit.

Reena, who saw the realization on his face, nodded in satisfaction, and returned to her painting.

"You know what to do," she threw over her shoulder.

Jonah turned and left. Terrence followed him, but not before aiming a grimace at Reena's head.

"One would think," he said on the stairs, "that a woman who is about as feminine as a punching bag wouldn't get so damn emotional."

Jonah swallowed. "Reena is a woman of many parts."

"Oh yes indeed," agreed Terrence. "Part bossy, part scary, and part crazy."

Jonah had to laugh at Terrence's assessment. "Now I wonder why I went to her for clarity."

Terrence sat at the kitchen, and began to sift through recipes he'd left there. "You should have come to me. I'm in complete agreement with you."

Despite how Jonah felt, he just didn't have it in him to tell Terrence that his support wasn't entirely heartening. Reena's reaction, albeit over the top, had made him see things a little differently. He settled on a nod of gratitude, and set off for Vera's room.

Vera's door was ajar. He raised his hand to knock, but something told him that that wouldn't be a good idea. So he peered in to see what she was up to.

Vera's back was to him, and she stood perfectly stationary. Jonah had no idea why she was like that, but then she slowly raised her arms above her, put her hands together like some sort of elevated prayer, and bent her knees. Jonah frowned at this odd behavior, but then remembered what it was. He'd seen Reena do it a couple of times. It was a Temple Pose. So Vera was exercising, not making random, unintelligible movements. Instantly, Jonah revisited the memory of when they'd first met. Just like now, she'd been in the middle of a workout, and he was at her door, confused, lost for words, and trying to get in her good graces.

Someone up there had a hell of a sense of humor.

Vera attempted to transition to another position, but soon discovered that she couldn't do it. Swearing, she came out of the move, turned, and finally saw Jonah.

"Jonah." There was an edge in her voice, which made Jonah very nearly shake his head. He thought a good night's sleep would have assuaged things. "What is it?"

Jonah swallowed. "I, uh, just wanted to say that I'm sorry."

"Forget it," muttered Vera, and she returned to her yoga position attempt.

Jonah frowned. "You don't want to talk about it?"

"Nope," said Vera without facing him. "Sure don't."

The conversation was over, and Jonah knew it. He felt his own temper rise as he pulled her door closed and headed back downstairs.

So that was the response he got for trying to make things right? After his conversation with Reena, he actually realized he'd made an error. But when he tried to admit his fault, he was met with a response so hollow that it might as well have been a joke?

This was not the way that he wanted to feel when he got to his job orientation.

Jonah hadn't had to worry much about money the previous year, because he saved most everything, he was the cheapest person he knew, and lived at the estate. Despite that, he needed more of a routine. Last thing he wanted was to be a recluse. So he'd picked up a part-time job at the bookstore on campus at LTSU, called Two Cents.

After having to hear the meaning of his university's name from someone who wasn't even an alumnus, Jonah vowed never to be in the dark about campus lore again. He'd found out that the campus paper, *Two Cents for the Local Hunter,* had their very first site in the building that was now the bookstore. As the school grew, so, too, did the paper. As the student body increased, the campus paper moved to a more spacious setting next to the Britton Building. The space they vacated became the bookstore, and was named *Two Cents* to pay homage to the humble beginnings. It was nice to be informed.

Jonah stepped into the store, which usually wasn't open on Sundays save the ones in the initial weeks of the fall semester. As with every new location he went to (he'd had no use of the place last year because Kendall's class had no text), he went into Spectral Sight. He grimaced as he closed his eyes and envisioned the curtain rising so the actors could perform. Thinking of plays made him think of the previous night.

There were several spirits and spiritesses about. They moved with patrons and employees. Some even perused Spectral books of their own. Their presence was a very good sign. Spirits and spiritesses tended to avoid areas that weren't friendly or contained sinister elements, so if this many moved about the place, there were no red flags.

"Welcome, Eleventh Percenter," drawled a man's voice.

Jonah turned, surprised. The spirit of an elderly man had just initiated contact with him. He wore a sweater vest, khakis, and loafers. What surprised Jonah was that the spirit was so opaque that he simply could have passed for another patron. If he hadn't greeted Jonah the way he had, he probably would have made a fool of himself and asked him what courses he taught.

"That was an interesting approach, sir," he commented. "Are you here often?"

The spirit nodded. "Quite often. My son's the manager."

He motioned to a man who'd gotten a book off of a tall shelf for a shorter woman, and with a jolt, Jonah recognized his new supervisor, Whit Turvinton. Another glance at the spirit, and Jonah had no doubts. The spirit probably observed Whit's features and personality and imagined seeing a younger version of himself, revisited through interactions with his son.

"A matter of months?" Jonah asked him.

"A year," corrected the spirit. "The opaqueness of my form shows you how well Whit took it."

Jonah knew the silent question that the man was asking him. He nodded without hesitation. "I'll help him out as best I can, sir."

The spirit smiled. Jonah deactivated the Sight almost at the same time as Whit noticed he was there.

"Afternoon, Jonah!" he said as he extended his hand.

Jonah took his hand, and noticed something in his eyes that he hadn't seen before. His father's spirit had been right; he hadn't taken the passing well. He'd probably thrown himself headfirst in his work so as to put off the moment he needed to grieve. He didn't know how bad it would be when that time came, and wanted to hold it off as long as possible. Jonah felt for him.

"I could have sworn that you were just talking to yourself," said Whit.

"Nope," said Jonah, who had a ready-made excuse for anyone who'd seen him as he conversed with the spirit, "I was saying the books that I needed under my breath, so I could remember the sections to find them."

Whit's questionable face cleared instantly. "No need for that," he said, "I looked up your class and got your books in a package. I do that for all the employees that are students."

"Wow." Jonah's eyes widened. "Thanks!"

"S'Alright," said Whit. "We're back here."

He led Jonah to an office in the back that didn't have the greatest lighting job. It put Jonah in mind of those poorly lit rooms in the old movies where gangsters cleaned guns and counted money. There were several people there; some underclassmen that Jonah didn't know, some people that Jonah didn't even think were enrolled at the school, and (Jonah sighed) Lola Barnhardt.

"Your package is right there, Jonah." Whit pointed, and Jonah's hands clenched. Of course it was next to Lola.

With a smile reminiscent of the one Vera gave the lady who'd helped them the night before, he sat down next to her.

"Hey, Jonah," she whispered. "What happened to your arm?"

Jonah looked down at his injured arm. Liz's healing had done a great job, so it was no longer incapacitated and in a sling. Even so, he still had it wrapped for soreness. "Weights."

Lola emitted a soft exhale. Jonah raised an eyebrow. Did she think that he was brave? Or a badass? If she'd seen what actually happened, her perspective would be very different.

Hmm, he thought suddenly, *maybe I should let her watch. Then maybe she'd forget her crush.*

Thankfully, the orientation wasn't long. The job was pretty clear-cut. But Jonah was interested in seeing one more person before he left, though.

Kendall.

He found her exactly where he thought he would, which was in her office finishing up plans and printing syllabi. They'd had more interactions because of her relationship with Reena, and despite the fact that Kendall kept most of her personal business to herself, he'd learned some things about her. One main thing was that she *never* brought work home if she could help it, and greatly despised group work and staff meetings. She and Kendall had been dating since before the previous year's Thanksgiving, but Reena still hadn't told her about the Eleventh Percent. Jonah did not want to be a fly on the wall when that conversation happened.

"Hey, Kendall!" he said. "How're you doing?"

She beamed when she saw him. "Hello, J," she said. "What're you doing here on a Sunday?"

"Orientation for Two Cents," Jonah explained.

"Ahh, okay," said Kendall. "Did you sign up for another class, too?"

"Yeah," said Jonah. "Narrative."

Kendall smirked. "You'll like that, I'm sure. It was my favorite class back in grad school."

"I wish I could be in your class again," lamented Jonah. "I learned so much in your class! You actually made college fun!"

"I appreciate that, Jonah," said Kendall, who truly looked flattered, "but you'll like Professor Ferrus. He's awesome; I promise you that. Now, how is Reena? I haven't seen her in few days, since I'm getting ready for the next semester."

Jonah shook his head. She'd just seen Reena last week; was a few days really that long? "She's lecturing me, as usual."

"What did you do this time?"

Jonah gave Kendall an abbreviated version of the previous night. When he was done, her eyebrows inclined slightly, which filled him with foreboding.

"Take it as a learning experience, Jonah," she said at last. "That's what I do whenever someone's offended by something I do."

Jonah sighed. That was it? Kendall was the best. "That's easy for *you* to say, Kendall," he said as he took an armload of her syllabi. "People don't get mad at you."

"Have you forgotten the ancients in my department?" asked Kendall. "Or Reynolda? Speaking of Reynolda, she got a job at *Rome's Ledger.*"

"What!" cried Jonah. "A paper gave Reynolda a job? A paying job?"

Kendall nodded, mock fear in her eyes. Jonah shrugged.

"Well, that's it, then," he said. "That paper will start seeing more fish than victims of the mob."

They shared a laugh, which was interrupted by a meditative voice from Kendall's door.

"Pardon me, Kendall."

They turned to see a woman there, a pile of syllabi in her hands as well. Jonah estimated that she might be in her mid to late forties. She also seemed to have a rather subdued demeanor, which was punctuated by eyes that gave her an abstract, unfocused air. Her shoulder-length brown hair would have been entirely unremarkable if not for the solitary streak of grey.

"I was wondering if Professor Ferrus was here," she continued in that same meditative voice. "I have his paperwork completed."

"He'll probably pop in soon," said Kendall. "Oh, Jonah? This is Charlotte Daynard, the departmental assistant. Miss Daynard, Jonah Rowe."

"Rowe?" said Miss Daynard, who looked surprised. "You're Jonah Rowe?"

"Yes," answered Jonah in a rather terse tone. "How do you know me?"

"I don't." Miss Daynard smiled and shrugged. "I read some of your assignments last semester. You have a very interesting view of life is all. See you later, Kendall."

She left, and Kendall eyed Jonah with curiosity.

"That was a clipped response," she commented. "What was the deal?"

Jonah dropped Kendall's syllabi on her desk. "Learning experience, right? Isn't that what you said?"

Kendall stared, and then laughed and sorted papers.

Jonah gritted his teeth. Kendall may have viewed it as facetious, but it was anything but. He'd learned his lesson. He wasn't going to be overly friendly with a female stranger again for a very long time.

6

At Home with the Decessios (All of Them)

Jonah seemed to thrive in the midst of routine, and as the weeks went by, he had a great new one. Training in the Glade was always an enlightening experience. While he longed to try that earthen explosion thing that Liz and Nella taught him again, he decided against it, because he couldn't imagine what damage it might cause if too many people were in the area.

Trip and his cronies could always be counted on for ire and discord, something that Jonah could not figure out for the life of him. He didn't think it was too much to ask for Trip to show him just a tiny amount of respect, particularly after Jonah helped to expose Trip's father's true killer. But it didn't happen. Trip was as adversarial to Jonah as he'd always been. Maybe even more so.

Oh well.

But an unexpected surprise happened in the form of Grayson Morris, one of Trip's buddies. He'd begun to act differently towards Jonah after he'd prevented Felix and Trip from destroying each other. Trip's other friends (Karin, Markus, Malachi, and the rest of them) treated Jonah with even worse disdain after that incident, but not Grayson. He no longer attempted cheap shots during trainings, and had even helped Jonah up after an unceremonious spill or two. Karin had looked over at him in unpleasant surprise, but Grayson simply turned his back on her. Weird.

"It's because he knows that the Blue Aura is capable of kicking his ass," said Terrence at the end of a training. "What else could it be? It's not like Trip gives them permission to think."

But Jonah wasn't so sure about the last part. Trip's cronies—one of them anyway—seemed to be growing an opinion of his own. He didn't know whether to panic or rejoice.

Work was great, too. There were no dull moments to be had. His first day included a great deal of levity when a freshman asked about ants, not realizing that *ANT* on his booklist referred to Anthropology. Another time, a sophomore got caught switching price tags on some of the pre-owned books. The work had been expertly done, but he hadn't factored in the fact that the register's scanner would expose his wrongdoing. Another crazy event occurred when a biology pre-med major came in to purchase a textbook on human anatomy and dissolved into tears because of the full load of courses she had.

"It's going to be alright!" Jonah suspended his new policy to be aloof with unknown females and patted her shoulder. "There is no need for all of that—"

"It *won't* be alright!" the girl shrieked. "I never should have taken such a full load! I'll be on academic probation before mid-terms!"

It took a very long time to calm the girl down, and once she'd left, Whit jokingly said that they should have used tranquilizer darts on her. They'd all shared a laugh, but Jonah wondered whether or not her professors might need them later on once the girl saw all of the syllabi that she had to keep up with.

Liz illuminated the situation at dinner that night, with a mixture of pity and irritation.

"That's Cynthia Kerner," she revealed when Jonah told her what happened. "She's a transfer from a junior college who's trying to go leftfield from her family, who are all business majors."

"How do you know about her?" asked Reena.

Liz gave an uncharacteristically wintry laugh. "We have the same advisor. The guy actually suggested that I be her mentor."

"Great idea!" said Jonah readily. "She'd really benefit from a mentor!"

"Indeed, she would," said Liz, returning to her ham. "A fact that I made very clear when I declined."

Jonathan was the one supervising trainings again, and Jonah hadn't had much conversation with him, which was cool. It was hard to worry about stuff with Jonathan around. He had that aura—no pun intended—of calm about him that was infectious. But when he opened his mouth at times, Jonah wanted to pull his hair out. He just didn't have it in him to tolerate the riddles at the moment.

"I've told you before that Jonathan is a man of two minds, Jonah," said Reena one evening as she forced a painting dry with a blow dryer. "With a head full of the things he's learned and seen, is the occasional riddle all that surprising?"

"If only they were occasional," muttered Jonah.

His narrative class was alright. Kendall hadn't been lying; Dr. Ferrus was great. Tall, bearded, and knowledgeable, the man really knew his stuff and seemed approachable. But his class just wasn't the breath of fresh air that Kendall's had been.

He made the course aims known very quickly, and seemed to be much more rigid with his structure, which was something that had chafed Jonah in the past. Ferrus also seemed partial to group assignments, which Jonah hated with a passion. The assignment he'd been forced to do with Reynolda Langford last year had only served to strengthen that hate.

Vera, much to Jonah's relief, was much warmer in her treatment of him in recent weeks. The terse responses and cool gazes had also ceased. Jonah was glad of that. He understood why she'd gotten angry, but he didn't understand why she'd stayed angry for so long. Hopefully, he'd never have to figure it out. He'd never see that woman Rheadne (Jonah hadn't meant to memorize her name) again. She'd been helpful, and disappeared into the night just as quickly. Jonah was happy to write her off as one of the many people that one met in life, had some interaction with, and were gone. A one-shot deal.

Jonah and Vera even had time to talk while placing milk out for the heralds one day. They'd touched on their dinner and *Let's Not Kill the Soprano,* and something in Vera's voice let Jonah know that they would not discuss any other events past those two.

"I want to switch gears," said Jonah, "and point out something funny. Whoever named the heralds shouldn't have left her out."

He pointed to a bright brown cat near Bast.

"How do you mean?" asked Vera.

"Think about it," said Jonah. "Bast, Anakaris, Isis, and *Laura*? They could have kept the theme going, don't you think?"

Vera gave it some thought. "Maybe it wasn't so much name legacies as it was a name that fit," she said. "Bast's name fits her—regal and majestic. Anakaris is focused and strong, so that works, too. Isis...flighty, speedy, and prone to change. Maybe that cat didn't fit any of those. Plain, not ambitious, quaint...just like her name. Laura."

The cat shot reproachful eyes at Vera. She didn't appreciate that assessment too much. But Jonah didn't care. It was just nice to be speaking to Vera again.

One thing that Jonah was looking forward to was LTSU's first football game of the season, which was scheduled to take place the first weekend of September. The opening game would be against the Warriors of Culvy Smits College, LTSU's sworn rivals. In all the excitement of that, Jonah was also excited to meet the oldest of Bobby's, Alvin's and Terrence's siblings, Raymond and Sterling.

"They always come to the first game of the season," explained Terrence. "It's my understanding that they're all quite superstitious about it. Bobby's been playing football since the age of seven, which was before I even knew them. They went to his very first game as an entire family, and Bobby's team had a winning season. So now, even if they can't make every game, we always go to the opener as a family. Ray and Sterling drop everything."

"What do Raymond and Sterling do for a living?" Jonah hadn't ever asked that question.

"Raymond teaches self-defense interventions to police officers, as well as practitioners of Spectral Law," said Terrence. "Sterling is a youth mentor."

"To Tenth kids?" asked Jonah. "Or Elevenths?"

Terrence smiled. "We all stay close to the Eleventh Percent in some way, shape, or form. He may come across Eleventh kids in his job. It doesn't matter; ethereal or no, the kids all need someone to give them some advice."

"That's quite a resume that your family has," commented Jonah with a smile. "Raymond the self-defense instructor, Sterling the mentor, Alvin the studious, Bobby the football star—"

"—and Terrence, the janitor who happens to cook," said a cold voice.

Trip had wandered their way. He finished Jonah's sentence as though he'd been waiting to use that one, and savored it hugely.

Terrence's eyes widened in cold shock, and he turned to Trip, steel knuckles on one hand. Jonah held him back, livid his own self.

"And the point of that was?" he demanded.

Trip shook his head, like he was dealing with small kids. "The point was I felt like it," he said. "And what's the point of your involvement, Mr. Author, But Not Quite?"

He didn't even wait for a response as he laughed and walked away. Jonah stared after the bastard, wishing he had his batons.

"Utterly unnecessary," he grumbled. "I shouldn't have gotten in your way, man."

He turned, and was surprised to see that Terrence was on a nearby stump, contemplating his knees. All of his anger was gone.

"Terrence?" said Jonah. "What's up?"

Terrence looked up at him, resignation in his face. "He's right, ain't he?"

* * *

The two-story brick house that was the Decessio family home, to Jonah, was the picture of what true family should be. Sure, Alvin, Bobby, and Terrence spent most of their time at the estate nowadays, but they all had nothing but fond memories of the place and made a point to drop in on their parents as often as possible. Jonah couldn't blame them. Mr. and Mrs. Decessio were easy to like.

When Jonah, Terrence, and Reena pulled into the driveway, they saw Mr. Decessio next to his station wagon, seemingly having an earnest conversation with no one.

"The hell is he doing?" wondered Terrence aloud. "Is he out here talking to the car?"

But as the rolled further up, they saw that Terrence's father was not conversing alone; his words were directed at someone underneath the car. Legs hung out in plain sight.

"Oh," muttered Terrence, who shook his head. "He just couldn't resist!"

Mr. Decessio finally noticed them and smiled, tapping the hood as he did so. The figure underneath pushed himself free came smoothly to his feet.

"Afternoon to you all!" said Mr. Decessio. "Jonah, you're the only one here who doesn't know my oldest son. Raymond, this is Jonah Rowe."

Raymond clapped Terrence's shoulder, gave a smile of recognition to Reena, and then shook Jonah's hand. With his medium-length hair, broad features, and wisdom-beyond-his-years eyes, the man could have passed for Mr. Decessio's twin if Mr. Decessio weren't burlier.

"Nice to finally meet you, Jonah." He even sounded like his father. "I can finally put a face with all the crazy stories."

At that moment, Mrs. Decessio came out of the house. She had damp rags in tow, presumably for Arn and Raymond to clean their hands. Jonah thought that that would be pointless without water (their hands were pretty filthy), but then a sloshing sound announced a new arrival, and a new figure rounded the house with a bucket of water in his hand.

By process of elimination, this must be Sterling. He was a bit of a surprise to Jonah. Apart from the brown eyes, Sterling shared no resemblance whatsoever with the rest of his family. He had closely-cut hair, an angular face, and a rather uncoordinated gait. In Jonah's opinion, he looked more like a treasured family friend. Jonah would have assumed that Terrence was an actual blood relative before he believed it of Sterling.

Sterling noticed Jonah's gaze, and nodded. "Yeah, I know."

"You know what?" asked Jonah.

"I know that I don't look like anyone," said Sterling. "Most folks see us together, and assume that I'm a cousin."

"That is not true, Sterling," said Mrs. Decessio firmly. "You're one of us! Look at your eyes!"

Sterling lowered the water bucket near his father and brother, and shook his head at his mother. "Mama, I have told you time and again that I'm fine with it. At least I don't resemble Aunt Monica! Hey, Reenie!"

Reena punched him in the shoulder. Jonah and Terrence laughed instantly.

"Do not call me Reenie!" she snapped through a grin.

"Why not?" asked Sterling innocently. "No matter how old you get, you'll always be little Reenie..."

He turned and fled, and Reena gave chase. Everyone else laughed.

"Sterling met Reena when she was fifteen, and got her name wrong all of the time," Arn explained to Jonah. "By the time he finally got it right, he'd been calling her 'Reenie' for almost a year, so he stuck with it."

"Reena shouldn't have ever shown me how much it bothered her," said Jonah in a devilish way.

"Jonah don't you dare," warned Terrence. "Reena will cold-spot all of our asses—oh, sorry Mama!" he added hastily when he saw Connie's face.

"Where are Bobby and Alvin?" asked Jonah.

Raymond snorted. "Right there."

Jonah turned around and saw what was so humorous. Bobby had just returned from sprints, a sweaty mess. The funny part was Alvin, who was with him. His hair was matted and his face was red.

"Oh, hey, Jonah—" said Bobby, only mildly winded, but Alvin spoke over him.

"Why—Why did I have to come with you?" he gasped.

"Because Ray was helping Dad, Sterling was helping Mama, and Terrence wasn't here yet," said Bobby. "So that left you."

"But did we have to barefoot?" demanded Alvin.

Jonah and Terrence looked down. They were indeed barefoot. Bobby's looked largely unscathed, but Alvin's were raw, and just as red as his face.

"I told you, big bro," said Bobby, "running barefoot toughens our feet and activates more muscles!"

"Oh they're activated," said Alvin, glaring at his brother. "They're freakin' screaming!"

"That's enough boys," moderated Connie, and Bobby and Alvin ceased at once. It was so amusing to Jonah that Terrence and all the Decessio sons were just like most men in the world when it came to their mothers.

"What's good for dinner, Mama?" asked Bobby.

Connie narrowed her eyes at her youngest son. "There is more to me than just feeding you bottomless pits," she said.

"Oh, of course, Mama!" said Bobby in a placating manner.

He made to drape a sweaty arm on her shoulder, which she swatted away.

"Get cleaned up," she ordered. "I'd expect you to be doing that already, seeing as how Lizzie is coming soon."

Since Jonah's childhood, no one he knew could duplicate his grandmother's cooking. While that was probably going to remain the case, Mrs. Decessio's cooking definitely came the closest.

Liz had joined them after leaving Nella with Vera and Maxine, and they all enjoyed baked chicken, bacon mac and cheese, cobb salad

(Reena was overjoyed), and honey-glazed biscuits. Terrence rounded off everything nicely with peach cobbler. Jonah sat and wondered, as he often did when he ate with Terrence, just where the hell he put all that stuff.

The topic, unsurprisingly, moved to football almost instantly.

"We are going to mercy kill those guys," said Bobby flat-out. "This will be nothing more than a scrimmage for us."

Arn looked at Bobby very seriously. "That's the wrong mentality to have, son," he told him. "You speak from a perspective of someone who has read the stat papers. Games aren't played on paper."

"Dad, it's no sweat," said Bobby. "Their star quarterback transferred to the University of New Mexico."

"Ian Nolte transferred?" asked Arn.

"Yep," said Bobby as he helped himself to more cobbler. "They had to grasp at straws, and replaced him with a second-string accident who can't throw a fit, let alone a pass."

"Why would that Nolte guy leave a situation where he was the centerpiece?" asked Jonah, baffled.

"Increased exposure," said Raymond promptly. "The boy thinks he'll be on T.V. more for the University of New Mexico than he would for LTSU. But I am willing to bet anything that he sacrificed his role as a centerpiece. He'll be lucky to crack third string at a university like that."

Mrs. Decessio questioned Liz about her workload, which Liz responded to with half a sneer.

"My lowest grade last semester was a B-plus," she said. "Not my best contribution, but I digress—"

"Elizabeth," said Mrs. Decessio incredulously, "your lowest grade was *B-plus?* What was that class?"

"Anatomy."

"Little girl, you need to be proud," said Mrs. Decessio. "Complain about a B-plus in General Studies or something, but not Anatomy."

Liz didn't look entirely convinced, but she smiled anyway. "Yes, ma'am."

"Bobby says that you're the most talented Green Aura at the estate," said Mr. Decessio. "Would you say that's true?"

Liz blushed. "I wouldn't say that. There is Ben-Israel, Akshara, Sherman, Noah, Willow, Gerald—and let's not forget Reverend Abbott up at the Faith Haven—"

"It's you," said Terrence, Reena, and Bobby simultaneously.

"Undoubtedly," said Jonah alone. "The Reverend is old-school. Man sewed me up like an old quilt."

They all laughed, and dispersed shortly thereafter. Alvin helped his parents haul dirty dishes to the kitchen, while Ray, Terrence, and Reena went to the family room. Bobby and Liz quietly left the house. Jonah snorted at the thought of them, and rose to follow Ray, Terrence, and Reena into the family room when someone gripped his shoulder.

It was Sterling.

"Wanted to tell you something, now that everyone's gone," he said. "Don't much care for too much conversation around other people."

Jonah made a face at that. "Aren't you a mentor? Don't you speak around other people on a daily basis?"

"Those are kids," dismissed Sterling. "But anyway, I wanted to thank you, personally, for what you did for my brother after that 49er business."

Jonah hadn't expected that. It went against the mood of the entire night. But he shook his head at Sterling. "You should be thanking Reena, man, not me—"

Sterling shook his head. "Reenie shot him up with some miracle juice, but *you* were the one who killed all those Haunts and stopped the 49er."

He looked at Ray in the family room, who was demonstrating a self-defense maneuver on Terrence while Reena looked on. Jonah thought that was kind of funny, because Reena looked as if she wanted to commit the move to memory so as to try it on someone later on.

"Bobby's the favorite, of course," he said. "We all know that. But if anything happened to Terrence, I truly don't think Mama or Dad would ever get over it."

Jonah nodded. "Terrence needs to hear you say that. He is under the impression that he's extra and isn't worth anything."

He told Sterling about Trip's jab, and what Terrence had told him and Reena about their Aunt Monica. Sterling's eyes hardened somewhat at what Trip had said, but when Jonah mentioned their Aunt Monica, he just sighed.

"Trip can rot in hell," he muttered. "But Aunt Monica needs to go somewhere, sit down, and shut up. Hate that woman."

Jonah glanced into the family room again and laughed. Reena had already mastered Ray's move, and Terrence was making excuses as to why he stumbled through it.

"You all really seem to dislike this woman," remarked Jonah when he returned his gaze to Sterling. "Do your parents hate her, too?"

"Not hate so much as simply don't like," said Sterling.

Jonah shook his head. "That's just sad. Sometimes people aren't satisfied unless they've reminded everyone of their opinion at least fifty times."

"Well, you know that old saying," muttered Sterling. "You can pick your nose, but you can't pick your family."

7

Pigskins and Perps

LTSU's season opener was an even bigger deal than Jonah thought.

"What is so important about this game?" he asked Terrence the morning of. "It's not like it's homecoming, or a playoff or something. So what's the big deal?"

Terrence looked at him like there was still so much he needed to learn about the world. "One, it's Culvy Smits College, and they may as well be the spawn of hell down here. Two, the last time LTSU played them, Culvy Smits won by a point, compliments of a twenty-six yard kick that Aunt Monica could have made. Three, everyone is anxious to see how they will do since their ace QB has gone for greener pastures in New Mexico, which is ironic, seeing as it's desert."

Raymond, who'd overheard all of that, snickered. "That was good, Terrence, and all true," he said. "Helven Torrington has some huge shoes to fill."

"Helven Torrington is the name of their new quarterback?" asked Jonah. "He sounds like he should be playing chess with Douglas, not anywhere near a football field!"

Bobby was clearly a distracted young man, torn between psyching himself up for the game and following Liz's advice, which was to relax and clear his head beforehand. Bobby was also eager to impress pro scouts, who could be at any game. An early draft bid was very possible. Jonah noticed that that eagerness wasn't shared by his parents. They had encouraged Bobby to finish his degree in the event that football didn't pan out due to injury or whatever other circumstance that could occur. Bobby had made it clear that he had no intention to abandon his sports medicine degree, but he wasn't too concerned with injuries. "My girlfriend is not only a pre-med major, but a Green Aura," he'd told them. "If I got injured, even badly so, it's nothing that couldn't be fixed either through medical or ethereal means."

Jonah had to admit that he took Bobby's side on the matter. He and Terrence had spoken at length about it, and were in agreement. If an opportunity to go pro came up, Bobby should go for it. Who knew where that opportunity could take him? Given his devotion to fitness and conditioning, he could most definitely thrive in the much more physical environment. He could be successful as hell, and Jonah knew that he'd treat Liz like a queen and then some. Hell, he could probably even buy his *own* estate.

But entertaining those notions got everyone way ahead of themselves.

The football stadium wasn't the largest one that Jonah had ever seen, but the people present didn't have to worry about comfort. Rome, North Carolina had between seven or eight thousand residents, and they all seemed to be there. And that number wasn't counting the families, supporters from other towns, or the faithful fans and LTSU alum who made the road trips to lend their support.

Jonah and Terrence found their seats, and then laughed at Reena because she and Kendall had a minute-long kissing interlude before they seated themselves (one would have thought they hadn't seen each other in a year, when it had just been several days). Most of their estate friends were there as well, with their own families. He spotted Douglas and sighed; the guy brought his chess club sign-up sheet to the game. Of all the naiveté. Spader made a point to look slightly more presentable, which only meant that he didn't want to be spurned when he took bets. Benjamin, Ben-Israel, Akshara, and Melvin weren't too far away from Malcolm and the rest of Bobby's family. Magdalena sat with her own family, and Vera, Maxine, Nella, and Liz had grouped together several rows down. Jonah even saw Trip, Karin, Grayson, Ian, Malachi, and Markus. They were situated near LTSU's band. Jonah wished that they had just sat on the opposing side. If there were such a thing as luck, he didn't want LTSU's chances to be tainted by their unsavory presence.

Just about all of LTSU's supporters wore the stark Hunter crimson of the school, so the whole side resembled a sea of blood. The other side was a maze of gold and black.

"Is it just because of what we've all heard, or does it look like Culvy Smits already knows that their number's up?" asked Terrence.

Jonah looked at the visiting team as they rushed onto the field amidst the cheers of their loyalists and the jeers of LTSU's faithful. Terrence was right. They seemed to be a dejected, listless bunch. It appeared that even their faces, hidden beneath gold helmets with swords emblazoned on both sides, they were not thrilled about this game at all.

"Seriously?" said Jonah. "All those guys on that squad, and it's all hit the fan due to the departure of one?"

"Never underestimate what the absence of one cog can do to an entire unit, Jonah," said Reena. "You already know that old saying about not knowing what you have until it's gone."

"Very true." Jonah returned his eyes to the field. "Let's see what this Torrington guy does with his chance."

Terrence had pointed Torrington out to Jonah. He wore number 12, and even from this distance, Jonah could see that he hung onto every word that his coach said. The kid looked unimpressive. There was no other way to say it. Jonah was not a football whiz, but he didn't need to be to see that this boy was not a great fit for the role that Ian Nolte's departure forced him into. If this had been a film, Torrington would be akin to an actor trying hard to make a role work as opposed to one who embraced the character.

Jonah gave himself a mental shake. It was unfair to write the boy off. How many people had written him off as the Blue Aura?

LTSU did their kickoff to Culvy Smits, and the player who caught the return got pulverized after a few measly yards. Jonah and Terrence looked at each other. This didn't bode well for the gold and black.

The game fell apart rather quickly, at least for Culvy Smits. Terrence pointed Bobby out to Jonah (number 63) at defensive tackle. Within the first few plays, he'd already sacked Torrington three times.

"Dear Lord," said Reena with concern in her voice after the third sack, which left Torrington woozy, "that's not defense. That's assault! Who is Bobby trying to impress?"

"Fifty-five percent of it is pro scouts," said Kendall, "the other forty-five is Liz. I swear it is."

Reena looked at her. "You think that a sweet spirit like Liz would enjoy that kind of barbarism?"

"Hey," shrugged Terrence, "there is just something about having your girl watching you do what you do. Trust me."

"Uh-huh," said Reena, "because you're *such* an authority on the matter."

Terrence's mouth twisted. But Jonah gave some thought to what he said.

Something about having your girl watching you do what you do.

Bobby was lucky. As an athlete, he had the luxury of Liz watching him. There was no way in hell a woman would watch Jonah write a book.

His thoughts went back to the game rather sharply, as a collective chorus of anger came from the supporters of Culvy Smits College. Their wide receiver had actually defied fate and made it into the end zone, only to have the touchdown nullified due to a flag on the play. LTSU's lead remained twenty-seven to nothing.

Jonah noticed at that moment that even some of the people on the Culvy Smits side were booing them.

"They're taking Nolte's departure personally," observed Terrence with mirth. "Look at some of those signs!"

There were many signs on their side, many of which were for the team. Others, however, had things such as *THIS BLOWS* or *BENEDICT NOLTE* or *DIE IAN DIE*.

"Okay, now those are unnecessary," snapped Reena, who hadn't noticed how amused Kendall was about her emotion. "So this Nolte guy made a personal choice, and they view it as a betrayal? That's immaturity!"

"No, Reena," said Terrence, "that is FOOTBALL!"

Mercifully for Culvy Smits, halftime came, but not before LTSU had abandoned further with two more touchdowns. The score was now forty-one to nothing.

"Snack time, Jonah," announced Terrence. "Let's hurry up before the lines get stupid."

With quick requests to Kendall and Reena to hold their seats, Jonah headed down with Terrence for hot dogs and soda. He didn't know what Terrence meant about hurrying, because going into the crowd was like a trudge through marshland. After going against the grain for what seemed like forever, they reached the concession stands. The guy that assisted Jonah looked so frazzled that Jonah contemplated leaving him be, but the intoxicating smells of food made that consideration falter.

"I wouldn't recommend the X-tra Large soda, Terrence," he warned. "You saw that line to the can."

"Ahl buh fun," said Terrence, which prompted Jonah to look at him in confusion.

The man had already started eating a hot dog. One of five that he held in his hand. They hadn't even left the concession stands yet!

"I'm sorry, my friend," laughed Jonah, "but could you grace my ears with that one more time, please?"

"I said that I'll be fine," he said. "I'm the resident bottomless pit, after all."

Jonah smirked, turned around, and bumped into a person near him in line.

"Oh, sorry—"

He froze.

The man had barely moved; Jonah's bump had been insignificant. But he had such a murderous glare in his eyes that Jonah didn't even finish the apology. For several seconds, he thought that he saw the man's fingers twitching, like he desired to throttle him.

But then, just as suddenly, the man's face cleared. "It's quite alright," he said in a curiously hollow voice. "I know that you didn't intend to do it."

He turned and left without any purchases. Jonah stared after him.

"Jonah?" came Terrence's voice into his ears. "Something wrong?"

Jonah slowly shook his head. This wasn't the time to tell the truth.

Because something was up. There had been something familiar about that pointed face, rust-colored hair, and unsteady walk that favored the left side…

When they returned to their seats, Jonah forgot the man easily. He was nearly in tears from the horrified look that Reena gave Terrence's four hot dogs, nachos, funnel cake, and XL soda. He decided not to tell her that there had been five hot dogs to start with.

But soon, Reena forgot Terrence's gluttony. With winning out of the question, Culvy Smits came out of the locker room intent on taking the low road. Their new goal was to inflict as much pain as possible.

Brandon Lewis, LTSU's running back, got undercut so viciously while rushing that he almost did a full flip before he hit the ground. But that was only the beginning. Fredrick Sanders, the quarterback and one of Bobby's closest friends, was the victim of a facemask penalty. A violent pass interference shook up their wide receiver. Culvy Smits received yet another flag for roughing up the kicker on a field goal.

"Oh for God's sake!" shouted Terrence after the kicker pulled himself from the ground, thankfully uninjured. "Is this necessary? They're still gonna lose! This hasn't gotten them one step further to a touchdown!"

Reena tilted her head from Kendall, so that only Terrence and Jonah could hear her. "That's not what I'm worried about," she said. "I'm hoping that Bobby doesn't channel ethereality in a fit of fury and cripple someone."

"Hmm..." Terrence's frustration faded somewhat. "That hadn't occurred to me."

Jonah looked at them. When he'd channeled ethereality while unendowed, he hadn't caused any serious damage. Why were they so worried?

"He doesn't have an endowment," he said. "What possible harm could he do?"

"Bobby's still an ethereal human, Jonah," Reena reminded him. "If he gets up enough emotion, he could—"

The clashing of helmets at the line of scrimmage pulled their attention back to the game.

Culvy Smits was on offense once again, smug about their roughhousing. The play began, with the center handing the ball off to Torrington. Bobby penetrated the line easily; he just about bowled over his opposer. Torrington looked for an open teammate, not that it would have helped him much anyway. Once he saw Bobby coming at him, completely unopposed, he abandoned trying to pass and fled. Bobby gave chase, and Torrington ran in earnest, nearing his own team's sidelines. His teammates screamed at him to throw away the ball to avoid another sack or sacrifice further yardage—

BAM.

Bobby connected with Torrington before he could give up the ball, but it was no mere tackle. He'd blasted the second-string with such barbarous force that he was actually knocked out of one of his shoes. The two of them slammed into some of Torrington's other teammates, and a few of them fell like bowling pins. Even Culvy Smits coach wasn't spared. He took an unceremonious spill when a falling player got knocked into him.

"Oh my God!" shouted Kendall, who was no louder than anyone else. The Hunter supporters were beside themselves with glee; the other team *did* just rack up penalty flags. But Jonah didn't share the giddiness of his fellow fans. Torrington wasn't moving. Bobby had knocked him out cold.

"*That's* what he can do," said Reena. She stared at the field, wide-eyed and fearful.

LTSU recovered the fumble, and the possession was theirs, but several people convened on Torrington's limp form. Jonah looked in the crowd where he could (since everyone was on their feet), and he could see that their fellow ethereal friends were also aware that that had been more than just a sick, nasty tackle. Douglas had actually dropped his chess club sign-up sheet. Bobby's entire family looked like they were ready to scoop him up and flee the scene. Liz, horrified, simply stared at the field.

And Trip was laughing.

Jonah, disgusted, pointed him out to Terrence and Reena. How could he laugh?

After what seemed like an hour, Torrington stirred, and people on the Culvy Smits side cheered. Even a few LTSU fans joined in once their bloodlust gave way to concern. Reena breathed a sigh of relief, and Terrence relaxed too.

"Okay," he said, "now we can resume the slaughter!"

Reena and Kendall looked at him in shock. He snorted.

"What? He's alright, ain't he?"

Jonah laughed at that.

Bobby's tackle seemed to scare Culvy Smits straight, and they pulled no more underhanded tactics. Since scoring wasn't an option, they took their beating like men. When the game ended, the final score was seventy-five to nothing.

"And that was the first game?" asked Jonah back at the parking lot.

"Yep," said Raymond. "Just imagine what it's like at homecoming."

They waited in the parking lot while everyone else filed out. Reena had gone to see Kendall to her car, and Jonah, Terrence, and the rest of the Decessios waited for Bobby.

"I thought Bobby had killed that boy!" said Mrs. Decessio. "How many players did he knock down?"

"Connie, they were fine," said Arn indifferently. "After little Helven was roused, there was no concern. It was almost karmic."

"Arn!"

"Mama," said Sterling with smile, "that stuff goes with the territory. That boy got knocked out. He didn't tear, sprain, or fracture anything. He's fine. If he didn't want stuff like that to happen, he shouldn't be on the team."

A muscle clenched in Connie's jaw. It was clear to Jonah that she didn't agree with that assessment, either, but she resigned herself to the fact that she had no allies amongst the men.

Bobby appeared, arm around Liz, and Jonah glanced at Terrence and Alvin with a grin. They had no doubts that he'd been soundly rebuked.

"I went and checked on Helven," he said, and it was clear by his tone that it hadn't been his idea. "I rung his bell pretty hard, but he'll be alright."

"Good," said Connie sternly. "At least we managed to instill some decency into one of you."

Bobby smiled that same strained smile he'd given Liz. "Yes, Mama."

"I'm glad," said Liz, giving him a quick on the cheek. "I'll see you all later; I've got to get back to Vera, Maxine, and Nella."

She clamped Bobby's hand one final time, and left.

"Mama, I'll head back with Jonah and Terrence," said Bobby hastily.

"And Reena, if she can manage to pry herself away from Kendall," said Terrence.

Jonah looked at Terrence, amused. Even after all this time, he was *still* annoyed by the fact that he never had a chance with Kendall.

Alvin and his parents piled into the family car, and Raymond and Sterling followed them in Sterling's car.

"You aren't really sorry, are you?" asked Terrence.

"Hell no, I'm not sorry!" spat Bobby, who looked repulsed at the very notion. "Those rat bastards went all martial law *first;* I even heard some of them planning that underhanded crap when we were returning to the field. So why should I be regretful if Torrington fell victim to poison his own team created??"

"I'm glad to hear it," said Terrence, who led the way to the car. "I thought you were afraid of pissing Liz off, being whipped and all."

Bobby's face flushed. "I am not whipped."

"Uh-huh, okay," said Jonah. "You say that now, but you were a study in servitude a few minutes ago."

"Those few minutes got me back in Liz's good graces," countered Bobby. "How long was it before Vera spoke to you again?"

Jonah stiffened. Terrence made a face, but said nothing.

Jonah's attempts at a comeback were a bust. He had nothing. Damn.

"That's—That's why you'll lose the next football game," was the best he could do.

As much fun as it was spending time with the Decessios, Jonah was glad when Sunday arrived. Everyone would be returning to their routines, and Jonah couldn't wait to return to the comedy sitcom that was his job at the university bookstore.

The only one what wasn't pleased was Mrs. Decessio.

"She adores these family get-togethers," explained Terrence. "One would think that she would want this house all to herself and Dad."

"She gets that enough," said Reena. "Don't blame the woman for liking it when all of her sons are around."

The thing that Jonah loved about Terrence's family was that they never got sick of each other. He was eager to get back to his routine, but it had nothing to do with cabin fever. It was also nice that he, Liz, and Reena were just as much family here as everyone else.

It was a few minutes past eight in the morning, and they'd all come to a silent agreement that they would allow Mrs. Decessio to have all of her sons around her for as long as possible, and not focus so much on having to leave. As such, Mr. Decessio and Ray put together the new bookcase, Sterling and Alvin trimmed the hedges, Bobby cleaned his room (he'd made it as junky as the one he had at the estate), and Jonah, Terrence, and Reena repainted the fence and mailbox.

"How is this for a laugh?" muttered Terrence after loading the paint roller for what he must have hoped was the last time. "Yesterday, we were barbarians. Today, we're homemakers."

"Oh, you love it," said Reena. "When we're back at the estate tonight, you're going to miss this. Especially the cooking."

"I can cook my own meals!" said Terrence. "Quite well, by the way!"

"But they aren't your mother's cooking," Jonah weighed in.

Terrence had no response to that. He knew they were right. So he did the only thing he could do, and returned to the fence.

Once all the chores were done, they all convened at Mrs. Decessio's table for a final round of her cooking. As they'd spent the entire morning working, she'd made breakfast food for them. Everyone was amenable to this. She'd even made spinach quiche for Reena, so that she wouldn't have to eat bacon, eggs, or waffles.

"You know, Mrs. Decessio," said Reena gratefully, "sometimes I wish you were *my* mother as well."

"I love that Reena doesn't eat wheat," muttered Terrence. "More pecan waffles for us!"

When that meal was over, Raymond and Sterling rose. They really wanted to get the driving out of the way so that they could get plenty of rest before work on Monday morning. Of course Mrs. Decessio had food wrapped up for them, like they were college students. Neither of them minded.

"It's been a pleasure, Jonah," said Raymond, shaking his hand. "Hope to do this again soon."

"Feeling's mutual, Ray," said Jonah.

He and Sterling said their goodbyes, and were gone.

"Okay, that's that!" said Bobby, cracking his knuckles. "There is a double-header today! Any takers?"

Mr. Decessio and Alvin rose to follow him. Jonah, Terrence, and Reena went to wash their plates.

"Bobby needs to take the occasional break from football," remarked Reena. "If he's not playing it, he's watching it. That's a recipe for burnout."

"He *does* take a break from time to time!" said Terrence. "That's when he lifts weights!"

They transferred their dishes to the pile, per Mrs. Decessio's request. Jonah took two steps away from the sink when the landline rang. Terrence glanced at it and frowned.

"What's up, Ter?" said Mrs. Decessio, who hadn't missed his expression.

"It says it's Sterling's cell," he said. "They've only been on the road fifteen minutes; maybe Ray left a watch or something."

Since he was the nearest, he went ahead and answered. "Hey big bro, what—?

Terrence took the receiver from his ear, looking more confused than ever.

"Terrence, what is it?" asked Jonah.

"He wants me to put him on the speaker," said Terrence.

He did as Sterling asked, and Connie spoke out to him.

"Okay, Sterling," she said, "what did Ray forget?"

"Mama." Sterling's tone of voice sent a chill down Jonah's spine. It sounded ominous, foreboding, and just plain *wrong*. Apparently, it had the same effect on his mother, who abandoned the dishes and turned to the phone.

"Sterling, what's the matter?"

"Mama, is Dad with you?" he asked, ignoring the question.

"No, he's—"

"Get him, Mama, now. Please."

Jonah and Terrence looked at each other. Reena, who now looked a little afraid, volunteered to go get Mr. Decessio. Jonah had no idea what Reena said, because when he got there, he looked as concerned as everyone else.

"I'm here, son," said Mr. Decessio. "Now, what's wrong?"

"Dad," said Sterling, "Ray and I stopped for gas, and…"

"What is wrong, Sterling?" demanded Mr. Decessio.

"Dad," repeated Sterling, whose voice almost sounded pained. "I think—I think you need to call some of your friends in Spectral Law."

Eighth Chapter

"Mr. Decessio is in Spectral Law?"

Jonah made that inquiry of Terrence as he and Reena joined him in the family room, where Mrs. Decessio, Alvin, and Bobby were already seated. The football game was on in the background, muted and long forgotten. They'd all figured that they may as well be comfortable while they waited for Mr. Decessio to return from whatever Raymond and Sterling had discovered.

"It wasn't anything glorious," said Terrence. "He worked as a consultant, much like Reverend Abbott did. But then he had a job behind a desk for a long while. He wasn't ever a full-fledged field Practitioner, because he didn't want Mama to have to deal with sleepless nights. But people always came to him for advice. Dad has always been great at putting pieces together; making connections where other people didn't even see connections. Maybe it was because he had the freedom to put facts together and not worry about the distractions of the chase and excess adrenaline and whatnot."

"He was highly respected from a desk?" Jonah was amazed at that.

"Everybody's got their functions, Jonah, you know that," said Reena. "I work behind a desk, but I still have layers."

"Point," conceded Jonah. "So when did he retire?"

"2001," answered Terrence. "He had already opened the body shop, and wanted to devote all of his time to it. But his buddies still ask him stuff from time to time."

Jonah was still quite fuzzy on the nuances of Spectral matters; they just hadn't been of much interest to him. Jonathan touched on the laws and guidelines concerning the Eleventh Percent, but he usually spoke on them from a spiritual perspective. Jonah supposed that was okay, since the Protector Guide was a spirit. It was only recently that he'd become more cognizant of the *human* upholders of ethereal code and law.

"Did he work with Reverend Abbott at all?" he asked.

"No idea," said Terrence, "but I'm sure that it's safe to assume that they knew of one another."

The front door opened, and Mr. Decessio, Raymond, and Sterling walked in. Jonah had hoped to see them again soon, but he hadn't expected it to be this soon, under whatever odd circumstances these were.

"Dad, what—?" began Bobby, but Mrs. Decessio gave him a quelling look. Mr. Decessio didn't look capable of withstanding a barrage of emotions just yet.

"Arn, what's happened?" she asked.

Jonah had never seen Mr. Decessio like this. He sat down in his chair, clicked off the muted television, and sighed.

"Just give me a second," he said at last. "I'm waiting for—welcome to our home, sir."

Jonah started, because Jonathan had appeared in the middle of the room. Though Jonah had seen the occurrence on many occasions, he'd never seen Jonathan do it into someone's home.

"Jonathan?" Mrs. Decessio was just as surprised as the rest of them. "I'm honored to have you in our home!"

Jonathan smiled. Jonah had just seen him at the estate before he had come to visit the Decessios, but he never got over just how reassuring it was to be in his presence. He was dressed as he normally was; beige shirt, tan slacks, and matching duster. The ensemble was completed by the silver necklace with figure-eight that was stemmed on either side. The ancient symbol of infinity.

As it was daytime, Jonah knew that Jonathan's strength was limited, and that made him *more* uncomfortable. What had happened that forced Mr. Decessio to request Jonathan's presence before nightfall?

"The honor is all mine, Constance," he said. "And Raymond, Sterling. It has been too long. But I doubt throwing around pleasantries is the reason that I was summoned."

Mr. Decessio slowly shook his head. "No sir. It wasn't."

"Tell me what you found," said Jonathan.

It seemed that Mr. Decessio seemed more assured in Jonathan's presence as well. But he still looked very unnerved. "My oldest boys here were about to get on the road when they stopped for gas at the BP near the highway ramp. Another customer walked a small distance to the diner next door for food, and made an abominable discovery."

Jonah felt a prickle of recognition in his memory. Why did a BP gas station in close proximity with a diner sound familiar?

"I hadn't even gotten the nozzle in the tank yet," said Sterling. "The guy ran back to the gas station, screaming and crying. We couldn't make head or tails out of what he was saying. Then I asked him again, and he said something about a bunch of bodies. Then he fainted."

Jonah winced. Terrence and Reena showed similar signs of alarm.

Jonathan's head cocked slightly to the left, which was what he did instead of frowning on occasion. "And you went to investigate?"

"No," said Raymond, "I did. Sterling was trying to get the man off of the ground."

"And you saw these bodies?"

A sort of shiver ran across Raymond's face. "Didn't have to. They guy left the door open when he came running out of the diner. I was within five feet when I caught the smell."

Mrs. Decessio shuddered.

"I couldn't go any further," said Raymond. "That smell just about made my stomach turn."

"I'm glad that you didn't see what lay within." Jonathan's expression didn't change as he spoke, but he fingered his infinity medallion. "But I am curious. Once the Tenth man had seen the carnage and ran back, the clerk at the gas station surely would have called the sheriff. What about it prompted you to call your father and ask him to call Spectral Law?"

Sterling took a deep breath. "When I saw how pale Ray had gotten, just from a smell, no less, I activated Spectral Sight, sir. A couple of spirits near the place said that something 'sinister' had occurred. So I called Dad. Ray didn't seem up to it at the time."

Jonathan turned his gaze once more to Mr. Decessio. "I'm certain that you didn't go in there alone, Arn, right?"

Jonah looked at Alvin and Bobby's faces. They looked as though this were some kind of ghostly tale. But the more Jonah thought on it, the more it seemed to be just that.

Mr. Decessio nodded to his sons, as if they'd done their part. Jonah was surprised that he hadn't just bombarded them with the whole story, but after seeing that gesture, maybe he figured that it would benefit his sons to tell their parts themselves so as to get the bile out of their systems. *Now* he'd take over. "No I didn't, sir. I called two of my closest contacts, Patience and Charles. We went in as a collective. It was just like the hysterical Tenth man said. They appeared to have been there several weeks. Patience had informed the Phasmastis Curaie."

"Sorry," said Terrence, "but there is something that makes no sense. If this diner was by the highway, it probably had people coming by every day. So why wasn't this crime scene discovered by some random Tenth who wanted a cheesesteak and some iced tea before now?"

"Nobody bothered to notice, son," said Mr. Decessio quietly, "because the Auric shielding just wore off this morning. Up until this morning, the Tenths saw an illusion of a sign that said *Closed until further notice*. Once that wore off, it just appeared like it usually did. That's why the Tenth man tried to go inside."

"How did you know that there had been Auric shielding?" asked Jonah.

Mr. Decessio half-shrugged. "Tools of the Spectral Law trade, son."

"Auric shielding." Jonathan closed his eyes. "Eighth Chapter."

Mr. Decessio nodded. Jonathan took a deep breath, with a look in his eye that Jonah couldn't place.

"Forgive this abrupt departure, people," he said, "but I must notify the other Protector Guides and the heralds. Arn, thank you for contacting me. Constance, thank you for welcoming me into your home."

He vanished with a soft gust.

"What the—? snapped Bobby, but Connie stopped him from saying the next (undoubtedly profane) word with another look. He faltered instantly.

"What does Eighth Chapter mean?" asked Jonah, still a bit shocked by Jonathan's abrupt disappearance. "Why is it such a big deal?"

Mr. Decessio cracked his knuckles. "The ethereal laws are mandated by the Phasmastis Curaie, enforced by practitioners of Spectral Law, and followed by us Eleventh Percenters," he began. "Ethereal crimes are a bit more multilayered than Tenth ones, so they are placed into Chapters based on severity. Keeping a spiritual endowment a little too long, unauthorized *Astralimes* travels, assault on an ethereal or non-ethereal human—they all go into the Chapters. They used to be one through seven, but some ethereal crimes within the past few decades have been so vile, grisly, and heinous that they were granted their very own Chapter. The Eighth."

Jonah's hands clenched. So a new Chapter had been created in the past few decades. Who else could have been the cause of that? "Because of Creyton."

Mr. Decessio nodded. "Eighth Chapter crimes were indeed the ones committed by Creyton."

"Not only Creyton," added Mrs. Decessio. "They also refer to the crimes of the Deadfallen."

"The Deadfallen?" said Alvin, confused. "What is that?"

"They were Creyton's most dedicated disciples," said Raymond. "You know those old medieval stories where kings and queens had their own elite fighting units that were a cut above even the royal soldiers? It was kind of like that, just sick, twisted, and evil."

"Wait a second," said Jonah. "I thought that Creyton's followers were called Spirit Reapers."

"No, Jonah," said Mr. Decessio. "A Spirit Reaper is simply any Eleventh Percenter who has turned evil. But the Spirit Reapers who devoted their physical lives entirely to Creyton, who bought into his B.S. about "death and dying?" Those are the ones to whom he granted the most loyal, most faithful name of Deadfallen."

"But why were they called Deadfallen?" asked Terrence.

"I can answer that, just from the context clues," muttered Reena. "Creyton termed them as the Deadfallen because they were the ones most likely to be responsible for a deadfall. Right?"

They looked at Mr. Decessio, who nodded. "More or less," he said.

"Sometimes they were brazen, but Creyton usually had them use subtler tactics," said Mrs. Decessio. "We'd hear incidents all the time of Tenths or Elevenths getting hurt or killed. Or stories of spirits and spiritesses being reaped and usurped. But they were hard to catch, because they worked from the shadows, much like vampires. I guess they were kind of like an ethereal Mafia, and Creyton was Don. He and his disciples were truly a bane to the Phasmastis Curaie and the S.P.G."

Jonah felt for anyone who might have been a victim, but he especially felt for the spirits and spiritesses. They deserved peace in the next life! "What happened to these people?"

"Some got caught by the Networkers," answered Mr. Decessio. "The rest...I don't know. No one except Creyton knew who they all were. Worked from the shadows, as I said. I had already retired when they all went quiet."

"The ones that got caught don't deserve to see Earthplane again," said Sterling nastily. "May the ones still physically alive continue to rot on The Plane with No Name."

Jonah whistled. The Plane with No Name was an entire plane pur-posed with holding imprisoned ethereal criminals. The Curiae didn't bother to name it, and its location was known only to them, the Pro-tector Guides, and the Networkers. No one but the upper crust knew; not even the other practitioners of Spectral Law were privy to the lo-cation. Terrence had told Jonah about the place a long while back at the Meadow Road Inn, but Jonah was so unnerved by the place that he'd filed it away.

Until now.

"So the 49er…Titus Rivers, Jr…were Deadfallen disciples," he mur-mured.

"Yes," said Mr. Decessio, "but there is no need to worry about either of them, of course. Patience already told me the Deadfallen disciple responsible for the massacre at the diner. He never went to The Plane with No Name."

"Yeah?" said Raymond. "Who is he?"

"Wyndam O'Shea."

"Wait," said Reena suddenly, "wait. I know that name. He was the lunatic, right?"

Despite the situation, Jonah snorted. "Reena, if the man followed Creyton, it's a foregone conclusion that he's crazy—"

"No, Jonah," said Mr. Decessio. "You misunderstand. O'Shea is true *lunatic*. He had these—fits—that coincided with the full moon."

Bobby sniffed. "A man who was crazy depending on a moon?"

"A man like that is always crazy, Bobby," said Sterling. "He is just…extra crazy at the full moon."

"And he never got caught." Reena loosened her hair, a sure-sign of stress. "I saw a picture of him in Jonathan's study when I was in my teens. I never forgot him…long face, belligerent eyes, that rusty mane of hair…"

Jonah choked. *What did she just say?*

"Jonah?" said Mrs. Decessio, concerned, "are you okay?"

"Yeah," said Jonah, but then he remembered manners. "I mean, yes, ma'am. I just need some fresh air. Been sitting a long time."

"That's true," said Mr. Decessio. "We've all been seated for a long while, and this is not light hearted information. Patience and Charles have notified their end, and Jonathan has notified his Guidemates. The right people are on Wyndam O'Shea's trail now. You kids get up, stretch, and don't let this consume you. As bad as O'Shea is, it's not Creyton that we need to fear."

Jonah shot up as though his seat had overheated underneath him and headed outside to his car, where he rested his weight on the side. He knew that Terrence and Reena understood, so he wasn't surprised when he saw them follow him outside a few minutes later.

"What's really up, Jonah?" asked Reena.

"Wyndam O'Shea," he said in a tense voice, "I've seen that guy. He was at Bobby's game yesterday! He was about to strangle me because I bumped into him at the concession stand!"

Terrence and Reena were stunned. Jonah didn't let the silence spiral.

"Reena, are you familiar with lunar cycles?"

"Who isn't?" asked Reena.

Jonah chose not to answer that question. "When was the last full moon?"

Reena narrowed her eyes in thought. "The most recent one? You weren't even here. That's when you were at Nelson's and Tamara's."

Jonah gritted his teeth and cursed.

"What's wrong now, Jonah?" asked Terrence. "You got a toothache, too?"

"*No*, Terrence," said Jonah. "There is something that I need to tell you guys that I didn't before."

He told them what happened with the whole Scius and Inimicus incident after he stabbed the 49er. Then he recounted Malcolm's explanation of their meanings and how he'd written it off as a myth.

"Fascinating story," murmured Terrence. "Truly. But what's got to do with Wyndam O'Shea?"

"I'm getting to that, replied Jonah, and he told them what he remembered about the diner, and how O'Shea had entered, and then the scene in that strange room.

"It had to be him under that hood," said Jonah. "He had that card. I know he is the obvious suspect, but dammit, he had that card. I think he might be Inimicus."

Now that Jonah had put all the pieces together for them, Reena's face looked stern.

"Why didn't you tell us before?" she demanded.

"The card thing wasn't important after it happened, because Terrence had been bitten by the vampire," said Jonah. "The rest...I—I forgot."

"You forgot?" said Terrence and Reena together.

"Yes, I forgot!" Jonah shot back. "It was like—like a dream or something. I think a Protector Guide was there, but he said I'd forget his name. And damn if I did forget it—"

"You experienced a Spectral Event?" said Reena, her irritation fading.

"What? No!" said Terrence. "He'd have forgotten by now! That's the rule!"

"The rule?" repeated Jonah.

"Jonah, Spectral Events happen to all Eleventh Percenters, but they are unreliable," Terrence informed him. "When you're Guided in a dream, you are not in physical form and therefore on a higher spectral wavelength than usual. But once it's over, you're lowered back into a three-dimensional mindset. The Spectral linkages are severed, so your waking mind forgets."

Jonah and Reena stared at him. Terrence threw up his hands.

"Will you stop gawking at me like that when I say something informative?" he demanded. "Just because I mop floors doesn't mean I'm a dumbass. I do have some use; no matter what Trip says."

"Trip—? Man, screw him," said Jonah. "And of course you aren't a dumbass! No one is saying that! It's just that I actually do remember things, despite this so-called rule. I remembered that diner that was next to the BP; I think there was a Meineke somewhere around there, too. I remembered Wyndam O'Shea. I remembered that there was a Protector Guide who told me that I'd forget his name. I forgot all those things, but seeing O'Shea yesterday and having these conversations today brought it back. Mostly."

"Maybe it's because of your aura," hypothesized Reena. "One of your gifts is balance. Maybe there is a balance between your wakeful and spiritual mind, which allows you to re-build memories if you have the proper triggers. That's pretty sweet."

Jonah frowned. Add that to the list of things he could do as the Blue Aura that people referred to as *cool*.

"Do you recall anything else?" asked Terrence.

"Not at the moment," said Jonah. "But if triggers can help rebuild, I think I might have a way to bring it back."

* * *

In light of the events of the day, they all decided to give Mrs. Decessio the pleasure of staying a few more hours. It also helped to calm everyone's nerves. By the end of it, Raymond and Sterling really needed to get back, but they promised to make no more pit stops. Jonah, Terrence, and Reena returned to the estate, followed by Alvin and Bobby. They retreated to their favorite spot, Reena's art studio. Jonah's plan was simple: He'd close his eyes and focus his mind. Terrence would call out a line from the paper, and the more Jonah focused, the more he could tie events to the lines.

By no means was it an instant success, though. Terrence had to repeat a couple lines three times or more, and Jonah's mind had nothing to give concerning the line about "*the 49er's screw up.*"

"I have a feeling that whatever the 49er screwed up is very important," said Terrence. "Do you think the screw up was losing to you and Trip? Was he supposed to turn us all into vampires or something?"

Jonah sighed. "I don't think the 49er was supposed to make *any* vampires," he said. "There is something else that I never told you guys. After the 49er was beaten, I had a conversation with Jonathan about how it all went down. Everyone was satisfied with the story about the 49er wanting to take Creyton's place, but there was one part that never sat well with me. When we first met Felix, he said that the 49er was storing lifeblood. His plan was to reach a certain number. Remember how you said that that number had to be fifty, Reena? Because that was logical round figure, or something?"

Reena had Jonah's full attention as she nodded.

"And then there was that vampire snitch up at LTSU right after the New Year," continued Jonah. "When we asked him about the lifeblood storage, he said that it—"

"—was the tip of the iceberg," finished Reena. "I remember. That was right before Felix came in and threw him into the sunlight."

"Right," said Jonah. "Anyway, those two pieces led me to believe that the 49er taking over Creyton's place wasn't the original plan. When he decided to go into business for himself, I think he—he deviated from what was supposed to be doing. Jonathan agreed."

Terrence and Reena were silent. Jonah did just drop some heaviness on them. He lowered his head to try to wrap his mind around stuff, but then he straightened.

"I just remembered something else from the Spectral Event," he announced. "From that strange room I told you about. The one that had the cold fire with...with Creyton's presence in it. Inimicus was pissed that the 49er had any involvement at all. They thought *they* should have been the one carrying things out all along."

"I still can't believe that Creyton's essence was in that fire," said Terrence, who shook his head. "He should be gone! Completely!"

"I know, man," said Jonah. "We said the exact same thing after I beat him in that graveyard at the Covington house. But he didn't cross to the Other Side. He somehow got a hold of Bruce Darden's remains and essence and posed as Roger."

"Right," said Reena. "But you stopped him there, too, before he could destroy Vera and manipulate her Time Item ethereality. You said that healing essence was too much for his incomplete form."

"It was," said Jonah. "That little disguise of his exploded the minute the baton with the healing essence touched him."

"Bearing all that mind," said Reena, "the question I pose is this: How did his essence get into that fire?"

Jonah fell silent. The truth was that he didn't know the answer. None of them did. He didn't know what happened to Creyton's essence after that night at S.T.R. He hadn't given it much thought other than the relief that the bastard was gone.

"But there is something that is equally important," said Reena, distracting them all from their thoughts. "The part that you remembered about Creyton's fire intimating to Inimicus about the '*lambs implementing their plans.*' God only knows what that means."

"According to Creyton's fire, those plans were already in place," said Jonah.

"So—what?" said Terrence. "Is Moonboy O'Shea actually Inimicus, then? Is he, I don't know, trying to merge himself with Creyton's essence in the fire or something?"

Jonah straightened at that revolting thought. But Reena answered for him.

"That can't work," she said flat-out. "A lunatic who has fits of psychosis that coincide with the moon merging with an essence in a fire? That's damn near possession. And that's not possible."

But Jonah had a twinge of uncertainty. Yes, it sounded absurd when Reena put it like that, but when one was an Eleventh Percenter, the word *possible* didn't hold much weight anyway.

"Fine." Terrence stood up. "I've got the perfect solution. So whatever is left of Creyton's essence is in a fire in a run-down house somewhere? We find it, go in there with a hose, and put that sucker out. Who's with me?"

Jonah threw himself into work and school. They were instrumental in centering his mind, and both did so in unique ways. Work provided an opportunity for him to continue familiarizing himself with university history, as research and history were two of his favorite things. So work time was a pleasure, even with Lola Barnhardt hovering around him. School forced him to focus on his coursework. Once assignments got underway, there was just no mental room for bits of essence in cold fires, Inimicus, partially constructed Spectral Events…or murder scenes in a diner.

Jonah had had a hard time filing that one away. He hadn't seen what happened with his own two eyes, and Mr. Decessio, in an effort to keep everyone's nerves as level as possible, had shared no details. But he had the very annoying habit of picturing whatever he heard. And after hearing about that diner, he'd done just that.

These were reasons why work and school had their benefits.

Jonah could always count on Douglas to distract him at school, too. He had agreed to meet Douglas for lunch after one of the latter's graduate courses. Jonah was interested in hearing about his class, as they'd had some guest professor, but Doug wanted to go on about his grandmother's displeasure about his decision to go to graduate school.

"Oh, and it gets better!" he said hotly after they refilled their sodas. "When I asked her opinion on whether or not I should continue my studies in Urban Regional Planning, she informed me that her interest in my studies ended when I walked across the stage the first time! I do not get what that woman's problem is!"

"You know, Douglas?" said Jonah in a serious tone. "It sounds like you're still clawing for granny's acceptance."

"Am not." Doug's answer came out far too quickly for it to be true. "Grandma has made it quite clear that everything I do is a failure, especially in comparison to my rugged, hardcore uncles and cousins. I hate that—" he stopped himself when he saw the expression on Jonah's face. They'd been down this road before, after all. "Um—I mean that I'd be grateful if my Grandma had more appreciation, that's all," he finished rather timidly. "Hey, do you want to do some chess club recruiting here in the caf?"

Training was always fun, and got more and more so each time Jonah did it. He loved no longer being the new guy anymore. But even after all this time, everyone still regarded him with keen interest, all because he was the Blue Aura. He found that part aggravating; hadn't he acquitted himself well over the years?

"Jonah, you're just as normal as the rest of us," said Liz when he touched on the subject one evening. They were in the middle of a training session as partners, and he'd just parried her attempt to hit a pressure point in his arm. "You're Blue, but you don't have to impress anyone. Especially not at this point."

Jonah attempted a wind attack, but Liz tricked him by getting into his personal space so that the maneuver would have incapacitated him as well. "It's just that being scrutinized gets tiresome," he muttered as he glanced at Trip and Karin, who eyed him with the usual disdain.

"We all get scrutinized, Jonah," said Liz. "But since it occurs so much from other people, we have no business doing it to ourselves. Besides, you passed the Nella test."

"The Nella test?"

"Oh yeah," said Liz. "My sister is just fifteen, and very sweet when she wants to be, but she is inordinately picky and selective about those she allows into her heart as friends. She is a great judge of character—you should have seen her at Sandrine's last Christmas party. Anyway, she adores you. Talks about you more than I do. Now Dad, Mom, and Sandrine want to meet you, and they aren't the types of people who actively do that kind of stuff!"

"Huh." It was hard to believe that the rest of Liz's family was so private and guarded when she and Nella were so bubbly and social. But the endorsement she'd given him lifted his spirits nonetheless. "Tell me; what was Nella's impression of Bobby? And the rest of your family's impression?"

"Glowing," replied Liz. "Not that I would have needed their approval to date him."

Jonah smirked, and they continued training.

After narrative class one evening shortly thereafter, Jonah returned to the estate to find that everyone had broken off into their respective activities. He laughed when Benjamin and several others wanted to watch reruns of *ScarYous Tales of the Paranormal* (Terrence abandoned them after telling them *Grave Messages* was worlds better). Reena had agreed to paint one of Malcolm's wooden swans. Liz attempted, yet again, to convince Bobby that detailed notes were better than the whole night-before cram.

Nella had begun to teach guitar to Vera and Magdalena. Reena had explained to Jonah that since Vera had turned Nella on to the theatre, it would only be right to show interest in something that Nella enjoyed as well. The women were having a rough time of it. Magdalena's and Vera's fingertips were raw; they looked like Alvin's feet had when he returned from jogging barefoot. Jonah supposed that's why Nella brought out the guitar picks. Those things seemed to be making the experience much more pleasant.

Nella looked so happy playing the music, which Jonah found refreshing. Up until that point, the only other Eleventh Percenter he'd met who'd had an affinity for music was Trip, and he scowled and brooded when he practiced (much like he did with everything else). Jonah had always imagined that if a person was musically inclined, it should provide pleasure. And Nella, unlike Trip, made it look fun the whole time. She even smiled when Magdalena dropped her picked for the fifth time.

Jonah saw that he wasn't the only one enjoying the proceedings. Jonathan stood near him, looking at them with amusement.

"Are you enjoying yourself, sir?" he joked.

"Extremely," said Jonathan. "I just wish that Vera and Magdalena would stop getting so frustrated. Nellaina has been playing guitar since she was four years of age. They, on the other hand, have been playing four hours."

Jonah snorted, but sobered somewhat. "Did you make those notifications to your other Guidemates, sir?"

"I did." Jonathan sobered as well. "All the other Protector Guides and heralds have been alerted and tasked with keeping a lookout for...other incidents."

"Are those likely?" asked Jonah.

"I've no idea, Jonah," said Jonathan. "I pray that O'Shea is contained quickly, and that he is acting alone. He is a very disturbed individual, much like the 49er."

Jonah winced. He hadn't told Jonathan about the remnants of Creyton's essence in that fire. He just didn't know how to breach the subject. It was bad enough that his little fire could be influencing Wyndam O'Shea, but when Jonathan mentioned others, it really rattled him.

"You think that he could be working with other Deadfallen disciples?" he asked. "Just how many of them slipped through the Curaie's grasp?"

"Well, Jonah, that's not a simple question to answer," said Jonathan, "because Creyton—"

Jonathan tensed.

The air pressure changed so suddenly that Jonah's ears popped. He noticed that everyone else got jarred as well. Magdalena even dropped her guitar pick again. Only one thing had that kind of range and power.

A Ghost Wave.

Trip and Karin burst out of the kitchen, with the former clutching his head like he had a headache.

"Titus," said Jonathan, his voice stern, "did you do that?"

Trip's eyes narrowed. "Jonathan, I am *here*. Right here, inside. That kind of range and intensity would have never come from indoors. It would have destroyed too many surfaces."

Jonathan's eyes flashed. "Someone is making their presence known outside."

Jonah's eyes widened. Trip was the only person he knew who used Ghost Waves. What the hell was this?

"Seems that way, sir," said Trip.

"Everybody outside," commanded Jonathan.

Jonah was the nearest to the door, so he led the pack as the residents poured onto the grounds. He had no idea what he expected to see out front, but it was definitely not a jet-black SUV.

Terrence and Reena came to Jonah's side, and looked at him in complete confusion. Had the driver of the SUV been responsible for the Ghost Wave?

Not a single one of them knew what to make of this.

"Is...Is someone in that thing?" asked Spader cautiously. "Because vehicles going on their own just ain't my gig. Reminds me of that *Christine* movie."

Jonathan didn't answer Spader's question. His face was a mask of calm, but Jonah was certain that he was angry.

What the hell *was* this?

The driver's door popped open, and everyone jumped (Liz actually pushed Nella behind her). A lean man stepped out from the driver's side, and shut the door behind him. It wasn't pitch-black dark just yet, so Jonah was able to make out a dark jacket, black cargo pants, and steel-toe boots. The man didn't acknowledge any of them as he ringed the vehicle and opened the passenger door. It was almost like some kind of red carpet treatment for a celebrity or something.

"I can't see much of anything," muttered Terrence. "Whoever is the closest to the porch, turn on the light!"

The nearest person—Maxine—clicked on the light, which didn't really help matters in Jonah's opinion. The man held the door for the passenger, whose movements were not as fluid as the driver's had been. It seemed that his exit was much more laborious as he exchanged words with other man. Together, they moved into everyone's line of sight.

The man who'd been the passenger was older. Much older; he was either in his eighties or nineties. He looked to Jonah like a man who'd been strapping, intimidating, and maybe even dangerous—at one time. But those days were clearly behind him now. His steps were calculated and deliberate, but he wasn't bent, nor did he have a limp. An ash-grey beard obscured a face that showed significant wear due to the pull of age.

The driver was clearly the man's son. There was no doubt in Jonah's mind that, at his current age, the man was not only in his prime, but at the place his father had been in his heyday.

"Evening to you, Jonathan!" said the father in a voice that carried strength that his body didn't.

Jonathan's face remained calm. "Gamaliel."

Now Jonah heard mutterings amongst his friends. Most of it was unintelligible, but he caught some things here and there:

"Gamaliel? As in Gamaliel Kaine?"

"*The* Gamaliel?"

"Legend?"

Jonathan didn't acknowledge any of them. His eyes remained on the visitors.

"And G.J.?" he said to the younger man. "You've grown into a strong man, son."

Unmoved, the younger man inclined his head rather stiffly. "Hello, Jonathan."

Gamaliel smiled. "It's been a long while, Jonathan. Do you still believe in blessings?"

"Every day is a blessing, Gamaliel," murmured Jonathan. "Life itself is a blessing. But I have to ask you about the Ghost Wave. Were the dramatics necessary?"

The old man hesitated, and then laughed. "I'd forgotten that you don't care for Ghost Waves."

"No, I don't." Jonathan appeared to be tired of the small talk, but kept his cool. "What is it that you need, Gamaliel? How can we help you?"

"We are in need of your wisdom and expertise, Jonathan." Gamaliel looked serious for the first time. "We wanted to know if you'd grant us haven to discuss things."

"Think before you do that, Jonathan," spat Trip. "Think hard and clear."

Jonathan took a deep breath. "Haven granted. Welcome to our home. How is Sanctum Arcist holding up? How are your students?"

"Why don't you ask them yourself!" said Gamaliel.

He nodded at G.J., who snapped his fingers. With a crisp wind, nearly thirty people stepped out of thin air near Gamaliel and G.J., having used the *Astralimes*.

"WHOA!" shouted Bobby in alarm. Several other people stepped back from the new arrivals as well.

Trip glared at Jonathan. "You just had to grant them haven!"

Reena tried to pull Jonah's arm. "Jonah," she hissed. "Jonah!"

But Jonah didn't hear her. Once again, the color drained from his face. Not because Gamaliel and son looked pleased as punch at their reactions. It wasn't even because the population of the front yard had just increased by about thirty-two.

It was because one of the people who'd appeared, near a man on G.J.'s right, was Rheadne.

Jonah looked around. His worst fear was confirmed: Vera had spotted her as well. He clearly saw a muscle twitching in her jaw in the porch light.

"We don't mean you any harm," said G.J., who placed a hand on his father's shoulder. "It's just that after what happened at that Crystal Diner not too far from here, we couldn't be too cautious."

9

Citizens Kaine

Innumerable pairs of eyes were now on Jonathan, whose facial expression never changed. As mysterious as Jonathan was, Jonah (once he tore his eyes off of Rheadne) thought that he could tell his thought pattern. Yeah, that G.J. guy claimed that he and his buddies didn't mean any harm. But that *Astralimes* move had been a power play. There was no other word for it. It also made the next question obvious.

Would Jonathan treat it as such?

Jonathan surveyed the group in silence for several moments. Trip looked as though he had a very definite opinion on how Jonathan should handle the situation, but he didn't say anything.

"You want to discuss things, do you?" said the Protector Guide at last. "Very well, then. Let's move to the courtyard, everyone. We'd best be comfortable and well-acquainted if we'll be matching wits."

The residents of the estate headed toward Jonathan's desired destination, casting wary looks at the new arrivals. Gamaliel lifted two wizened fingers and beckoned his own group forward. Vera contemplated Rheadne with a cool expression, and then glanced at Jonah. He pretended that he didn't see it. This wasn't the time for that.

He fell in step with Terrence and Reena, who were nearer to the back of the group of residents.

"Okay," he said. "Tell me something about that old man that I don't know."

Reena cast the group another wary glance. "That old man, Jonah, is Gamaliel Kaine. He is pretty noteworthy."

"Pretty noteworthy?" chimed in Terrence, who looked at Reena in disbelief. "Jonah, Gamaliel was probably the best Networker in existence."

Jonah did a double take. "That guy was a Networker?"

"Yeah," said Terrence. "People in Spectral Law swore by him. Remember how we learned that Felix's dad had been a great Networker? I wouldn't be surprised if he learned everything he knew from that guy."

Jonah looked back at the older Kaine, who obviously wasn't moving as crisply as his younger counterparts. His son G.J. and another man stayed in close proximity to him. Jonah had always had respect for the elderly, and found himself cautiously intrigued.

"He's got to be at least in his mid-eighties," he remarked. "How long was he a Networker?"

Terrence pulled out his favorite jelly beans, and tossed a couple into his mouth. "I remember that Dad said that Kaine retired from their ranks when he began his consulting job for the S.P.G.," he replied. "He would have hashed out another campaign, but he had to go."

"Campaign?" said Jonah with a frown. "What, they have to be voted into the Networkers or something?"

Since Terrence had taken the reins of most of the story, Jonah was surprised to hear Reena scoff.

"The Networkers make a career of corralling Spirit Reapers," she said. "You know that time doesn't really matter to spirits, and the Networker's tenures aren't recognized as years, but as campaigns. Seven years equates one campaign."

"Right," said Terrence. "Gamaliel Kaine there did four campaigns, two years."

Jonah did the mental math, and then nodded. "Wow. That's quite a time frame! But you said he had to go, Terrence. What did he do after thirty years that made him get canned?"

"He wasn't canned, per se," said Terrence. "Dad told us that Mr. Kaine remained old-school. He wasn't able to change with the times. He thought the methods of the Networkers needed to remain old-school, too. He even pushed to become head of the pack. That wasn't gonna happen."

They reached their destination, but no one seated themselves, since Jonathan had desired everyone to get acquainted. Terrence lowered his voice and continued.

"He had to be dealt with, or something, but they weren't willing to screw him out of his job—"

Terrence immediately fell silent, and Jonah was about to ask why, but then Reena's eyes darted to a direction behind him. Jonah wheeled around, and found himself face to face with Kaine himself.

"Jonah Rowe, is it?" he asked. I was wondering if we could converse while everyone, ah, complies with dear Jonathan's request."

"Certainly, sir," said Jonah respectfully, and Terrence and Reena gave them privacy. Gamaliel seemed to regard Jonah with some sort of underlying scrutiny that he couldn't place.

"Forgive me, sir, but how did you know that I was Jo—?"

"You're the only one here that fits Rheadne's description," said Kaine. "She told me all about how she bailed you out in the middle of the night."

It took Jonah a moment, but then he understood. "Oh, that. My arm was injured at the time, and—"

"Spare me," said Gamaliel edgily, which surprised Jonah. "I was quite intrigued to learn that you mastered the Mentis Cavea."

Jonah raised an eyebrow. That had been such a random statement that he didn't know how to react.

"It was an interesting thing for a layman like yourself to want to learn," said the old man.

"I'm sorry, but what?" The intrigue that Jonah had for this man faded with each passing word. "My physical life was in danger. We'd been Haunted! If Felix hadn't shown me—"

Gamaliel made a wry face. "Felix Duscere. The sazer drunk. He taught you."

"Sazer drunk?" repeated Jonah. "Did something happen for you not to trust him?"

"I don't trust anybody," replied Gamaliel. "And I certainly don't trust sazers who trade Networker secrets among novices."

Anger flared up inside Jonah. "You—"

Gamaliel turned his back on him. G.J. wasn't too far away. Jonah could only assume that he had heard the whole thing, as a smug little smirk was on his face the entire time he escorted his father to his seat.

Jonah took a leveling breath. That living relic had some nerve putting him down like that. Jonah would have loved to have seen his archaic ass fight off fifty-something Haunts.

Attempting to locate Terrence and Reena, he turned into the direction they had gone. He hadn't made it two steps before someone said, "Jonah."

He paused, closed his eyes, and steeled himself. It hadn't been this harrowing when he'd met Creyton for the first time. "Rheadne. So I'm guessing that you knew that Vera and I were Eleventh Percenters that night, huh?"

"Not that night, no," she responded. "When I got back to Florida, I told G.J. about helping you, and he said your description sounded like the Blue Aura who lived at the Grannison-Morris estate. Who'd have guessed that I'd have run into you, of all people?"

Jonah ran his tongue across his teeth. He didn't care for people noting that he was the Blue Aura before they noted anything else. Yeah, it went with the territory in the ethereal world, but he had no appreciation for the label always preceding him.

Rheadne hadn't finished speaking. "It did make some things make sense, though. Your essence was far too developed to be one of the Ungifted."

Ungifted. That term sounded like it might have negative undertones. It just didn't sound right. But there was something else in

Rheadne's statement that gave him pause. "My essence was developed?" he asked. "Are you an essence reader?"

"God, no." She laughed. "That power would suck to have. I'm skilled at ethereal tracking. I can sense the presence of other ethereal beings. But I wouldn't have needed essence reading to feel the tension between you and your dainty little friend over there. What was that about?"

"I—" Jonah hesitated. He wasn't comfortable explaining his and Vera's situation, or whatever it was, to a woman he barely knew. "She isn't my *dainty little friend*. We were on a date that night."

"Really?" Rheadne glanced Vera's way with doubt in her eyes. "It wasn't just an outing of two friends?"

"Two—why—no—why would you think that?" sputtered Jonah. Hadn't it been obvious that he and Vera had been on a date?

"I took the hint from you," shrugged Rheadne. "You were the one who introduced her as simply *Vera*, after all."

With a final grin, she went off and sat next to two of her friends, which left Jonah alone.

Now he felt awkward as hell. When he'd introduced Vera that way, he did so out of respect. He didn't want to place a label on her that they hadn't yet established. But it didn't sound so great when it came from Rheadne. Was that how Vera had interpreted it, too?

"Jonah, you look as if you've encountered a Spirit Reaper," said Reena, who'd found him again.

"No," muttered Jonah. "Worse than that. That woman you chewed me out about? Where you said I disrespected Vera? That's her."

He pointed Rheadne out to Reena, whose confused expression cleared. Jonah also saw comprehension on her face.

"So that's why Vera got so frigid all of a sudden," she said.

Jonah looked at Vera. She seemed to be having a forced conversation with Ben-Israel and Magdalena while determinedly not looking at him or Rheadne. "Reena, I still don't fully get—"

"Of course you don't," interrupted Reena, who looked at him sadly. "You're a man."

"Seriously? You—"

"Attention, everyone," called Jonathan, whose voice carried impressively over the din.

Jonah finally seated himself next to Terrence and Reena while giving an irritated look to the latter. His irritation faded, however, when he noticed the seating arrangements in the courtyard. Most of the residents sat among each other, as they usually did. Trip and his clique sat amongst themselves, also as usual. But Kaine's people sat entirely away from them. If a bystander happened to see the way they'd segregated themselves, they would have thought that the residents of the estate carried some infectious disease.

Jonah shook his head. No matter how old people got, they were always inflexible about moving beyond their comfort zones. Most everyone out here was grown, yet they still exhibited such childish behaviors.

"There are those of you who are already aware of who our guests are," continued Jonathan, and Jonah could tell that he had regained his composure. "But for those of you that are not, this is Gamaliel Kaine, Sr., who is the founder and instructor of Sanctum Arcist, which is based on the outskirts of Fort Lauderdale in Florida. This is his son, Gamaliel, Jr.," he indicated the younger man who attended Gamaliel, Sr. so closely, "and there is his other son, Gabriel."

Frowning, Jonah looked in the direction that Jonathan pointed. Gabriel Kaine had barely even acknowledged the introduction. They were definitely family, but Gabriel was neither as strapping as his brother nor had the presence of his father. Jonah wondered why no one seemed to treat Gabriel with more respect, seeing as how he was the second son of the Big Boss. But he just looked like another one of the pack.

"According to Gamaliel," Jonathan went on, "the residents of Sanctum Arcist have been noticing strange occurrences around their dwelling place same as we have."

Gamaliel cleared his throat. "There had indeed been an upsurge in untoward activity within these past few months. My son G.J. began cleaning up what was initially believed to be small pockets of vampiric activity. The beasts had become much bolder all up and down the coast until the disappearance of the 49er."

Jonah, Terrence, and Reena glanced at each other. They all knew the circumstances of the 49er's disappearance. It hadn't been a secret, after all. Jonah couldn't take all of the credit, however, as it had been Trip that had doomed the traitorous vampire to be a transient, vegetative wraith.

"It turned out that they weren't vampires," continued Gamaliel. "The savagery was identical, but the crimes turned out to be Eighth Chapter."

Jonathan's eyes narrowed. "Deadfallen disciples."

"Indeed," nodded Gamaliel.

"So would it be safe to assume that you spent several evenings trying to stamp out imaginary vampires?" asked Jonathan, which took Jonah by surprise. He'd never heard Jonathan take jabs at anyone. What was it about this guy that made him do that?

It turned out that Gamaliel hadn't missed the sarcasm. G.J. glared at Jonathan, instantly angry, but his father forestalled him with a raised hand. "We made a logical choice to act," he said calmly. "The gifts that we have are meant to be used. What would you expect us to do? Converse with the Guides and then sit on my hands?"

The man had baited Jonathan, but Jonathan only reacted with a small chuckle.

"Opinion noted," he said.

"Pardon me," said Reena, who rose. "I've got a question. It was unnecessary for you to have been in the wrong for so long. Why didn't anyone correspond with the experts on vampires? I'm certain that Felix Duscere, for one, would have told you everything you needed to know."

Jonah's mouth twisted. Reena didn't hear the scathing comments Gamaliel had made about Felix.

When they heard Felix's name, both Gamaliel and G.J. made sour expressions.

"Duscere's help was not required," said Gamaliel. "As I said, the crimes were Eighth Chapter, not vampiric."

Reena didn't look pleased with that answer, nor did Jonathan.

"When you made the discovery that they were Deadfallen disciples," said Jonathan slowly, "what actions did you take then?"

"We attempted to destroy them," said G.J. "But that quickly became impossible."

"May I ask why?"

G.J. took a reluctant breath. "The Deadfallen that we encountered have become more vicious in their actions," he said. "We figured out that three of them, India Drew, Matt Harrill, and Reese Dixon, had terrorized a town that was completely inhabited with Ungifteds."

There was that word again. Jonah was about to ask, but Jonathan beat his question.

"I have made my thoughts very clear on that term," he said sternly. "We do not refer to Tenth Percenters 'Ungifted' simply because they are not ethereal."

G.J. rolled his eyes. "Kindly do not impose your views on me, Jonathan," he said. "It's just a word. Anyway, Pop sent Drover and Green to look into it. They never came back."

"But why would they be so riled all of a sudden?" asked Spader. "Between the three you just named and the Moon Man O'Shea, it sounds as if they've been emboldened for some reason."

G.J. looked at Spader. "You know of Wyndam O'Shea?"

Jonah was surprised by that revelation as well, and he looked at the ratty boy, stunned.

"Yeah, I do," said Spader. "He disfigured a friend of my Dad's when I was about five years old. He was one of the ones that never went to The Plane with No Name."

G.J. appraised Spader without words for several moments. "They are angry," he said at last. "Angry and vengeful. When they discovered that the 49er, one of their fellow disciples, attempted to take their beloved Transcendent's position, it caused a great deal of outrage. They probably would have torn him limb from limb and then staked him, but Trip over there made him impossible for them to locate."

Almost mockingly, he inclined his head in Trip's direction, but Trip didn't reciprocate. Jonah spoke up now.

"Did you just say Transcendent?" he asked. "Because I know for a fact that Creyton's followers called him *Master*."

"Know it for a fact, do you?" Gamaliel's eyes slid Jonah's way. "Then your knowledge is poor. Those stupid minions were the ones that referred to him as Master. But his handpicked disciples referred to him as their Transcendent in reference to what he believed he had done, and what they believed they might one day achieve."

Jonah closed his eyes. Creyton referred to himself as *Transcendent*? Messiah complex, much?

"Jonathan, sir," said Douglas suddenly, and many heads turned his way, "who are these Deadfallen people? Why are we not familiar with them?"

"Trust me, Douglas," said Jonathan, "most Eleventh Percenters are familiar with them. But no one knows all the names."

"Where are they?" asked Douglas.

"Integrated." Trip spoke up this time. "A bunch of y'all here might as well be babies, but your family members might know. When the Curaie tried to close in on Creyton, a bunch of those Deadfallen bastards either got killed, or got caught and put on the Plane with No Name. But another bunch of 'em were never apprehended. Creyton put them into Integrated Status, but they could return to him at any time. I suppose you could refer to them as on-call workers, or something. When he started that whole vessel thing some years back, he started using the minions. Much tighter leash there."

Gamaliel gave a mock applause. "Expert Deadfallen knowledge straight from the son of the inner circle!"

"Don't raise your voice too loud, Gramps," snapped Trip. "You might dislocate a hip."

That aroused the ire of many of the Sanctum residents, but G.J. was the one who rose.

"You want your ass kicked, Rivers?" he whispered.

Trip stood up. "I'm right here, Shit Face. Step up. Do me a favor."

"That is enough, you two," growled Jonathan. "Gamaliel, if you want our assistance, corral your boy here and keep the venom to yourself. Trip, no one here is a Shit Face. Drop it. *Now.*"

The young men seated themselves, staring daggers at each other. Jonah stood up, dumbfounded.

"I'm not even worried about all of the tension," he announced. "I'm still on those psychopath Deadfallen. They just integrated back into society right under the Curaie's noses?"

"Jonah, they didn't *become* integrated," said Jonathan, "they were already integrated. They lived everyday lives just like everyone else, but they had secret lives as Creyton's disciples. If their Transcendent told them to lay low, they did it. Only Creyton could name them all, and he also knew every detail of their private lives."

Jonah looked around at those around him, ashamed of himself for the nasty urge to question whom he could trust. He knew these people. They were his friends. Most of them, anyway. But he knew that he wasn't alone. There was suspicion in the air.

Jonathan sensed the shift, and his eyes narrowed. "That was not an invitation to suddenly start second-guessing dear friends. We are friends and family here."

"Can you be sure of that, Jonathan?" queried Gamaliel as he extracted a can of peach snuff and piled some into the left side of his jaw (Vera pulled a disgusted face). "We all know that you are an unflappable paragon of virtue, but can the same be said of your students?"

"Can the same be said of your folks here?" demanded Nella at the top of her voice.

It shocked most everyone, and Liz widened her eyes at her sister in warning. But Nella shook her head and rose to her feet.

"No, I won't be quiet, Liz," she said. "This man is encouraging Jonathan to doubt us, so is he willing to doubt his own people, too? They're just like us!"

"In ethereality only," scoffed a tall, brown-haired woman leaning on a tree near Gabriel.

"That isn't necessary, Penelope," said Gamaliel, though Jonah could tell by the look in his eyes that he didn't appreciate being told off by some girl decades his junior. It made Jonah laugh, and he saw smirks on Terrence's and Reena's faces as well. Bobby even looked at his girl-friend's younger sister as though she had bigger ball than LTSU's defensive line.

"With all due respect, Gamaliel," said Jonathan, "Nellaina's inquiry is a valid one. Can you vouch for your pupils?"

"I would my trust my students to the ends of the earth," said Gamaliel coldly.

Jonah and Terrence glanced at each other. That was a truly bold statement, but Jonah didn't agree. He wouldn't trust these people to the ends of the grounds.

"Admirable," said Jonathan. "But you have yet to answer my question. I appreciate the information you've given us. But we still do not know your reason for being here."

Gamaliel stood, and spat out a revolting arc of snuff onto the ground. Some of the residents shuddered. "I felt that the recent misfortunes have birthed an opportunity. I felt that it was necessary to pool our knowledge. Between your considerable tenure as a Protector Guide and my years of combating all things detrimental to the ethereal world, we just might quell this insurrection."

Many eyes turned to Jonathan, who looked pensive for several moments. Finally, he nodded.

"That could work," he said. "But Gamaliel, the logistics of the thing puzzle me. Is it your plan to coordinate this togetherness from Southern Florida?"

"Not at all," smiled Gamaliel. "We will take advantage of your gracious granting of haven."

He gave a gesture, and all of his counterparts tossed twigs on the ground. Jonah stood in alarm. In their experience, no one who used twigs as portals had good intentions. These people lowered in his eyes further. But Rheadne was one of them. That had to mean something, right?

Where each twig had landed on the ground, camping equipment appeared. Supplies for tents, sleeping bags, battery powered lamps, and many other things appeared before their very eyes.

"Do you see this right now?" demanded Terrence. "Did these...these people just invite themselves into our domain?"

"They didn't invite themselves, Terrence," said Reena. "Jonathan granted them haven. That includes housing, quartering, and generous protection."

"Generous protection?" said Jonah. "Do these people look like they need protection?"

Reena sighed. "Jonah, generous protection is their protection from *Jonathan*. As long as the haven agreement stands, that old bastard could burn down the backyard, and Jonathan couldn't touch him."

"What?" Jonah frowned at that. "Jonathan wouldn't be stupid enough to tie his own hands like that. He must have a way around it. He must know something we don't."

"He always does," said Terrence.

"I agree," said Reena. "I pray that nothing bad comes of this...arrangement."

Jonah glanced over at Jonathan, who'd just got done instructing the people of Sanctum Arcist to fracture the twigs so as to close their connections. "Switching gears," he said to Terrence and Reena, "do you think that Wyndam O'Shea is Inimicus?"

"I don't know, Jonah," said Reena. "It's difficult to say now. There are too many variables now."

"But he was the one who killed those poor people in the diner," snapped Terrence. "Why couldn't he have been the one who went to that fire and bragged about it?"

"Terrence, we just heard the names of three other disciples—"

"And none of them kill in accordance with moon phases, Reena," said Jonah.

Reena sighed. "You got me there," she conceded, "but we can't worry about what a trace of Creyton's essence in a fire is commanding a person who might be Inimicus to do right now. We don't have the time."

"What do you mean, Reena?"

"These people." Reena jabbed a finger at the group now constructing campsites. "I just hope that Jonathan knows what he's doing."

Jonah noticed several people conversing, while many headed back to the estate so as to speak away from prying eyes and ears.

"We can talk more about it tomorrow," said Reena. "I want to call Kendall before I got to sleep."

"I'll head back up with you," said Terrence. "All this excitement has made me quite hungry. Interested in a club sandwich, Jonah?"

"I'd love one," said Jonah, "but I'll come behind you guys in a few. I want to tell Jonathan something really quick."

Terrence and Reena left, and Jonah headed in Jonathan's direction when someone grabbed his wrist.

It was Rheadne. The sight of her gave Jonah another one of those jolts. Why did that keep happening?

"Come to my tent whenever you can," she said quietly. "Tonight, tomorrow—whenever. It's the red one with the tiger on the side of it. And don't bring your buddies."

10

Friction

When Jonah returned to the estate, he was unsurprised to see that no one had gone to bed. They were still talking about Gamaliel Kaine and Sanctum Arcist. He knew where Reena would be, so her absence wasn't a surprise to him, either. He had half a mind to join Terrence for some food when, in a room off the den, he heard something that did surprise him.

"Jonathan, if Kaine wanted your assistance, then there are proper channels he could have taken." It was Trip speaking. "I'm not disputing your influence, but there are all kinds of other Protector Guides between here and Florida. Kaine bypassed all of them, and the Curaie, and dumps his shit in your lap? And let's take a closer look at something else as well, shall we? Gamaliel and G.J. want your help? Fine. Why did they not share this information privately? They shared this information in front of everyone like a damned panel discussion. The whole thing stinks to high heaven."

Jonah frowned. He actually agreed with Trip. The man had a point. Was Hell going to freeze over?

"In many ways, Gamaliel's approach was quite intelligent, Titus," said Jonathan. "Had he put the information through the proper channels, who knows what integrated Deadfallen disciples could have heard it? India Drew, Reese Dixon, and Matt Harrill could have easily slipped back under the radar if they'd gotten wind of it. O'Shea could

111

have as well. As for dumping things in my lap…you didn't see the carnage in that diner. You think I'd sweep those concerns under the rug? I will not dispute Gamaliel's track record. His aid could be beneficial."

"An interesting observation, Jonathan," said Trip in a rather sardonic tone, "considering the fact that Kaine cost you—"

"Shut your mouth, Titus," said Jonathan sharply. "The past is the past. It cannot be changed. Do I trust Gamaliel Kaine? I have no answer for that. If he is sincere, then a united front between us may very well prevent further loss of physical life. If he is not sincere, then my granting him haven keeps him close, where he is unable to bring any harm to his students, my students, or himself."

There was silence for a few minutes.

"You want me to watch them, don't you?" asked Trip.

"Yes," said Jonathan.

Trip laughed. "I knew you didn't trust that fucking shanty town that's in our backyard now."

"It's not a matter of trust, Titus," said Jonathan. "It's a matter of common sense. As a Protector Guide, it behooves me not to take my role lightly."

"Whatever you say, Jonathan," snorted Trip. "But as for keeping an eye—or in my case, ear—on these new fools, consider it done."

"Thank you, Titus."

Jonah hurried away, well aware that that was the end of it. After all the surprises of the night, he didn't want to get caught eavesdropping.

What had Trip meant when said Kaine cost Jonathan something? Gamaliel had called Jonathan an unflappable paragon of virtue, but that had obviously been sarcastic. What did he know about Jonathan? Or (given the fact that Jonathan told Trip that he wanted to keep Gamaliel close), should Jonah be asking what Jonathan knew about Kaine?

When he finally made it to the kitchen, he overheard another heated conversation.

"I don't like it," said Bobby. "I don't like how they just showed up at night in those numbers and have been given room and board."

"Ain't nobody got room and board," said Spader, who absent-mindedly moved a jack of spades across the table. "Jonathan gave them access to a wing of bathrooms and showers here that no one even uses. That's it as far as coming in here. For everything else, they've got their own crap—"

"Yeah, they do," interrupted Bobby, "and they transported said crap via twig portals! People who use those things are never up to any good, Spader!"

"Bobby, just because an object is used for dark purposes doesn't mean that the object is evil," Spader spat. "Twig transports were commonplace once, right?"

Bobby made a face at Spader. "Impressive," he muttered. "Who'd have thought that a gambler could be philosophical?"

"Bobby. Spader." Terrence sighed and flicked away a card of his own. "Just drop it. I'm sated and satisfied, and you two are ruining it."

Bobby rolled his eyes and departed. Spader left seconds later, wondering aloud about whether or not someone in Sanctum Arcist knew anything about cards. Jonah lowered himself in the recently vacated seat.

"Those two will come to blows sooner or later," muttered Terrence. "They should just have their duel and be done with it."

"It wouldn't be a duel," replied Jonah. "Well, *Bobby* would be dueling, but Spader would be flailing around and screaming."

Terrence nearly spat out his water. Jonah laughed at him.

"So," said Terrence, "you got any more opinions about these people?"

"I've got several opinions, but not too many of them are nice," admitted Jonah. "I even found myself agreeing with Trip, for God's sake."

When Terrence raised an eyebrow, Jonah filled him in on what he'd overheard.

"I wasn't even trying to be nosy," said Jonah. "But, in all honesty, Trip wasn't exactly speaking quietly."

Terrence gave no criticism, and stared off into space. "So he wants Trip to watch 'em. Huh. What could that old man have ever cost Jonathan? He barely looked capable of standing."

"He wasn't always old, Terrence," said Jonah. "And Jonathan has been around a long time himself. If he were alive, what would he be? One hundred seven? They could have had a falling out long before any of us were even in the world. But whatever happened was enough to make Jonathan lose composure when Trip brought it up."

Terrence nodded. "Jonathan hasn't even really volunteered information about his past," he said. "He never really came across as secretive or anything, but he hasn't ever given too much of himself. Maybe Reena might know something."

Jonah rose and made his own sandwich, finally. "Well, we won't find out tonight, because she's on the phone with Kendall. But let's just hope that, despite her apprehension, that whole thing doesn't turn out badly."

"Nah." Terrence seemed deep in thought again. "It won't be all bad."

"Yeah?" said Jonah, who put the finishing touches on his sandwich and went to close Malcolm's bread box. "Why do you say that?"

"Some of the women were fine," mumbled Terrence.

Jonah shook his head. "Were you hoping for a nightcap with that one named Penelope?"

"I'm not interested in her." Terrence shook his head. "I had my eye on another woman. Reena told me her name... what was it... Rheadne?"

Jonah fumbled with the breadbox, and spilled several slices of bread into the sink.

* * *

"You are one distracted guy," commented Whit.

"What gives you that idea?" Jonah tried hard to sound nonchalant.

"The book you're reading," said Whit without hesitation.

"What's wrong with—? Oh."

Jonah looked down and realized what Whit meant. He'd been thumbing through a Neuroscience textbook for the past several minutes, and hadn't taken in a single word.

Whit laughed. "I imagined that you wouldn't get insights for your Narrative class from that book."

"You imagined right," said Jonah, who closed the book and returned it to its proper place.

"Are you alright, though?" Sincerity flooded Whit's previously amused voice. "Feeling the weight of your midterm?"

"I guess you could say that." Jonah was evasive, but he wasn't worried. Whit never asked too many questions.

Whit nodded. "Why don't you take some of the self-imposed pressure off of yourself? Take a night off from studying. Catch a movie. Hey, when's the last time you been on a date? You probably haven't noticed, but Lola Barnhardt really likes you."

I noticed that before you *did,* Jonah thought. "They all sound good, Whit. You have my word that I will do at least one of those things."

Whit nodded in approval. "Say, why don't you get some fresh air right now? Ten minutes won't hurt anything."

Jonah took him up on that offer, and walked around to the corner of the Two Cents for extra privacy. When he was certain that he was alone, he closed his eyes, took a deep breath, and willed the curtain in his mind to open while he summoned a spirit at the same time. When he opened his eyes, his favorite spirit, the middle-aged war veteran, stood in front of him.

"Hello, sir," said Jonah respectfully.

The spirit smiled. "It's always a pleasure, son. Are things going well?"

Jonah really enjoyed his interactions with this spirit. He always had a kind word, was helpful whenever possible, and (most importantly to Jonah) referred to him as something besides *Eleventh Percenter*, which was the handle all the other spirits and spiritesses used. "The short answer is yes, I suppose," he answered, "but the long answer is that my life has just added some extra variables that may not mesh well."

The spirit nodded. "Factors such as those present themselves on an almost daily basis, young man. It's just a matter of choosing what has right on its side."

"But that's the thing," said Jonah. "I'm not sure how to do that. How do I know? How will I know?"

The soldier's spirit shook his head with a smile. Jonah had a feeling that if he'd been tangible, he'd have placed a hand on his shoulder. "I asked that question many times when I was in the war. At that time, I had some pretty concrete perceptions of right and wrong, but during my time in Spirit, I've learned one important thing."

"And what is that, sir?"

"That right is a matter of perspective," he replied. "Yes, people can *tell* you, but that's merely an imposition of their doctrine onto someone other than themselves. What's right can be fluid, much like time. A right decision on Monday may not be a right one on Tuesday. It all comes back to personal perspective."

The explanation was something straight from Jonathan's playbook, but Jonah got the gist. It was a relief to know that it was okay for him to be confused. "Thank you, sir," he said. "It was nice to exchange a few words about it all to someone who is impersonal."

"It's an honor, son." The spirit smiled, and disappeared.

Class was enjoyable, and Jonah was back home before eight. Although he couldn't see the Sanctum people from the front of the place, he had no trouble at all feeling the tension in the atmosphere. He headed upstairs to drop off his bag, with a vague inclination to journal or blog to clear his head.

That plan was dashed the minute he reached his room, which was occupied by Terrence and Reena.

"Relax," said Reena. "Nothing is wrong. We've just been waiting for you."

"Oh. Okay." Jonah dropped his bag. "You could have done that in the family room or kitchen."

"No we couldn't," said Terrence. "We're free from nosiness here."

That piqued Jonah's interest. "So I take it that Terrence filled you in, Reena?" he asked her. "So, do you have any information on Jonathan's past?"

Reena shook her head apologetically. "Jonathan is as much an enigma to me as he is a mentor," she told him. "But that's not why we're here. We're here about training tonight."

"What about it?"

"Kaine wants to do a combined one."

That gave Jonah pause. "I'll admit that I'm a bit intrigued, but what's the big deal?" he asked. "You look concerned."

"Yes, Jonah," said Reena, "I'm quite concerned. Somebody might get hurt."

"Reena, we all get banged up and bruised at trainings," Jonah reminded her. "What's the big deal about Sanctum?"

"Jonah, these Sanctum people treat every fight like it's a real duel for physical life," said Reena. "I've even heard that some years back, some people even got killed when training got carried away."

"What?" demanded Jonah. "Are you serious?"

Terrence glanced out of the window, as if someone might be eavesdropping there. "Jonah, do you remember your very first training? When Jonathan was explaining the Eleventh Percent?"

"Yes, of course."

"You remember asking if we fought spirits, and how Bobby and I told you that we weren't freedom fighters that sat around waiting for fights?"

"Of course," said Jonah.

"Well, that's what Sanctum does," said Terrence. "Kaine has got them thinking that they are some rugged band of survivalists. Like they're the ethereal world's last line of defense against a Spirit Reaper uprising or something."

Jonah slowly shook his head. "So, they're vigilantes? Like, ethereal vigilantes?"

Reena nodded. "Remember when Nella said that they were just like us, and that Penelope bitch said that it was in ethereality only? That's what she meant. I'm sure of it. They are likely under the impression that Jonathan's stance of fighting as a last resort has softened and spoiled us."

"Great," mumbled Jonah. "Just great. So we've been using weapons for practice only all this time, while they have been training as if a risk was a stone's throw away."

"Yeah," said Terrence. "But we have done our share of dangerous shit. No one could ever accuse us of weakness."

"Terrence," said Reena sternly, "the insanity that's happened to us was not a product of us looking for trouble. We were preserving our physical lives, which we have a human right to do. But these people? They traipse around like guns-for-hire."

"All opinions are noted," said Jonah, who reached for a sleeveless T-shirt. "Now, let's go out there and hopefully prevent a massacre."

Twenty minutes later, they were in the Glade. Jonah had seen Bast patrolling, and she looked to regard the new arrivals with indifference.

Gamaliel and his people from Sanctum were already there, trading holds amongst themselves while already endowed. Maybe it was because Jonah had been forewarned, or maybe it was the fact that his eyes didn't lie; these Eleventh Percenters *were* pretty vicious.

Jonah looked at the faces of his friends, and saw anxiety there as well. The only faces that lacked it were Bobby, who looked thrilled, Spader, for a reason unknown to Jonah, and Trip, who looked like he simply wanted an excuse to critically injure someone. Gamaliel, seated near the lights, spotted their faces and gave a smile, which was lopsided on account of the copious amounts of snuff in his mouth.

"We've been waiting for you kids!" he said cheerfully. "Now endow yourselves and let's begin!"

"Gamaliel," said Jonathan, who'd appeared not far from the trees, "I will thank you to leave the instruction of my pupils to me."

He didn't look angry or even annoyed, but Jonah thought his gray eyes were more piercing than usual.

G.J. contemplated Jonathan scornfully, but his father merely inclined his head.

"Begging your pardon, Jonathan," he said graciously. "I didn't intend to rock the boat."

"Like hell you didn't," grumbled Malcolm under his breath. It always surprised Jonah to hear Malcolm angry. As such a quiet man, he was probably the most likely to flip out if things got bad.

Jonah took an endowment from an elderly spiritess, and readied himself. The ratio of residents to guests gave the residents an advantage in numbers, so he wasn't surprised to see many people partner up amongst themselves. Others, like Bobby, Malcolm, Terrence, and Reena, decided to brave some of the Sanctum Arcist people. His eyes fell on Rheadne, but with Vera nearby, he didn't go anywhere near her. He needn't have bothered the contemplation though, because a man with spiky black hair moved in front of him.

"Name's Brock Tenta, Rowe," he announced quietly. "Twenty-seven years old, gray aura. Interested?"

The way he introduced himself was a little off-putting to Jonah. He had half a mind to sarcastically shout for the man's name, rank, and serial number. "Alright, Brock, I'm Jon—oh, wait, you already know that. Whatever. I'm game."

"Hands and holds?" asked Tenta. "Weapons?"

Jonah was about to mention that he had no interest in weapons when he noticed Tenta's heavily taped wrists and hands. What did he think they were about to do? Bare-knuckle boxing?

Unfortunately, Tenta took Jonah's inspection of his hands as an indicator of his preference, and smirked.

"That's perfectly fine," he said.

He threw a punch that Jonah wasn't ready for. His left fist collided with the side of Jonah's head, and Jonah fell to a knee. His left ear was ringing, and pain radiated from his neck to his temple.

"What the HELL!" he snapped as he slapped a hand to his ear. "I hadn't even said anything!"

"I just assumed you were ready to go," shrugged Tenta. "Course, if you're already incapacitated, I totally understand—"

Jonah didn't miss the insult, conjured mist to enshroud his fist all the way up to his forearm, and then smashed that forearm into Tenta's jaw.

It seemed that Jonah wasn't the only whose situation unraveled at that time. The entire training went straight to hell. Bobby, who had partnered with some guy who called himself Cisor, had gotten incensed after a short joke and shoulder-tackled him. Terrence had matched with a guy named Iuris Mason, and that situation deteriorated after Mason threw a handful of earth into Terrence's face just to get in a cheap shot. Grayson and a Sanctum man were at each other's throats, but then wound up crashing through a bench seconds later. Trip had altered the sound around his opponent almost to the point of nausea, and then beat him down. But, even amidst all of the chaos, the straw that broke the camel's back was the matchup between Reena and Penelope. Penelope was deceptively strong, but so was Reena. They'd been evenly matched for the most part; Penelope had even had the audacity to be surprised. She had attempted to knock Reena's legs out from underneath her, but Reena prevented that with her speed. Penelope's momentum carried her too far, and Reena sought to take advantage with a cold-spot trick. But the second she extended her hands, Penelope stiffened her fingers and did a knife-edged thrust directly into Reena's throat. With an abbreviated scream, Reena fell to the ground, her breath coming in troublesome gasps.

Jonah's mind nearly blanked when he saw what Penelope did and he would have rushed her right then and there, but—

"ENOUGH."

Jonathan's voice rang across the entire Glade, a fact made eerie by the fact that it hadn't risen. Everyone froze where they were. Not even the people from Sanctum Arcist disobeyed him.

He went to Reena, and placed a hand on her shoulder. "Relax your breathing," he commanded. "The agitated muscles will remain constricted if you continue trying to force air through them. Steady it, and relax." His eyes then snapped to Penelope, who stifled a flinch.

"Penelope Pulchrum, I cannot think of anything to say right now that could excuse your tactic."

"What!" said Penelope defiantly. "She extended her hands! I know that move; she was gonna displace the balance between heat and cold! No way was I experiencing that. No way!"

"Did it occur to you to grab her hands?" demanded Jonathan. "Or to invade her personal space so that she would be affected as well? Or even to flee?"

"My kids don't know how to flee, Jonathan," said Gamaliel. "And I must request of you the same thing you asked of me earlier: Leave my kids to me."

The old man winked at Penelope. Jonah saw it; there was no mistaking it. Jonathan, who had returned his attention to Reena, hadn't noticed.

"Terrence," said Jonathan, and Terrence nodded.

He lifted Reena into his arms, which made Jonah frown. Reena really must have been incapacitated for that to happen. She had very little tolerance for male gallantry.

Reena cast wintry eyes on Penelope from over Terrence's shoulder. "I'm going to tag you back," she whispered. "I stake it on everything I love."

Very deliberately, Penelope turned her back on Reena and cracked her fingers. "Wherever and whenever, bitch."

"Shut up, Pulchrum," growled Jonathan, which took some people by surprise. "Terrence, take Reena up to the infirmary. Ben-Israel and Akshara will see to her. Nellaina, help them, and when she gets up there, help your sister."

Jonah looked around, so distracted that he didn't notice the vengeful gaze Tenta gave him for nearly dislocating his jaw. What had happened to Liz?

Then he saw her, several feet away. She had a bloody nose and a rather distracted, detached air. Vera gently helped her to her feet. He headed over to them.

"What happened to her?" he asked.

"Concussion," said Vera in a tone that was none too friendly. "Courtesy of your friend."

"You mean Rheadne?"

Liz stumbled, and Vera prevented her from falling. For a moment, Jonah thought she had given her full attention back to her best friend, but then she muttered, "Oh, is that her name? I didn't commit it to memory like you did, you see."

It took some effort, but Jonah brushed that aside. "Why would Rheadne have hit her hard enough to give her a concussion?"

"I suggest you ask her," snapped Vera.

"What is up with you, Vera?" Jonah asked with impatience. "It was probably an accident. Why didn't you ask her?"

Vera gave Jonah a look that would have rendered the Sahara Desert an icy wasteland. "I don't know, Jonah! Maybe it was because I'm not on a first-name basis with the woman, or maybe I was more concerned with my best friend's welfare than I was with playing a goddamned game of Twenty Questions! But why don't *you* ask her? Wouldn't that just make your night? Weren't you looking for an excuse to be in the presence of your perfect, unblemished, and unscarred lifesaver? Well, here's your chance! GO!"

She turned her back on him and guided Liz up the path, where Bobby assisted by taking Liz's other arm.

Jonah stared after them for several moments, stunned and shocked. What had gotten into Vera? Where did all that come from? What had he done that was so wrong?

But he couldn't bother with that now. He needed redirection.

More importantly, he needed an explanation.

He didn't even release his spiritual endowment. He stalked off, a red tent with a green tiger claw as his destination.

Jonah's anger hadn't abated in the least, but it had been tempered by caution. Maybe in his stunned haze, he had imagined that the campers would have all taken to their tents and gone to sleep. But once he reached them, he saw that that was not the case.

Several Sanctum campers were still awake, and walked the camp. Some compared notes, while others seethed about the abrupt end to the training.

Jonah nearly blew it when he tripped over a tree branch, which caused an ear-splitting crunch. A young woman whipped around to the sound, alert and wary.

"What was that?" she said. She looked straight at Jonah, but thank God above, the shadows of the night concealed him.

"Calm down, Aloisa," said Penelope. "There isn't a damn thing here that's a threat to us. Believe that."

The one named Aloisa relaxed, if only slightly, but she didn't drop her gaze. "Maybe it was one of those heralds."

"Heralds," said Penelope with scorn. "Some stinkin' cats know a few tricks, and suddenly they have special names."

"Well, I thought it was kinda cool—"

"To be dependent on damn animals?" snapped Penelope. "Mr. Kaine was right when he said reliance on domesticated housecats was asinine."

"Pens," said Aloisa, "why don't you just calm down?"

"Why?" Penelope eyed the younger woman. "Because I should be ashamed for my scathing rebuke from The Ghost of Christmas Never? Not my fault that island girl couldn't take a hit."

Aloisa looked at Penelope. "Look, I'm on your side, Pens, but a knife-edged thrust was a little extreme—"

"If she had been a Deadfallen disciple, it might not have been enough," interrupted Penelope. "But don't worry, my friend. She is being protected as we speak."

Jonah's temper rose. This woman was talking about his best friend, after all. He almost missed Aloisa's response.

"What do you mean? You think that guy that carried her up was her boyfriend?"

Penelope scoffed. "I meant Jonathan, Aloisa. Boyfriend…please. Island girl doesn't like men. Wasn't it obvious?"

Aloisa frowned, confused. "Uh, no."

Jonah leaned in closer, wanting to know exactly how it had been obvious, but someone grabbed his left hand, and covered his mouth. Jonah nearly protested, but another familiar voice whispered into his ear.

"Don't struggle! They'll come and inspect!"

Jonah relaxed. Sort of. It was Rheadne. Just the person he wanted to see.

"Why are you spying on Aloisa and Penelope?" she whispered.

"I'm not," whispered Jonah defensively. "That wasn't supposed to happen. I was looking for you."

Rheadne's expression cleared. "Came for me, huh? I'm pleased, but you would have met disaster this way. My tent's on the other side of camp. Come with me."

She released him, and cautiously took off. Jonah followed her. They maneuvered around the camp with nary a sound; Rheadne was excellent at stealth. Jonah caught words from some other people as well. He glimpsed Tenta again, who was still seething over his injured jaw. Jonah clearly heard *Blue Dumbass* when they went near him. When they neared Rheadne's tent, they saw G.J. snapping harshly at Gabriel, whose mouth was tightly set, as if he didn't trust himself to respond. Rheadne rolled her eyes at them.

"He should have kept his opinion to himself," she commented once they'd entered her tent.

"What are you talking about?" asked Jonah. "What was all that?"

"When that excuse of a training was done, Gabriel told Gamaliel and G.J. that they ought to treat Jonathan with more respect," said Rheadne. "The way G.J. reacted, you'd have thought Gabriel pissed himself in his tent."

Rheadne lit three battery-powered lanterns. Jonah noticed that the tent was very large for just one person, but whatever. Maybe Rheadne figured that if they would be here for the foreseeable future, she wasn't going to be claustrophobic.

He situated himself into a comfortable seating position. The purpose of this meet was back in his head. His indignation, dulled by all the stealthy movements, returned to its previous level.

"Now—" began Rheadne, but Jonah cut across her.

"This isn't a social call, Rheadne," he said in a low, sharp voice. "You banged up my friend pretty badly out there."

"What?" Rheadne looked to be racking her brains. "Oh wait—you mean that Elizabeth girl?"

Jonah's mouth twisted. "Yes, that Elizabeth girl," he answered. "You concussed her! You bloodied her nose!"

"Jonah, shit happens," said Rheadne. "That girl realized that she'd never drop me in a straight-up fight, so she tried to subdue me with a nerve strike. That would have thrown off my equilibrium for hours. I defended myself."

Jonah remembered that Liz was adept at exploiting nerves and pressure points, and just how jarring it could be when she hit them. But that didn't alter his mood. "Did you have to hit her so hard, though?"

"I panicked, Jonah," said Rheadne. "I am truly sorry. But if you want my honest opinion, she's far too delicate for training."

Jonah, who had actually felt the same way about Liz, regarded Rheadne when she said it. "How do you figure?"

"She fought intelligently," Rheadne explained. "She fought intelligently, and was so cognizant of weak spots that I ascertained that she is a Green Aura. A medic. Medics have no business in a fight."

Jonah looked at her. She'd figured out Liz's aura just by watching her fight? "Liz would probably disagree with that assessment."

"Oh, I bet she would," said Rheadne. "But you weren't delicate when you knocked Brock on his ass."

Almost by reflex, Jonah looked down at his forearm. It had been completely unscathed due to the mist that had shrouded it during his attack. The left side of his head, on the other hand, was still sore. "He went nuclear on me. He acted like a stupid cyborg, belting out his information at the beginning like that."

"Our Official Designations," said Rheadne. "Mr. Kaine taught us that the most important information needs to be short and sweet."

"Huh." Jonah shrugged. "So what's your official—thing?"

She snorted. "You already know that my name is Rheadne Cage. Twenty-eight years of age, cerise-colored aura."

"Cerise?" said Jonah. "Hmm. That's kind of pink, right? I've never seen a pink aura before. Does that aura signify anything?"

Rheadne grabbed Jonah's left hand and extended it, inspecting his palm as though it had a cut or a burn. The action seemed rather odd to Jonah; he began to think that his palm had some abrasion that he couldn't see.

"What are you doing?"

"Stop talking, and just hold on a second," said Rheadne without removing her eyes from his hand.

Jonah nearly asked another question, but then his hand began to elevate in temperature. It felt like that part of his body had suddenly become feverish.

"There," said Rheadne, who sounded pleased with herself. "Hold this with that hand."

She handed him an unplugged alarm clock. When Jonah took it, it began to blink **12:00** in huge, blue numbers. Five seconds later, it sparked and shorted out.

"Oh, damn," he muttered. "I didn't do that on purpose—"

"Forget it," said Rheadne. "It was a gift from Gabriel, and I hated its alarm. But anyway, that's what a pink aura signifies."

Jonah thought on it. "You're an...amplifier? You make people stronger?"

"Not quite," she answered. "I can focus ethereality that you already have. I can fine-tune it. For example, there was so much power in your hand that you could direct it to your fingers and use them as tasers."

"Nice!" Jonah was impressed. "So if I want to physically tase someone, I need to seek you out?"

"Not at all," laughed Rheadne. "You can do it on your own. You just needed it brought to the surface. It's a nifty little trick, if you're ever without your batons."

"You know about my batons?"

"I know about many things concerning the Blue Aura," Rheadne responded.

Jonah raised an eyebrow. That was a tad bit odd.

"I'm attracted to you, Jonah," said Rheadne with no reservation. "There, I said it. If you were expecting me to be flirtatious and coy about it, you're going to be disappointed. That brainless shit is for little girls. I find you sexy, intriguing, strong, and driven. And you're remarkable in the most profound sense. The Blue Aura. The potential harbinger of significant upheaval. It's all so captivating to me."

Jonah said nothing. Of all the things that he expected to come out of Rheadne's mouth, that hadn't been on the radar at all.

"I'll tell you something else," Rheadne went on. "I kind of regret the fact that Jonathan found you first. Mr. Kaine has taught us so much, made us so aware of our ethereality...I have no doubts that he could have made you even more formidable than you already are. Be that as it may, you still need help. More help than you've been receiving here. With these brazen remnants of Creyton's Deadfallen disciples rearing their ugly heads here and there, it's always best to have to the right people on your side. I can help you. All you have to do is let me."

Jonah blinked. No underlying innuendo, no double entendres, no flirty interludes...Rheadne was one hundred percent direct. She had been so unabashed and so unapologetic that he was speechless. He would have been lying if he said he didn't find it kind of attractive.

"Take your time with it," said Rheadne with a half-smirk. "There are no hurries. I have a feeling that we'll be here for a while. 'Night."

She gestured to the entrance of her tent, so Jonah exited. It almost felt like an out-of-body experience. Despite his disconnected frame of mind, he still had the wherewithal to retrace his steps around the camp so as to avoid prying eyes.

So Rheadne found him attractive. No, she said *sexy*. She didn't toil with the thing at all; she just put it out there. She wanted to help him become a better Blue Aura? She wanted him to *let* her make him a more effective Eleventh Percenter? Huh.

And to think, he'd been angry when he first sought Rheadne out. He'd had a purpose to see her. Now that he'd actually seen her, though...

"Where have you been?" said a voice.

Jonah looked around, and saw Terrence eying him suspiciously.

"Terrence? What are you doing here?"

"I was looking for you," said Terrence. "I thought you'd like to know that Reena's injury was minor, and she's breathing normally."

"Really?" Jonah's head cleared at the good news. "That's great! How is Liz doing?"

"Fine," said Terrence. "Concussion. She'll need to stay awake for several hours, so Bobby's got her watching action movies."

Jonah snickered. Terrence didn't.

"Where have you been, Jonah?" he repeated.

Jonah shrugged. "Nowhere, really, I was right behind you actually, but—"

"You were *nowhere really* for over an hour?"

Terrence looked beyond Jonah, and put two and two together.

"Were you with Rheadne?"

"Yeah, we exchanged some words," chuckled Jonah. "Now wait till you hear this—"

"For a whole hour." Terrence's interruption was cool, and he looked anything but amused. "Despite the fact that one of your best friends had a tracheal injury, and a girl you've called your baby sister had a concussion."

Jonah took a step back and frowned. "I knew that Reena would be okay under Jonathan's care," he said slowly, "and I knew that Vera would see to it that Liz would be attended to, as would Nella, and of course, Bobby. Angel on the shoulder, and all that, you know? But I actually went to talk to Rheadne so I could find out why she brained Liz so hard…"

Jonah's voice trailed off when Terrence's face hardened. It was a foreign expression.

"Why do you have to have everything, Jonah?" he asked.

Jonah looked at him, taken aback. "What did you say to me?"

"Seriously, must you have everything?" demanded Terrence. "What, are you picking over Vera like food?"

"Picking ov—? What are you talking about, Terrence?"

"Is that what Vera is?" Terrence continued. "Some slab of meat that you stash away while you try to dine on something new?"

"Are you on crack, Terrence?" asked Jonah, dumbfounded. "Have you been partaking in Vintage?"

"Don't be a smart-ass with me, man." Terrence actually got in Jonah's face. "Who do you think you are? You're already the Blue Aura, and you've already started experiencing the glory that comes with it—"

"Glory?" demanded Jonah. "Have you lost your fu—?"

But Jonah's swear word was cut off when Terrence simply gored through his words as though there'd been no interruption.

"—but you've got to be a player now, too? Has your status as the Blue Aura given you that high of an opinion of yourself?"

Jonah felt his eye twitch. "I don't think I like your tone, Terrence," he said coldly. "You're making me sound like I'm treating women like playthings—"

"You just owned up to it!" Terrence fired at him. "And I just told you that I was interested in Rheadne!"

"Oh for the love of Christ!" Jonah almost shouted. "That's what this is about? I didn't swoop in like some bird of prey on what you wanted, Terrence! Rheadne started liking me back when my tire blew out—"

Terrence's eyes flashed, and Jonah realized the mistake he'd just made. Terrence hadn't ever known that—

"*Rheadne* was the one that helped you and Vera out?" he whispered. "You knew her already? And you didn't tell me?"

"I assumed Reena told you, because she knew—"

"You know what they say about those who assume—"

Jonah interrupted Terrence with a wave of his hand. He had never ever wanted to punch his best friend in the face, but it was a distinct possibility at this moment. "Terrence, I didn't know her. You can hardly call talking to someone for ten minutes knowing them—"

"But you knew who she was, Jonah!" barked Terrence. "You already called her cute, and now you just want to slither in like a damn snake."

Jonah felt hell in himself like he never had before. "You know what, Terrence? I didn't ask for any of this. It just happened. You get that? It's not my fault she said she was attracted to me, and didn't frickin' notice you—"

Terrence drew back to hit him, and Jonah yanked a baton from his pocket, thankful he was still endowed. He was ready for whatever Terrence threw at him.

But nothing came. Terrence caught himself halfway to Jonah's face, and then lowered his fist and loosened his fingers. His eyes, however, remained as hard as iron.

"Go fuck yourself," he said.

"I should tell *you* that," responded Jonah, "seeing as how that's pretty much the only action you'll ever see."

A muscle twitched in Terrence's jaw, but he turned his back on Jonah, and marched off toward the estate.

Jonah just stood there, clutching his baton so hard that he barely felt it.

First Vera.

Now Terrence.

And on top of it all, he still had his a midterm.

11

The Grind

Jonah had one of the most screwed-up dreams ever. He'd been in a glass cage that was perforated with holes for breathing. Vera and Rheadne were bidding on him, as though he were some prize animal. But there was a catch: the more they dueled with their bids, the more the glass walls closed in on him. Terrence stood behind the cage, with some switch attached to the outside clasped in his hands.

"You'd better move it along, ladies!" he crooned. "I'll be forced to put him down if these walls close any further!"

He shot up in his bed, only to realize that there was no cage. That was a relief.

But then came the additional realizations. The relief was short-lived, as he still felt caged.

Vera was unlikely to bid on him at any auction. She'd just as soon slap him.

Terrence may not him put down, but he probably wanted to.

The only person in that dream that he was on good terms with was Rheadne. A woman who was about as subtle as a land mine.

Jonah looked at the clock. It was a little before five in the morning. For a few moments, he actually caught himself wondering if he'd preferred being asleep and caged to awake and confused.

Exercise was out of the question, because Terrence would be in there before he headed to Trand High School for work. Of course, he would make breakfast for anyone interested, but Jonah suspected that there would (conveniently) not be enough for him. But that was fine. He wasn't going to eat anything cooked by Terrence Aldercy. So he simply went to get dressed.

The fact that Jonah didn't have to see Terrence was a relief, but he should have known his luck wouldn't hold. Before he reached the stairs, someone stepped out of a steamy bathroom, freshly showered. Jonah, who was deep in thought and not paying attention, bumped into her from behind.

"Oh I'm so sorry—!"

But then Vera realized who had bumped into her, and her expression frosted over.

Jonah was not in the mood for further excoriations, so he lowered his head, murmured, "I'm sorry, too," and ambled on past her while trying to ignore the scent of rose oil that emanated from her.

Luckily, Jonah ran into no one else from there to his car, and he high-tailed it to some ma-and-pa diner, which took some steel resolve, as he hadn't forgotten the Crystal Diner. He got it to go, and that was that. Minutes later, he sat in his car, crunching down waffle fries as he waited for the creative writing department to open for the day. He knew full well that Reena wouldn't have approved of his breakfast of fried sausage, waffle fries, and toasted pecan twists with extra icing, but he couldn't have cared less.

Unfortunately for Jonah, sitting cooped up in his car on a quiet morning provided a great deal of time to think.

And thinking was the absolute last thing he wanted to do.

He had approached Rheadne with the intent of letting her have it for injuring Liz. The fact that he left the conversation confounded, mystified, and flattered wasn't really the issue.

The issue was that Terrence found out that he had had a conversation—one damned conversation with the woman—and had gone completely off the handle.

Where the hell did that come from? Terrence had made up his mind that he was right, and didn't even bother to hear anything else on the matter. That had played a part in Jonah losing his own temper, because he hated it when people formed full opinions on partial information.

Vera thought of him as an opportunistic playboy.

Terrence thought of him...as an opportunistic playboy.

He half-wished that he knew who Inimicus actually was just so that he could find him and pick a fight.

"Jonah?"

Jonah looked over. Mr. Dagg, one of the groundskeepers, was near his window. Jonah was relieved to see a face that wasn't scowling at him, but disappointed because he knew Mr. Dagg didn't have keys to the building.

"Are you alright, son?" asked Mr. Dagg.

"Morning, sir," said Jonah. "I've been better, but all is well."

"You're never here this early, son!" commented Mr. Dagg. "Isn't there someplace else that you can have some peace?"

While the word *No* blared in Jonah's mind, he said aloud, "Less distractions here, sir."

Mr. Dagg nodded, bade him a good rest of the day, and went on about his duties. Jonah was glad to see him go. The exchange of pleasantries was fine; he just wasn't interested in it after a few minutes.

Just then, a car pulled up next to him, driven by a person who could let him into the building.

"Hey, Miss Daynard," he said.

She got out of her car and pushed the gray strand of her hair behind her ear. "Charlotte, Jonah," she said in that meditative voice of hers. "Please call me Charlotte. Why are you here so early?"

"Less distractions," he said without skipping a beat.

Charlotte gave him a look, but then shrugged. "Okay, then. Will you help me transport some reams of printer paper, please?"

Jonah reached to accept some of the load. Charlotte extended a few, but then paused, and looked at him with curious eyes.

"Who was the lady you were with this morning?" she asked.

Jonah looked at her in surprise. "What?"

"The woman you encountered this morning," she said. "Who was she?"

"I…haven't encountered any women this morning," said Jonah, puzzled. "Except you, of course. I've only seen Mr. Dagg."

"Uh-huh," said Charlotte as she lowered reams of printer paper in Jonah's arms. "And between you and Mr. Dagg, which one of you wears rose oil?"

Jonah stiffened. He'd smelled rose oil on Vera that morning, but he'd only bumped into her for a second. And Charlotte Daynard had picked up that scent off of him? Even after sitting in a car that smelled of sausage and fried potatoes for over an hour? "Must be in the air," he shrugged. "I haven't smelled roses, and I haven't been around anyone who has any."

Charlotte held his gaze a moment longer, and then grinned. "My mistake."

She headed up the stairs, unlocked the door, and held it open for him. He took advantage of her courtesy and walked inside.

He didn't quite know why he lied to Charlotte. He couldn't place why he felt the need to do so. Maybe it was because she was mostly a stranger to him. Maybe it was because he didn't want to talk about Vera.

Or maybe it was the fact that Charlotte picking up on such a miniscule scent was just creepy.

Since Jonah was already on campus, he was early for work as well. Fifteen minutes into his shift, however, he knew that using work and school to distract himself, while beneficial in the recent past, might be a challenge at the current time.

Whit was so overly positive that it was nauseating. Jonah knew the man was covering grief from the passing of his father, but damn. Then three students got busted trying to walk out with blue books stashed in their pockets. Lola hurt her ankle trying to catch one of the thieves, and then milked the injury for all it was worth when Jonah ran over to help her. When he saw the approving look that Whit gave him, he realized that the guy was still on that tip about Jonah asking her out. He sighed. Everyone seemed to have a bead on what he needed to do except him.

He had lunch with Douglas, which was a good thing because he didn't have to spend time corralling the thoughts in his head. But then Douglas had to ruin it and talk about Sanctum.

"I don't think I've seen such savagery in my entire life," he kept saying. "You would think that everything in their life is about some war. They've got the whole rebel without a clue motif down to a science."

"Mmm hmm," mumbled Jonah.

"And that cantankerous man and his oldest son are ridiculous," Douglas went on. "The way they go on with that self-righteousness, you'd think they were two parts of the Trinity. No wonder Gabriel sneaks away from that camp most every night."

Jonah, who'd been on autopilot up to that point, sat forward. "What, now?"

Douglas looked up. "What?"

"Gabriel Kaine. He slips from the camp most nights? How do you know that?"

Douglas shrugged. "Remember that I have my grad courses four nights a week. When I get home, I go into Spectral Sight right before I drive into the gates."

"What for?"

"Random precaution," said Douglas quietly. "Those vampire incidents way back when made me paranoid. Anyway, I've seen him some nights, near the outer woods, just standing there. It's like he's waiting for something."

Jonah looked at Douglas intently. "And he is out there alone?"

"Usually."

"Usually?"

"Sometimes he's out there conversing with spirits and spiritesses," replied Douglas. "And two nights ago, I even saw him with some heralds I hadn't ever seen on the grounds before."

"Heralds?" said Jonah. "You're sure about that?"

"Of course I'm sure," said Douglas. "We are all on a first name basis with every cat that calls the estate home, remember?"

"It's just odd, isn't it?" said Jonah. "I overheard that Penelope woman telling another woman named Aloisa that Gamaliel spoke out against working with heralds. He tells them that all the Eleventh Percenters need is themselves."

Douglas frowned. "Why would any Eleventh Percenter hate having heralds around?"

"No idea," muttered Jonah. "But since when were *you* so perceptive and watchful, Doug?"

Douglas crunched some ice. "The estate is my home," he said. "And these people are our guests. My Uncle Carroll always said that guests are like septic tanks; they are only welcome on your land when they work right. Jonathan might be watching, but the more eyes on them, the better."

After narrative class, Jonah grabbed a sandwich from school—he'd been avoiding the kitchen at all costs—and headed home. When he reached the gate, he remembered his and Douglas's conversation. He drove in, parked, and headed back. It was his turn to see if people took up residence near the entrance.

The walk didn't take very long, and proved fruitful. Gabriel was about to leave, but flinched when he saw Jonah.

"And just what are you doing?" said Jonah in a cold voice. He had already had less than favorable interactions with Kaine, Sr., and it was safe to assume that Kaine, Jr. had the same opinion. As such, he saw fit to brace himself with their other family member.

"I wasn't doing much," said Gabriel quickly. "I was just getting some fresh air. But it's nice to officially meet you, Jonah Rowe."

Jonah was caught by surprise. Gabriel's voice was inordinately deep for such an unremarkable individual. It was weird to hear such a low register from such a slight form.

Gabriel extended a hand, also a surprise, and Jonah shook it. Then Gabriel shook his head.

"Oh yeah," he laughed to himself, "I almost forgot. Official Designation is Gabriel Kaine, twenty-two years of age, auburn aura."

Jonah looked at him, confused. "Why are you introducing yourself?" He even forgot to put the hardness in his tone. "Jonathan took care of intros."

"This is a personal conversation, where we converse with just each other," explained Gabriel. "No one is speaking for me now. Pop and G.J. act as the mouthpieces of the masses, so people that we usually come across assume that we all have the same mind."

"And you don't?" Jonah couldn't help but to ask.

Gabriel shook his head, but didn't elaborate. He simply sighed. "Let me get back to the camp before I'm missed," he said. "Again, it was nice to speak to one of you guys myself for once."

With a nod, he pocketed his hands and departed, leaving Jonah as curious as when he first arrived.

Jonah checked on Liz in her bedroom. He was happy to see that she was making a steady recovery from the concussion. The estate was empty except for the two of them, but that wasn't a surprise. Everyone else was training in the Glade. Whatever.

He went to his room, half of his mind on homework, and found Reena seated at his desk.

She eyed him inscrutably. Her black and scarlet hair was in graceful curtains around her face, which Jonah found surprising, but then he understood. She wore her hair down to cover the bruise on her throat area.

Jonah braced himself. He should have just stayed in Liz's bedroom.

"I'm curious," said Reena in a slow, scratchy voice, "as to why you are avoiding me, too."

Jonah stared.

Reena raised her eyebrows. "Well?"

"I, um, wasn't thrilled about you tearing me out a new one as well," admitted Jonah.

"I wasn't going to do that," said Reena with narrowed eyes. "I was merely wondering how has distracting yourself with other aspects of your life been working for you."

"So you don't think that I'm a subhuman man-whore?"

"Of course I don't," scoffed Reena. "What I would like, though, is to hear things from you."

Relieved, Jonah told Reena everything. When he finished, she nodded without hesitation.

"So you had other intentions," she said. "Makes sense."

"So that's it?" said Jonah, hardly daring to believe it.

"Jonah, I believe you wholeheartedly," said Reena, like it was the most obvious thing. But Jonah wasn't annoyed by it. At least *she* was acting like she had good sense.

"That's nice to know," said Jonah. "I was expecting you to throw your nose up and make a condescending remark about all men."

"Already have," smirked Reena. "But it wasn't aimed at you this time around."

"Small comfort," muttered Jonah. "I just can't get why Terrence went so crazy."

Reena's eyes, which had been on the window, lowered to Jonah. "Isn't it obvious?"

That was the second time in two nights that Jonah heard that question, and the answer to that one had been no more obvious than the answer to this one. "Nope."

Reena sighed. "Jonah, you're the Blue Aura. You've proven yourself an exceptional ally on more than one occasion. You pull crazy, wild, unfathomable solutions from thin air, and make them work. And they work well. Now let's look at Terrence. Or more accurately, let's look at how Terrence views himself. He is an unparalleled, matchless... cook. He didn't go to college; he only has his G.E.D. A lot of people have gone the same route, but in Terrence's eyes, that puts him low on the totem pole. He had a biological family that didn't want him, and then had an adoptive family that sucked even worse. He was blessed to find a family that loved and accepted him, but in doing so, he inherited four brothers to compete with. Let's not forget the other brother that he has, who is football royalty, and who strikes gold with everything he touches. Imagine having to deal with all that—and then being friends with the Blue Aura. Look at all you've done, Jonah. My God, sometimes *I* envy you—and then I get over it," she added when Jonah widened his eyes. "Now a beautiful, strong-willed woman, who is neither brainless nor submissive, comes into the picture. Terrence thinks she is worthwhile, but that woman wants you. When you put it all into perspective, it's obvious, Jonah."

Jonah blinked several times, because that had not resembled an easy train of thought. But he wasn't an idiot. "Terrence imagines that I have it better than him," he said slowly. "This is a man who can make a feast out of anything. A man who can eat five frickin' hot dogs and a pound of fries, and not only doesn't have to spend the rest of the week on a toilet, but also doesn't gain any weight. A man who listens to alt-rock, and actually understands what the hell they're talking about. And yeah, I get the family piece, but look at my own situation—"

"Jonah, as a person who experienced screwed up familial relationships, I would never diminish your childhood experiences," said Reena quietly. "But look beyond that. Your parents weren't around, but you had a grandmother who told you that you were worthwhile from the cradle. Terrence didn't get anything like that until he was a teenager. So if we look at it—just from the surface—you have had it better. And...I suppose that Rheadne was the last straw for him."

Jonah didn't say anything. Sure, Reena had put things into a clearer perspective, but Terrence was still off-base. He was a great guy! He had definable talent! The residents of the estate got to enjoy his culinary talents almost daily. Jonah's progress with writing was so start-and-stop that he returned to school so as to fine-tune his focus. Terrence hadn't gone to college? Jonah had a Master's degree that he wasn't even using. It was quite unfortunate (okay, *more* than quite) that Terrence had to go through two families to finally find one that loved and accepted him, but he had that now. Jonah had only had his grandmother, and now she was beyond his reach.

It made Jonah angry that Terrence couldn't see the other side of the coin. He hadn't factored in the fact that Jonah had had a shitty past as well. The fact that their fallout was over a woman, after all they'd been through, just made him even angrier.

Jonah noticed that Reena didn't have on her dampener, so she'd probably just read the entire episode that had just run through his essence.

"This is gonna get worse before it gets better, right?" he asked through clenched teeth.

"That's for you and Terrence to decide," said Reena.

"Uh-huh," said Jonah, his tone heavy. "Can you apply your logic and theories to Vera?"

Reena rolled her eyes. "I refuse to waste my breath on that. Someone blind, deaf, and dumb could figure that one out."

"I'm not a veteran at this, Reena," murmured Jonah. "I've spent most of my life having women remind me that I was unattractive and worthless. I had an on-again, off-again girlfriend named Priscilla Gaines from eleventh grade to junior year of college, but other than that, the female connections I have had were pretty much hook-ups here and there, no strings attached."

"So you're practically a late bloomer," commented Reena. "It's not unprecedented. But there are always mature avenues to take with it."

"Maturity." Jonah grinned. "Says the woman who vowed to tag Penelope back."

"That bitch doesn't count," said Reena, her pensiveness fading at once. "I will pay her back in kind, so help me God."

Jonah laughed. "I heard her conversing with another Sanctum girl named Aloisa," he revealed. "Aloisa thought that Terrence was your significant other after he took you to the infirmary, but Penelope explained just how obvious it was that you were gay."

Reena's eyes narrowed. "One of those, is she? It will make hurting her that much sweeter."

Jonah smirked. Conversation with Reena had served to siphon some of the bile from his mind. Some of it.

He brought his sandwich to his mouth, but Reena pelted an ink pen at him.

"Not on my watch," she declared. "Come downstairs with me. We can have vegetable lasagna and salad."

Jonah sighed. At least one of his friends hadn't done a one-eighty.

Over the next couple weeks, Jonah did the best he could to sort of coast through things, but the forced activity of it was likely to drive him insane.

He had his associates at work and school, spoke to Kendall when he could (because of the Sanctum presence, Reena went to her place all the time, so Jonah didn't see her around the estate), and even had some pleasant exchanges with Charlotte Daynard, who was an okay person once he got over the creepy rose oil-sniffing incident and adjusted to the meditative, musical voice.

Inimicus was never far from his mind. He spoke with spirits on his breaks, eager to know of any strange activities. The spirits and spiritesses didn't know anything of note, and Jonah believed them. Their compositions were strong and distinct, which meant they weren't being forced to lie. He was relieved for that part, but disappointed because of the lack of information.

Work and school were manageable.

Home was another matter.

He had to keep up with training; that was a must. He couldn't be out of practice if he had to spar with another Sanctum person. And he couldn't keep buying school sandwiches, either. Neither Reena nor his budget approved of it.

So he had to go back among everyone. And he had to face Terrence and Vera. And Rheadne.

Life was just so much fun.

The first part of resuming his home routine was fine because it provided options. He could rely on Bobby, Benjamin, Malcolm, Alvin, and Spader for variation. Ignoring Terrence was simple. Mostly.

Reena had been diplomatic at first, but she quickly soured on being the rational one. She was vehement in her refusal to be a middle ground of communication, but that was fine. Terrence had nothing to say to Jonah, and Jonah had nothing to say to him. It was what it was.

"If you only sat down like men, you could probably rectify it all!" snapped Reena after Jonah let Malcolm give him a double-leg takedown on purpose so as to not have to dodge near Terrence. "You are acting like fourth graders!"

"This is not one of those cute little sitcoms that came on in the nineties, Reena!" Jonah shot back. "Issues aren't resolved in thirty minutes or less in the real world! I was not the one in the wrong!"

"You told him fucking himself was the only action he'd ever see—"

"Did you forget the fact that he told me to go fuck myself before that?"

Reena took an exasperated breath. "Why am I friends with you again?"

"Because I am the only who employs your health tips," Jonah joked.

Jonah's situation with Vera was even stranger. She had ceased the sharpness, but when they had to speak, she was distant, and oddly formal. She was tactful, and maybe even civil, but it was so dispassionate. So emotionless. It was like talking to a cyborg, or something.

Rheadne was anything but. She loved conversing with Jonah. They often spoke at length about subjects that weren't even the point of their conversations. She hadn't been lying; she was helpful to him in regards to improving his ethereality. The taser thing was just the start of it. Soon, Jonah was capable of more things while unendowed, figured out that his balancing power could also balance his own immune system, and Rheadne had also taught him a neat trick that involved charging ethereal weapons. If he touched an ethereal steel weapon of any kind, and focused his essence into it, he could make the weapon's impact significantly more powerful. It wore off after an hour or so, but it was still cool to Jonah.

"How did you know that could work?" he asked her after successfully charging up his batons.

"Because that trick was created by a Blue Aura," Rheadne answered. "Guy named Silas Marcellus Burke. He passed into Spirit in 1812."

"Really?" said Jonah, intrigued. "Did he do anything else?"

"His life wasn't too remarkable," said Rheadne. "He made a career as an Ungifted—"

Jonah winced, which made Rheadne hesitate.

"Sorry. I mean to say *Tenth*—Constable. He lived to be one hundred and sixteen years old. You did know that Elevenths had longer life expectancies than... Tenths, right?"

Jonah nodded. Rheadne kept her gaze.

"Please realize that there truly is no negativity intended when I say Ungifted, Jonah," she told him. "It's just a word—"

"It just doesn't sound right," said Jonah seriously. "I mean, *Ungifted*? Did Kaine come up with that?"

"No," answered Rheadne. "It's a common ethereal term that simply means there are some people in the world that weren't born with the gift of the Eleventh Percent."

"And that's a bad thing?" asked Jonah.

"Jonah." Rheadne placed a hand on his shoulder. "Is it insulting when someone is called unfamiliar? Or unmitigated? Or unaffiliated? No; they're just terms. They only contain the meaning that you place upon them."

Jonah didn't embrace that, but he wasn't willing to have any spats with Rheadne. They'd just have to agree to disagree.

Liz, of all people, came to Jonah in all seriousness one evening with the air of someone about to confide the location of a drug exchange or a stolen goods cache.

"You need to watch yourself, Jonah," she told him. "I warn you."

Jonah was taken aback, but then he got her meaning. "You don't have to worry about me, Liz," he promised her. "I've simply made a new friend."

Liz's green eyes brightened. "Uh-huh. Friend. Well, your new friend didn't get that memo."

Jonah rolled his eyes. He loved Liz like family, but he wasn't about to go that route with her.

The subsequent trainings were less explosive, but tense just the same. Gamaliel began to dole out advice, wanted or otherwise. Jonah had to give the man a modicum of credit; he'd probably forgotten more than any of them would ever know. But his delivery was the problem. Yes, his wisdom was vast, but he gave out instruction as though he addressed lesser beings. Jonathan had to put him in his place more than once.

After Bobby rather forcefully dropped a Sanctum man named Darius, Gamaliel made no secret that he was unimpressed, and advised him to improve his conditioning, as his "exploder strength" would betray him in a real fight. Reena had a chance to attack Penelope, but did not do so. She gave her a sweet smile instead, and moved on to Magdalena, Maxine, and Akshara. When Jonah questioned her about letting the woman walk, she simply said, "It'll be on my terms."

Jonah also noticed that Trip met with Jonathan several times, but their conversations were never long. He must have things to report from spying on Sanctum Arcist. He couldn't glean much from their interactions, because once they were done, Jonathan remained poker-faced, and Trip remained...Trip.

Jonah and Terrence had common ground one night during training. They'd squared off with other people, but then got upended by G.J., who shook his head in disgust at them.

"A very poor performance," commented Gamaliel. "You two have no awareness. With disregard like that, you would blindly walk through a Threshold of Death."

"What, now?" grumbled Terrence.

"A Threshold of Death," said G.J. "Surely, Jonathan told you about those?"

"We don't dwell on things concerning death here, seeing as it isn't real," Jonah threw at him.

Gamaliel and G.J. looked at each other. The latter sighed.

"A Threshold of Death is a door that can be linked to a place foreign of its origin."

Jonah looked at them. Terrence wasn't doing much better.

G.J. and his father looked at one another again, but this time, they smiled. Jonah didn't like those smiles. They sent fire through his guts.

"Let me break it down to the simplest common denominator," said G.J. "Your bedroom, for example. Say I wanted to get into that room, but didn't want to go through your house to do so. So I would perform a Threshold of Death to make a pathway. The room can be linked to wherever I am; I cross the Threshold, walk into the room, and boom. I'm in the house, no *Astralimes,* no front door—nothing."

"It works the other way as well," said Gamaliel. "A house can be ethereally linked to a room, and crossing the Threshold can also put you into a house, from that room!"

Jonah and Terrence looked at each other. That sounded sick. Scary sick.

"Why exactly are they called the Threshold of Death?" Jonah wanted to know.

"A flawed belief system." Jonathan was suddenly behind them. "It was initially known as a Threshold of Life, because life can happen anywhere. Also because, medics could link up a room to wherever they were, walk across the Threshold, and assist someone in need of healing. But it got rechristened, and I used the term very loosely, as the Threshold of Death, after its usage became notorious for Creyton's acts of horror."

Jonah couldn't imagine such a thing. Couldn't imagine walking into a room, and suddenly being in a different house. Or leaving a room and suddenly being in a different house. How confused did one have to be to fall for a trick like that?

"But you needn't worry of such things," said Jonathan. "The mere creation of one, let alone using it, will get you placed on The Plane with No Name for the duration of your physical days."

Jonah swore that Jonathan said it like it was more than just mere information. It sounded like a threat.

"Right you are, Jonathan," said Gamaliel as he stuffed more snuff in his jaw. "Right you are."

G.J. helped his father away, and Jonathan moved to aid Liz, Nella, Melvin, and Magdalena.

"You know," said Terrence, "I never actually hated old people till I met him. And he's a legend."

"Well," sighed Jonah, "it goes to show that even legends can be ass-holes, too. Don't they remember that they had a purpose for coming here? Can't they pool information, drop some Deadfallen, and then haul their asses back down to Florida?"

They both laughed at Jonah's words. Then they looked at each other, and the laughter faded.

Terrence turned away, and engaged Ben-Israel in a grapple. Jonah turned, and hailed Bobby and Alvin.

Trip wasn't just performing spy duty for Jonathan. He also maintained his primary goal of causing Jonah as much grief as possible.

"I'm surprised that you aren't bosom buddies with the Sanctum Arcist people, Rowe," he remarked. "They are sanctimonious glory hogs, much like yourself. Or maybe that's it—you aren't keen on them because you all are so much alike."

"Funny," mused Jonah, "because I thought they were more similar to *you*. The way that they fight so viciously and hardcore, you know? Clearly, they must be overcompensating for something else. You've got a wealth of experience with that, no?"

Trip scowled.

Jonah came to the realization that if he didn't get a mental break away from estate soon, his brain might explode. Someone up there liked him, though, because at the beginning of November, he got the chance.

Nelson called him with an interesting request.

"Tamara and I are road-tripping for a few days," he explained, "and we wanted to know if you'd watch our house."

Jonah raised an eyebrow, even though Nelson couldn't see him through the phone. "Watch your house?"

"Yep," said Nelson. "For four days, five at most."

"Nelson, I'm glad that you thought of me and everything," said Jonah, "but why would you need someone to watch the house for such a short amount of time?"

Nelson hesitated. Jonah could tell it, even over the phone. "I'll tell you when I see you. Okay?"

Now, Jonah had to do it. What was wrong with Nelson?

"See you in a day," he said.

Hours later, Jonah recounted the brief encounter with Reena, who looked strangely eager.

"May I come with you?" she asked.

"I don't know about that, Reena," Jonah told her. "I didn't actually get the green light to bring friends into their house."

"Oh, I don't want to stay there with you," said Reena. "It's just an excuse to surprise Kendall. She is staying at the Marriott in the same city for a conference."

Jonah folded his arms. "So I'm merely a tool to get you to your girl-friend?"

"Pretty much," said Reena.

"Gee, thanks," said Jonah, but he laughed.

"Just one thing, though," said Reena.

"What's that?"

"We're dealing with Tenths," she reminded him. "So it's not a two-step process, but a three-hour drive."

Jonah and Reena threw their bags into Jonah's car the next day after Jonah shot Dr. Ferrus an email that he'd miss that week's class, as well as informing Whit that a personal matter required his presence out of town. It wasn't his business that the matter was not an emergency. But after Nelson acted the way he did over the phone, it just might be.

They were about to get in the car when Terrence pulled up. He looked a bit dirty, like he'd been fixing something. Jonah nearly growled in his throat, and tried to remember Felix's breathing techniques.

"Where are you two going?" he asked them.

"Away," replied Jonah. "Why are you so dirty?"

Terrence breathed through his nostrils. "Me and my dirt are minding our business, and leaving yours alone."

Jonah shook his head and shrugged. "Whatever."

He hoped Terrence would go away, but he didn't do so just yet. Instead, he lowered to look at Reena in the passenger seat.

"Make yourself scarce when Jonah goes on the prowl, Reena," he warned. "If you don't respect men who are chauvinists, you certainly won't respect seeing Jonah at work."

Reena, who was determinedly silent during their exchange, sighed. Jonah ignored it.

"That's cute," he muttered. "Now, don't let us hold you up any further. I'm sure that you need to go and get cleaned up, so you can listen to all your Incline Down music while you make a nice, intimate meal for all one of you."

Terrence actually winced; Reena whispered, "*Damn, Jonah.*" He lowered himself into the driver's seat, and he and Reena were on their way.

"Jonah Rowe, that was a kick to the balls, and you know it," said Reena.

"Whatever," said Jonah indifferently.

But as he focused on the road, he realized that the indifference wasn't as concrete as he wanted it to be.

"Hey, Jonah!" greeted Nelson some hours later. "It's always a pleasure, man! And you were at our wedding—Reenie, right?"

"It's Reena," Reena corrected. "But it's great to see the both of you again."

Jonah shook Nelson's hand while Reena embraced Tamara, but both of them were on alert. Nelson was friendly and boisterous, like always, and Tamara didn't act out of character, either. But still, something was off. Reena had even removed her dampener to better gauge things.

Jonah took it from her and pocketed it. He didn't want a repeat of what happened the last time he wore it and then gave it back to her.

"Alright, Nelson," he said after they'd seated themselves. "Let's hear it, friend."

Some of the laughter left Nelson's face, and he sighed. "First and foremost, Jonah, we didn't ask you under any false pretenses or anything," he said. "We really did want someone to watch this place while we took our trip."

Reena looked at Jonah, and then back at Nelson and Tamara. "Why do I get the feeling that your sudden vacation isn't just due to stress?" she asked.

Tamara frowned. "That's amazing," she said.

"Yeah, it was," concurred Nelson. "You psychic, or something?"

He looked at Jonah, who raised his eyes with impatience.

"You may not understand this, Jonah, because you are the most normal person we know—" Jonah didn't look at Reena when Nelson said that, "—but it seems like something...odd is in the air."

Jonah sat forward. "Has anything been happening to you guys? What feels off in the air?"

Nelson seemed to steel himself. "Jonah, Langton's wife just checked him back into the hospital. He's getting worse. He's lost like eighty pounds."

Jonah furrowed his brow. "That's unfortunate, and I mean that, despite how I feel about him. But is that what's bothering you? His poor health?"

Tamara shook her head. "Jonah, it just didn't feel right. I saw the guy last week, when I brought Nelson some lunch. He looked like he was...dying slowly."

Stranger and stranger. As bad as the story was, Jonah didn't see why *they* were so alarmed. But Tamara continued.

"And do you remember that woman that you and Nelson can't stand? Jessica Hale?"

"Yeah," answered Jonah. "What about her?"

"We haven't seen her in three weeks," said Nelson. "She's taken a leave of absence from work."

"My God," said Reena dully, "sounds like she has a stalker."

Neither Nelson nor Tamara said anything. Reena's eyes bulged.

"She—oh my God, I didn't actually mean—"

"Somebody is stalking Jessica?" Jonah demanded.

"Yes," said Nelson. "Started a while back. Ant let slip that Jessica started noticing some guy in one of the clubs she frequents on the weekends. No one thought anything of it at first. We didn't care—it would only make sense that Jess would get the wrong attention given the way she dresses. Then Mrs. Souther started getting these weird messages at the office for her. From some guy. Then she started coming to work later and later. She said that she wanted to come when the streets were busier. She even started wearing pantsuits, Jonah. Pantsuits. Because she didn't want to draw attention. Then she got her leave of absence. We haven't seen her at the office since, and Ant ain't talking."

Jonah looked over at Reena again. "Let me get this straight," he said. "Langton's decline in health coincided with Jessica's situation, and you guys needed time from all of it. Is that right?"

Nelson nodded.

"Get out of here," said Jonah, who now desired nothing for them *but* vacation. "You guys have rescued me from stress, and now I'll do the same for you. Go. I've got your place."

They looked so grateful that Jonah didn't even mind that they wanted to leave without another word. But Reena wasn't done.

"Really quickly, guys," she said. "Do you know anything about the guy at all? I mean, he made the blunder of a lifetime by calling the office."

Nelson nodded, as though that were a fair question. "You would have thought that, especially after the police got involved. But it seems like he was even too smart for them. Of course they weren't telling us anything, but Ant had another slip of the tongue and told us about one of those freaky messages."

"Sounds like something he'd do," muttered Jonathan. "He can't keep his mouth closed worth shit. What was the message?"

Nelson shrugged. "He told Mrs. Souther to tell Jessica that she looked beautiful in the moonlight, or something."

Jonah tensed. *What?*

It was pure luck that he looked at Reena at that moment. She'd reacted the same way to Nelson's words, but she locked eyes with him and told him without words that Nelson and Tamara didn't need any other information. He got it.

"Thanks for that, Nels," he said. "I pray, for Jessica's sake, that they catch this dude soon. Now get out of here. Go clear your heads. I promise that the house will be in one piece when you get back."

Nelson and Tamara didn't need to be told twice. They got their bags from by their front door, and were gone.

Jonah sank into a chair once they'd left. Reena joined him, disbelief all over her face.

"That moon freak, Wyndam O'Shea is stalking Jessica, Jonah," she whispered. "How the hell can that be?"

Jonah felt hollow. He almost found himself hoping against hope that it was a bad dream or some sick joke. "But why, though? How did he happen across her? Why Jessica?"

"He did not happen across her, Jonah," said Reena. "Don't even entertain that notion. This is about you."

Jonah raised his head. "How do you figure?"

"Jonah, that stupid skank is bait," said Reena. "He probably figured that he had a snowball's chance of getting to you at the estate, so he did some digging and found your first job."

"Wonderful," said Jonah. "Just frickin' wonderful. He's got to be Inimicus, then."

"There still isn't enough evidence for that, Jonah," said Reena. "For all we know, Inimicus could be one of those other Deadfallen disciples that Gamaliel mentioned. Inimicus could be giving them orders."

"Or they could be getting orders from that trace of Creyton in that cold fire," Jonah reminded her.

Reena took a breath. "Oh yes. That's possible, too."

"And O'Shea just had to pick the person that I hate with every fiber of my being," Jonah ground out. "Those Sanctum fools should have set up shop here in the city."

He stood up, and pulled a baton from his pocket. Even without an endowment, it heightened his sense of security. "I'll get you to Kendall tomorrow morning, Reena. Just like I promised."

Reena regarded Jonah. "What are you going to do after that, Jonah?"

"I can't believe these words are going to escape my mouth," he said. "But I'm going to go talk to Jessica."

12

The Gates of Hale

Jonah dropped Reena off at the Marriott, where Kendall greeted her with an exuberance that he knew she wouldn't feel at the conference. Reena was thrilled to be with Kendall, but she was still leery of leaving Jonah on his own, especially if Wyndam O'Shea was around. But Jonah laughed her off.

"It's daytime," he said. "And I even bothered to check the moon phases when I printed off the directions to Jessica's place. It's a half moon tonight. He's at his craziest at the full moon."

Reena relented only after Jonah promised to alert her if anything untoward happened. But he wasn't going to do that. Reena deserved her fun. The whole of this was on him.

But when he left Reena there, he realized just how alone he was.

It wasn't fear or loneliness or anything. He'd been on his own since he was eighteen, after all. But a great deal of things had changed since that time. Hell, things had changed since he'd gotten his damned first job at Essa, Langton, and Bane.

He didn't dare go to Jessica's house this early. At nine in the morning, a victim of stalking would likely physically injure anyone within ten feet of them. So he killed some time at the Shining Brews, which was the coffeehouse near his old bookstore job. He couldn't resist the urge to look at the former site of S.T.R. It was cleaned and vacant now, but it brought back great memories, like Mr. Steverson recounting stories about either his sharecropper parents or about Vietnam. Or like Amanda Gomez, the meticulous bookkeeper, who told anyone who listened about how badly she wanted a baby. Or like Harland LaGrange, who brought coffee for everyone before resuming his usual quiet, aloof behavior. He and Malcolm would have gotten along great.

And then there was Roger, the enigmatic bookworm who was actually Creyton in a sick disguise. He'd stationed himself at the bookstore (with the aid of the 49er, one of his disciples) so that he could read up on the Time Item, who turned out to be Vera—

That jarred Jonah from his thoughts. That night when Vera said she trusted him, and he saved her physical life seemed like a long, long time ago now. Now, she was mad at him. As was Terrence. A woman whom he had considered such a joy to be around now barely spoke to him. And his best friend, one of the few men in the world that he considered a brother, was angry at him, too.

He rose from the table, tossed down some dollar bills, and left.

Idleness begat unpleasant thoughts.

Finding Jessica's house wasn't hard, but Jonah did have to turn around twice because two places were one-way streets.

Directions could be annoying like that, but he'd be damned if he invested in a GPS. The last thing he needed was some seductive female voice to tell him, "*Turn right here,*" and send him off a cliff.

Jessica's residence was a cozy home that was plain white in color, with trim hedges beneath lilac shutters. It was neatly perched between two similarly patterned homes on either side. The house looked as though the owner was some sweet considerate person. Looks could be very deceiving.

Jonah flattened his slightly disheveled hair as best he could. He didn't want to look like a shady element.

He had just stepped out of the car when a surprised voice said, "Rowe?"

Ant Noble stood nearby with coffeehouse purchases. Jonah considered him with alarm.

Worry had taken away that stupid grin that Jonah remembered so clearly, and the youthful air that he had come to regard with such scorn and disdain was no more. It looked like Jessica's plight had aged Ant into a more serious, mature individual. When Jonah knew Ant back at the accounting firm, he would have applauded such a change, but not like this. Not this way.

"What are you doing around here?" asked Ant suspiciously.

"I—" Jonah had to re-gather his thoughts. Seeing Ant's transformation had been disconcerting. "I found out about Jess's situation."

Ant tilted his unevenly bearded face. "Nelson," he murmured. "It was Nelson, wasn't it?

"What if it was?" asked Jonah.

"So why are you here?" Ant asked him again. "Are you here to gloat while my baby's down?"

Jonah was suddenly furious, but he caught himself. Although imbecilic comments were flashes of the Ant Noble he knew and hated, he realized that this was a man reacting out of fear and worry. "Ant, I want to help if I can," he said with sincerity. "I may—I may have an idea who is messing with Jessica."

Ant's expression cleared at once. "Really? How would you know?"

"He's—he's done some bad things around where I live, too," said Jonah quickly.

"You mean that place in the sticks?" asked Ant.

It took all of Jonah's resolve not to roll his eyes. "Yes, the place in the sticks."

"Have you given any information to the police?"

"Well, the Tenth—I mean, the police tend to work better when they have more information," said Jonah, knowing that Ant wouldn't be suspicious. "I was hoping to talk to Jess, and see if we could compare notes."

"Of course!" nodded Ant. "Come in!"

Jonah hesitated. "Ant, you do remember that Jess and I hate each other, right? She won't be eager to talk to me. To be honest, I'm surprised *you* are talking to me."

Ant looked completely unperturbed. "If you know anything that will make Jess safe again, then the past doesn't matter."

He actually lowered his purchases on Jessica's stoop and fumbled in his pocket. Jonah thought that this was unusual behavior for someone about to knock on a door, but then Ant produced a key. Jonah's eyes widened in disbelief. There was *no way*.

"You two have exchanged keys?" he demanded.

"Yeah." Ant hadn't even noticed Jonah's reaction. "A month and a week ago. Greatest night of my life, and then this happened."

Despite the moment, Jonah had to frown. How could Ant be so enamored with a woman who treated him so badly?

Ant unlocked the door, gathered his purchases, and walked inside. Jonah followed.

Jessica's living room walls were the same lilac color as her shutters, but beyond that, the place was a sty. Unkempt laundry lay piled in places, empty water bottles and paper plates were strewn all over the floor, one of which (Jonah thanked God above that it was unlit) was perched atop a scented candle. None of these things bothered him, though. It was easy to understand that someone dealing with a stalker wouldn't be too concerned with the state of their house. Even so, Jonah still noted that such a display was the complete opposite of the mental picture that he had of Jessica Hale.

"I was going to clean all of this today," said Ant, embarrassed. "I meant to do it last night, but Jess didn't want to be in her bed alone at night. Least I could do. Excuse me."

Jonah just stared after Ant. This poor, deluded fool was nothing more than a star-struck slave.

Then, he swore to himself. Since Jonah had discovered he was an Eleventh Percenter, he had a strict policy to go into Spectral Sight whenever he came to a new location. Ant's appearance had distracted him from doing that. He decided to take advantage of his momentary privacy. Closing his eyes and willing the stage to rise would only take—

"WHAT IN THE ACTUAL FUCK?"

Jonah jumped. He didn't even complete activation of the Sight. He turned in the direction of the primal shrill, and realized too late that Ant wasn't accompanying him at the moment. His jaw dropped.

Ant had not looked to his usual standards. The interior of this house had been nothing to brag about, either.

But neither of them prepared him for the sight of Jessica.

Jessica had always kept herself immaculate. Everything was always in place when she looked down her nose at everyone. At this moment, however, Jonah would bet cash dollars that *that* Jessica would look down her nose at *this* one. She was a wreck. There was no other word for it. The chin-length bob hairstyle was now a rat's nest, and had the consistency of wilted leaves. There was nary a trace of makeup on her blotchy, neglected skin. Her formerly French-tipped nails were chipped, jagged, and looked every bit as sorry as her wardrobe, which consisted of an ill-fitting tank top, pajama shorts, and an oversized bathrobe.

As Jonah gawked at her on the stairs, Jessica only exhibited rage.

"TONY!" she shouted.

Ant tumbled back into the room, visibly horrified by his mistake. Jonah hoped that he could rattle off an explanation, but unfortunately, Ant couldn't seem to string together anything but ludicrous exclamations.

"Jess! Baby! Hey! I can explain!"

"Why did you let him into my house, Tony?" demanded Jessica, who bounded down the final stairs with no regard for coordination or obstacles. "You haven't even cleaned up yet, and you let him in! I should take something and knock you in the head—"

"But, baby—"

"I didn't give you that key to bring people into my house at your leisure!" snapped Jessica. "Least of all this b—"

"Now hold on, Jessica!" interrupted Jonah. He knew what he would deal with, sure, but if Jessica was going to cut to the chases with her rudeness, he could very well forget that he wanted to help her. "Ant is only trying to help—"

"He can help by inviting you out, and then cleaning this house!" snapped Jessica.

"I know what's been happening with you, Jess! He's—!"

"You know nothing, Rowe! You need to mind your own damn business!"

"For God's sake, would it kill you to show some decency?" demanded Jonah.

"Get out of my house before I call the police!" roared Jessica. "No doubt they have dirt on you already—"

"YOUR STALKER IS ALSO A MURDERER, DAMMIT!" shouted Jonah.

Ant looked as though he'd been punched in the gut. Jessica blinked.

"He is a killer, Jessica," Jonah repeated. He really hated to pull that card, but Jessica was making it hard to want to aid her. Shocking her was the only alternative he had. "Remember that backwater place where I live now that you badmouthed? He's been there. He's killed before; he just massacred a diner this past summer. Your bitch exterior and armor won't save you, Jessica. This man is a loon. Literally. Now, I need to know if you have information besides the sightings and the messages from Mrs. Souther."

Jessica looked like she had ingested some disgusting medication, but she was silent. Jonah didn't even want to blink.

Had he gotten through? Was she finally going to see sense, if only for a matter of minutes?

He was about to breathe again when Jessica pointed a chipped-nailed finger at her front door.

"Get out of my house, Rowe." Her voice was barely above a whisper. "And stay out of my affairs. If I see you around here again, *I* will be the killer."

Jonah stared at her in disbelief, while Ant stared at him hopelessly.

He had actually wanted to assist Jessica, if it had been possible. He actually had. But he was not going to stand there and convince her to save her own physical life. Jessica Hale had only one frame of mind, and that frame of mind was *bitch*.

"May whatever happen to you, happen to you," he said. "I swear to frickin' God that I couldn't care less now."

Ant took a horrified breath, but Jonah turned his back on the both of them. Wrenching open the front door, he strode out, vowing never to darken it again.

13

Journal of a United(?) Front: First Entry

Jonah fulfilled his role as a house sitter, spending the time bingeing on *Arrow* and *Supernatural*, as well as catching up on schoolwork. He allowed Reena as much time with Kendall as possible, picking her up only after he'd finished with Nelson and Tamara when they'd returned from North Myrtle Beach. Once they were back on the highway, Reena asked how things had gone with Jessica. Jonah muttered the only word that encompassed the whole thing.

"Disaster."

Reena sighed, as though that didn't surprise her at all. "Were you able to even get it out?"

"I was forced to jump the gun, actually," admitted Jonah. "It was the only way to get a word in edgewise."

"What about her boyfriend?"

"You mean the Labrador Retriever on two legs?" Jonah sighed. "She was beyond angry with him. I wouldn't be surprised if she put him over her knee."

Reena closed her eyes and brought her fingers to her temples. "So what do you plan to do about it?"

"What the bitch told me to do," said Jonah instantly. "Stay out of it."

Reena's eyes flew open, and she looked at Jonah in pure horror. "Jonah, you cannot mean that."

"Like hell I can't," snapped Jonah. "If she thinks she can deal with Wyndam O'Shea on her own, let him tear her to pieces. I couldn't care less."

"I don't believe you," Reena fired back. "Jonah, you cannot allow our knowledge to just sit there. If you felt that way, you never would have gone to see her in the first place! Even if she is a solipsistic, bitch-born whore, she doesn't deserve to be stalked and possibly murdered. Tell me you don't care, Jonah. Tell me that I've read you wrong, and that you can stand idly by while a Deadfallen disciple takes a victim that you actually had the power to save."

Jonah made a wry face as he changed two lanes. Leave it to Reena to make him feel guilty and ruffled. It was times like these that Terrence's presence was truly missed, because he would have relished in calling Jessica names that he daren't repeat in front of his mother.

"Tell me I read you wrong, Jonah," repeated Reena.

"Where did this desire to protect Jessica originate, Reena?" he asked her. "When did you feel the need to become the Defender of Skanks?"

Reena shook her head. "I have no love for the superficial bitch."

"She ain't so superficial now," murmured Jonah. "Believe that."

"But she is a human being," continued Reena, "and a Tenth Percenter who is in way over her head. Yeah, she is a bitch. But she has the right to live, Jonah. Was she frightened?"

Jonah took his time maneuvering into the right lane. "Yeah, she was scared. I could tell."

"Thought so. I'm almost certain that eighty percent of it was a front, seeing as how her personality is one of the things that she hasn't lost control of."

Jonah said nothing. Now that his anger had faded somewhat, he had realized that he couldn't abandon Jessica to a grisly fate. She and her well-developed bitchy attitude had blinded him, which wasn't a surprise. He just didn't know how to help her now.

His protracted silence prompted Reena to look at him with narrowed eyes.

"This is the part where you say you will discuss it with Jonathan, because he has the ability to work unseen and cause no further indignation."

Jonah heaved a sigh. "Yeah... that thing you just said."

When they got home, though, an announcement was made that momentarily distracted Jonah from Jessica and her plight.

To everyone's interest, there was finally evidence of a point to Gamaliel's presence at the estate. To everyone's disgust, it required a grouping of estate residents and members of Sanctum Arcist.

"It's simple," said Gamaliel. "We have discovered activity that is congruent with Eighth Chapter behavior, but the spots are in four different locations. So four groups should suffice. I suggest four two-and-ones."

"No," said Jonathan flat-out. "You will not come here to my domain and dictate strategy. It will be fair. Two twos-and-one, and two ones-and-two."

Jonah raised his eyebrows at the number play, and Reena shrugged. He also realized that their friends and even some of the Sanctum people were confused. G.J. poised himself to explain, no doubt condescendingly, but Jonathan never gave him the chance.

"It means there will be four groups," the Guide explained. "All of the groups will have three people; two groups will have two residents and one Sanctum representative, while the other two will have two Sanctum representatives, and one resident."

The residents looked amongst themselves. They weren't thrilled about this. Jonah wasn't surprised to see that even some of the Sanctum people looked reluctant to take this on.

Neither Gamaliel nor G.J. looked amenable to Jonathan's arrangement, but Jonathan looked intractable. Trip smirked at their irritation, but then again, he enjoyed drama.

"Your arrangement is illogical, Jonathan," said G.J. "This is a possible engagement—"

"It is not an engagement, G.J.," said Jonathan calmly. "Because you are not soldiers, and this is not war."

"As long as it's Eighth Chapter crimes, it's war!" insisted G.J. "And, truth be told, I think that Pop's idea is by far the best one—"

"Of course you do," yawned Trip. "And that's because you're so far up your daddy's ass, I'm surprised you can breathe."

G.J. and several others rose, including Penelope and Rheadne. Trip did the same, as did some of his buddies.

"Please," Trip whispered. "Please allow me the privilege to beat your ass into the ground."

Now Jonathan rose. "Everyone sit down. Now."

There was that emanating power voice again. The one that no one could defy. Everyone complied. Jonathan returned his eyes to G.J.

"I am already aware of what you wanted to say," he told him. "You wanted to say that Gamaliel's plan was superior to my own because my students have only used weapons for practice. This is precisely why an evened out approach is the best one, because while my students have indeed only used weapons for practice, all of you at Sanctum Arcist have trained toward past memories and moments of glory. None of you have experienced true ethereal war."

"He's got a point, Pop." Gabriel spoke for the first time ever in the group. Jonah had already heard it, but the other residents were in awe of him, as they'd yet to hear his baritone voice. "We came here for a conjoined effort, and Jonathan's way shows appreciation of our respective strengths—"

"Gabe," said Iuris Mason, "was anybody talking to you?"

Jonah frowned. Terrence reacted to it as well. Gabriel had just been shot down, and his father and older brother hadn't done a thing about it. Nothing.

Jonah thought of the Decessios, who were so supportive of each other, even when they disagreed. He thought of Liz and Nella.

What kind of family would leave their own in the cold like that?

Gabriel swallowed hard, and fell silent. Gamaliel threw a glare at him before he spoke.

"Now," he said, as if his son hadn't said anything, "Jonathan, not to beleaguer the point—"

"I insist upon this," said Jonathan. "Two twos-and-one, and two ones-and-two. Balanced teams, versatile strengths. The collectives will have access to equal representation as well as diplomatic awareness and the ability to defend themselves."

"Hold up." Rheadne this time. "If I may sift through all that, did you just say that we may need your help resolving things diplomatically?"

"Precisely, Rheadne," said Jonathan.

"We stamp out fires with fire to protect our right to be civilized," said Rheadne.

"And it is the mark of a primitive mindset to protect the right to be civilized through resorting to savagery," said Jonathan.

"Damn," said Douglas, looking at Jonathan with admiration, "that was good!"

Several people laughed. Rheadne rolled her eyes, but didn't respond. Jonah felt for her. As awesome as she was, a meeting of the minds with Jonathan was never a good idea.

"Fine, Jonathan," said Gamaliel. "You win. We pick the groups now. The—ah—non-engagement is two weeks from now."

"Why then?" Douglas blurted out.

"That is the next full moon," answered Reena. "I'm guessing that they want to bait O'Shea, see if he is the ringleader."

Many of the Sanctum people regarded Reena with awe. Reena rolled her eyes, as though the information was obvious.

"Very well done, Reena," said Jonathan, who grinned her way. Then his eyes returned to Gamaliel. "Pick your twos-and-ones," he practically commanded.

Gamaliel looked over at his charges. "G.J., Iuris—" then he looked at the estate residents, frowning.

"And Royal Spader," said G.J. for his father.

Spader looked like he'd been given a great honor. Alvin, who was seated near him, acted as though he gagged.

"Very well," said Gamaliel. "Moving right along... Cisor, Rheadne, and—"

"That guy, Pop," G.J. pointed at Terrence. "Thomas, I believe?"

"My name is *Terrence,* man," said Terrence, irritated. "But yeah, I'll do it."

Jonah looked at Reena. That had been a very random choice. Why did G.J. do that?

Then, plain as day, he locked eyes with Jonah and gave him a smile so smug it should have been criminal.

Jonah couldn't believe it. G.J. had done that to spite him? There might be Deadfallen psychos terrorizing places, and G.J. wanted to play petty games? Who did he think he was? Rheadne's father?

Rheadne hadn't looked pleased with the arrangement either, but she made no objections.

"Now to you, Jonathan," said Gamaliel.

"Malcolm, Elizabeth, and Gabriel will be my first group," said Jonathan without hesitation.

Jonah wasn't the least bit surprised that Jonathan had chosen Malcolm instead of Bobby. Bobby had a tendency to be rash, and he was extremely overprotective of his girlfriend. Bobby wasn't thrilled, but by the look in his eyes, he had come to the same conclusion.

"Jonah, Reena, and Pene—"

"Oh hell no!" Penelope blurted out. She actually rose from her seat as if that would accentuate the point. "No way. Take *her.*"

She pointed at Aloisa.

Jonah glanced over at Reena, and was surprised to see her smiling. It was actually a little frightening; her smile was so cold and calculating. Then he understood. Penelope hadn't forgotten Reena's declaration, and she wasn't going to make things easier by being anywhere near her. Reena probably got immense pleasure out of the fact that she had the woman sweating.

Jonathan's grey eyes narrowed, but he didn't look surprised. "Are you agreeable with that, Miss?" he asked Aloisa.

After giving her friend a curious look, Aloisa nodded.

"Very well, then," said Jonathan. "That is that. No training tonight, everyone. The evening is yours. Do with it whatever you like."

People dispersed, and Aloisa moved closer to Jonah and Reena. Penelope used the opportunity to slink away. Reena tensed when she saw the girl, but Jonah tapped her shoulder.

"She's cool," he said. "At least I think."

"Comforting," muttered Reena.

"What's comforting?" asked Aloisa as she seated herself.

"Never mind, never mind," said Reena. "It's a pleasure to talk to you personally, Aloisa."

"The pleasure is mutual," said Aloisa with a smile. "Official Designation is Aloisa Oxendine, twenty-one years old, orange aura."

"Right," said Reena. "Well, I'm Reena, age unimportant, and my aura is yellow."

Aloisa almost laughed.

"Oxendine," said Jonah thoughtfully. "Are you Lumbee?"

"Yeah, actually." Aloisa looked at him, mildly surprised. "I'm originally from Pembroke."

"How did you wind up in Florida?"

"Family retired there," Aloisa explained. "Met up with Mr. Kaine when I was about ten, after I messed up and told some of my teachers that I saw spirits, and they thought I had a mental disorder. So Reena, did I see you training with a javelin?"

"Yes," said Reena.

"Ever wonder how helpful it'd be in a real fight?"

"Thought crossed my mind a few times," said Reena. "But I'm not a soldier, so I don't worry about it too much."

"I saw the selenite and Jarelsien," observed Aloisa. "Are you an essence reader?"

"Yes," said Reena.

"What's your range?"

Reena looked surprised. "I can read the essence of everyone here, should I wish to."

Jonah saw Aloisa mouth, "*Wow,*" and decided to detach himself from this budding hero worship.

"Pardon me," he said. "I need to speak to Jonathan."

He hurried over before Jonathan could vanish.

"Hi, Jonah," said Jonathan. "How may I be of assistance?"

"Jonathan, I have a problem," said Jonah.

"Oh?"

"Well, it's not me, actually," clarified Jonah. "It's someone else."

He told him about the things he'd discovered in the city, including the failing health of his former employer. Jonathan took the information almost dispassionately, like he wasn't paying attention. But when Jonah finished, Jonathan's gaze sharpened.

"This has been going on for a month, you said?"

"Yes, sir."

"Has Jessica involved the Tenth Police?"

"Um, I can't really say, sir," said Jonah. "Ant mentioned giving information to the police at some point, but I'm not sure they did too much with it, as it was inconsequential. Also, Jessica is—well, forgive me, sir, but she is a stubborn bitch. She is of the mind that it will all just go away if she hides in her house long enough."

Jonathan nodded. "It may be a good thing that the Tenth authorities' influence has whittled away," he said.

"It—it is?" said Jonah, taken aback.

"Yes, it is, Jonah," said Jonathan. "This way, I can get the S.P.G. to investigate since the Tenth authorities haven't muddied up the waters too much. Thank you for telling me, Jonah. I will alert them now. Your fr—ah, former colleague will never know that they are in her affairs. Most of the work will be done out of the sight of the Tenths, and if they are seen, it will simply be assumed that they are regular law enforcement."

Jonah nodded eagerly. He knew that Jonathan would know the best course of action.

"You will need to speak to Jessica again, Jonah," said Jonathan.

Jonah misheard Jonathan. For a moment there, he thought the spirit said that he had to talk to Jessica again. "Come—come again, sir?"

"You heard, son."

"But, Jonathan! We hate each other. That—woman— threatened me to stay out of her business!"

"Your plight is not unnoticed, Jonah," said Jonathan. "But fear is a powerful motivator. You put the possibility into her consciousness, and she won't forget that. Feelings are raw now; she is acting out of fear. But give it some time. I would not be surprised if you get another opportunity to speak with Jessica."

Jonah had heard of optimism, but this? This didn't even have a term. "Right," was all he could manage.

Jonathan nodded. "I'm going to alert the S.P.G. now. Prayerfully, O'Shea will be apprehended long before Jessica wastes away in her home."

He disappeared, leaving Jonah to figure out the best term for the Protector Guide's optimism.

"Fold." Douglas dropped the cards, which left Jonah, Cisor, Spader, Iuris, and Benjamin in the game. How the co-existence piece had lasted this long was beyond Jonah, but he wasn't engaged in any conversation. That may have helped things a bit.

Spader looked across the table, his face completely free of emotion. He looked at each of his remaining opponents in turn. Jonah couldn't tell if the kid was reading them or what, but he knew that he wasn't getting anything from Spader.

"Check," murmured Benjamin.

Spader remained emotionless.

"Damn it, raise," snapped Iuris.

He pushed some chips forward. Spader looked at him.

"Why are you raising?" he asked calmly. "All you've got are some measly-ass face cards."

Iuris widened his eyes, but then tried to smooth over his expression. Unfortunately, Spader caught the slip, and Iuris knew it. He let his cards fall in disgust.

"Thanks much," grinned Spader. "And Jonah?"

Jonah looked at his own hand. There wasn't a damn thing he could do. All he had was a high card of an ace. "Done," he said.

Everyone else folded in front of Spader, who then laughed, and revealed his hand to be pure garbage. Jonah's eyes flashed. He could have actually beaten the bastard with the high card!

"Sorry, people!" said Spader gleefully. "Maybe next time! Come back whenever you're ready."

Jonah and Benjamin rose from the table, and Benjamin went upstairs. Jonah was about to go downstairs when he heard new conversation. He hid, and listened.

"That was a little too crafty, Royal," said Cisor. "Admit it. You mark the cards."

"Nope," said Spader. "I don't mark cards. I'm a winner. It's what I do."

"It was brave of you to clean us out without any of your friends around," said Iuris. "We could tune your ass up if we so chose."

Jonah's eyes narrowed. Were they seriously about to assault Spader?

"That'll never happen," said Spader without the slightest trace of fear. "You've been granted haven. Touch me, and you risk the relinquishment of the granting."

That was cleverly played, but Jonah knew that these were some mean-spirited people. He really hoped that they wouldn't double-team Spader, regardless of the consequences.

"I'll give it to you, kid," said Cisor. "For your age, you've got a set. How old *are* you, actually?"

"Eighteen in three weeks," said Spader.

There was a bit of silence, which prompted Jonah to brave a glimpse from behind his wall. Iuris and Cisor seemed to come to some sort of understanding, while Spader finally looked confused. So Spader, the Reader of People, met some people that he couldn't read. Huh.

"That would be young enough," murmured Cisor.

"Young enough for what?" asked Spader.

"For rehabilitation, of a sort," said Iuris. "When this whole deal is over, you can come back to Sanctum Arcist with us."

Jonah's eyes widened. Evidently, Spader felt something similar.

"Go to Sanctum Arcist?' he asked.

"Yep," said Cisor. "I don't have any doubts that G.J. would vouch for you. He's already said that you have more drive and initiative than just about anyone else here."

Jonah was experiencing a mind war. Were they serious about this?

"But—but the estate is my home," said Spader slowly. "I've been hanging around here since I was ten."

Iuris grunted. "That doesn't really add up, does it, Royal?" he asked. "How can home be a place where you just hang out?"

"Do they even respect you around here?" asked Cisor.

"I—well—I suppose many people view me as immature and sneaky—"

"Not what I asked," said Cisor calmly.

Spader had no answers for them. Jonah closed his eyes. Spader wasn't very respected. He was viewed by most everyone as a conniving, thieving creep, which Jonah knew for a fact wasn't a lie. But at the same time, he knew what it was like to be ignored, or to receive negative attention if one received any attention at all. He'd have loved to have had solace at seventeen.

But this wasn't solace. This was defection.

"I didn't think that you had any answers." Cisor had a sort of quiet triumph in his voice. "Come with us when we're done here, Spader. I swear that old Jonathan probably won't even notice that you're gone."

They left Spader; Jonah heard the scrape of chairs across the kitchen floor. He glanced at Spader from his hiding place again.

The kid simply looked shocked. Jonah left, not wanting to be caught by Spader when he left the table. But that wasn't his main concern.

It seemed that Aloisa Oxendine wasn't the only one fascinated by strangers.

"Rowe!"

The insistent call made Jonah jerk his head up. He'd fallen asleep in class. *Shit.*

"Was your slumber an indication of my effectiveness as a professor?" Professor Ferrus demanded.

He stared at Jonah with intense, scathing eyes. Several people in the class were as well. Jonah felt even more self-conscious, and hoped that he hadn't snored.

"No sir," he mumbled. "I just—I apologize."

There was no point in explanations. It made more sense to just concede and be done with it.

Dr. Ferrus didn't look to be in a forgiving mood, but he looked away from Jonah. If he wasn't going to forgive, maybe he could just let it go, Jonah supposed. It wasn't like Jonah was slacking. He'd gotten an A on that godforsaken midterm, hadn't he?

"As I was saying," said Dr. Ferrus to the class at large, "your papers on effectively interweaving ideas into stories are expected next class. Kindly see to it that they are gripping. Perhaps we can gauge their effectiveness by Mr. Rowe's attention span."

Jonah took a breath through his nostrils. He'd done wrong. He'd messed up. But the man didn't have to take that route. That was just petty and damn childish.

Class dispersed. Jonah wasn't worried. He had a good grade in the class, so he needn't dwell on the screw-up. Even so, he'd do his best work on the paper. Maybe if he turned in a stellar paper, Ferrus would let it go.

He saw Miss Daynard on his way out of the building, but was careful not to get too close. Her voice was so meditative that he just might fall asleep again.

When he returned home, he saw Liz, Nella, and Vera, who had just finished with something dealing with plants (Jonah couldn't imagine what, because it was too dark to be gardening). As usual, Liz brightly acknowledged him, while Nella flashed him a sweet smile.

Vera's greeting was as mechanical as ever. Jonah just shook his head and walked on.

Terrence met him by the door, which Jonah assumed to be a coincidence. But when he attempted to edge past him, Terrence didn't move.

"Reena is up in the infirmary," he told him.

"What?" said Jonah, all senses on alert. "Why?"

"She nearly got mugged today."

Jonah frowned, but then glanced back at Liz, Nella, and Vera. If Reena had been mugged, then why were they out here, so cheerful?

"She didn't tell them." Terrence answered the question for Jonah. "She just told me. She didn't tell Liz because she'd make a big deal of it, and she'd didn't tell Ben-Israel because he'd go by the book, and tell the whole of the known world. She got Akshara to look her over."

"What's her injury?" asked Jonah.

"Sprained wrist."

"Damn," said Jonah. "What did the guy do?"

Terrence looked at him in confusion. "He got away. Ran away, actually. Reena injured her own wrist when she broke his jaw."

Jonah laughed. Then he realized the situation. The laughter melted from his face. "Thanks for telling me," he mumbled.

"Yeah," said Terrence. "I just thought it'd be great for you to visit your friend before you ran off to get help from Rheadne this time."

"Not doing this with you, Terrence," said Jonah. "I ain't got the time, or the energy."

Jonah left Terrence without another word, dropped off his bag in his room, and then headed to the infirmary. Reena looked great; she wasn't even on a bed. She sat on a chair reading something on her phone. Her wrist was snugly wrapped, but it didn't seem to bother her at all.

"How're you doing, Reena?" Jonah still had to ask.

"Fine," said Reena idly. "Just wanted to stay here while Akshara's balm took effect."

Jonah nodded, and sat near her.

"Did you really break the man's jaw?"

"Yeah, I did," said Reena. "I felt it break."

Jonah could tell something wasn't right. It was in Reena's voice. She wanted to be brave, but she seemed disturbed.

"Why did you get Akshara to fix your wrist and not Liz or Ben-Israel?"

Reena took a deep breath. "I didn't get mugged, Jonah," she said. "The guy was a Deadfallen disciple."

Jonah gawked. "Are-are you sure?"

Reena looked rattled. "Positive."

Jonah looked at the door and made sure they were alone. Then he turned back to her. "How are you positive?"

Reena checked their privacy as well, which really concerned Jonah, as he'd just done that. What had Reena acting like this? "When Terrence's parents—" Reena glanced at Jonah when she said Terrence's name, but Jonah was too concerned about her to react, so she needn't have worried, "When Terrence's parents told us about the Deadfallen, I wanted to know more. So I—"

"—went to Jonathan's study, and looked them up," finished Jonah. "Please continue."

Reena shook her head. Maybe she didn't realize that she was that predictable. "Right. I discovered that Creyton never used identifying insignia, or anything. He loathed things that could identify his disciples so much, he made it so they could contact with a phrase that only they could say. No one else."

"How would that work?"

"No idea," said Reena. "But Jonathan told me that Guides, Networkers, and Spectral Law Practitioners did figure out a recurring attribute."

"What was that?" asked Jonah.

Reena pointed two fingers toward the upper portion of her throat. "Residual bruising at their pulse area," she said. "Apparently, most Deadfallen disciples, if not all of them, have it."

Jonah sat back from her. "Did Jonathan tell you why they have bruises on their throats?"

"No," said Reena. "He might not even know himself."

Jonah doubted that one, but he didn't say anything. He also thought he knew the connection of Reena's story, but felt that Reena needed to say it herself so as to begin the process of healing from the negative experience. So he decided to accommodate her. "So how were you sure that he was Deadfallen?"

Reena looked at him, once again, like the answer should have been obvious. Jonah clenched his teeth. He knew that would happen. It was the price he paid for being a good friend to allow it. "He approached me, thinking that I was an ally because of this bruise that bitch put on my neck," she answered. "He came up to me, revealed his matching bruise, and said what I presume is the common phrase they share."

"What was that phrase?" asked Jonah.

"I told you that I can't say it," responded Reena.

"Oh come on, Reena." Jonah had a little impatience by this time. "It's just us."

Reena shook her head. "You don't get it, Jonah. I literally can't say it. The Deadfallen disciples are the only ones who could. So, this guy said it, and I answered, 'What?' And then he tried to go nuclear on me. He made the mistake of going for my throat, and I flipped out. I snapped his jaw."

Jonah couldn't help but smile, despite the situation. Reena had indeed been in danger, but that crazy bastard didn't know about Reena's leftover anger towards Penelope. "Jonathan would want to know about this, Reena," he told her.

"You're right." Reena nodded in agreement. "And I will tell him...after tomorrow night."

Jonah raised his eyebrows.

"I'm not being pulled out of our outing, Jonah," Reena informed him. "If the man I saw today can lead us to his stupid nest, maybe we can stop this crap."

"Oh yeah..." Jonah had almost forgotten that entire arrangement, which was an example of Gamaliel Kaine actually having a point to be present at the estate.

So much for getting an early start on his narrative paper.

"Say, Jonah," said Reena suddenly, "Terrence was the only person that knew about this, other than Akshara, of course."

She looked at him expectantly. Jonah didn't know what she expected, though.

"Yeah," he admitted, "he was the one who told me."

Reena raised her eyebrows. "And?"

Jonah rose from his seat, shaking his head. "And nothing's changed."

Reena rolled her eyes in irritation, and slumped in her chair. As he left, Jonah heard her mutter, "*Goddamned men.*"

The next evening arrived in the blink of an eye, but Jonah didn't feel much fear. He was aware that it wasn't a funny situation, but there were too many things that he didn't know. What they'd find was unclear. Maybe he should have been thankful for the confusion, because it didn't leave room for fear.

The four groups met on the front porch as the final traces of daytime waned. The front porch would serve as their communal *Astralimes* point. The Sanctum people wanted to use their twig portals, but thankfully, Jonathan shot that down. Jonah saw that Reena, whose javelin looked like a baton in its dormant form, looked uncomfortable. He knew she'd had fights with sazers and a couple vampires when she was a teenager, but that was forever ago. The look in her eyes elevated his uneasiness just a few notches. To Jonah's surprise, Aloisa didn't look too much more composed than Reena. After that first night and that disastrous first conjoined training, he expected them all to be hardcore wannabe warmongers who spent their time salivating for fights—Cisor, G.J., Iuris, and many others in Sanctum seemed that way—but Aloisa looked to have anxiety. Terrence, who avoided eye contact with Jonah, didn't seem to be ready for a fight so much as ready to be done with the briefing bit. Rheadne threw a sly grin Jonah's way (Terrence, who'd been ignoring everything, managed to notice that), but was all business seconds later. Malcolm's face was emotionless, as usual. Liz had a serious expression that wasn't becoming on her usually sunny face. Gabriel simply looked ready to move.

"As I'd mentioned before, there are four locations," said Gamaliel. "Investigate them thoroughly; fine-toothed comb. If you come into contact with pockets of resistance, squash it. G.J., Iuris, Royal, here—" he passed them a note. "Go to that address. Cisor, Rheadne, Terry—"

Terrence raised a finger, but sighed in resignation and didn't correct the old man as he slid the three of them a slip of paper.

Jonah wondered why it was necessary for Gamaliel to be so clandestine. They were Eleventh Percenters being sent to investigate potential threats, not Special Forces.

"That ought to do it," said Gamaliel. "And remember, as long as you are breathing, you are capable of fighting."

Jonah raised an eyebrow. That wasn't a notion he wanted to think of while doing this. He saw Terrence's slight frown; even Spader's expectant face faltered somewhat. G.J., Iuris, and Cisor nodded.

"Let's get to it, people," said G.J.

He, Iuris, and Spader used the *Astralimes,* and with brief breeze, they were gone. Cisor, Rheadne, and Terrence followed shortly after. Jonah couldn't help but feel a pang of concern for Spader and, damn it all, Terrence.

Gamaliel looked to Jonathan. "I think it's safe to assume that you would like to dole out these particular orders, old friend," he said.

There was a bite in his voice, and Jonah thought he understood. The cantankerous buffoon was still ticked off about the fact that Jonathan overrode him. Jonathan gave the two remaining groups his full attention.

"Look after yourselves," he said. "I have no doubts in any of your abilities, but if you can obtain fruitful information with minimal risk, that would be preferable. Elizabeth, I'm counting on you to keep yourself as safe as possible. If your skills prove necessary—"

"Don't worry about me, sir," said Liz seriously. "I'll be fine; you already know that it's a mistake to underestimate me. I just had this conversation three times with Bobby."

Jonah recalled Rheadne's opinion on the matter. *Medics have no business in a fight.*

He hoped that that was wrong.

Jonathan gave her another look of concern, but then nodded. "Your address is 1208 Winity Lane," he said to their group. "See what you find, and report back. Gabriel, I pray that we have an understanding."

"We do, sir," said Gabriel in a calm voice. "We do."

"Very well," said Jonathan. "Malcolm, best foot forward."

"Always, sir," said Malcolm.

They used the *Astralimes*. Jonathan finally turned to Jonah, Reena, and Aloisa.

"Your address is on Route 6," he told them. "Take care of yourselves."

Jonah nodded. "We've got this, Jonathan."

The Protector Guide nodded, and stepped away. Before Jonah used the *Astralimes* with Reena and Aloisa, he saw Jonathan look over to the woods. Trip was there. Jonathan nodded at him, and Trip acknowledged it with a small nod of his own before looking away. What was that about?

"Jonah, we got to roll," said Reena.

Jonah gave himself a mental shake, and used the *Astralimes* with the two women.

Seconds later, they were on the front lawn of a farmhouse. Jonah was sure that it was unremarkable in the daylight, but in the evening, it's stark whiteness, sprawling acreage, and dark windows made it unsettling and eerie.

"You ever watch those shows where they talk about hostile spirits?" asked Aloisa, uncertainty in her voice. "It seemed like all the houses in those shows were big and white, just like this one."

"Spirits and spiritesses have far more effective ways to get people's attention than haunting their homes," said Reena. "Surely, you know that spirits abhor that stereotype. What are you thinking, Jonah?"

Jonah looked from the house to the large barn, and then looked at the garage. Of the trio, the garage seemed smallest. That made it the most logical place to check first.

"I don't know about pulling weapons yet," he muttered. "It'd give us away almost instantly."

"Where are your gloves?" asked Aloisa curiously.

Jonah looked at her. "What?"

"You don't wear gloves on engagements?"

"No, because we don't go on engagements," said Reena. "We're not soldiers."

Aloisa raised her hands. "I'm not making a jab, I promise!"

She hastily dug into her pants pocket and tossed pairs of gloves to Jonah and Reena.

"Mr. Kaine instructs us to always wear gloves on engagements," she explained. "You can be incognito for as long as possible, but when the time comes to fight, the fingers come off of them, so you don't have to waste time ripping the whole thing off."

Jonah put them on. Reena did the same.

"Nifty trick," he commented. "How many times have you done this?"

Aloisa looked away. "Never," she admitted. "I know what I know from hearing G.J. and Cisor and Rheadne and the others."

"Wait a second." Reena seemed to forget their plan for a moment. "Never? Pulchrum threw you out here, just like that?"

"We all have to learn sooner or later, right?" asked Aloisa.

Jonah threw a look over at Reena. She didn't buy that, either. Penelope was leery of Reena, they knew that. So she threw Aloisa out here, so that she could feel Reena's rage.

He had a fleeting thought of introducing Penelope to Jessica. Just lock them in a room, and let them massacre each other.

"We've done enough running our mouths," said Jonah. "Let's get this started. Stay close together."

They moved toward the garage, which, like everything else, was bathed in the light of the full moon. Jonah reached for the side door, which opened easily. Before he could step forward, Reena stopped him.

"What?"

Reena removed a pocket knife from her vest and made rather dramatic slits on the threshold. "I researched those Thresholds of Death things. The functionality of one will cease if the threshold has been mutilated."

Briefly pausing to marvel at Reena's knowledge, Jonah stepped inside the garage. He willed the bulbs to come to life.

"Lazy," commented Reena. "The light switch is right there."

The whole place could be taken in one glance, and Jonah didn't see anything out of the ordinary. He was about to suggest moving on to the barn when Reena said, "Whoa."

Jonah moved nearer to her and Aloisa, not seeing what they saw at first, but then he saw it.

It was blood.

It wasn't a great deal of it, but its presence was disturbing nonetheless. Jonah noticed that Aloisa looked like she really didn't want to be here now.

"Is this old?" he asked Reena.

"No." Reena's voice was so sharp and strong that it was unnerving. "We have to get of here."

"Reena—?"

"Jonah, this blood is—"

Aloisa, who'd backed away in disgust, suddenly screamed. Jonah and Reena whipped around in alarm, and in Jonah's panicked state, he lost his will over the electricity. They couldn't see what was happening to Aloisa.

"LET ME GO!" she screamed.

"Jonah!" shouted Reena. Yellow illuminated the dark, which meant that her endowment-powered javelin was ready. "Gloves off! Literally!"

Jonah ripped the fingers off of the gloves, and had his batons in seconds.

"Aloisa's gone!" he shrieked.

"They took her up to the house!" cried Reena.

"How the hell do you know?" demanded Jonah.

"Essence reader, Jonah!"

"Oh, right!"

They nearly injured themselves when they burst out of the door at the same time, and tore off for the farmhouse. Jonah noticed that the distance between them didn't seem this far when they first saw it.

"How did they move so fast?"

"Easy!" gasped Reena.

"Are they Deadfallen disciples?" gasped Jonah.

"No!" said Reena. "Sazers!"

Horrified, Jonah redoubled his efforts, and they hit the porch at the same time. At the door, Reena cried, "Jonah, the door—!"

"Not waiting, Reena!" roared Jonah.

He bashed in the front door. An almost bestial exclamation met his arrival, and before he knew it, Jonah was in a battle for his physical life. The sazer grabbed him at the wrists and wrenched them in an attempt to make him drop his batons. The bastard knew exactly what to disable. Jonah dropped one of them, but gripped the other so tightly that his hand was almost numb. The guy was strong as hell, and Jonah struggled to free himself.

"Reena!" he spat over the bastard's head, "go find Alo—"

Another sazer leapt from the staircase and jumped Reena, making them both crash to the ground. Her javelin clattered away from her, sparking out the second it was free of her endowed hands. Great.

Worried about Reena, Jonah kicked his own opponent in the groin. The sazer collapsed as though he'd been shot, and Jonah tried to go in the last direction he'd seen Reena before it went dark. He shouldn't have taken his focus off his own opponent, because he grabbed Jonah by the ankle and brought him down. Not even a kick to the balls incapacitated a sazer in Red Rage, it seemed.

The bastard tried to mount Jonah before he could turn on his back. Jonah remembered what Rheadne taught him about charging his weapon, and focused as much essence as he could into the baton he still held. When he felt the sazer's hot, rotten breath on the back of his neck, Jonah swung backward.

The guy howled as he got propelled off of Jonah's back and crashed into a table. He was out.

One down.

The temperature dipped considerably, and Jonah scrambled to his feet and raced toward Reena's direction. She must have tried to disorient her opponent with her cold-spot trick, but the thing must have been too riled to feel the cold, because it didn't let up. Jonah attempted to grab the man from behind, but he swung a punch that sent him into the wall and his remaining baton out of his hand. That hurt like ten kinds of hell, but he ignored it as best he could. Reena screamed in rage. She was having trouble with the other Red-Raged sazer, a situation that was compounded by the darkness. Jonah focused so hard on the electricity that he accidentally blew the top bulbs out. Mercifully, a lamp stayed on, and the television popped on as well. Even this paltry amount of light was a boon, because Reena finally managed to grab a flower pot and hit the sazer, who had straddled her, in the face. It had little effect, but the sazer was temporarily blinded by the dirt. Jonah tackled him off of Reena, which sent them into the TV stand. Yep, the TV fell and rolled across the crazed sazer's back.

Jonah looked at the sazer in disbelief. He was still conscious!

"Jonah!" Reena spat blood from her mouth. "Grab his feet!"

Jonah did as she asked without thought. Reena scrambled to the sazer, battled back his flailing hands, and wrapped him in some sort of leg chokehold Jonah hadn't ever seen before. The Red-Raged sazer's strength was unbelievable, but Jonah hung on to his legs for dear life with a combination of a tight grip and body weight.

Eventually, the combination of his injuries and Reena's unforgiving pressure on his windpipe made the sazer's struggles wane. His legs ceased thrashing, as did his struggling arms. Reena had done it.

But she didn't let him go.

"Reena!" Jonah hopped up and tugged at her arms. "REENA! Stop! He's out! He's done! We have to find Aloisa!"

That made Reena relent, and she freed herself of the sazer. Jonah retrieved his batons and kicked her javelin her way (the lamp hadn't gone out during that last skirmish).

"Come on, Reena!" he told her. "Upstairs!"

Reena's anger hadn't fully abated, but she followed Jonah's lead up the stairs without a word. When they reached the first landing, they raced to the third room, where the door had been smashed off of its hinges.

The sazer girl was seconds away from digging into Aloisa's flesh with the girl's own hunting knife, but the arrival of Jonah and Reena took her by surprise. When she saw Jonah's blue-gleaming batons, her eyes widened.

"The Blue Aura!" she spat. "But that's not right! They promised—!"

Reena had heard enough, and charged the girl with the butt of her javelin, using her ethereal speed the whole way. The force knocked the girl through the window, where she bounced sickeningly on a corner of the roof before she hit the ground with a thud.

Jonah looked at her, wide-eyed. "Damn, Reena."

"Sazers are made of stronger bodily materials, as we just found out downstairs," said Reena, who didn't even look remorseful. "She's still physically alive. Probably."

Jonah went over to Aloisa and helped her to her feet. Her shirt had been ripped and she was covered in scrapes and bruises, but she was otherwise okay. The poor girl hadn't even gotten her gloves off so that her endowed fingers could touch it.

"J-Jonah," the girl was frightened out of her mind, "Reena. She said they were going to—to eat me."

Jonah glanced at Reena, who still had her eyes on the downed sazer outside the window. "What?"

"That's what I was trying to tell you earlier," said Reena. "That blood in the garage belonged to the owners of this farm."

"What!" Jonah couldn't believe what he'd just heard. "How can you be so sure?"

"The lifeblood was still fresh enough to have traces of their essence in it," said Reena. "Those sazers…they wiped out the whole family. I could still read their fear in that lifeblood."

"I—I thought you were an essence reader, Reena," said Aloisa. "Are you like—like a lifeblood reader, too?"

"Aloisa," Reena seemed to be regaining her composure now, "life is in the spirit, which encompasses everything about us. Our essence is just as tied to our lifeblood as our spirit, because our lifeblood aids in sustaining physical life. So I could read the essence in their lifeblood as if they were still there. It will fade soon, of course, but it hadn't just yet."

"Never mind that!" said Jonah impatiently. "Why are they doing this? I thought sazer's didn't have a vampire's thirst!"

"They don't, Jonah," said Reena. "These sazers are cannibals. They didn't care about the lifeblood so much as the meat that came along with it. Thirst wasn't the issue here; it was the hunger. But that's not the issue here."

"It's not?" said Jonah and Aloisa together.

"No," said Reena. "That sazer that you helped me put down? His essence was laced—and I do mean laced—with something like betrayal. And that one—" she tilted her head toward the broken window, "—said that someone *promised* something."

Jonah could see Reena's direction clearly. "You think that this was a trap."

"I know it was a trap," said Reena shortly. "I think that whatever Deadfallen disciples that were around here unleashed these cannibals sazers on this poor family and then told them that they could have free run of the place. And then we showed up and wrecked the party."

"Explains why you sensed betrayal in the essence," said Aloisa.

But Jonah stopped registering words after *trap*. If he, Reena, and Aloisa walked into a trap, then—

"Terrence," he whispered.

Reena's eyes widened in fear. "My God. They could have walked into a trap, too."

Jonah punched a nearby wall in frustration. "And we don't know where they went! Kaine had to be so damned secretive—"

"I can find him," said Reena.

Jonah stared at her. Reena had her talents, but to pull locations out of thin air? That might be a stretch. "How would you go about that exactly, Reena?"

"Terrence is my best friend, Jonah," said Reena tersely. "Don't think I can't peg the essence of one of my closest friends with the proper focus and concentration.

Jonah's misgivings faded at once. "Then find him. Now."

Reena closed her eyes and took a deep, centering breath. Then she grinned. "Done."

"Okay," said Jonah, "let's—"

"You aren't leaving me!" said Aloisa loudly. She finally ungloved her hands, and her hunting knife shone with orange brilliance. "I'm coming to help!"

"Aloisa—" Jonah didn't even try to conceal his doubt, but Aloisa cut across him.

"I choked here," she said. "I got grabbed, almost got us all killed. Let me make it right."

"But—"

"If I don't succeed, I've failed," she said flatly. "That's what Mr. Kaine always says; it's his primary admonition. I failed here. Let me fix it. Let me help."

Jonah nodded. He wasn't entirely comfortable with it, but they were wasting time standing here. "Fine. Reena, guide us."

"Gladly," said Reena. "Let's go."

They followed Reena's lead. Her focus was so strong that Jonah didn't even need to know the location. He just needed to grab Aloisa's hand and bring her along the pathway, the wind, and the second step—

They were in an abandoned warehouse. Jonah didn't even know where it was. The place was a mess. It seemed that every object in the place had been overturned or smashed. He looked around, but didn't see anyone.

"Are you sure this is the place, Reena?"

"Yes," said Reena with conviction. "Now, we need to find Cisor, Terrence, and Rheadne—"

"HERE!" someone shouted.

Jonah wheeled around. Terrence was behind them, partially buried under some broken objects. His left foot was lodged underneath what appeared to be a large filing cabinet.

"Help me!" he snapped, but there was no anger there. "We need to get out of here; some stupid cannibal sazers—!"

There were roars of rage. Speak of the devil.

At least five sazers, all emaciated but feral as beasts, came out of the darkness and were about to converge on Terrence's trapped form.

"Help him!" cried Aloisa, who ran to their right, and began to scramble up a shelf. "I have a plan!"

Not knowing or caring what her big plan was, Jonah and Reena raced to Terrence before the cannibal sazers reached him. Jonah hoisted up the cabinet, and Reena yanked Terrence's leg free. He swore loudly; his foot was turned in a nauseating direction. Jonah didn't like their chances of guiding Terrence a safe distance away with hungry sazers feverishly wrestling through all the broken crap—

"Heads up!" called Aloisa from somewhere above them.

Jonah looked up, puzzled, but Reena's eyes widened in alarm.

"We need to get out of the way!"

"Reena, Terrence's foot—!"

"Just trust me!" Reena cried.

Once they got Terrence to a standing position, Reena hurried between them, and used her ethereal speed to race them to the clear.

Not a moment too soon. Not only would the sazers have reached them, but they would have been in the direct path of Aloisa's big plan. Once they were clear, a massive, metallic rack leaned precariously, and Jonah caught the briefest glimpse of Aloisa, who'd propped herself between the wall and the rack. She pushed with all of her strength, and the rack fell forward. Their predatory pursuers were crushed underneath it. They didn't have a chance.

The good news was the fact that the positioning of the rack provided a containment of sorts for its products, so they didn't crash all over the place. The bad news was that once the rack crashed to the floor, a shard of iron shot up in the air like a bullet, and sliced across Jonah's upper arm, leaving a deep gash.

"DAMMIT!" His arm felt like it had been stabbed with the world's hottest knife, but at least he maintained the presence of mind to hold on to Terrence. Reena winced at the cut.

With a feline's grace, Aloisa dropped from her perch, and grinned at them. "Done good, didn't I?" she asked.

Even though his brain urged him to say something else, Jonah managed a smile. "Very nice, Aloisa. Very nice indeed."

"Are you crazy?" hissed Terrence. "What if that had been your face?"

"Shut up, and let the girl feel good about herself," muttered Jonah. "Long story."

Thankfully, Aloisa didn't hear any of that.

"Terrence," said Reena, "where are Cisor and Rheadne?"

Jonah was thankful Reena asked the question, and not him.

Terrence's face darkened. "Cisor gave chase after we were ambushed. Didn't even give me a second thought. Rheadne tried to get my foot free, but she wasn't strong enough to lift the thing alone. So she used a twig portal to go find help."

"Oh no," said Aloisa, "Mr. Kaine would have told her to cut her losses."

"Jonathan would never stand for leaving someone alone," snapped Reena. "How long ago did she leave?"

"Couple minutes before you guys showed up," answered Terrence. He wasn't pleased about Cisor and Rheadne leaving him. It was written all over his face.

A nerve worked in Reena's temple. She wasn't pleased with what Cisor and Rheadne had done, either. Jonah didn't get the rage, seeing as how Rheadne at least went for help. Cisor's dumb ass was the one who wanted to go be Rambo.

"Let's just get back home," said Reena at last. "We all need medical attention. And we can tell Rheadne that there is no need to bring anyone."

"But what about Malcolm and Liz?" said Jonah. "Spader?"

Reena closed her eyes. "Let's get home," she said. "We can regroup there. We are of no use to anyone here. Here is the plan: Aloisa and I will use the *Astralimes* to the Glade. That's where everyone will be, and probably where Rheadne will have gone to look for help. Jonah, Terrence, you two use the *Astralimes* straight to the infirmary. Terrence needs to get off of his foot, and you need to get that wound dressed. I'll send someone along, and we'll do all the explaining and everything."

"Alright," said Jonah. "Hang on, Terrence. Away we go."

They carefully used the *Astralimes* on account of Terrence's ankle, and moments later, they were in the infirmary. Jonah aided Terrence to a bed, and assisted him with positioning his bad foot. He then grabbed a bunch of paper towels, and applied pressure to his gash. He didn't care that it was crude; he was just tired. They didn't even have to wait for Liz to return with Gabriel and Malcolm. Ben-Israel, Sherman, Akshara, Kendra, Barry—they were all out in the Glade somewhere. He knew that Malcolm would have taken care of Liz, for Bobby's sake. If he had read Gabriel correctly, he could be relied on as well.

Terrence's eyes were in the opposite direction. There was a trace of a grimace on his face, but that very well could have been because of his foot.

"Does it feel any better now that you're off of it?" asked Jonah.

"A little bit," said Terrence, still looking the other way. "How is that cut? Were you able to staunch the blood flow?"

"Kinda sorta," said Jonah.

More silence. Then—

"I have to ask," said Terrence suddenly. "What was that Aloisa girl thinking when she kicked down that thing on all our heads?"

Jonah snorted. "We saved her earlier, see. Sazer was about to fillet her ass—literally—and Reena stopped it. She figured that since she failed then—"

"—she should overcompensate, and save you by almost crushing all of us," finished Terrence. "I'd have preferred the sazers, personally."

They shared a laugh, and then went back into silence. Twenty seconds later—

"Rheadne came on to me, man," said Jonah.

"I know that." Terrence finally stopped staring off into space. "*Now.*"

Jonah took a deep breath before he said the next part. "I'm not sorry about hanging out with her, man."

"You shouldn't be," said Terrence. "You ain't stupid, are you?"

Jonah didn't ask what made Terrence finally understand. Or what made him finally accept it. It didn't matter. "I swear," he told Terrence, "all this foolishness has got me famished. I could do with some of your mom's bacon mac and cheese."

Terrence nodded. "That would be great right now. But you know what would be better? Some pizza."

Jonah raised an eyebrow. "Pizza?"

"Yep, pizza," said Terrence. "With extra *olives.*"

Jonah grinned. He got the metaphor.

"Would you be game for that?" asked Terrence.

Jonah checked his makeshift bandage of paper towels and tape. He took his time with it. Eh, what the hell. "Yeah," he said. "Pizza with extra olives would be cool."

Terrence nodded. That was that.

But then, at that exact moment, Reena stormed into the infirmary, with nary a Green Aura with her. She was just as bruised up as Jonah was, but her hair was down, and her eyes were ablaze.

"ALRIGHT, DAMMIT!" she shouted. "This has gone on for far too long, and it is over! DONE!"

Terrence's eyes widened. "Reena—"

"No, just listen," Reena snarled. "Terrence, you were the first Eleventh Percenter to greet Jonah at this estate! He's been there for you more times than can be counted, right?"

"Yeah, but—"

"And Jonah," Reena's voice was even louder, "you have eaten Terrence's food, hung out with his family, and have even broken bread—wheat bread, no less—in his mother's house, yes?"

"Yes, Reena, but—"

"Not finished!" She raised a hand to shush him. "We all know how crappy families can be. It's an earned title, blood and obligations be damned. We've earned that title. All of us. You two are my brothers. And I will no longer have a rift between my brothers."

Jonah and Terrence looked at each other. Reena hadn't ever called them her brothers before. She wasn't fond of most men as it was, so it was a rather huge deal. Touching, even.

"I am not telling either of you how to handle this Rheadne situation," Reena continued. "It's not my business, and truth be told, I really don't care. But I do know one thing: women are a poor reason to dispense with the bonds we've built. So, as of this moment, your conflict is squashed. Got me?"

Jonah and Terrence looked at other once more. After a tirade like that, there was only one thing they could do.

Let Reena have this one.

"Squashed," they said in unison.

Reena took a steadying breath. "Good. Now, I'm going to go get Liz and Ben-Israel so they can fix us up."

She left. Jonah and Terrence watched her leave, and then laughed their heads off.

14

Per Mortem, Vitam

The pain in Jonah's arm was irritating as hell. Yeah, it was healing now, but Liz explained that, due to the deepness of the cut, the ache would last for a bit. When Jonah asked about her experiences with Malcolm and Gabriel, he saw a lingering fear in her eyes, but she praised Malcolm.

"He dropped two sazers before I could even attempt to find one of their pressure points," she said. "He said he wouldn't have let me fight anyway because he had my back as a friend, and he considered it a solid for Bobby. But I've got him pegged. I know he views me as a little sister as well. He wouldn't have wanted me to fight either way."

Jonah nodded. Good things. "And Gabriel?" he asked. "You didn't mention Gabriel."

A slight frown came across Liz's face as she returned her vials to her healing satchel. "Gabriel was as helpful as Malcolm was. But he seemed...preoccupied."

"I'm sorry?" said Jonah, confused.

"Yeah, I know," said Liz. "He said that Malcolm gave a good accounting of himself. He also said that he was sure that I could protect myself, but it wasn't like a compliment. It was like—like an assessment."

Jonah didn't know what to make of that. It sounded as though he'd been right in assuming Gabriel wasn't a jerk like the other men in his family. But what Liz said was a bit strange.

190

But he couldn't discuss anything further with Liz. If he kept on, he'd likely lose most of his thoughts, which would have helped nothing at all, especially not too long from then.

Jonathan wanted them in his study to discuss the night, and see what could be taken from it. Jonah had heard Reena reference the place many times, but Jonah hadn't ever seen it. Whenever he needed his mentor, he could just summon him and not have to wait for him in any room. This night was full of new things.

As Sanctum took their ever-loving time (they'd refused any assistance from the estate's Green Auras), and Liz and Reena were assisting Terrence with crutches, Jonah got to the study first. It was a spacious place, with wall to wall books covering every subject Jonah cared to name. If Jonathan allowed it, he might just stay here after the meeting and peruse some of the books.

Jonathan's desk was a glossy ebony wood, without a single trace of dust. On its surface was an interesting collection of neatly-placed items: an empty picture frame that looked as ancient as the room, an aged wallet, several papers rolled up scroll-style, a Masonic bible, a forty-year-old calendar(?), and finally, a spherical crystal full of what looked like amber. In the center of the crystal was the same infinity symbol as Jonathan's medallion. It looked to be made of gold.

Jonah looked around to make sure that he was still by himself, and then he picked up the crystal sphere. It was the temperature of hot chocolate; hot to the touch, but not unbearably so. The smoothness almost made it feel wet, but Jonah noticed that his touch left no marks or fingerprints. He wondered if it might be another random possession, but given its prominent place on the table, it had to mean something.

"Do you like that?" asked Jonathan.

Jonah started, and the crystal slipped from his hands.

"NO!" he shouted, but miraculously, the crystal fell right back on the table, in its original position. It was just like a cat that landed on its feet.

"Huh?" said Jonah aloud, and Jonathan laughed.

"Very interesting, isn't it?" he said. "It is called the Vitasphera. It is an eternal crystal symbol of Life that proclaims someone as Overseer of this estate, which is currently me."

Jonah nodded, eyes still on the sphere. "So it's passed down, then?"

"It is," said Jonathan. "It usually occurs when an Overseer passes from physical life into Spirit. I was able to maintain it, as I became a Protector Guide."

Jonah had to ask the question before everyone else turned up. "Why didn't it break? I mean, I'm glad it didn't, but why didn't it?"

"It is eternal, Jonah," said Jonathan. "Of spirit. And spirit cannot be broken."

Jonah managed to tear his eyes away from the thing at those words. "Um, Jonathan? I really hate to disagree with you, but spirits can get very, very bro—"

"Not true, Jonah," said Jonathan. "Eternal means eternal. Life and spirit are eternal, because life never ends. What cannot end also cannot be broken. Scarred, abused, beaten down, yes, but never truly broken."

"Ever the sage."

Gamaliel shuffled in, accompanied by G.J. The others filed in as well. Jonah saw Aloisa and Spader look around with the same wonder he'd had, but he also caught Iuris', G.J.'s. and Cisor's scans as well. With all the differing personalities, he was reminded of the staff meetings at his old job.

"Welcome, all of you," said Jonathan. "I am thankful that everyone has returned largely unscathed. Make yourselves comfortable."

As usual at the estate, the number of people had no effect on the room's comfort at all, but Jonah saw that the mentalities did not change despite the private setting. G.J. took his usual place near his father, and Iuris and Cisor sat close to them. Resignedly, Gabriel remained on his feet. Rheadne seated herself without a care in the world, but not before she looked Jonah over (he didn't know if it was an injury assessment or an appraisal). Terrence frowned her way; he still hadn't gotten over being abandoned. Malcolm stepped back so as to offer a chair to Liz in a gentlemanly manner. Liz took it, and yanked Reena down next to her to spite Spader, who'd tried to sit next to her. Aloisa seated herself, and Jonah let Terrence have the last seat on account of his recently set foot.

"Right then." Jonathan seated himself in the chair behind the desk. Jonah had to admit that it was an impressive display, and far more imposing than Gamaliel's side profile, complete with his action-figure fool of a son. "First and foremost, how is your foot, Terrence?"

"Healing, sir," answered Terrence. "It was a full break, but Ben-Israel set it, and Akshara gave me a tonic to bolster white blood cells or something like that. She said the break would be healed in a day or so."

"Very good," said Jonathan, pleased. "Elizabeth, it is my understanding that you had to do some fleeing this evening. You did not experience any lingering effects from your concussion, did you?"

Discomfort crossed Rheadne's face, but Liz's smile had its usual radiance.

"None at all, sir," she said. "And I had no cause to feel threatened, thanks to Malcolm."

"Gabriel did well, too," added Malcolm hastily, but Gabriel only half-acknowledged the praise. Jonah figured that he didn't get complimented often.

"Jonah—" began Jonathan, but Gamaliel interrupted him.

"If I may, I'd like three of my guys to designate themselves, just so everyone knows everyone."

Jonathan blinked very slowly. "Very well. Go on."

Gamaliel nodded to them, and they went into their asinine routines.

"Gamaliel Kaine, Jr., thirty-five years old, red aura."

"Iuris Mason, thirty years old, white aura."

"Knoaxx Cisor, thirty-three years old, silver aura."

Reena sighed, Terrence gagged, and Liz looked as though she found this unorthodox roll call tiresome. But Jonah barely registered any of that, not even Cisor's weird first name. There were two things that stuck out to him: G.J.'s stupid "designation" was irrelevant, as Jonathan had already introduced him the first night they met him. Why did he have to do it again?

Second thing, Gamaliel skipped over Gabriel, yet again. Sure, Jonah had heard his designation thing, but his father didn't mandate that he do it, like he had for G.J. and the others. He treated the man worse than Jessica treated Ant.

"Excellent, Gamaliel," said Jonathan. "Jonah. I would like very much to hear your exploits with Reena and Aloisa first."

Jonah rattled off what had happened at the farmhouse on Route 6, while Reena added things from time to time. Aloisa was silent at first, probably still ashamed, but Reena tapped her arm.

"Aloisa, you were just as brave as the rest of us," she said sternly. "You have no right to be ashamed."

"Like hell she doesn't," said Gamaliel, who rose and almost displaced his mouthful of snuff in his fury. "What is the creed, Aloisa?"

Aloisa hung her head. "If you don't succeed, you fail," she muttered.

"But she didn't fail," insisted Jonah. He had been taught to have more respect than he exhibited now, but Gamaliel pissed him off so easily. "Aloisa unleashed a trap on about a half-dozen sazers. Wiped them out. Unorthodox, sure, but if she hadn't done it, they would have buffeted on Terrence."

"Hold up," said Spader as he cast a scathing eye on Aloisa, "didn't her trap also result in taking a chunk of flesh out of your arm, Jonah?"

Scowling because Spader wasn't helping anything, Jonah rolled up his sleeve and showed Spader his stitched, bandaged arm. Liz's skills were effective. The injury was still sore, but it looked even better than when it first got dressed. "It's getting better, Royal," he snapped. "Let it go."

Spader frowned. Jonah had never called him by his first name.

"Let me ask *you* something, Spader," said Liz suddenly. "What were you attempting to do with your dig on Aloisa? She freely admitted to being attacked, but then she redeemed herself! What did you do when you, G.J., and Iuris discovered that you walked into a trap, huh? Did you wow the sazers with your matchless ability to draw an ace of clubs?"

Spader looked incensed, but Jonathan raised a hand.

"Please people, let's keep this civil. Terrence, you were rescued by Jonah, Aloisa, and Reena, is that right?"

"Yes, sir," said Terrence. "I'd have been picked clean by those cannibal sazers."

"Would you agree that Miss Oxendine leveled the playing field with her trap?"

Terrence fought with himself, because he hadn't much cared for Aloisa's tactic. "I would have to say yes, Jonathan," he murmured at last. "Aloisa saved our asses back there."

Aloisa looked so grateful that she seemed to forget Gamaliel's earlier shaming.

"Tell me this, Cisor and Rheadne," said Jonathan, "why did Jonah, Aloisa, and Reena have to be Terrence's saviors? What occupied the two of you?"

Cisor didn't seem to keen on answering Jonathan's question, but as he was now on the hot seat, he didn't have much choice. "We had been attacked by nearly eight sazers. They were a threat, but they weren't as strong as some I've seen—"

"Lucky for you," murmured Jonah, who remembered the vile beasts he, Reena, and Aloisa fought.

Cisor threw him a look, and then continued. "We fought off a few, but some broke away and fled. I chased after them to stop them, because I feared they'd get backup."

"And Rheadne freakin' abandoned me," snapped Terrence.

Rheadne's eyes flashed. "Look, Terry—"

"My name is *Terrence*."

"Whatever! But I told you that we needed help! Cisor went after the sazers who ran! I tried hard to get that thing off of your foot, you know I did. I had to go for help."

Jonathan looked at Rheadne. "You came back here for help, Rheadne?"

"Yeah, I did," said Rheadne.

"I didn't see you."

Rheadne swallowed. "That's because I went to Mr. Kaine."

Gamaliel looked at Rheadne coldly, but Jonathan threw up a hand again.

"Keep talking, girl," he commanded.

Jonah frowned at the edge in Jonathan's voice. It was new. Rheadne's eyes widened slightly at it as well, but continued.

"He said to cut my losses," she muttered. "I wasn't particularly comfortable with that, so I was about to find some of your estate people. But before I could, Reena and Aloisa were back, telling us that they'd gotten Terrence out."

Iuris and G.J. looked about ready to rip Rheadne's head off. Jonathan had a similar expression, but his gaze was on Gamaliel. Reena took the time to speak.

"Jonathan, I think this entire thing was an elaborate trap," she said. "I know that that seems obvious at this point, but I don't mean trap as in easy meat. I mean gift-wrapped and expertly lured."

Jonathan's eyes slowly slid Reena's way. "What makes you say that, Reena?"

"Two things," said Reena. "One of which I haven't yet revealed. I was attacked by a Deadfallen disciple last night."

"What?" This news was met with great alarm from all of Reena's friends, save Jonah and Terrence, who already knew. Jonathan momentarily forgot his anger at Gamaliel. "Are you alright?"

"Yes, sir," said Reena hastily, "no worries. I broke the guy's jaw."

She didn't mention Akshara fixing her wrist. She didn't want to get her in trouble.

"How did you know that he was Deadfallen?" demanded Cisor.

"He had the bruising at his pulse, did he not?" asked Jonathan, who cut wintry eyes at Cisor.

Jonah saw confusion on his friend's faces; even Gabriel, Rheadne, and Aloisa were puzzled. Jonah looked at Terrence and mouthed, "*Tell you later.*"

"Yes, sir," said Reena. "And he approached me because he saw the skin discoloration on my neck from training with that—with Penelope.

He said the phrase and I couldn't repeat it, so he attacked me. I fought him off."

"I'm missing something," said Spader.

"Per usual," murmured Liz.

Spader ignored that. "But what phrase are you talking about?"

"There is a phrase that the Deadfallen use to identify each other," said Reena. "One disciple says it to another, and they say it back. Creyton made it so they are the only ones who can say it. No one else can—"

"*Per mortem, vitam,*" said Jonathan.

Reena looked at him in pure shock. Gabriel looked frightened. Jonathan's expression didn't change.

"I can assure you that I have no dealings with the Deadfallen," he said calmly.

"Then how can you say it?" asked Gabriel.

"The dark ethereality that Creyton placed on the words only applies to physically livings beings," Jonathan explained. "I'm in Spirit, so it's fair game for me."

Jonah saw the suspicion melt from Gabriel's face. "Right. Of course. Sorry, sir."

Terrence tapped Jonah's arm. "*Wouldn't Gamaliel and 2.0 have filled him in already?*" he asked in an undertone.

"*Nope,*" Jonah mouthed back. "*They treat him like a piece of shit.*"

"Jonathan," said Reena, once she recovered from hearing the phrase again, "what does that phrase mean?"

"We are blessed to have a Latin expert in this room," announced Jonathan. He raised his eyes to Malcolm. "You won't be able to say the phrase itself, but I'll bet that you'll have no problem revealing its meaning. If you please."

Malcolm nodded, and rattled off the meaning as if he'd wanted to the entire time they'd been in the study. "Through death, life."

There was a brief silence after those ominous words. Jonah knew that Creyton had always believed that not being physically alive was death. It wasn't that much of a stretch to assume that he'd taught his disciples the same. But to hear that Latin phrase make it sound so eloquent, so poetic…that just wasn't right.

"But we've strayed from the point," said Jonathan. "Reena, you kept this information of your attack from me because you hoped the Dead-fallen disciple would lead you to the nest of them we seek, correct?"

"Yes sir," nodded Reena. "I thought that it might have even led to Wyndam O'Shea, since tonight was a full moon and all. I am ashamed to say that I outsmarted myself."

"That's not true, at all," said Aloisa of all people. "You just said that I had no right to be ashamed after the way I blundered. If that's the case, then you certainly can't tear yourself down, friend."

Aloisa elevated many notches in Jonah's eyes. That was a very kind thing to say.

"Friends?" Clearly, G.J. didn't share Aloisa's sentiment. "Why don't you just jump over and join them, Oxendine? Then you can be one step above Ungifted, too!"

"Silence, Gamaliel," said Jonathan sharply. "And if you use that slur in my presence again, I swear on all things ethereal that I will rescind your haven, and cast you off of my lands." He turned back to Reena. "There was a second thing that you wanted to share, Reena?"

"Yes, there was," said Reena. "Tonight, before I knocked the sazer out of the farmhouse window, she screamed that somebody made her and the other sazers a promise of some kind."

"Hang on," said Malcolm suddenly, "what was that, Reena? Did you say something about a promise?"

Reena nodded. Jonah took the opportunity to assist.

"I heard it too, Malcolm," he said. "The sazer lady saw us coming to help Aloisa, and said everything was wrong or something, and that someone made her a promise."

Malcolm lowered his head, features screwed up in thought. "One of the sazers we saw said something similar," he revealed. "What was it, Lizzie? Your brain is nearer to photographic memory than mine."

Liz's eyes widened. "That's right! It was the scraggly sazer boy! He said something about a promise being broken!"

"I'm sorry," said Spader, who seemed determined to contribute, "but that sounds like *they* were betrayed, not us."

"A two-way betrayal?" asked Gabriel.

"Spader may be on to something," said Terrence. "I mean, it ain't the first time two parties got screwed by someone else."

"But that doesn't make sense!" Gabriel was adamant about his point.

"Shut up, Gabe," said G.J. coldly. "You're looking for spirits that aren't there. They are obviously repeating the ravings of a lunatic—"

"No," said Reena, just as coldly as G.J. "*Wyndam O'Shea* is the lunatic, and he was nowhere to be found tonight. These were cannibalistic, Red-Raged sazers. In a word, crazy. When crazy people say the same thing in two different places, it makes you think. What else have you got, Gabriel?"

"I mean, a two-way betrayal is an awfully complex thing to put in place if the goal was just to guarantee fresh meat to sazers," said Gabriel. "What is the end goal of that? Who benefits? Who would have no love for two groups of Eleventh Percenters, but also promise the sazers meals that they wouldn't get?"

Jonah stiffened. Gabriel had asked a great question. He glanced at Terrence and Reena. They all knew who would benefit from an arrangement like that.

Inimicus.

Jonah prepared to divulge, but then Gamaliel spat in his cup and sighed.

"Gabriel, that is the stupidest thing I have ever heard," he said. "My God in Heaven, I have always told you that you talk when you ought to listen. I wonder if *you* should have been abandoned in this Terrence boy's stead—"

"Don't say that!" said Jonathan, aghast. "That's your son!"

"You don't have to remind me!" Gamaliel fired back. "There is no need to be cruel!"

"ABANDONING YOUR FAMILY IS NOT THE WAY TO ACHIEVE YOUR ENDS! CUTTING YOUR LOSSES LEADS TO FAILURE AND RUIN, KAINE, AS YOU VERY WELL KNOW—"

Jonathan stopped himself. There was complete silence.

Jonah stared, eyes wide. That outburst had come from Jonathan. The Protector Guide, their mentor, the one who always maintained his composure and never raised his voice because he never needed to.

But he just did.

It hadn't been a normal shout, either. If it had been a normal outburst, Jonah would have been shocked, but he'd have gotten over it. But it wasn't normal. Jonathan's voice had taken on some kind of otherworldly bass; it had achieved some ethereal range that the room couldn't have achieved if they had tried it at the same time. It hadn't just washed over them, it cascaded. Books had flown off of the shelves, the Masonic bible had been blown open, and the Vitasphera had rolled from its place of honor.

But the people in front of Jonathan were the most affected. Jonah learned that G.J., Iuris, and Cisor's faces could achieve a facial expression other than scorn. Rheadne looked as if a teacher had just rebuked the class. Malcolm and Gabriel had actually backed themselves flush against the wall. Terrence had toppled from his chair, Liz looked as if she'd been backhanded, and Reena tightly gripped her seat, and Spader and Aloisa had actually clamped hands.

But old man Gamaliel was terrified. His bearded, wrinkled face was frozen in silent horror, and his eyes were wider than they'd probably been in years.

"Forgive me," he said in his normal voice, and with a wave of his hand, all of his materials went back to their places. "I shouldn't have done that. I meant what I said, but as a Protector Guide and Spirit with responsibility to this estate, I freely admit that it was wrong to lose my composure." He pointed a finger at Gabriel, though his eyes were on Gamaliel. "Apologize to your son," he ordered. "Now."

Gamaliel's face unfroze, and he closed his mouth with a pronounced swallow. Jonathan kept his glare on him, and didn't lower his hand.

"Gabriel, I apologize," said Gamaliel.

"You do?" said G.J.

"You do?" Gabriel demanded.

Gamaliel didn't look happy about it, but he also looked as though he had no desire to test Jonathan again. "I do."

Jonathan's eyes narrowed. "Good. This meeting is adjourned. I have much to think about."

* * *

"What the hell happened in there?" demanded Jonah.

They wanted to go to Reena's art studio, but no one wanted to subject Terrence's mending ankle to stairs too much, so they went back to the infirmary. Jonah was certain that everyone else that had been in that study was off somewhere discussing what had happened. He, Terrence, and Reena were no different.

"I have no idea," said Terrence, "but in my personal opinion, Jonathan has officially reached badass status."

Reena was still recovering from the tirade, which was saying something, because she had been a bystander and it hadn't actually happened to her. "I have known Jonathan for going on fourteen years, and I have never seen him do that. To anyone."

"Not even Trip?" asked Jonah.

Reena looked Jonah in the eye. "Not even Trip, Jonah."

Jonah couldn't believe it. It just seemed so out of character. "The way that Gamaliel just went with it…did what Jonathan asked him and apologized to Gabriel…it was so creepy that I couldn't even properly appreciate the emasculation of it."

"It's good news for Gabriel, said Reena, "that's probably the first time anyone's ever stood up for him in his entire life."

Terrence shook his head. "The way that he's treated by his so-called friends…and then his dad and brother just jump right in, and go with it! It's just foul."

"I overheard G.J. tearing him down the night they got here," said Jonah, who didn't feel the need to mention that he'd been looking for Rheadne at the time, seeing as how he and Terrence had just squashed things that very evening. "And it was all because Gabriel said that they ought to treat Jonathan with more respect."

"Wonder how they feel about that now," uttered Terrence.

"I had a conversation with him later on," Jonah went on, "and he seemed alright. But there is something off about him."

He told them about his conversation with Liz from earlier. Terrence shrugged.

"I can't say that I'm interested in him so much as what Jonathan knows about old man Kaine," he said.

"What are you talking about?" said Jonah.

"Come on, Jonah," said Terrence. "That thing we just saw? Not even a bully can pull that off. We have all come to the conclusion that something has gone down between them. You think that Jonathan has dirt on him?"

Jonah hadn't given that any thought, but Reena waved a hand.

"If Jonathan actually had dirt on Kaine, he'd never use it," she said in a matter of fact tone.

"We also thought that he'd never use anything other than an inside voice," Jonah reminded her.

"Jonathan is not that petty," insisted Reena. "Kaine rattled his cage, but he would never dangle a dagger over anyone's head. He hasn't ever acted like that."

"Just because he has never done it in your presence doesn't mean that he isn't capable, Reena," said Terrence. "But—but I don't think Jonathan would do that. He kept Trip's secret, after all."

The words *Trip* and *secret* triggered a memory in Jonah's head. "Before we went to our different spots, I saw something odd," he said to them. "Trip and Jonathan made eye contact right before we went through the *Astralimes*. They gave each other a nod. I wondered what that was about. I told you that Jonathan wanted Trip to watch Sanctum. I wondered if it had something to do with it."

"Could be," said Reena. "And I truly don't mean to disregard you or write you off right now, Jonah, because we might have to revisit that whole Trip and Jonathan thing soon, but I'm more concerned about something else. Before Gamaliel became the target of Jonathan's rage, I got the feeling that you were going to bring up Inimicus in there."

"I was," admitted Jonah. "It seemed an opportune time. It was the answer to Gabriel's question."

Reena fingered her dampener. "I'm glad that you got interrupted, Jonah."

"Huh?" said Jonah.

"You heard," said Reena. "I don't like the thought of discussing Inimicus around Sanctum Arcist."

Jonah's eyes widened, but Terrence was the one that posed the question.

"You think that Inimicus might be among them?"

"Doubt that," said Reena, "but I think that Inimicus, whoever that is, might have an informant."

Jonah stared at her. Wrapping his mind around her last words required brainpower he wasn't sure he had. "You think Inimicus has a spy? The spy has a spy?"

"It makes sense, Jonah," said Reena. "How did you say that Malcolm described Inimicus? The embedded enemy? The one you don't know you don't know? Wasn't that it? That requires an intricate level of secrecy. A person couldn't very well function from the shadows while showing their face, could they?"

Jonah said nothing. Reena made her point, as only Reena could.

"I'll go with it," said Terrence. "Do you have any idea who it could be? This informant?"

"Yes," said Reena. "We've just made mention of him. Gabriel."

"What!" said Jonah. "How long have you thought this?"

"Since I've figured out how badly his father and brother treat him," replied Reena. "I've watched him. Read his essence. He is full of anger—"

"Can you blame him?"

"No, I can't," said Reena. "I can't help but think of my own parents when I think of him. Which is why I started suspecting him."

What the hell, thought Jonah. "Douglas told me that Gabriel wanders off from the Sanctum camp most nights," he revealed. "I even ran into him one night when I was done with class. He said that he just needed to get away. I didn't think much of it, because most of his comrades are such idiots, but now…Reena, are you sure?"

"Not a hundred percent," admitted Reena. "I'd never be that bold. But like I said, I've watched him. He's been so quiet and downtrodden, and suddenly he's vocal? Then you said that Liz said that he was assessing her and Malcolm? And in Jonathan's study, he posed the question of who would benefit the most from a two-way betrayal. It's all very suspicious."

Jonah couldn't argue with her. But a part of him still wanted to believe in Gabriel. The way he got bullied by his own family engendered sympathy. It did. He had every right to be angry. Maybe even vengeful. But if his plan for retaliation involved working with whomever Inimicus was…

"You suspect him because he kinda did a one-eighty," said Terrence.

"I don't believe in one-eighties," said Reena. "Evil people who suddenly do good things were always capable of doing good. Good people who suddenly do evil things were always capable of doing evil. It all depends on what aspect of themselves they choose to explore."

Before Jonah could wrap himself around that one, his phone began to vibrate. He grabbed it from his pocket and looked at the unfamiliar number. Who the hell was this?

"Hello?"

"Rowe," said a tearful, female voice. "Is this you? Have I gotten it right?"

"Yeah," said Jonah. "Who is this?"

"Are you around anyone?" the woman asked.

What kind of question was that? "Um, what if I am?" asked Jonah.

"Get away from them," commanded the woman through the tears. "I won't talk with anyone around you."

Jonah's eyes widened. He recognized the person now. He only knew one woman who could be one quarter bossy, three quarters bitchy. But she would never call him. Not ever…

He held up one finger to Terrence and Reena, and stepped out of the infirmary.

"Jessica?" he hissed. "How the hell did you get my number?"

"Are you around—?"

"I'm alone, okay? I'm alone. Now answer my question!"

After seconds of silence, Jessica answered. "I got your number from the directory at the office. It hasn't been updated."

"Are you serious right now?" asked Jonah in disbelief. "I haven't been with that damned company for almost two—"

"Look, Rowe." Jonah heard Jessica attempt to raise her "bitch" back up to its usual level, but she failed. "I hate you, and you hate me. But Tony has been driving me insane about getting your help. I've fought him about it. But—but I might need it now."

Jonah's eyes narrowed. "You don't listen to anything Ant says," he said shrewdly, "and you actually threatened my physical life—"

"Physical life?" said Jessica, puzzled.

"Um, my life," amended Jonah. "My life. The point is, why are you listening to Ant all of a sudden? Why are you changing your tune?"

Jonah distinctly heard Jessica's breath catch. "Because I'm scared, Rowe. I'm goddamned *scared.* This guy that's been following me has figured out where I live. He's been putting notes in my mailbox that say how easy it is to get to me. I'm at Tony's now."

Jonah cringed. As much as he hated Jessica—and he did hate the bitch—the stalker had found her home.

No. Wyndam O'Shea, lunatic and Deadfallen disciple, had found Jessica's home.

God, if he sent some of those cannibal sazers after her—

"Are you serious, Rowe?" Jessica's voice was accusatory. "Did you really want to help me get out of this mess? Do you really know things about this guy?"

Jonah breathed through his nose. Why couldn't he be a belligerent bastard, like half of Sanctum Arcist? "Yeah, I do."

Five seconds. Fifteen seconds. A minute. Then—

"I'll give you a shot," said Jessica finally. "What choice do I have? Tony will be delighted. I will call you back. We can meet at a place we both know, because I don't want you at Tony's, and you damn well aren't coming to my house again."

She hung up.

Flabbergasted, Jonah lowered the phone and walked back into the infirmary, wondering if this was what it felt like to survive a concussive blast. Terrence and Reena were alarmed by the look on his face.

"Jonah? What is it?"

Jonah looked at them, and actually laughed incredulously. "Guess what? On top of everything else, hell has frozen over."

15

Fire, Fire, and Ice

As Jonah knew it would, the news of Jonathan's outburst flew not only amongst estate residents, but also throughout the campsite of Sanctum Arcist. Gossip was like that.

No one was surprised that the Elevenths in Sanctum Arcist were furious. For a reason Jonah couldn't understand, they kept up the conjoined trainings, and to no one's surprise, there were skirmishes. They got stamped out easily enough, but Jonah and Terrence noticed that when things got tense, Penelope was always a million miles away from Reena.

Alvin and Bobby had been in tears when Terrence told them about what Jonathan had done to Gamaliel, but Jonah couldn't fully appreciate the humor. If he'd heard it secondhand, he'd have laughed his ass off. But he had been there. And it hadn't been a pleasant experience.

Cutting your losses only leads to failure and ruin, Kaine, as you very well know.

Those were the words Jonathan shouted at the old man. Whatever Gamaliel had done to get on their mentor's bad side, must have been damn near unforgivable.

"I want to know what it is," said Magdalena after Liz had said she was glad that Kaine didn't have a coronary out of fright. "Call me nosy, I really don't care. But Jonathan has always told us that emotional control was paramount. Yet that old man makes him *loco.*"

"I don't think Jonathan is a hypocrite," said Vera. "Instead of asking why Jonathan neglected his own advice, we ought to wonder what Kaine did to *make* Jonathan neglect his own advice?"

"Does it even matter?" asked Bobby. "Kaine's been begging for it ever since he graced us with his presence. What better person to do it than the Master of the House?"

Even Douglas, who generally avoided gossip because he couldn't keep secrets worth a damn, was pleased to hear about what happened.

"This is Kaine, right here," he demonstrated by knocking over a chess piece. "As an added bonus, I should take him to my house and barricade him in a room with my grandmother. She can peg someone's inadequacies in a second."

Jonah, Terrence, Reena didn't really participate in these conversations, but some comments by (who else?) Trip prompted them into it one day.

"I'm in full support of Jonathan's actions," he was quick to point out. "So he punked that old bastard? That's beautiful. But Spader says that Jonathan threatened to rescind G.J.'s haven and cast him out. He should've done that! He should have banished all of those goddamned bastards, and been done with it!"

"It's not as simple as that, Trip," muttered Jonah against his better judgment. "They're not all like Kaine. It's not possible for all of them to be the same. If we can tolerate a few of them long enough to—"

"Why am I not surprised that you want this combined farce to continue, Rowe?" said Trip with a derisive laugh. "You usually need additional help just to luck out, anyway."

Jonah narrowed his eyes. "Maybe you could have schooled me on how to better handle myself, Trip, but Jonathan didn't put you in any of the groups."

"I had a gig, Rowe," snarled Trip. "You knew that."

Jonah remembered that eye contact and nod between Trip and Jonathan, but didn't bring it up. "Yeah, I did," he said. "But I wonder if your time had been better served elsewhere. How much did you make that club? Two dollars?"

The kitchen erupted into laughter, while Jonah turned his back on Trip, and left. As a writer, he knew that paying dues for one's art was necessary. But Trip had to be an asshole as usual, and unwittingly left an opening. Therefore, Jonah-1, Trip-0.

Jonah spent some time bringing Terrence up to speed on things that they had learned after they'd had their falling out. To their surprise, Terrence had been busy himself during that time.

"I conducted an investigation of my own during that time," he revealed. "After you mentioned remembering a fireplace in that Spectral Event, I took some sick days and started searching out abandoned mansions, starting with the Covington House."

"You were checking out abandoned mansions?" asked Reena. "You put yourself in danger like that?"

"Like I haven't done that before," murmured Terrence. "But yes. I wanted to find any clues that I could. Luckily, mansions in this area aren't too numerous. Problem was, I had no way of narrowing them down. They all had fireplaces."

"Was that why you were dirty that day Reena and I went into the city?" asked Jonah.

Terrence looked away for only a moment, but nodded. "Yeah. That was why."

Jonah nodded, not wanting to bring up what they'd squashed, either. "So, what did you find?"

Terrence frowned. "I found something very interesting when I searched my seventh mansion. Near that particular fireplace, I found shavings."

"Shavings?"

"Yep," said Terrence. "Ethereal steel shavings."

That got Jonah and Reena's interest. Terrence savored the attention for a second or two, and then continued.

"I collected some of them, and then took them to Dad," he explained. "I told him that I had—had come across them, and wondered what to make of them. He said he had a way to trace the aura color of the last person who handled the steel. He said their ethereality would be present, even in the shavings."

"How did Mr. Decessio trace the aura color of an Eleventh Percenter who wasn't holding the steel?" asked Jonah.

"Never mind that," said Reena. "How could he track it down using only shavings?"

"Dad only said that he used the tools of the trade, like he always does," shrugged Terrence. "Anyway, he came back to me and told me that the last person who handled whatever this metal was before it got filed to shavings…had an auburn aura."

Jonah took a deep breath. Reena looked at Terrence as though he were a gripping lecturer who'd yet to reach the salient point.

"After Dad told me that," continued Terrence, "I went back to all the other old mansions. It wasn't that tedious, because I knew what to look for. These shavings were near the fireplaces of each one. So now we know that Inimicus has been starting fires in each one of those fireplaces, and also that whoever it is has an auburn aura."

Jonah couldn't help but marvel at his friend. Terrence had done some sharp work!

"The auburn aura thing is interesting," said Reena. "And the transient fireplace visits make sense. Once Mr. Decessio contacted Jonathan, and then Jonathan got Spectral Law involved, Inimicus couldn't keep making fires in one place. They had to switch it up. You did some awesome things, Terrence!"

Terrence snorted, but he was pleased. A blind man could have seen it. "Like I said, I'm not an idiot. Plus, being around the two of you, I'm gonna learn some stuff."

"You were always capable, Terrence," said Jonah. "Kudos for finding this new stuff. Now, I'll finish explaining everything else to you."

Jonah meant to tell Terrence everything once they buried the hatchet, but after the meeting in the study, there had only been one prominent subject on the entire grounds. But now he had to explain everything once he received the phone call from Jessica. Terrence was shocked at O'Shea's looking into Jonah's past, and his audacity to stalk a Tenth Percenter.

"Why would he go after someone in your past, though?" he asked.

"No idea," said Jonah. "Maybe he thinks he can play with my head like the others ones did with Kaine down in Florida."

"But if he wanted to play with your head, why did he choose Jessica?" demanded Terrence. "You hate that bitch."

"He had no way of knowing that," sighed Jonah. "It's not like I want him to stalk one of my actual friends; hell, I don't want the man stalking anybody. But—but I wish with everything in me that it wasn't Jessica. And, speaking of playing with people's heads..." He told Terrence and Reena about Iuris' and Cisor's offer to Spader. Reena looked coldly surprised, but Terrence just nodded.

"Saw it coming, actually," he said.

"You did?" asked Jonah.

"Uh-huh," said Terrence. "Spader and his folks ain't really the tightest unit in the world, but I know for a fact that he was messed up by what happened to his father's friend. I'm not even sure that Spader's dad got over that, so he had to see that his whole life. Then here comes old man Kaine, who indulges in extremes for everything. His little foot soldiers offer Spader a far more violent and conniving approach than anything Jonathan would ever condone, and there you go."

"There is no way Spader could be that fickle!" said Reena. "Jonathan has been nothing but good to him, despite his questionable legal choices sometimes—"

"Reena," interrupted Terrence, "there is another reason, too. Liz."

Jonah hadn't even thought of that, but now that Terrence had mentioned it, it made perfect sense.

Apparently not to Reena, though.

"Liz?" she said. "You've got to be kidding. You can't think that his crush is that far gone."

"Spader is practically her unrequited love slave," said Terrence. "And we all know that those feelings will never be reciprocated. Liz is hopelessly devoted to Bobby and detests Spader because of his gambling, thievery, and slob tendencies."

"Spader is a lot of things, but stupid ain't one of them," added Jonah. "He knows how Liz views him; you saw how she treated him in the study. Granted, the treatment was valid, but still. Those are some powerful motivators for a seventeen year-old, hormone-crazed rebel to pick up his bag and leave.".

Reena had no words. Jonah and Terrence both made good points. She sighed. "Terrence, you've said it before, and I'm saying it again," she muttered, "never a dull moment, is there?"

Reena couldn't have been more right. The events of a Thursday three weeks after that conversation were testament to her words.

* * *

Jonah looked forward to the couple of days' free time he'd get for the Thanksgiving Holiday. He returned from class that night, excited about a Netflix binge he'd planned. Terrence would be back later, as he had to be one of the janitors on hand for the high school autumn dance. Reena was out with Kendall.

Jonah saw Gabriel again when drove into the gate. The man stood with his eyes closed, mumbling to himself. It was weird, but Gabriel was a weird guy.

He parked his car and reached for his bag, but unfortunately was too zealous with the reach and knocked some books to the floor. Swearing, he reached to pick them up.

Then something that sounded like a rapid hail of bullets jerked him upward so fast that he slammed his head on the car roof. Barely registering the sting in his head, he freed himself from the car and looked around wildly.

"Jonah!" boomed Gabriel's voice from nearby. "I'm glad you're here! Come with me!"

Jonah was apprehensive (Reena's words against Gabriel rattled around in his head), but something told him that this was legit. He caught up with Gabriel.

"What did you do?" he demanded.

"Nothing!" Gabriel shot back. "I was whittling away time and I saw sparks in the woods!"

Gabriel pointed ahead of them, and sure enough, there were orange-ish sparks popping intermittently through the darkness.

Jonah vaguely remembered a story where Jonathan killed some Haunts outside in a wave of what was described as "golden fireworks." But these sparks were orange. And he certainly didn't want to see Haunts tonight. He wasn't endowed and didn't feel up to conjuring a Mind Cage.

They were about ten feet away from the source of the lights when they faded, along with the sounds. Then, as suddenly as Jonah's and Gabriel's ears were given a reprieve, their noses were attacked by horrible odor.

"Shit!" struggled Jonah, blocking his nose. "What is that?"

"Shit," said Gabriel as well, but his was much lower and fearful. "Jonah...you smell burning flesh. It's Michael Pruitt."

Jonah was about to ask who that was, but upon further inspection, he no longer felt the need to care.

A black man who looked to be about his own age lay on his back, sprawled and unconscious. On one hand, Jonah was thankful that the guy was still breathing. On the other hand, when he looked at the lower half of the guy's body, he saw that, breathing or not, his nightmare had just begun.

There were burns all across Michael's thighs, lower torso, and legs. Some looked inconsequential, some looked more serious, and others looked as though they'd been created by hellfire.

"I—I don't know how to help him," said Gabriel, who seemed to be fighting nausea. "Dear God..."

"Shut up, Gabriel," commanded Jonah. He knew what to do, and the first thing was to admit the fact that he didn't have a clue, either. "I'm going to go into Spectral Sight."

He closed his eyes to take the deep breath and will the curtain open when he overheard Gabriel still speaking to himself.

"Dear God…Aloisa…"

The name popped Jonah's eyes open. "Aloisa? What's she got to do with anything?"

Gabriel's eyes didn't leave Michael's form. "This is her fiancée, Jonah," he murmured.

Jonah's body went cold. Then he closed his eyes, and activated the Sight with more effort. Stage was there, curtain was lifted.

When he opened his eyes, he saw one spiritess. One. She'd do. Jonah would take anything he could get.

"Spiritess, he said, "this man here has been grievously injured, and the two of us are unaware of how to help him. But I know some people who can. Hopefully, at least. Please go and alert a young woman named Liz Manville—"

"And please get a girl from the campsite behind the estate named Aloisa Oxendine," added Gabriel in a tense voice.

"And Liz might need a lot of help," said Jonah. "Please also find Ben-Israel Larver, Akshara Bhandari, and Kendra Eller. And please, please find Jonathan."

The spiritess nodded and vanished.

"What do you think happened?" demanded Jonah.

"I don't know," answered Gabriel. "I was up there near the gate, and I saw your car right before I heard the noise."

"It was frightening," said Jonah, "sounded like gunfire. Or maybe…"

Jonah's voice trailed off when he saw a charred remnant of a firework near Michael's damaged left leg. He picked it up with a frown, and glanced at Michael's pocket. There was evidence of others.

"Aw, hell," he said.

"What is it?" asked Gabriel.

"The guy had a bunch of fireworks in his pocket," said Jonah in a hollow voice. "Somehow, they got lit. There was no way he'd been dumb enough to have matches near his pocket—"

"Could it have happened because of a cigarette?" asked Gabriel.

"Maybe," said Jonah. "Why do you ask?"

"Because there are a few over here," said Gabriel slowly. "'Bout five, actually."

Jonah moved nearer to Gabriel. There were cigarette butts near their feet. Four were sufficiently extinguished, but one was still smoldering...

Jonah took a deep breath and stamped the butt. Anger wouldn't help anything. But it didn't take away from the face that he still was angry. Damn it, Trip...

"Jonah?" said Liz from behind them. "Gabriel? That spiritess, Florence, told me that you needed me—"

Her eyes fell on Michael, and the blood drained from her face.

"*What happened to him?*"

"It was a terrible accident, Liz," said Jonah. "He had firecrackers in his pocket and—"

A dreadful scream interrupted Jonah again.

If Gabriel hadn't stopped her, Aloisa would have flung herself onto Michael, which would have only worsened things. She was sobbing and speaking incoherently while Gabriel tried to calm her.

"Aloisa, he's still physically alive, calm down—you're no help to him like this—"

"Jonah." It was Jonathan. "What happened to this boy?"

"Jonathan," said Jonah as Liz ran green-tipped fingers across Michael, "this was a freak thing that was caused by stupidity and carelessness—"

"Jonah," said Jonathan, "maintain your composure, and tell me what happened."

Jonah took a moment to take in what Jonathan just said. Pot calling the kettle black much? "Like I said, it was a freak accident. Gabriel and I found him. He had a collection of firecrackers in his pocket. He must have sat or knelt or something near that cigarette there."

He pointed. Jonathan looked at the butts, and then back to Michael. Jonah could see him putting two and two together. For several seconds, the only sounds were Aloisa's sobs.

"Titus," said the Guide, and Jonah saw the anger in his eyes. He prayed that if another outburst came, it would be aimed at Trip.

"Titus did this?" said a voice that signaled that the evening was about to get a whole hell of a lot worse. "Titus Rivers did this to Michael?"

Gamaliel and G.J. had joined the party. Jonah figured that it was too much to ask for them to stay at the campsite when Aloisa left it. But at least it was just Daddy and Son as opposed to the whole Douche Pack.

"Indirectly, Gamaliel," said Jonathan quietly. Jonah still saw anger there, but he trusted Jonathan not to blow up again, since he regretted it so much last time. "Trip's vice indirectly caused this."

Gamaliel made a sour face. "Then you know what you need to do."

"You're right, Gamaliel," agreed Jonathan, "I need to ensure this boy's well-being."

Jonathan turned to Liz, presumably to ask her what she'd gleaned, but Gamaliel bristled.

"Your assistance is neither desired nor required," he said shortly. "It is necessary for us to remain here for the foreseeable future, but I can summon two of our own Green Auras from our home to retrieve Michael—"

"YOU WON'T!" cried Liz unexpectedly. She actually abandoned Michael entirely and got in Gamaliel's face. "You can't use the *Astralimes* to transport him! It will only make things worse!"

G.J. opened his mouth angrily, but then Aloisa cut across him without realizing it.

"What do you mean, Elizabeth?" she asked.

Liz looked at her. "Aloisa...Michael has burns across the board; there are even signs of eschar. I just did an assessment of his internal systems; his heart rate is a mess, and there is also peripheral vascular resistance. We can't risk the *Astralimes* because the change in air pressure might expedite the releasing of catecholamines and increase the risk of hypovolemia. I think that his best bet is keeping him here and entrusting him to us."

Jonah understood so little of what Liz had just said that he felt idiotic. He could tell that Gamaliel and G.J. wanted to find loopholes in it, but to his delight, they couldn't do it. Nella had shut them down the first night, and now Liz had, too. Gabriel looked at Liz with something like fear. Jonathan regarded her with such a fierce pride that a bystander may have thought he was a proud father.

But Aloisa only had eyes for Liz. It was as if the conversation was between the two of them the whole time anyway.

"Are you good at this?" she whispered.

Liz looked her into the eye. "I'm one of the best, so they tell me."

"Then fix him," said Aloisa. "Please."

Liz took a deep breath. "I will do my level best."

Jonathan smiled. "I trust your skills wholeheartedly, Elizabeth," he said. "Tell me what you'll need."

"Excuse me," snapped Gamaliel, "I have not given the green light to any of this—"

"You have, actually," said Jonathan calmly.

"Jonathan," growled Gamaliel, "you may have disarmed me once, and I may not think as sharply as I used to, but I would be aware if—"

"You green-lit things such as these when I granted you haven," said Jonathan. "Since you have haven, you are blessed with quartering, lodging, and generous protection, but that agreement only remains valid as long as you are compliant with the statutes of the dwelling place where you have haven. Moreover, as the person who granted said haven, I have responsibility to assist you in providing ideas for successful interactions and medical assistance, should the need arise. As a decorated former Networker, I know that you are cognizant of the fine print."

Gamaliel was utterly speechless. G.J. was angry, but that was likely due to the fact that he couldn't argue with guidelines.

Jonathan abandoned the need for dick measuring and returned to Liz. "What do you need, Elizabeth?"

"Help," said Liz instantly. "Lots of it. Please get Ben-Israel, Noah, Akshara, Barry, and Nella. I'll need Jonah, too—"

"You have been endowed, Jonah," said Jonathan, and Jonah welcomed the surge of power in his body.

"Thank you so much, sir," said Liz. "The only thing I know that might work for Michael requires an amplifier's help—"

"Rheadne is one," said Jonah before anyone could say anything else. "She can help us."

Gabriel and Liz looked at him questionably, but Liz nodded.

"Awesome," she said. "I'll also need Vera."

Jonah's eyes narrowed. He didn't know if Liz had deliberately timed that to be after he mentioned Rheadne or what.

But Liz was back to Michael and not focused on him at the moment.

"Gamaliel, G.J.," said Jonathan, "your presence is no longer required here. Will you require Gabriel's aid, Elizabeth?"

"No, sir," said Liz without lifting her head.

Jonah winced. Liz didn't even know it, but she had just subjected the poor man to the rage and frustration of his father and older brother. Iuris and Cisor too, once they were informed of it all. If Reena was right, and Gabriel was an informant for Inimicus, he didn't need to be handed fuel this way.

"Very well," said Jonathan. "I will go and deal with Titus. I bid you all good luck."

He vanished. A seething G.J. helped his father (who wasn't faring much better) back to the campsite. Gabriel, who probably knew what awaited him, walked in the other direction. Jonah, Liz, Aloisa, and Michael's unconscious form were alone now.

"Is there a reason why he hasn't awakened yet?" Jonah asked Liz.

Aloisa's breath caught in fear, but Liz placed a hand on her shoulder.

"He is an ethereal-induced sleep," she answered. "I don't like doing that because it doesn't seem fair, but he'd be in hellish agony if I hadn't done it. Now Jonah, I estimate that Noah and Barry will be here with a stretcher in about—"

"Now," announced Noah. He and Barry, a bald, stodgy-looking guy, had just appeared from nowhere, stretcher in tow.

"Excellent," said Liz. "Now Jonah, please help them get him on the stretcher. And please, please be as careful as you possibly can."

As if Liz needed to tell Jonah that. He and the Green Auras slowly and deliberately worked Michael Pruitt onto the stretcher, and then he assisted then in lifting it up.

"So far, so good," said Liz, "now let's get him up the infirmary."

"I can't do this. I can't help you."

Nella had taken one look at the burns on the lower half of Michael's body, dropped the medical utensils, and shrank back in horror.

Jonah placed his hands on her trembling shoulders. Liz had already briefed him about the fact that his balancing powers would be invaluable during this procedure. The others would be able to steel their wills, but Nella, at fifteen, had not had her healing talents weathered and tested in a sickroom as much as her sisters and the other Green Auras.

"Yes, you can, Nella," he told her. "Yes, you can. Just hold on a second."

Everyone that Liz had requested was present. Noah and Barry, after carefully depositing Michael onto an infirmary bed, joined Liz and Ben-Israel in proportioning salves, tonics, and balms. The first part of the procedure required traditional (i.e. Tenth) surgical methods, which were being performed by Akshara and Kendra. Vera, after gathering towels and water, sat near the door, where she administered her Time Item ethereality to the infirmary only. Vera rarely used her powers, because they could be quite dangerous, but she'd been given special permission from Jonathan to manipulate time in the infirmary so as to accelerate Michael's healing time.

Liz hadn't yet revealed what she had in store for Rheadne, so she assisted Vera with the towels and the water.

But Jonah had all of his focus on Nella.

"Nella, listen to me," he said. "You've said that you aren't as good as Liz and your oldest sister. Your mom told you that practice and passage of time would take care of that. This marks the beginning of those times. Times like these will make you stronger, tougher. They will also make you better, just like you want."

"Jonah, please don't make me—"

"I'm not, sweetie," said Jonah. "You're not being made to do anything. Your skills are ready-made for such a time as this. You're needed."

Something stirred in Nella's eyes. Her fear hadn't faded in the least, but something about Jonah's words gave her the strength to work in spite of it. She wiped her tears and nodded.

"Okay," she said. "Okay. I can do this. No time like the present, right?"

"Our procedure is done," announced Akshara. "You can now apply your balms and salves, Liz."

"Thanks, Akshara, Kendra," said Liz. "Ben-Israel, let's do this."

"Always up for a medical challenge, Lizzie," said Ben-Israel.

In Jonah's mind, Liz and Ben-Israel's work took longer than Akshara's and Kendra's. He couldn't imagine doing what they had to do to apply those things. He'd turn tail and run the first chance he got, and that was with all the disgusting things that he'd seen.

And he had just given Nella words of courage?

"How are we doing with the time, V?" Liz asked Vera without looking up from Michael."

"I'm great, Lizzie," said Vera, who looked as though she was trying to sift through complex thoughts. Hell, maybe manipulating time went along the same lines. "Just keep up your work."

After what felt like forever, Liz and Ben-Israel were done. Ben-Israel went to clean his hands, while Liz straightened up, and took a deep breath.

"Nella, you're up," she said. "I need you to come to the foot of the bed here and keep Michael's heart and central nervous system regulated."

Nella moved to her designated spot and slowly raised her hands, and her fingertips gleamed green.

"What does she need to do that for?" asked Jonah.

"For you," said Liz. "This is where you and Rheadne come in."

Jonah swallowed. Did Liz have to say it like that in front of Vera?

He thought he saw Vera's brow crease for a second, but she maintained her concentration on her own job. But then his thoughts returned to Michael, and all petty things melted away. "What do you need me to do, Liz?"

"All of the things we've done needed to happen," explained Liz. "Akshara and Kendra needed to perform traditional Tenth surgery to close the wounds and sort them out. Then Ben-Israel and I had to apply the balms and salves to replenish Michael's blood cells, re-grow skin, and reverse the effects of the eschar. But there is a catch."

"Catch?" That wasn't a word that Jonah wanted to hear in a situation like this.

"Yes, a catch," said Liz. "In order for all of our work to come together, Michael has to be awake. The physical healing takes place only in harmony with emotional healing."

"Wait," said Jonah, wide-eyed. "Wait. You're telling me that I have to help him process his trauma for all of this to come together?"

"Precisely," nodded Liz.

Suddenly, Jonah wished that he could have traded places with Kendra or Akshara when they did the traditional Tenth surgery. Liz could *not* be serious.

"Liz, I am not that powerful," he protested. "My way with words is not that awesome."

"That is a lie," said Liz. "You're probably the most powerful Eleventh here."

"But you said he'd be in hellish pain if he woke up!"

"True," said Liz, "that's why Nella is at the foot of the bed, keeping his vitals level. And you will have help." She finally focused on Rheadne. "Rheadne, I need you to amplify Jonah's balancing power. Michael has to stay calm while Jonah talks him down. In order for him to heal, he cannot thrash or panic."

Rheadne cracked her fingers. "Understood."

"Can you amplify in close proximity?" asked Liz. "Or does it require physical contact?"

"Physical contact is always preferable to proximity," said Rheadne. "Trust me on that."

Liz didn't look like she bought that. Jonah didn't even look at Vera. All he knew was that it had been physical contact the last time Rheadne had amplified him. And he didn't much mind her touching him.

It was all about helping Michael, right?

But Jonah couldn't help but feel just a bit awkward when Rheadne slowly and deliberately clamped his shoulders with her hands. With Vera in the room, it kind of felt like he was being forced to steal out of a wallet while someone took pictures. But he gave himself a mental shake as he focused on Michael.

"Okay, Jonah," said Liz quietly. "I'm going to bring him out now. We've done all that we can do. It's emotional now. And when he is in emotional harmony with his physical body, he will heal. Five—four—three..."

She mouthed the last two numbers and flashed Jonah a thumbs up. Michael opened his slightly bloodshot eyes.

"Wh-what...wh—where..."

Jonah took in a breath. "Hey, Michael. Michael Pruitt, right?"

Michael looked at Jonah, confused. He looked at the others and seemed to realize that this was a sickroom. That was when his eyes widened. "No," he said. "No no no—"

"Michael, calm down, man," said Jonah hastily. "All is well, and it will just get better, okay? We're helping you. Healing you. How are you feeling right now?"

Michael frowned, deep in thought. "I feel scared as hell. But I also feel this calm above it. It's almost like that's what I should be feeling, not the fear. It's good."

Rheadne tightened her grip on Jonah's shoulders, as if she wanted to denote that their ethereality worked well as one. He'd celebrate when this was done.

"What happened in the woods?" he asked Michael.

"I was just taking a walk," began Michael. "I had some stiffness from being in my tent too long. I saw Gabriel, so I went another way, just to leave him be. I tripped over a root or something in the woods, and my wallet fell out of my pocket. When I picked it up, a fuse from one of my firecrackers came loose from my other pocket. It got lit on a burning cigarette. I didn't know even know anything was wrong til the firecrackers started going off in my pocket. It burned, man. It burned everything, my pants, my back, my legs…it just burned everything."

At that moment, Jonah felt a resistance against his balancing. When Michael recalled his terror, the trauma began to fight the peace.

"Get back in control, Jonah," whispered Nella. "I'm doing everything I can to prevent a spike in his heart rate."

"Cool it, Mike," said Jonah, making his voice as serene as possible. "There is no need to go to a dark place in your mind. You're healing now. Just keep talking, alright?"

Jonah attempted to match the trauma's strength. Rheadne's amplifying helped him put a lid on it. He hoped it could last long enough for this to work.

Michael calmed somewhat in response to Jonah's voice, and continued. "I thought about Aloisa. I didn't think I'd survive that. The burns hurt so bad, man. And I wanted her to know that I was sorry for leaving her behind…all because I was dumb enough to have firecrackers in my pocket."

Jonah tightened his focus. He could do this. He had to do this. "You don't have to be scared about leaving Aloisa behind, Mike. Because you didn't. You're not in Spirit; you're right here, with us. The time for panic is over. Gabriel got me, and we found you and got you help. You are healing right now, but we've got to finish it. Let the fear go. This will work."

"But it *won't* work," said Michael, his voice a little tenser. "I'm disfigured. I'll never be right again. I've failed Aloisa by screwing myself up like this."

"Michael, have you not been listening to me?" said Jonah, prepared to lay it on thick. "You won't be disfigured. My Green Aura friends are *that* damn great at what they do. You might not even have scars. Let's finish it, man. Aloisa will need you strong and whole, especially for when your wedding day comes along."

The words *wedding day* took all of the tension away from Michael's face. The trauma decelerated. "I'm really going to be alright?" he asked. "I'll be better for Aloisa?"

This was it.

"Yes, Michael," said Jonah emphatically. "You will be healed. Aloisa is waiting for you right now, ready to see just how healed you are."

Finally, Michael looked calm. Jonah felt the trauma lose its hold.

"Yes!" whispered Liz, who almost sounded enraptured. "The burns are healing! It's taken hold!"

"Vitals are stable, too!" said Nella gleefully. "Vera, what have you done for us?"

Vera stood with a grin. "The prep, traditional, and ethereal procedures took about thirteen hours," she said. "But those hours passed in this room only. Once we get out of here, only about forty-five minutes will have passed. It's just a little past midnight."

"You are the best in the world!" grinned Liz.

Vera grinned, but it slipped slightly when her eyes reached Jonah, whose shoulders were still in Rheadne's grip.

"And...healed!" announced Liz. "Completely healed!"

Vera relinquished her power over the time and left the infirmary. Just like she said, all the clocks, which had showed that ten hours had passed, all wound back. Jonah shook his head. *Man, that was a scary power.* He was glad Vera didn't care to use it like that often.

Vera returned with Aloisa, who looked at Michael with equal parts fear and hope.

"He's alright?" she asked.

"Just like before!" beamed Liz. "It's so awesome that I had the people available that I did. A healing process like that would have taken weeks were it not for all of us, plus an amplifier! You're great at that, Rheadne!"

Rheadne finally took her hands off of Jonah's shoulder and gave Liz a look of gratitude. "All in a day's work, Lizzie."

Once all ethereality had dissipated, Michael blinked and looked around at everyone. "I—I had the most terrible dream," he said. "And how did I get here? I remember being in the woods."

Now that Michael was healed, the mood was considerably lighter, and everyone grinned.

"You can fill him in, Aloisa," said Jonah. "Take this seat."

Everyone left the couple on their own. Jonah detached himself from them all and went to the kitchen. He was tired, but Gatorade was calling his name. He got a glass of the fruit punch kind and took it down in a swallow.

He wondered if he'd stay awake long enough to tell Terrence and Reena that no matter how tedious (Terrence) or wonderful (Reena) their nights had been, they couldn't hold a candle to his own.

"Whatever," Jonah yawned to himself. "They'll be here later. I am going to bed."

"Seriously?" said a voice. "You're thinking about sleep right now?"

Jonah whirled around. Rheadne leaned against the back door, her arms crossed. So she hadn't made it back to Sanctum's camp yet.

"Of course I am," said Jonah. "Aren't you? That took a lot out of me."

"You made it look easy," said Rheadne. "You truly are incredible, Jonah."

"Incred—? Nah," said Jonah. "I'm not incredible. What happened was a team effort."

"Elizabeth did her part, just like the other Greens, and Vera's time control was a nice touch," conceded Rheadne. "But you were the one who brought about perfect equilibrium."

That was some high praise, but Jonah honestly felt that he was only a part of the whole. "Liz made it happen," he said. "And the perfect equilibrium part? God only knows if I could have done that alone. Joining my ethereality with yours was what made that perfect."

Rheadne left the door and stepped into Jonah's personal space. "Exactly."

And she kissed him. There was nothing gentle about it. It was intense from the start. Jonah was stunned for only a second, but he recovered nicely. It was easy to adapt to Rheadne's fervor, and easier than that to enjoy it. As his hands found the small of her back, Jonah realized one thing. Rheadne Cage kissed the same way she lived her life: Forthright and unapologetic.

They parted, and Rheadne ran a slow, deliberate finger across her bottom lip.

"You can still go to sleep if you feel the need to," she told Jonah.

Jonah's eyes narrowed. "Like I can go to sleep after that."

Rheadne grinned, and backed to the door. "Subterfuge is necessary, because of the tension of tonight," she said. "But still—don't keep me waiting."

She left. Jonah stood there, just for a moment.

His decision was made. It didn't even take a second's deliberation. If that kiss was a prelude to what was to come…then what the hell was he still doing in this kitchen?

He went to the refrigerator, got another cup of Gatorade, and then left out of the back door.

Even though subterfuge was a must, finding Rheadne's tent didn't take long at all. Jonah didn't think that it would, anyway. It had been a while since he had had sex, so patience wasn't a virtue at the moment. When he tapped the entrance, Rheadne invited him in. He entered, and stopped in his tracks.

Rheadne had been seated, and, were it not for some black, boy-cut shorts, she'd be completely nude. When Jonah was inside, she rose. Again, she stopped Jonah in his tracks. She was quite a sight, and the fact that a great deal of her scars had been artfully and tastefully covered with tattoos was an added touch. But Jonah wasn't even paying much attention to her tats. She smirked at the scenic route his eyes took over her body.

"Yeah," she said to him, "I know. Just wait till you feel what you see."

Jonah shook his head. "You are one of the most direct women I've ever met," he remarked. "It's refreshing as hell."

"Yeah, just as I suspected," said Rheadne, who seemed to be enjoying the banter, though the look in her eyes denoted that she couldn't hold back much longer. "All this time, you've never had a real woman. A mature woman, who knows what she's doing, and doesn't have to quibble with preliminaries and fluff. You needn't worry...I'll take good care of you."

She and Jonah were inches apart when she clutched his arms. His shirt faded away, as though it were an illusion. He looked down at his bare torso, stunned.

"How did you do that?" he wanted to know.

"Come on, Jonah," said Rheadne, whose resolve faded more and more with each passing second. "Ask me the right question."

Jonah was quick on the uptake. He didn't have much resolve left, either. "Can you do that for my jeans?"

Rheadne gave him that confident grin again. "Now, *that* is the right question."

* * *

Jonah returned to the same back door he'd exited, and laughed to himself. He didn't know how long he'd been gone, and didn't give a damn about that fact, either.

Rheadne was far more effective—and fun— than any training in the Glade. She was as good as her word—she *didn't* bother with tedious preliminaries...she knew exactly what she wanted. And Jonah was a fast learner; adapting to her desires was as easy as adapting to her kiss. And that amplifying power she had made the sex infinitely more amazing. Upgraded it from a sex session to an adrenaline-laced thrill ride.

Well, *three* adrenaline-laced thrill rides, to be exact.

That had to happen again. Very soon. Thank God, Rheadne was amenable to that. She made that clear before he left her.

Jonah felt renewed heat in his body just thinking about it. He opened the back door, walked in the kitchen, and froze.

Vera stood near the sink, a glass of water in her hands.

She looked at Jonah in surprise, but then looked beyond him, to the back door. Jonah saw the moment that she put two and two together, because that was when her eyes hardened.

"Wow, Jonah." Her voice was quiet, cold, and menacing. "You—just—wow."

She dropped the glass roughly onto the countertop—it actually cracked. But she gave it no notice as she turned her back on him and left.

Jonah swore under his breath. Did he have to run into her in the middle of the night?

16

Sazers and Suites

"So, all in all, a wild night."

After the three of had rested from their own respective nights, Jonah, Terrence, and Reena met up in Reena's art studio. As Terrence's ankle was one hundred percent again, all was well with taking the many stairs again. Just like Jonah had predicted, Terrence's night had been full of aggravations, spills, and then making sure the bathrooms were clean, as well as empty, of students. Reena didn't talk much about her evening, which meant that it had gone well. Once they'd recounted their stories, Jonah told his own. At least up to a point. He took a page out of Reena's book, and didn't tell them about Rheadne. As far as he was concerned, his private moments with Rheadne were his own, plus there was the fact that he enjoyed being on the same page with Terrence again too much to brag about sex with the woman he'd had a crush on before she'd abandoned him in a fight.

Once all the stories were out there, Terrence made the comment about it being a wild night, which they all thought was pretty accurate.

Jonah had already heard the praise and compliments that had been doled out to everyone involved in Michael Pruitt's healing. There had even been some savage levity from Bobby. "I always said that Lizzie was my better half," he'd said. "Had it been me in the same situation and old Kaine said he wanted to take Michael away, I'd have let him cart his ass off and waved at the back of him while I did it." But after that, Jonah kept the conversation to Terrence and Reena. There were plenty other participants in last night's rescue to regale everyone else.

"I'm just glad Gabriel and I found him," said Jonah. "God only knows what would have happened if he'd been out there for hours."

Given her opinion of Gabriel, Reena held her tongue on him. "So the whole thing could have been avoided if Trip hadn't been smoking?" she said instead.

Jonah nodded. "Jonathan saw to it that Liz would have everything she needed, and then said he would deal with Trip."

"Huh," said Terrence. "Any idea what that entailed?"

"Nope," said Jonah, "but whatever it entailed wasn't enough for Gamaliel. He wanted a punishment that involved bodily harm."

Terrence shook his head. "Trip should smoke some more."

When Jonah and Reena looked at him, horrified, he shook his head and raised his hands.

"Just hear me out," he said to them. "Let Trip smoke some more, and have no one in harm's way. Then let Gamaliel or G.J. catch him at it, recall the anger, and have them duke it out. I'd bring popcorn for it!"

Jonah and Reena shared his laughter once he'd made that clarification. Then Terrence rose.

"All these recollections have made me hungry," he said. "See you guys upstairs."

He departed, and Jonah made to follow him, but Reena grabbed his arm.

"What, Reena?"

She eyed him in a very shrewd way. "Was Rheadne good, Jonah?"

"Huh?" said Jonah, and then cursed. He really had to get that under control.

Reena smiled and released him. "Gets you every time," she said.

"How could you possibly know, Reena?" he asked her.

Reena grabbed a paintbrush and twirled it in her fingers. "Jonah, your essence is on fire," she answered. "Mine was the same way when I had sex with Kendall for the first time. Plus, it was clear that there was something about last night that you weren't telling us."

Jonah shrugged. It wasn't like he was ashamed. "Alright, fine. Good is too small a term," he allowed. "She was fucking amazing. But that's all you get. I'm not big into the whole kiss-and-tell thing. It may be old-fashioned, but it is what it is."

Reena nodded. "I completely understand. I didn't want details, anyway. I just knew that there was more to last night than you let on, and I didn't want to ask you in front of Terrence."

"You have my thanks for that," said Jonah. "But I will tell you one thing, Reena. I don't think Vera is ever going to speak to me again."

He told Reena about running into her after he'd returned to the kitchen. Thankfully, Reena didn't scold, criticize, or judge. She simply shook her head.

"I hope that you believe in miracles, Jonah," she told him. "Because that's about what it'll take to fix that one."

Jonah heard some of the most hilarious and ridiculous things he ever had around the estate. It seemed that Gamaliel and G.J. just couldn't bring themselves to be grateful for Michael's steady recovery, and opted instead to harp on Jonathan's "humiliating" them and the fact that none of it would have happened had Trip not been so careless with his cigarettes. Reena simply laughed about it with Jonah and Terrence.

"The male ego is more dangerous than drugs," she said. "The only difference is with the male ego, there is no rock bottom."

"She's one to talk, ain't she?" muttered Terrence. "Put her around someone who is brilliant, and let's see how well her ego holds up."

One thing that was great was the fact that nothing was awkward between Jonah and Rheadne. Quite the opposite. The best thing about it was when Rheadne told him in the Glade the night after Michael's rescue that the people in Sanctum's camp were returning home for Thanksgiving, and they'd be back the Sunday afterward. And she had no interest in entertaining family while she was, as she put it, "in need." Jonah was more than happy to assist her with relieving tension, and spent every night with her up until the time the Sanctum crew used the *Astralimes* the night before Thanksgiving. On Thanksgiving morning, the estate looked interesting, especially pertaining to the numbers. On his first Thanksgiving holiday there, it seemed as if everyone had brought their families there. The place hadn't been jam-packed by any means; the estate comfortably accommodated everyone like it always had. This year was different. The majority of the residents left to spend the holidays with their own families. When Jonah queried Terrence about it, he waved a hand.

"It's not uncommon," he said. "Remember when I told you that a lot of Elevenths aren't full-time residents here? They're free to hang with their families whenever they want. But I don't think that's the reason a lot of people decided to spend Thanksgiving with their families. I think that they jumped at the chance to have time away from those Sanctum fools."

Jonah sniffed. So their thoughts were along the same lines. "That's what I thought, too. Even if Sanctum did leave for Florida for the next few days. Hopefully, our friends will have the chance to recharge their batteries before they come back here and have to see Sanctum again."

Douglas got invited to his Uncle Karl's house, much to his pleasure.

"He and my Aunt Emma only have one daughter, and she's my age, so I don't have to hear about fabulous gifts that she got from Grandma," he explained.

Liz and Nella went to their parents' house, where their oldest sister, Sandrine, would be as well. Vera went with them, which was fine with Jonah. They hadn't spoken since the night she'd seen him in the kitchen and had cracked that glass, and neither of them needed that kind of tension in their consciousness on the holiday.

It went without saying that the Decessios came to the estate, complete with Raymond and Sterling. That had been a huge surprise, especially for Mrs. Decessio, but Sterling treated it like a no-brainer.

"Eating dinner somewhere is easy," he said. "But home-cooking? Wouldn't miss it for the world."

Of course, Terrence, Reena, and Mrs. Decessio covered most of the cooking. Reena was probably in higher spirits than even Terrence, because for a second Thanksgiving, Kendall would be joining them. Jonah laughed when he saw her that morning.

"Sometimes, I feel like you're tailing me," he told her.

"Not in the slightest," said Kendall, playing along. "I see this as being at my girlfriend' house. I'm not here to see *you* at all."

Terrence, who still held mild irritation that Reena had scored such a catch, made generic pleasantries and returned to cooking.

At about three, the spread was out, which elevated the mood of an already familial, elated atmosphere: A half-dozen turkeys, five different types of dressing, macaroni and cheese, cranberry sauce, mashed potatoes, cornbread, pumpkin pie, chicken salad, hams, and deviled eggs weighed down the tables. Terrence had even sweetened the pot with bread pudding and traditional eggnog.

After everyone joined hands family style and observed Reverend Abbott's blessing (which was mercifully not long), people began to dig in. Multitudes of conversations were going on at once, but where Jonah, Terrence, and Reena were seated, the conversation got on Sanctum Arcist, because of course.

"I'm glad to be free of them, even if it is a little while," said Bobby. "But wasn't it a little annoying for Gamaliel to call it leave, like they're actually true military or something?"

"And they emptied out their belongings, but left the tents," said Maxine. "Here's to hoping that they don't blow all over the earth."

"But how long will they be here?" Magdalena demanded. "I still don't get why they're here at all. Forgive me, but that is still unclear."

"They are trying to curtail a Deadfallen threat, Magdalena," said Spader coldly. "Or were you not paying attention when they said that?"

"I was more occupied with the obvious bullying tactics they were pulling, so no, I guess I wasn't," Magdalena shot back. "And when exactly are they going to help us curtail things, Spader? 'Cuz all they've done so far is slap around some sazers."

"Um, pardon me," said Kendall, who lowered her fork with a frown, "but am I missing something here? What is Sanctum Arcist? And what exactly is a sazer?"

That portion of the table got silent. A pin drop could probably be heard in the silence. Jonah actually felt his palms moisten on the table. Magdalena and Spader were so nervous that their argument came to a ceasefire. Terrence glanced at Reena and mouthed, "*Handle it!*"

"Kendall, Sanctum Arcist is another estate, like this one," she said uncomfortably. "Boarding place, just like this. They came up for a—conference."

"Really." Kendall raised an eyebrow. "Conference must be going badly, the way Magdalena is talking. So what are sazers?"

"It involves this crazy game," said Jonah hastily. "It's an RPG that some of us play together. It's really competitive, and sometimes brings out the worst in us. Wouldn't you agree, Spader? Magdalena?"

As if on cue, they both nodded rigorously.

Kendall would have asked more questions if there hadn't been a well-timed knock at the door, which Jonah answered.

It was Michael and Aloisa, who both tried not to look awkward or apprehensive. That was no small feat, seeing as how they were now subject to multiple puzzled faces.

"What's up?" said Jonah.

Michael took a deep breath. "You don't require Official Designations, do you?"

"I'd much rather you didn't, to be honest," Jonah replied. "What's up?"

"Well, everyone's gone back for the next few days," said Michael, "and we didn't want to do that. I just got completely healed, and I didn't want to—aggravate any of that. No conspiracies, no ulterior motives. We were just wondering if you had room for two more."

Jonah raised an eyebrow at the fact that Michael felt the need to preface it like that, as if he thought that's what they'd suspect. He also felt a little ashamed, because that's exactly what he thought at first. But in the end, he shrugged. "Nobody deserves to be at a campsite eating burgers, dogs, and s'mores on Thanksgiving," he said. "Come on in. Just be mindful," he added in an undertone, "we have a Tenth in here, so easy on the ethereality talk."

Aloisa beamed. Many folks were more festive than suspicious. That had to do with the fact that Michael and Aloisa were never antagonistic, like their peers. Magdalena, after visibly turning it over in her mind, offered them seats next to her.

"I got to ask you," said Alvin, who hadn't wasted much time returning to his plate, "we've been eating for a while now. Why did you just show up at this time?"

Aloisa looked down and muttered something about not knowing how well they'd be received.

"You didn't have to hide out there," said Mrs. Decessio. "Trust me, no one cares, so long as you haven't slit anyone's throats."

"Mama!" said Raymond, any everyone laughed.

Jonah didn't care at all. He liked Michael and Aloisa, and they didn't have that air of superiority and contempt some of the other Sanctum folks had. Truth be told, they weren't much different from his friends at the estate.

He went to the head of the table with his mind set on another helping of sausage stuffing when someone else knocked at the door.

"Man!" he exclaimed. "Aren't we the popular ones?"

He opened the door, and was pleasantly surprised to see a grinning, toboggan-headed, long-haired boy in his late teens wielding two apple cobblers.

"Prodigal!"

"Hey, friend!" said Prodigal cheerfully. "I almost miss when you used to call me '*Boy!*' "

Many people rose from the table to greet him, and Reverend Abbott took the cobblers off of his hands so that he could properly reciprocate the greetings. Jonah looked over him with pride. When he first met the boy, he was an unnamed, transient vagrant who lacked sufficient nourishment and proper hygiene. Now, the boy (who'd taken the name Prodigal after hearing a piece of the Prodigal Son parable from Reverend Abbott) was an entirely different person. His cheekbones had faded, as proper nourishment had filled out his face. His hair no longer looked like a stringy, matted biohazard; it was trimmed, freshly washed, and looked straight under the toboggan. His sleeveless hoodie and khakis made him look like an extra from an old Pac Sun commercial.

"What are you doing here?" grinned Bobby.

"Been a while, so I thought I'd drop in!" said Prodigal. "Now, I'm really not too familiar with Thanksgiving foods other than the turkey, but I think dessert is prevalent. Did I get it right? There is a heavier focus on pies and cobblers, not cakes and cookies?"

"Cobbler will do just fine, believe me," said Terrence, who'd already gotten a saucer and new fork. "Now pull up a chair, get anything you want, and bask in the ambiance of your first Thanksgiving!"

When dinner was over, people left the dining room for their respective places of interest. Most of the men, led by Raymond, Alvin, and Bobby, went to the family room to enjoy football. Malcolm went upstairs to talk to his mom, who'd just discovered Skype. Spader went off…somewhere. Michael and Aloisa were about to return to their tents, but Jonathan shot that down and told them to take a room upstairs. Magdalena, Akshara, and Benjamin swooped on them, recruiting them into the dishwashing brigade.

Kendall, who had family to see the next day, bade Reena and everyone else goodbye, mercifully asking no further questions about Sanctum or sazers. Jonah knew that Reena was sad to see her go, but they had a welcome distraction in the form of Prodigal.

"So where have you been, man?" asked Terrence.

"You name it, I've been there," said Prodigal. "I've never sat anywhere too long. It's just not my nature."

Jonah could easily believe that Prodigal had trouble keeping still. Even now, he kept his hands busy by drumming his fingers on his knees.

"You definitely look like life is treating you better," commented Jonah.

Prodigal looked himself over. "You mean the threads?"

"No one says *threads* anymore," snorted Terrence. "But no, it's not just your clothes. It's you. Your whole demeanor has changed! How much money did Felix give you to get you off the park benches and gas station bathrooms?"

"He gave me enough," said Prodigal vaguely.

Reena surveyed him shrewdly. "Hmm. A subject that you aren't open about."

"I'm not being rude, Reena, I promise," said Prodigal hastily. "It's just that Felix taught me a lot of stuff about money management, and told me that the best way to maintain money is to never talk about how much you have. I really took that to heart."

"Wise policy," shrugged Jonah.

"While we're on the subject of Felix," for some reason, Prodigal massaged his left leg at that moment, "let's talk about your recent run-in with those sazers."

Jonah glanced at his friends. Under normal circumstances, he would have been suspicious. But this was Prodigal. If he found out helpful information, he would probably relay it to Felix to do something about it.

And something needed to be done about those cannibals.

"We were investigating in different spots," began Jonah. "Reena, me, and this Sanctum woman named Aloisa got sent to a farmhouse—"

"Really?" Prodigal looked at Terrence in confusion. "You weren't with them? You didn't cry foul, and beg Jonathan to complete the usual trifecta?"

Terrence looked awkward. Jonah wished that Prodigal hadn't even posed the question. No one wanted to rehash that crap. "We were mandated to switch things up," said Terrence lamely. "They had us on four different teams; a mixture of the two factions."

"Oh, okay." Prodigal didn't look as if he needed too detailed an explanation. "Sorry to cut across you, Jonah."

"It's alright," said Jonah, relieved. "To nutshell it, they were all traps. All deliberate traps. Each place was filled with cannibal sazers."

Something changed in Prodigal's face. "Cannibals."

Reena tensed, and Jonah knew why. Prodigal was a sazer, prone to Red Rage if his anger reached a certain level. But Prodigal noticed their alarm, and smiled.

"Calm down," he said. "No anger towards you. You showed me kindness; I'll always be grateful. It's just that... that's bad."

Jonah rolled his eyes. Understatement, much?

He was about to point that out when Prodigal tilted his head to the side, and said in a slightly elevated voice, "What's your take on that?"

Jonah, Terrence, and Reena looked at each other, confused.

"Prodigal?" said Reena, "What're you—?"

But Prodigal shook his head at them, and pushed back his hair back on the left side, revealing a Bluetooth. Jonah stared at it in wonder. How much money *had* Felix given this boy?

Reena's eyes narrowed. "Is that Felix on the phone?"

Prodigal nodded quickly. "Wanted to listen in."

"Put him on the speaker," Reena commanded.

Prodigal removed his phone (revealing what Jonah had thought was a massage to be activating the phone), and placed it on the arm of the chair.

"Felix," said Reena, coolness in her tone, "the spying tactic was unnecessary. Why did you send Prodigal as your errand boy?"

Prodigal laughed, as did Felix on the speakerphone.

"That wasn't the case at all, Reena," said Felix. "Prodigal was coming to visit you anyway, complete with sweet treats, so I thought this would be a good idea."

"Why?" said Jonah.

"I wanted to glean information in an unobtrusive way, answered Felix. "But I think we need to speak face-to-face. Is your schedule clear on Sunday afternoon?"

Jonah hesitated. The Sanctum Arcist people returned on Sunday, meaning he'd see Rheadne again. That didn't instill much desire in him to see Felix that day. Unfortunately for him, Reena correctly interpreted his hesitation, even if Terrence didn't.

"Yes, Felix," she said.

"Come to the Milverton Inn and Suites," said Felix promptly. "We'll talk then."

"Felix, I'm confused," said Terrence. "I'm completely cool with visiting you at that place. But why all the mysteriousness, man? Why don't you hop on I-40 and come to the estate? It's Thanksgiving, after all."

Jonah realized in that moment that he had never told Terrence Felix's opinions, but Felix spared him the trouble, and added a surprise remark to boot.

"No mysteriousness intended, Terrence," he said. "I do it this way for three reasons. First, I don't celebrate Thanksgiving. Second, I don't want to lay eyes on Trip if I can help it. Finally, it's my understanding that Kaine's little club is returning on Sunday. I'm allergic to Gamaliel Kaine."

The estate residents who'd gone home for Thanksgiving began returning Friday. Douglas was in high spirits, as he had avoided his grandmother and her criticisms. Liz, Nella, and Vera returned shortly after Douglas did. Vera was her usual self—until she saw Jonah. Liz had no such qualms, and flung herself into Jonah's arms like the little sister she was to him. She told him, once again, that he needed to meet her parents and older sister. Bobby brightened when he saw Liz, and whisked her away. Jonah saw Alvin shake his head. He knew that Alvin remained amused as ever at just how smitten his brother was. He also knew that Alvin, of course, would have called Bobby whipped.

The people from Sanctum Arcist returned on Sunday afternoon, an hour or so before Jonah, Terrence, and Reena planned to head to the Milverton Inn and Suites. The strange thing about it was the fact that it was a new contingent.

A larger new contingent.

When they'd first descended upon them, it had been twenty-four of them. Now there were at least thirty-five of them, all new except for Gamaliel, G.J. Gabriel, Iuris, Cisor, Penelope, and Rheadne.

Michael and Aloisa, who'd just had breakfast at the estate with Jonah and everyone else, were just as baffled as estate residents were.

"What the hell?" said Michael, frowning.

"What, you don't know these people?" asked Bobby.

"'Course we know them," said Aloisa. "But we had no idea that Mr. Kaine was going to change things up. He didn't tell us that before he left."

Reena's eyes narrowed in a way that let Jonah know that she suspected something already, but she didn't say anything.

"What are you thinking?" Jonah asked her bluntly.

"Nothing nice," she responded. "Let's just go see Felix."

Jonah, Terrence, and Reena knew exactly where they were going when they got to the Milverton. Many families were checking out, having stayed for the duration of the holiday. Jonah figured that these people were probably lovely folks on the eve of Thanksgiving, but that wasn't the case now. The departing patrons were as frazzled as the people at the front desk. It was easier for them to just walk to the elevator, ignore people as much as possible, and go on to Felix's suite.

The elevator opened on the much quieter hall ("It's almost like a different world up here," commented Terrence), and Jonah knocked on the door to the suite, which was opened almost instantly.

"Very nice to see you all again." Felix gave them all an approving glance, and a half smile. Jonah did notice that Felix's demeanor had improved, which might be attributed to a clearer conscience nowadays.

Felix had spent almost twenty years thinking that he murdered T.J. Rivers, who had been Trip's father, as well as a Deadfallen disciple. He'd thought that his Red Rage had gotten the best of him and he'd killed the man whom he'd believed had killed his own father. It had been Jonah, Terrence, and Reena who had unearthed the truth, discovering that both murders had been committed by the 49er, another

Deadfallen disciple. The revelation resulted in Felix's record being expunged on both the Tenth and Eleventh sides of the law.

The tight waves in Felix's hair were still as sharp as ever, and his beard was still pencil-thin, and precise. Although it was common knowledge, Jonah still couldn't believe that Felix was wealthy. He just seemed so down to earth and had a solid bead on reality. Many rich people didn't look like they could walk and talk at the same time.

"By all means, sit down," said Felix, motioning to the sofa in front of the widescreen. "May as well take advantage of the splendors of this fancy suite."

"Felix, this isn't like you," commented Reena. "Staying in suites, and all that. What are you up to?"

"Quieter up here," said Felix. "Easier to concentrate. It's not like me, Reena, that's true. But it is nice; I'll concede that. Have you guys ever been in this suite before?"

"Not this one," said Jonah. "But we have been in the one down the hall. The Apex Suite."

Felix lifted an eyebrow, inviting Jonah to go on, but Jonah had gone as far as he was willing to go. None of them, especially Terrence, had any interest in revisiting that. After a bit, Felix shrugged.

"It's your business," he murmured. "That's cool."

He sat near them and placed a bottle of Distinguished Vintage on the table. Felix explained that even though he was a recovering alcoholic with eight years of sobriety, he kept a corked bottle of Vintage with him to remind him that some things were stronger and more powerful than he was as a sazer. Jonah still questioned the risks of that, but if Felix had gone this strong for so long, he had a good handle on it.

"Where is Prodigal?" asked Terrence.

"Moved on." answered Felix. "He said he still has friends in the sazer underground, which is likely a thinly veiled way of saying that at least one of his friends is a girl he cares about."

Reena smirked. Terrence did, too. Jonah, however, pressed on.

"So why did we have to talk after you find out the sazers we saw were cannibals? I thought Prodigal might blow his stack."

A shadow crossed Felix's face. "Jonah, sazers are an extremely oppressed population," he said. "They refer to the homeless and low-income Tenths as an invisible population? No slight to their plights, but they are *blessed* compared to sazers. The Tenth World labels us volatile, throw their ever-changing DSM diagnoses at us, and declare us lost causes. The ethereal world is no better. They tolerate us so long as we don't upset their *natural order*. If sazers could be educated from an early age on how to manage themselves and their anger, and stop needing to defend their lives and actually have lives, they could be an integral part of society, ethereal or otherwise."

Looking around at this suite, Jonah had a fair amount of difficulty viewing Felix as oppressed, but then again he wasn't a sazer and had no idea. Reena, on the other hand, nodded.

"As a gay person, I take your point concerning oppression," she said. "But how does that tie to these cannibals?"

"I'm getting to that," said Felix. "There are sazers, like my father, who buck all the grim odds and thrive. My father had a wonderful marriage with my mother, who was a Tenth. Prodigal lives off the grid, but he tries to help the sazer friends that he has as best he can. All positive things, see? But then there is the dark side. Just like good Elevenths and Spirit Reapers, there are those who don't want to be saved. Who love stealing, destroying, and killing to eat. Some sazers have actually eaten their own. I've got stories. But to cannibalize Elevenths and Tenths...that brings attention to us all. The absolute worst kind. From the Tenth Police and their courts, to Spectral Law Enforcement, to the Networkers and the Curiae. The actions of a few bring about consequences for the many."

"Man," said Terrence. "I knew that sazers got a bad rap for the most part, but when you put it like that..."

Felix nodded. "You get the point. But I'm not quite through. Sazers, even the bad ones, don't want that attention. They will only bother to cross the line if protection was assured."

"Protection..." Reena's eyes widened.

"Felix," said Jonah eagerly, "when we went out on that mission, the sazers Reena and I came across said something about a promise. Malcolm and Liz said that the sazers they ran into said something similar."

Felix, who had moved at a light pace while he spoke, ceased and snapped his complete attention to Jonah. "Promises?"

"Yeah," said Jonah. "But when we briefed in Jonathan's study, Gabriel Kaine, that's Gamaliel's—"

"I know who he is," said Felix promptly. "Please continue."

"Right. Well, anyway, he kind of suspected that it was a two-way betrayal."

"Did he, now?" nodded Felix. "He can be quite brilliant when his dad and brother give him permission to speak."

"Reena thinks Gabriel is an informant to one of the Deadfallen running around," Terrence blurted out.

Reena looked at him coldly, but Felix looked pensive.

"If that's true, it would be bitterly ironic for old self-righteous Gamaliel Kaine," he said. "But given the way that he treats him…"

"Can you tell us more about the Deadfallen disciples?" said Jonah. "Terrence's parents were uncomfortable and scared just talking about them, and Jonathan and Gamaliel's conversations these days…"

Felix seated himself again. "Have you heard any names beyond T.J. Rivers, the 49er, and the lunatic who massacred the Crystal Diner, Wyndam O'Shea?"

"You knew about that?"

"Of course," said Felix.

"We've heard some more names," said Reena. "India Drew, Matt Harrill, and Reese Dixon."

"Ah…" Felix nodded. "You know the ones who've run into the Networkers in the past. I got to tell you, though, many of them got away. A bunch of them are on The Plane with No Name, like Lance Harkness and his common law wife, Athena. They were some pretty efficient murderers who took the thing about couples doing everything together way too seriously. Lars Davidson was a Gate Breacher who loved the thought of Creyton blocking the path to the Other Side, because it meant that spirits would come to Breachers like him for freedom. Mont Dancy graduated high school with me, and was almost as good with the Haunts as the 49er. Harold Gibson, Jano Riddick, Davis Powell—I can go on and on. But there were many who weren't ever found. Just be lucky you kids came along when the Networkers began to close in. By the time you were in your late teens, Creyton was transitioning to minions."

"Kids?" Terrence said heatedly. "Felix, you may be fourteen, fifteen years older than us, but do not call us kids. We get enough of that with Kaine."

Upon hearing the name again, Felix actually made a rumble in his throat that sounded like a growl. Jonah knew to be leery with Felix as well in regards to anger.

"What is your beef with Kaine?" he asked. "Fill us in. You already said that you were allergic to him."

Felix took five deep breaths. Ten. Fifteen. Jonah thought that maybe the query took things too far, but in a low voice, Felix began to speak. "He pushed to change my diminished mental capacity charge to murder in Tenth Court. And he was also vehemently against my father's nomination into the Networkers."

"What?" said Jonah.

"You heard," said Felix.

Jonah looked to make sure that Felix's eyes hadn't reddened. The look on his face was already bad enough.

"Kaine was a Networker, and because of his clout and status, he was damn near untouchable," said Felix. "He was influential in getting Creyton's and his followers' crimes reclassified as Eighth Chapter. It was a bold approach, you see, because there had only been seven chapters for centuries on end. Now Creyton comes along and gets his own chapter? Fine, whatever. But it gets better. He pushed for the Eighth Chapter crimes to also carry their own special set of consequences."

Jonah thought he knew where this was going. The destination wasn't a pretty picture, either. "Kill on sight?"

"Kill, period," said Felix. "Self-defense, premeditated...whatever. If the person was guilty of an Eighth Chapter crimes, he wanted them gone. And that was unheard of. Even when fighting evil, the code has always been that since life never ends, the law should be practiced in such a way that neutralized threats while maintaining the utmost regard for preservation of life. Cute in theory, but Creyton followed his own rules. So Kaine pushed to fight fire with fire, not realizing that all that approach would do was guarantee creation of hell on Earth and Astral Plane."

"I'm guessing that the Curaie was against that?" Reena didn't ask so much as comment.

"Oh yeah," said Felix. "The Curaie was against it. Jonathan was against it. Spectral Law, the Protector Guides—everyone. And Kaine began to go down in people's eyes. I mean self-defense is one thing, but he was saying that if you saw a Deadfallen disciple in the street, just kill 'em. With no regard to Tenth or Eleventh witnesses. Imagine the chaos it would cause if Tenths saw stuff like that. They wouldn't know that these were Creyton's Deadfallen disciples. They'd just see people killed in the street. Think about the Elevenths, who'd be so scared that they'd get caught in the crossfire that it would create more hysteria, and therefore create more victims. Then Dad came."

Felix allowed pride in his eyes and his trademark half-smile to come across his face. "Preston Duscere. Sazer who had mastered all of his impulses and base-level emotions. A man who hadn't disowned his son for being a problem child. And he became a Networker, despite Kaine saying that he couldn't be trusted just because he was a sazer. Nothing else. But Dad became a big deal despite him. He rallied against Creyton and the Deadfallen. Some got killed, but it was last resort and the passing of innocents into Spirit were at an all-time low. And when my Dad started making a difference, Kaine went out of his mind with hate. Then the bullshit happened with the 49er. Dad got killed, I got framed, and then labeled a drunken loon. And then Kaine made a speech in front of the entirety of the Networkers and Spectral Law Enforcement that since Creyton worked with sazers, then they were all evil and should be put down. He even said that my father's murder wasn't bad, because it was the necessary deed that could, as he put it, *shock* everyone back to the natural order of only Elevenths in Spectral Law."

Reena actually stood up, incredulity and anger on her face. Jonah wished that he hadn't heard it, because he already hated Kaine enough. Terrence shook his head and murmured, "*Asshole.*" Felix went on.

"Keep in mind that the ethereal world has never really been fond of sazers, but for Kaine to just get in front of everyone and be so brutal and vicious like that was bad for business. So he had to go. Due to his wonderful service and achievements, however, they didn't want to fire him. So they went underhanded. His appeal to get my charge updated? Nixed. Kaine resigned in disgust, bought land near Fort Lauderdale, and created Sanctum Arcist, where he teaches that sazers were born bad and the Ungifted Tenths are to be pitied. He became a husband and father late in life, and has Junior and Gabriel, or should I say, the Heir Apparent and the Accident."

Felix fell silent, and looked at the bottle of Vintage like he wanted nothing more than to drink every drop. He began to employ the breathing techniques again. Jonah sighed. He wondered if Felix had ever shared those things before. After all the things that Felix had taught him about unresolved anger, it turned out that he had some of his own. That bile had been sloshing about inside Felix for years.

He'd seen Terrence wince when Felix had labeled Gabriel an accident. Reena was angry herself, but Jonah wasn't worried about her. She wasn't the one who could knock folks through walls.

"No wonder you consider it ironic if Gabriel is a spy," he said to Felix.

Felix was on his feet now. "So tell me," he grumbled, "how many skirmishes have you guys had since Kaine and his pack of maniacs has been there?"

Now, it was their turn to spill. They told Felix about the dramatic arrival, the blessing of haven, that disastrous first conjoined training, and Jonathan's outburst. Felix raised an eyebrow at that.

"Jonathan lost his composure? I didn't think that was possible. What brought it on?"

"Gamaliel said that I should have been abandoned when my ass was in the fire, so as to cut losses," Terrence grumbled.

Felix shook his head. "I wasn't even aware that Jonathan and Gamaliel had a history," he said.

"You weren't?" said Jonah, disappointed. He hoped that Felix could shed light on things. Oh well. "There was a funny thing, though. One of them, Michael Pruitt, got burned all to hell, courtesy of lighting fireworks in his pocket due to a cigarette that Trip didn't put out. But Liz assembled a team of us and did an elaborate healing process, and he made a full recovery. I think some of them began to see that we weren't the wimpy cowards Gamaliel made us out to be."

Felix looked at him. "And you brought that up because—?"

"Because Kaine came back with a new bunch of his people," said Jonah. "The only ones that he brought back were the ones who didn't like us."

"But that doesn't include Gabriel," said Terrence, "or this woman named Rheadne. She's cool, apart from leaving me in a warehouse with hungry sazers."

Jonah glanced at Reena. Given the fact that she had opinions on both Gabriel and Rheadne, he expected her to add something. But she didn't touch it, choosing another tack instead.

"It's obvious, isn't it?" she said coldly. "The decent or even *semi*-decent ones began to warm to us, and then most of them are taken back, to be replaced with ones that are still hard-wired to hate."

"As if we didn't have enough to worry about with Inimicus," muttered Jonah.

Felix, whose eyes had been on the Vintage again, jerked them back up to Jonah. "Inimicus?" he demanded. "What do you know about Inimicus?"

"I—" Jonah was taken aback by Felix's forceful inquiry, "I—I—"

"Talk, Rowe," thundered Felix.

"Put the beast back in the box, Felix," said Reena in alarm.

"I'm not worked up, Reena," Felix shot back, though his voice had lost some of its edge. Some. "Tell me what you know about Inimicus, Jonah."

Relieved that things were back to center, Jonah told Felix what he remembered from the Spectral Event, the cryptic message he penciled out right after, the cold fire and hooded figure with the card. He also touched on the revolving door of people Inimicus could be, none of whom were a perfect fit. Terrence also threw in the piece of his own investigation of the multiple fireplaces and the residual ethereal steel shavings that were last handled by an auburn-colored aura.

"Why do you care?" asked Jonah. "What was the big deal when you heard the name?"

Felix ignored the question. "You remembered portions of a Spectral Event?" he asked.

Jonah took savage pleasure ignoring Felix's question this time. "What were you so up in arms about, Felix?" he asked again.

Felix looked awkward. "I didn't know that anyone knew about Inimicus," he relented. "I think that Inimicus—Creyton's unseen spy—is the one who's riling the sazers. The one who might be promising them protection."

Jonah looked at Terrence and Reena. They hadn't thought that, but it was definitely in the forefront of their brains now.

"Are you trying to figure out who Inimicus is, too?" asked Felix.

Jonah nodded.

Felix rose, and paced again. He was going to work a trail in the carpet if he wasn't careful. "I don't know how a trace of Creyton's essence got in that fire," he said, "but it's in all our best interests to keep those fires out, lest it intimate grislier orders to Inimicus."

Jonah didn't know why the situation had Felix acting this way, but he was ready for Felix to get to the point. He was ready to see Rheadne again.

"I might know a little bit of information that could help us both," said Felix. "This did not come from me. Kaine would shoot it down if he knew, and make your lives more miserable. I would advise you to go to

Jonathan and um…give him information that a vampire who got vanquished by nameless vampire hunter let slip that he'd been supplied lifeblood by a Deadfallen disciple right before he got skewered through his heart. That Deadfallen disciple was Matt Harrill, one of your Inimicus candidates. He was last seen in a town named Wilkesville."

"You mean Wilkesboro?" said Reena.

"No," said Felix, "I mean *Wilkesville*. About an hour from here, give or take. It's a town that's lost a lot of economy due to textile mills sending jobs overseas. The abandoned mills are perfect hideouts, though. He was last seen around there. Jonathan can…*suggest* another one of your little conjoined team missions there."

Jonah half-smiled. Reena and Terrence looked just as eager.

"We'll handle it, Felix," Jonah told him. "We'd better get back. It was a pleasure seeing you man."

They all rose to leave.

"Take care of yourselves," said Felix quietly. "Reena, I hope that you're wrong about Gabriel, but watch him. Be careful around Kaine's group of brand new haters, too. And Jonah, tell Vera I said hi."

He gave Jonah a meaningful look, which Jonah tried very hard not to return. So he wanted to be like that, huh? And Jonah hadn't even told him that Gamaliel had referred to him as a *sazer drunk*.

Once they were back in the lobby, Reena stopped them from going to the door.

"Need some liquid courage before we go home," she said.

"Seriously?" asked Jonah in surprise. "Did you stare at that Vintage bottle too long?"

"Not liquor!" snapped Reena, appalled. "I meant a virgin daiquiri!"

Jonah breathed a sigh of relief. That was the Reena they knew, and occasionally loved. "Go on, friend," he said. "We'll be right with you."

Thankful that Reena had on her dampener, he turned to Terrence when she left. "Inimicus scares Felix," he told him. "He tried to hide it with an anger outburst, and he almost fooled me."

Terrence nodded slowly. They were on the same page, it seemed.

Jonah had never seen Felix show fear; the only time he'd seen him overreact was in a state of fury. But the one that they'd just seen was convincing... right up to the point that he gave them the information about Matt Harrill and made the remark about Creyton's fire needing to stay out. He was probably concerned that if Inimicus was riling sazers, vampires could be riled as well. No one wanted an episode of crazy cannibal sazers and vampires on the Earth and Astral Plane.

"Jonah," said Terrence, "I've said it a million times. Well here's a million and one. What have we gotten ourselves into?"

17

The Unpleasant Surprise

Jonah, Terrence, and Reena got Bast to summon Jonathan as soon as they returned to the estate. They usually discussed things in the Glade, but because of the prying eyes and ears of Sanctum, it was better to meet their mentor in his study. As an added bonus, Bast monitored the door, along with Anakaris and Laura. Jonah loved the heralds.

Jonathan listened to all of the information with rapt attention. When they finished, he simply nodded, not giving away whether or not any of it was surprising to him.

"And this came from Felix?" he asked.

"Yes, sir," said Jonah. "He stressed that we come to you with it, so that you could wrap the information in a detailed package."

Jonathan smirked. "And by saying that, what you really mean is that he wanted the data to come from me, otherwise Kaine would dismiss it as the wild ramblings of yet another sazer."

"H—?" began Jonah, but Reena rammed her foot into his ankle so quickly that the betraying word became an anguished grunt.

"That's exactly right, sir," she said as she cut an eye at Jonah.

Jonathan caught Reena's action, and he smiled again. "There wasn't any need for that, Reena," he told her. "I assure talking about Gamaliel will not make me angry again."

"Not that I don't believe you, sir," said Reena delicately, "but—but—"

"Reena, please speak freely," said Jonathan.

251

Reena took a deep breath. "Okay, sir. It's not that I don't believe you. But it's obvious that going into detail about that man is a sore subject for you. Perfect example of that is when you called him *Gamaliel* just now, but before that, you called him *Kaine*."

Jonah half-expected Jonathan's eyes to flash or harden or something (damn Reena and her inane proclivity to be observant), but none of those things happened. Jonathan merely nodded once again.

"That I did, Reena," he said. "You needn't have worried; no offense taken. It is, after all, no secret by now that Gamaliel Kaine, Sr. is not one of my favorite people."

"Can we ask you why, sir?" risked Jonah. If Reena could test the waters, why couldn't he?

But it wouldn't happen. Jonathan shook his head.

"I will not tell you that, Jonah." He was neither annoyed nor perturbed, but still very firm. "It is a personal matter that is many years removed from relevance."

Jonah gritted his teeth. Fine.

"Jonathan, is it true what Felix said?" asked Terrence. "Did Kaine really create Sanctum Arcist to spite Spectral Law Enforcement?"

"Not entirely, but about ninety-eight percent," said Jonathan. "Gamaliel always wanted power, and he received an exorbitant amount of rank, clout, and pull during his time as a Networker. But even that wasn't enough. When he was put out to pasture, he built Sanctum Arcist, and it became his Heaven on Earthplane. He was finally in a situation where he was in total control and his word were absolute law."

"How cool was the Curaie with that?" asked Jonah.

"*Cool* is the most accurate term," said Jonathan. "They were cool on the idea from its inception. They were never thrilled about his little fiefdom, and none of his justifications could warm them to it. Engagah—she's the head of the thirteen Spirit Guides, as well as Overmistress of the Phasmastis Curaie—only permitted it because they couldn't actually stop him. He wasn't declaring war on anyone."

"But Jonathan," said Reena dully, "his methods—"

"Are merely offspring from his training during his time in Spectral Law," said Jonathan. "Laced with his own beliefs, of course. Think of it as cafeteria ideology, if you will. Teach the modalities that you pick and choose, and while ignoring what you don't like."

Jonah's eyes narrowed in disgust. "He was completely alright with teaching his students what he learned from the Networkers," he groused, "yet he was pi—sorry, sir—P.O.'d when he found out that Felix taught me how to do a Mind Cage."

"Ah, Jonah, but your situation was vastly different," said Jonathan, making his voice sardonic. "He could teach those principles because he was once a Networker. Felix picked up the skills second-hand, therefore his teaching them to unqualified Eleventh Percenters was most abhorrent."

Jonah was still miffed, but he calmed somewhat after hearing Jonathan's mocking tone. He, too, thought the logic was ridiculous.

Jonathan rose from his seat. "I will help you," he said. "I will present this information to Gamaliel as my own findings, and coordinate another mission."

It was clear that Jonathan still wasn't entirely on board with these missions, but Jonah knew that he wasn't willing to deprive his students of opportunities to expand their knowledge. Even if there may be danger involved. Jonah could respect that stance, but after those cannibal sazers, he didn't know whether or not to think of it as a privilege or a, dare he think it, death warrant.

"Terrence, Reena," said Jonathan suddenly, "please allow me a private moment with Jonah."

The two of them rose and exited the study.

"Jonah," said Jonathan as soon as they were gone, "have you heard anything further from Jessica Hale?"

Jonah pulled a face. He'd nearly forgotten that. "I have, sir. Apparently, her situation has worsened, and she is willing, in her words, to '*give me a shot.*' I'm awaiting her call. She said she'd give me a meet-up spot in the city that we both know, because she doesn't want me in her house again."

"When you see her again, please do not allow personal history to hinder your heart," he warned. "If Wyndam O'Shea is indeed the key to this, then aiding Miss Hale may not only save an innocent life, but also play an integral role in resolving this whole matter."

Jonah thought of what Felix said. If Wyndam O'Shea was indeed Inimicus (he still had his money on him), and he was taking orders from that trace of Creyton's essence in that cold fire and coordinating all of this hell, Jonathan just might be right. But still. "Jonathan, *innocent life* might be a stretch," he said. "You have never met this woman."

"I have not," agreed Jonathan, "but I have met people like her. One of them currently has haven on my grounds."

When Jonah met up with Rheadne, he only wanted to talk. Truly. His plan was to navigate a path through these people's tents, and figure out what the deal was with the new crew. That was it.

He didn't think about that plan again until he was lying on his back next to her, steadying his breath and covered in sweat.

"Christ Almighty, Jonah." Rheadne had to steady her own breath. "One would think you hadn't seen me in a year."

"Ditto," breathed Jonah. "How the hell is it hot in here? It's late fall; chilly as all get-out outside. It feels like you have central heating in here. Is it like this in all the tents?"

"Yeah it is," answered Rheadne. "As for the process—that's a long story. One that I promise that you don't want to hear."

That triggered Jonah's mind again. "That may be true, Rheadne, but there is another thing I wanted to talk to you about."

Rheadne chuckled. "You want to converse when I can barely catch my breath. That's cool. Go for it."

"Why did Kaine change up the people?"

Rheadne had had her eyes closed as she centered her own breathing. But when Jonah posed that question, she opened them again and was one hundred percent still. "I didn't know that he would shuffle up the group," she said.

"Not what I asked," said Jonah.

Rheadne sat up. Jonah mirrored that action.

"I have no idea why he did it," she told him.

Jonah regarded her. Her naked body tugged at his attention, but he fought himself, and focused. "Honestly and truthfully, you don't know?"

"I swear on my eyes, Jonah," said Rheadne. "And that's a big deal, because I truly fear blindness."

Interesting sentiment, but it did the trick. Jonah was convinced. "I believe you. It's a good thing that Mike and Aloisa stayed behind; they're almost convinced that if they had gone back with you all, they would have stayed back with everyone else, too—"

"They're probably right." Rheadne's response was instant.

Jonah didn't miss that. "So you *do* know something."

"Jonah, I don't know what Mr. Kaine meant by bringing others among our friends here," insisted Rheadne. "I am referring to Mikey and Aloisa. Mr. Kaine and G.J. were furious about the way Jonathan pulled rank like that, and then Aloisa just went along with it...he considered that a blatant undermining of his authority."

"Undermining—? Rheadne, her fiancée had just sustained severe burns. Can you blame her for not thinking about a damned chain of command during that time?"

"No," she admitted. "No, I can't. But Mr. Kaine...no one questions him. Ever."

Jonah fought the urge to grab her shoulders. "What is with you guys? Gamaliel is not the be all end all!"

"Mr. Kaine saved us, Jonah," said Rheadne, conviction in her voice. "He not only taught us about endowments, but also that life never ends because we earn the right to live. We earn the right every day."

"Earn the right?" repeated Jonah. "Earn the right? Rheadne, everyone deserves to live!"

"That line of thinking is your first mistake, Jonah," said Rheadne. "We don't get the things we deserve; we get the things we're dedicated to. One of the things we're dedicated to is living, so we train our minds, our bodies, and our ethereality every day. Mr. Kaine is hard on

us sometimes, but that's life. And with us Eleventh Percenters, sometimes a hard line is the best line. Regular Reapers, Deadfallen, minions, Haunts, vampires, sazers... you can't beat them by glad-handing
and pacifism. Mr. Kaine is a visionary. A genius. Without him, we're
wolves without an Alpha."

Jonah stared at her. What was he supposed to say to that?

"These are the things you'd understand if Mr. Kaine had gotten hold
of you before Jonathan did," Rheadne added.

Okay. Jonah had something to say to that. "Rheadne, Jonathan is—"

Rheadne forestalled Jonah by kissing him, and pulling him back
down to a prone position. He shouldn't have let that slide. He should
have been stronger than that.

Yeah. Well, that didn't happen.

"Checkmate."

Jonah hung his head as Douglas beat him for the third time at chess.
Maybe he had trouble focusing, or maybe it was simply because Douglas was an inveterate player.

Their friends were all around them, doing their usual activities to
unwind. Nella had actually made headway in teaching Magdalena and
Vera guitar; she'd even given them two rudimentary songs. It was refreshing to see a smile on Vera's face as she fumbled notes, but he
made no effort to be noticed beyond that. That smile belonged there,
not the dark frown that she'd reserved just for him.

Liz had been woebegone due to the lack of gardening in the late
autumn, but Akshara had convinced her that she could while away the
time by assisting her with making beaded necklaces. Since it wasn't
tonic creation or the explanation of systemic bodily functions, poor Liz
was completely out of her element. But she approached it with usual
zeal that most novices had. Bobby and Alvin, who played PS4 nearby,
couldn't resist grinning at her from time to time.

"Hang on!" she said excitedly. "I think I got it! I—!"

Another bead, burgundy this time, flew from Liz like a slingshot and bounced off of Maxine's (who had her usual Anime in her hands) glasses. Several people laughed.

"Sorry, Max," said Liz, embarrassed. "How many is that now?"

"Just eight, Lizzie!" said Maxine, who checked her glasses for nicks or dents. "No biggie!"

Reena sketched the whole scene from the corner. She was somewhat detached, yet engaged enough to make small talk when necessary. Terrence had borrowed Jonah's laptop, so that he could check something involving Duke basketball. Benjamin, Melvin, and Ben-Israel anxiously looked over his shoulder, undoubtedly hoping that whoever they played beat them.

Jonah returned his attention to Douglas. "I am up to here with you beating me all the time!"

"Well," said Douglas, who tried hard to hide his glee, "you could always focus a little bit more. Did you have a rough night?"

Jonah didn't answer. "How're your graduate courses going, Doug?"

"Great," said Douglas proudly. "How about your class?"

"Wish it were more fun," admitted Jonah. "But it's going well just the same. I'm more concerned with life 'round here."

Some of the mirth left Doug's face, and he leaned forward. "Speaking of things around here," he said, "I'm concerned about Spader."

Jonah kept his face impassive, but all his senses instantly keened. "Why?" was all he said.

"He's changed," said Douglas lamely.

Jonah's senses dulled somewhat, and he returned his gaze to the chess pieces. "Forgive me, Doug, but that's the most useless piece of information—"

"Have you noticed that he hasn't tried to pull fast swindles on us anymore?" interrupted Douglas. "He spends all that time with Kaine's oldest boy, and Cisor, and that Mason guy. You'd think that he'd gone through his whole life with them, and not us. It's like he wants to be one of them."

Jonah said nothing. Douglas Chandler had too many slips of the tongue for him to confide anything.

Douglas paused in the event that Jonah would respond, but when it didn't happen, he continued. "He even slipped up and called a Tenth girl Ungifted in the marketplace the other day."

Heat traced Jonah's insides. "Are you serious?"

"Oh, it gets better," said Douglas. "Or worse, I suppose. He said that Thanksgiving was the last straw."

"Nothing happened on Thanksgiving," contested Jonah. "I ought to know, because I was there."

Douglas shrugged. "He told me that it had to do with Prodigal."

"Prodigal?" Jonah frowned. "What did he do to Spader?"

"No idea," said Douglas. "I asked Terrence, Magdalena, everybody—and they said that he was nothing but his usual cool self. Spader said you guys just worshiped him."

"We didn't worship—" Jonah paused as understanding engulfed him.

Douglas caught the change, and he looked at Jonah concernedly. "What's wrong with you?"

"I figured out Spader's beef," he snapped. "Prodigal is about his age, with the same slouchy style and fashion. But everyone treats him *well*. It's frickin' jealousy, Doug. Spader must feel that there is only room for one vagabond at the estate. Well I can tell you, Doug, here and now…people were nice to Prodigal because he was nice to *them*. Thanksgiving was the last straw, my ass."

Douglas probably hadn't expected Jonah to get as agitated as he did, but Jonah didn't care. If Spader saw fit to act in that manner, he had no problem with emotionally meeting him in kind.

The funny thing about Spader's recent behaviors was that they actually made *Jonah* feel a need to be reckless. He couldn't channel it. Journaling didn't do it. Weight training with Bobby, Alvin, and Terrence didn't do it. Mock fights in the Glade in the increasingly cold temperatures didn't do it. Even the nights with Rheadne didn't channel it. Entirely.

Luckily, a potential opportunity for risk-taking came in the form of an unexpected text message, which Jonah received when he left Two Cents one afternoon. He paid for a sandwich, brought up the text, and read:

Rowe. The Pointe.12:30 Thursday. If u have plans, u better break them b/c u only get 1 chance.
<JH PrivilegedEternal>

Jonah snorted. *JH Privileged Eternal…*
She must have come up with that stupid text signature in happier times.
This was an opportunity for reckless behavior. But it was frickin' Jessica.
Of course, Jonathan's words rattled around his head at that moment. The ones about not allowing his personal feelings to hinder his heart.
"You'd better be glad, Jessica," mumbled Jonah to himself. "You'd better be glad I'm a good person."

* * *

Jonah had to give Jessica credit for her choice of meeting places. Under other circumstances, he wouldn't have chosen a spot outside for any reason. Especially if he'd had a stalker. But this was The Pointe.
The Pointe was a wide park in the city where Jonah used to live. It was situated across the street from the First Municipal Building, about a block from Jonah's old accounting job. The First Municipal Building wasn't the only building nearby; the Pointe was surrounded on the other three sides by a civic center, a cultural arts museum, and a four-level parking deck. About two blocks away, several restaurants catered solely to the hours of the business crowd, and even on late fall days like this one, the colder afternoons still saw numerous people at the Pointe grounds just for time away from their offices. Bright daylight, vehicular traffic, and an open, public space full of people at the peak of lunch hour. Wyndam O'Shea would have been a quintessential imbecile to try something here. Kudos to Jessica, if only this one time.

But Jonah didn't go to meet her just yet.

He had to make up for the mistake he'd made back at the farmhouse back on Route 6.

He closed his eyes, and visualized the stage curtain lifting and the actors performing.

Jonah could breathe easily here. The spirits and spiritesses were plentiful in this place. There was no tension in their faces at all, which was a great thing. If a spirit or spiritess was tense, afraid, or angry, it was almost a sure-shot bet that they were being attacked or threatened. None of these beings had those emotions.

Terrence and Reena had wanted to come with him, but Jonah didn't want extra company to spook Jessica, nor was he willing to allow his friends to use sick days this close to Christmas. He, unlike them, had the ability to tinker with his schedule, and he got Whit to put him on a weekend shift at the bookstore to make up for this day. So he was alone, no harm done to anyone.

He deactivated Spectral Sight and crossed the street to the discolored grass of The Pointe. To his left, a hot dog vendor feverishly racked up fare. Thirty yards in front of him, mutts and masters had fun with Frisbees and fetching sticks. To his right, seated on a bench and sipping at a coffee, was Jessica.

Jonah walked up to her.

Despite the chilliness, Jessica wore her usual short skirt and open-toed shoes. Despite her sunglasses, Jonah could tell that she had done her makeup, so she looked far different than she had last time. She missed it with the nail polish, though; the toes protruding from those shoes were deep plum, while the tips of the fingers clutching the coffee cup were cherry red.

Eh, well. Made no difference to him.

Jonah seated himself next to her. Jessica hadn't even acknowledged a second presence on the bench.

"Jess," he murmured.

Jessica's tone was an inch above a whisper. "Rowe."

Jonah could already see this heading downhill, so he changed tactics. "Why have you changed your tune, Jess? You said that you were scared, but you were scared when you threatened me, too. So what made you want to listen to Ant?"

Finally, Jessica turned to face him. Jonah didn't have to see her eyes to know that something bothered her, even beyond the obvious. "This is how this will work, Rowe," she said in a bitchy tone that fooled no one. "You will tell me everything you know about this man who is ruining my life. Everything you know."

Normally, Jonah would have gone on the defensive, and adhere to the usual facets of the relationship that he and Jessica had. But there was something in her voice that wasn't shielded by her snippy façade. It was an insistent, urgent cadence that only made Jonah feel inclined to comply. He imagined that she was truly that desperate for peace of mind. "His name is Wyndam O'Shea," he said after scanning the scene once more. "Some—Some friends of mine came across some things he'd done in the town where I live now."

"How do you know his name?" asked Jessica.

Jonah hesitated. Jessica was a Tenth, after all. "It—it became known to me when he caused some trouble in my town. Apparently, he has history of crimes, and he's back on the grid now."

Jessica made no sound, though her fingers seemed to clutch the coffee cup more tightly. "You said that he was a killer. Does that history you speak of involve killing people?"

Jonah swallowed. Why would she ask such a question? "Yes."

"You also mentioned the messages that Marguerite got at the accounting firm for me," murmured Jessica. "How did you know about them?"

Jonah wasn't about to throw Nelson under the bus like that. Not when he was the one that still had to work with Jessica after this. "I still have friends at the office, Jess," he offered. "And it's no secret what you're going through. Maybe something slipped. Who knows? But Ant confirmed a lot of things, too, so it doesn't matter how I know if it means it could prove helpful, does it?"

Jessica's eyes seemed to glare lasers through Jonah; it was evident even through the sunglasses. Then she looked back at the park. "So I guess you know about him saying that I look nice in the moonlight," she said.

Jonah had no idea how this conversation had taken this route, but felt the need to see it through. Stopping O'Shea meant possibly stopping Inimicus. Jonah could only think of that cold fire. He never wanted it to burn again. So he decided to level with her somewhat.

"That's how my friends figured out who he was," he told her. "The mention of moonlight. He is a lunatic, see."

"So he's crazy, Rowe?" scoffed Jessica. "You have an astute grasp on the obvious."

Jonah took a breath as Jonathan's words flashed in his brain again. "You misunderstand, Jessica. He is the textbook definition of a *lunatic*. The bad things that he does to people coincide with the full moon. That's why he said you looked nice in the moonlight."

Now Jonah saw Jessica's fingers trembling on the cup. A part of him was apologetic for taking it there, but if there was any information that made her take this seriously, then so be it.

"Are you a P.I. or something, Rowe?" she asked.

Jonah looked at her. "Where did that come from?"

"You are really informed," she commented. "You don't have any connection with this guy, do you?"

There it was again, that insistent, urgent cadence that Jonah associated with her fear and desperation. Despite their past, and despite that veiled accusation, he wasn't angry at her. For once. "Jessica, I want to help you," he said. "Maybe you can take this information to the cops and they can stop him." Since there was no chance that would happen, Jonah decided to sprinkle in some truth, however vague. "I also know that the—authorities— in my town will act on it, too."

Jessica's mouth tightened. She looked as though she still had misgivings about Jonah's sincerity. Once again, he successfully fought off aggravation.

"Yeah, Jess, we hate each other," he said, "but you don't deserve this. No one does. I can look you straight in your eye, and tell you that I have no connection to Wyndam O'Shea whatsoever."

Jessica gave Jonah an assessing look, as if she were physically attempting to see the truth radiate off of him or something. Or maybe she wanted to know that she could trust someone.

Her fingers still trembled on the cup. She put it down between them.

"I'm glad to hear it," she said quietly, "because I'm going to tell you something. Something that only Tony knows, and he won't tell a soul."

Jonah straightened. Jessica was confiding in *him*? When he said hell had frozen over, he meant it a jest. "What's that?"

"I bought a gun," said Jessica.

Jonah's eyes widened. "What?"

"You heard me the first time I said it," snapped Jessica.

"What did you do that for?"

"Because this man O'Shea deserves to die." There was a bloodthirstiness in Jessica's voice that frightened Jonah. "I will take your information to the cop on my case, but in the event that they continue to do all the *nothing* they're doing, I'll be ready."

"Jessica, you can't do this!" cried Jonah. "You're talking about murder, for God's sakes—"

"HE KILLED MR. LANGTON, ROWE!" Jessica shouted.

Jonah's mouth stopped working. There was suddenly a disconnect in his whole being; the only thing that still worked were his eyes, which registered the tears sliding down behind Jessica's sunglasses.

"Yeah, that's right!" she snapped. "Mr. Langton is dead, Rowe. O'Shea killed him in the hospital. And I will not be next!"

18

Journal of United(?) Front: Second Entry

"Confirmed, sir."

The reply was dry, but serious. The response back matched it in seriousness.

"You are certain? Absolutely certain?"

"Yes, sir, I am. One hundred percent. The information Rowe was given cannot be questioned."

Several months ago, Jonah had been near stupefied based on the fact that he'd found himself in agreement with Trip. But now, on the brisk afternoon that marked the last day of the first week of December, the tables had turned. Now Trip was in agreement with him.

He and Trip were with Jonathan in the Protector Guide's study. Jonathan was seated behind the desk, his long fingers joined and his gray eyes solemn. Trip stood near the edge of the desk, alert and disdainful concerning Jonah as usual, but Jonah saw human emotion beneath the cold. It was concern. He'd never seen concern on Trip's face, and the sight was not a welcome one. The fact that this situation actually invoked human emotion in Trip actually bothered Jonah more.

"I went to Anders Langton's hospital room," said Trip. "It was easy to do, I willed myself to not be seen. His body hadn't been there for a while, of course, but the dark ethereality was still there. It was present in the sound anomalies. The airwaves had been tampered with, and the official story in the hospital is that he was poisoned."

Jonathan's eyes stayed on Trip. "Time?"

"It took about the usual time you would expect," said Trip. "And given his condition, it was quite simple."

Jonathan closed his eyes.

"I'm sorry, but what took the right amount of time?" demanded Jonah, confused.

"It is an act that is called a Bloodless Sever, Jonah," said Jonathan, eyes still closed. "It is a most grisly form of dark ethereality, perfected by Creyton himself, who then taught it to his disciples. It involves the bodily organs undergoing the damage they would during massive blood loss, much like they would if someone gets severed with a blade of some kind. The physical body becomes so grievously affected that the spirit is forced to abandon it."

Jonah felt as if the wind had been knocked out of him. That was just sick. Trip ran a hand over his face. Clearly his thoughts were a mile a minute.

"Does that mean that O'Shea usurped Mr. Langton's spirit?" asked Jonah hollowly. "He didn't get to cross to the Other Side?"

"You don't have be summa cum laude to figure that out," snapped Trip, his trace of human emotion fading.

"Titus," said Jonathan, "you are still on thin ice because of the incident with Michael Pruitt. Calm yourself, now."

Trip complied, but it was obviously reluctant. Jonah was intrigued, despite himself. None of them knew exactly how Jonathan had *dealt* with Trip after his poorly disposed cigarette caused such damage to Michael, but given the fact that Trip had increased his band gigs, trained more savagely, and spent more time with Karin and his other buddies than ever, Jonah figured that it had most unpleasant.

He didn't have to be summa cum laude to figure that one out, either.

"You said that it was easy," Jonah said to Trip. "Why did you say that?"

Inimicus

"Your former boss had a history of obesity, hypertension, and heart disease," grumbled Trip. "A Bloodless Sever would be a nasty experience for even a person of optimal health, but for him..." That concern was on his face again. "If I can be excused, sir," he said tersely.

"Carry on," said Jonathan. "And thank you, Titus. You are the only one that I could trust with this."

Trip nodded once, and left. Jonathan immediately cast blazing eyes on Jonah, but they were neither angry nor accusatory. He, like Trip, looked concerned. And Jonah liked this situation less and less.

"Jonah, this was not a mere murder," he said flat-out. "This was meant to send a message. I am well aware that you nursed deep hatred for your former place of employment, but—"

"I hated him," said Jonah at once. "Mr. Langton and Jessica made the whole office uncomfortable, and they had a mad-on for me in particular. The man was a condescending blowhard. But—but I'm sorry that he's gone."

Jonah heard himself say it, which surprised him. With a further jolt of surprise, he realized it was true. He hadn't been just saying it.

Jonathan looked as though he were acutely aware of Jonah's internal conversations. Even though Jonah trusted Jonathan wholeheartedly, it was unnerving when he did things like that. "This makes acting on Felix's advice concerning Matt Harrill even more urgent," the Guide told him. "I'll announce it in the courtyard tomorrow."

He closed his eyes again. Jonah knew that his mentor didn't approve of the combative stance that Gamaliel Kaine had. He didn't view his students as soldiers.

"Sir—" he began, but Jonathan shook his head.

"Jonah, return to your day," he told him. "I must go Off-plane for a time."

He vanished, and Jonah left the study, but not before noticing how the interior of the Vitasphera seemed darker than it had been last time. But now wasn't the time to contemplate trinkets. He had to find Terrence and Reena. He had to tell them about his mistake...the mistake he didn't even reveal to Jonathan.

Finding them both was easy enough, but a place to converse? Not so much. Reena's art studio was too far from the study, and his own room was in no state for company, as it was laundry day. So they decided on Terrence's room (Jonah would just have to grin and bear it when he saw that Duke Blue Devils poster). He told them about what happened when he met with Jessica at The Pointe, even augmenting the story with the information he'd just learned from Jonathan and Trip concerning the truth, and the official Tenth ruse of poisoning. After going over the sheer brutality of Langton's murder, he got to the point.

Reena's eyes widened, but Terrence's narrowed.

"She's bluffing," he hypothesized. "Prissy things like that don't lug around firearms. She was trying to mask her fear with toughness."

"I wish that were true, Terrence," said Jonah, "but you're wrong. She has a nine millimeter. She showed it to me, from her purse."

"She dared show that to you in a public park?" Reena whistled. "Wow, Jonah. That could have been bad for you both. She is at the end of her rope."

"I agree," said Jonah. "O'Shea has driven her out of her mind with fear. And I don't know how to help her."

"What are you talking about, Jonah?" asked Terrence. "She isn't going to ask you again! You told us that she said you were only getting one shot—"

"This wasn't about help, Terrence!" Jonah burst out. "Jessica didn't even want help from me. She talked me into dropping a name so she could go Annie Oakley on her stalker the first chance she gets. I can't believe I gave her his name!"

"But this isn't your problem anymore, Jonah," said Reena. "It's not like you're one of Kaine's people, who take it upon themselves to go looking for trouble. Wyndam O'Shea wiped out a diner. Now he's killed your former boss. He is on the S.P.G.'s radar more so now than he was before. Maybe Jonathan—"

"No, Reena," said Jonah quietly. "I'm on the hook now, because if Jessica takes matters into her own hands, it will be based on information that I gave her. The only thing that Jonathan needs to do is hurry it up with that announcement tomorrow. Then we can find Matt Harrill. Jonathan can bind his ass in chains and torture O'Shea's location out of him for all I give a shit."

Jonathan congregated everyone in the courtyard the next day. It was much like that first night Sanctum swooped upon them, yet dissimilar in many ways as well. Summer had just ended back then, and the only thing chilly was the mood. Now the mood was matched by the day itself. Christmas was a little over two weeks away, and daylight faded much more quickly. As Jonah sat next to Terrence and Reena, he hoped that Reena wouldn't put her hands together by accident or something. If she did her cold-spot trick, it would make things even worse.

Sanctum Arcist, of course, segregated themselves from them yet again, but this time, it made Jonah angry. When Kaine had brought along his first batch of lackeys, Jonah and his friends managed to make progress with some of them. Gamaliel fixed that and brought these new reinforcements, while conveniently keeping around the ones whose ire never wavered: G.J., Iuris, Cisor, and Penelope. Aloisa and Michael (who made no secret that they considered the estate residents their friends now) had only been spared because they didn't leave with them on Thanksgiving. Gabriel...Jonah just didn't know. Reena had her opinion, and Jonah hoped that she was wrong, but something wasn't right about that guy. Rheadne was confusing. Jonah was aware that she was a believer in Kaine's approach and was loyal, but she just didn't seem to be as antagonistic as her counterparts.

Or maybe that just applied to Jonah. Their situation was a little different, after all.

He gave himself a mental shake and focused on Jonathan, who surveyed them with an all-encompassing gaze.

"I have a vital piece of information," he announced. "One that I believe mandates another joining of our two parties."

Gamaliel gave Jonathan a suspicious look. "Before you subject us to placing our physical lives in danger, I must ask the source of this information."

Instantly, Jonah was annoyed and concerned. Annoyed because it was obvious who Gamaliel meant when he said *us*, and concerned because he had no idea how Jonathan would let this play out. Felix had made it clear that under no circumstances could Kaine know that he was the source. How would Jonathan handle it?

"*Por dios!*" snapped Magdalena, which shocked everyone except those for those who'd been present during her rant at Thanksgiving. "May I ask you what right you have to be so suspicious of everything? When you sent people out to those bottom-feeding sazers, no one questioned the source of your—"

"That's enough, Magdalena," said Jonathan. "I have no problem revealing my source to you Gamaliel, because the source is me."

Jonah almost smiled. He'd have believed it had he not known otherwise. Jonathan hadn't scrambled, hadn't slipped in composure, and kept hit gaze on Kaine the entire time with a smile on his face, though the smile didn't get to his eyes.

"If that is the case," said Gamaliel, still not convinced, "why didn't you just say that from the beginning?"

Jonathan shook his head. "I was unaware that I needed to adhere to a hitherto unknown code of revelations, Gamaliel," he said. "I have been doing this job longer than you've been a grown man, after all."

Jonathan and Gamaliel looked each other straight in the eye. That look meant something, but Jonah didn't know what. Gamaliel ceased speaking.

"Matthew William Harrill is in Wilkesville," said Jonathan as though he'd never been interrupted. "Apparently, he has been there for quite some time."

Some of the people in the crowd made the connection, but others weren't familiar with the name.

"Is he one of those integrated Deadfallen you told us about, sir?" asked Liz.

"Indeed he is, Elizabeth," said Jonathan.

"Why would it be a problem to find him?" asked Bobby. "If he is a known integrated Deadfallen, immersed in the Tenths, the Networkers could find him, right?"

"Under normal circumstances, yes," said Jonathan. "But Harrill's situation is a bit unique. He is not just wanted and known by Spectral Law, he also has outstanding warrants with the Tenth Law circles as well. So he is on the lam."

"Odd that some of the other Integrated Deadfallen disciples haven't been helping him out," commented Terrence.

"Not really," muttered Gabriel, and once again, people were jarred by his deep voice. "The Deadfallen disciples on The Plane with No Name serve as examples for the ones that Creyton integrated. Now that Creyton is gone, they aren't willing to threaten their peaceful existences—"

"Yet they have been engaging in illicit ethereal activities to the point that Mr. Kaine and the rest of you guys had to come here, Gabe," interrupted Spader of all people.

Jonah leered at him. He'd definitely grown a set since his eighteenth birthday.

Spader looked at Gamaliel, whose face was shrewd. Iuris and Cisor looked at him with approval.

Jonah saw anger in Gabriel's eyes when he fell silent. That unnerved him.

Please don't be in league with Inimicus, man, he thought. *Please don't release all that bottled anger on Spader's dumb ass.*

"Both of you make valid points," said Jonathan, who shot Spader a stern look. "Gabriel, the integrated Deadfallen would not want their tranquility threatened, but, as Royal says, they have been acting with much more frequency. It leads me to believe that they are emboldened due to the figurehead that caused the first point of mayhem in the summer. Wyndam O'Shea."

Jonah's eyes widened. That was so masterfully done that all he *could* do was sit and stare. Jonathan had just taken Felix's information and merged it with the O'Shea situation. The tactic even had Sanctum peo-

T.H. Morris

ple looking discomfited. Terrence smirked, and Reena hid her grin as she stood.

"Let me see if I understand you, sir," she said in a controlled voice, "they want to rally behind O'Shea, who is probably trying to pick up where the 49er left off."

Jonathan had a smile in his eyes as he nodded. "I believe so, Reena. That makes Harrill integral. If he is located, he can likely lead us to O'Shea, and we can end this."

Jonah, along with everyone else present, heard the silent words that Jonathan spoke: "*And we can end this damnable arrangement with Sanctum as well.*"

G.J. took a deep breath. "So Harrill is in Wilkesville, and you probably suspect that he is using one of the abandoned textile mills as a hideout, am I right, Jonathan? So you want another mix and match?"

"No," said Jonathan. "Five groups of four. Two groups of my students, two groups of Gamaliel's students, and a final group made up of heralds. This will be December 18th."

"Those cats." Penelope didn't even try to hide her distaste. "What exactly could they do to benefit us?"

"Ascertain travel patterns via the *Astralimes* and twig portals, engage the Wilkesville spirits and spiritesses to assess illicit ethereality, and pull off a more stealthy approach than sixteen Eleventh Percenters can perform alone," said Reena. "It wasn't obvious, Pulchrum?"

Terrence snorted. Liz, Nella, Maxine, and Magdalena silently applauded. Penelope's wintry mask was merely a front; she had made the connection with what Reena had said. She was probably fearful that Reena knew of her conversation with Aloisa. Jonah looked at his sister with pride. He had never been so pleased to have been an eavesdropper in his life.

"The groups will be made now," said Jonathan. "Group one from our contingent will consist of Bobby, Alvin, Karin, and Titus. Questions?"

Not a single one of them looked pleased with that grouping, but they didn't say a word. Trip's look from the Decessio boys to Jonathan did all of the speaking for him.

Jonathan ignored every look of indignation. It was clear that he viewed the threat of the Deadfallen as a much more pressing matter. "The second group will consist of Jonah, Terrence, Reena, and Vera."

Jonah looked at Jonathan in horror. His expression could have rivaled Trip's. Why would Jonathan make such a group? Did he know that Vera hated him at the moment?

Then Jonah thought about it. If Jonathan didn't care about Trip's misgivings, then he wouldn't care about Jonah's personal dreck, either.

He looked at Reena, who shrugged. Terrence simply looked apologetic. A glance Vera's way yielded nothing. She stared at any and everything except Jonah.

But he did notice one thing. Rheadne. She gave Vera a look that was so reminiscent of hatred that it wasn't even funny. It was downright scary. It wasn't going to be pretty when Reena finally got her hands on Penelope, so he didn't even want to imagine what a fight would be like between Vera and Rheadne. Ethereal Tracker versus Time Item. Good Lord, perish the thought.

"We will play it your way, Jonathan," said Gamaliel, as though he had a choice in the matter. "My first group is my son, Iuris, Cisor, and Penelope. The second group is Rheadne, Hart, Logan, and Lia. Goodnight."

People dispersed. Rheadne caught Jonah's eye and mouthed, "*Midnight.*" Jonah nodded in a way that only she caught, and then returned his attention to Terrence and Reena.

"Did you hear that?" said Reena in disbelief. "'*My son.*' Like it was a formality. Like it was a foregone conclusion that he meant G.J., and not Gabriel. My God, if I'm right about that guy…"

Jonah wondered just how deep the hole was that Gamaliel and G.J. were digging with Gabriel. If the younger Kaine was the spy of Inimicus, then he was willingly plotting against his own family. Part of Jonah couldn't blame him. But getting in bed with people tied to the teachings of Creyton was serious shit. Was Gabriel evil? Or had he just reached the breaking point somewhere in there? Seeing as how his father and brother viewed him as a lifelong non-entity, he could have betrayed them at any time. He sighed. "We've got to watch Gabriel," he told Terrence and Reena. "He usually treks out to the estate entrance before he goes to bed. He might be communicating with O'Shea then."

"I know what to do," said Terrence suddenly. "Why can't we intimate to Bast to do a double route around the front gate or something? There is no way that Gabriel would ever notice her."

"That might work," said Reena. "But we will have to do that soon. That way, if O'Shea or Harrill give him new information or whatever, they won't have much time to do anything with it."

Jonah took a deep breath. "December 18th. Here is to hoping that Christmas miracles can come a week early."

* * *

After giving the matter further thought, Jonah couldn't understand why Jonathan had seen fit to make this a week before Christmas.

The tension was such that when Jonathan's annual transplanting of the large Christmas tree from the grounds was a welcome sight. It served to siphon off the anxiety, and people attempted to go about pleasurable routines. Liz was still stubbornly attempting to master beaded necklaces, and, truth be told, she'd made some progress. Maxine just learned to stay a mile away when she saw Liz working. Bobby didn't have football practice to distract him, so when he wasn't in the gym, he either chased his gridiron love vicariously through *Madden* or goaded Alvin into going on barefoot runs.

"Have you lost your mind?" demanded Alvin several days before Wilkesville. "It's forty-nine degrees outside!"

"Meaning what?" said Bobby, indifferent. "Fitness is eighty percent mental."

"And you're one hundred percent psychotic," grumbled Alvin.

Jonah channeled his own stress by multitasking, which had its benefits and drawbacks. He was out of school for winter break, but was left to his own devices because Terrence wasn't off from the school for Christmas just yet, and Reena had to work straight up to Christmas Eve. He spent most of his time journaling or researching Wilkesville, trying to find what would be the most logical hiding spot for Matt Harrill. He had a lot more energy than usual. Since Rheadne was in one of the groups who'd be on this Wilkesville mission, everyone spent time prepping late into the night, which meant no late evening rendezvous. Reena laughed when she saw the fervor in which Jonah did some things, but he paid her no mind. He never judged her when she didn't have her nights with Kendall.

The same day that Bobby dragged Alvin out barefoot into the cold, he went and bought Christmas presents for his friends, just like he had the previous year. That list included Rheadne, and for a reason he didn't quite know, Vera. He almost laughed (almost) when he thought of the last Christmas, where he'd been in a pseudo-duel with Felix about who got Vera the best present. Despite Felix's glitzy and rather ostentatious present, Vera admitted that she treasured Jonah's much plainer gift just as highly. That had been a pleasant revelation.

But a lot of things had changed since then.

Back then, Rheadne hadn't been in the picture.

Back then, Vera hadn't hated him.

Back then, Inimicus hadn't been a threat.

Back then, Jessica was simply a woman he couldn't stand. She didn't have a stalker, and wasn't itching to channel her inner Charles Bronson.

Jonah shook his head and looked at the purchases he'd gotten for his friends. But it was the two on top that got his attention.

For Rheadne, he got a circle scarf that was the color of her aura. For Vera, a thick chronicle of prominent female playwrights.

He sighed. Wasn't the Christmas season supposed to bring good cheer?

"Wilkesville will go great, Jonah. We've done stuff like this a million times for Sanctum."

Jonah wiped his brow and massaged his temples. It was the night before Wilkesville, and Rheadne, in her trademark forthright way, had sought him out before he'd left the Glade. He'd never say no to a night with her, but after they were clothed again, a sort of apprehension regarding the unknown overtook him.

"I want to believe you, Rheadne," he told her. "Truly, I do. It's just—it's just a feeling."

"This is why I wish that you were one of us, Jonah," said Rheadne. "Danger wouldn't be so unnerving."

Jonah narrowed his eyes. "I've been in danger before, Rheadne."

"Yeah, you have!" said Rheadne, who spread her hands. "So what's so different this time?"

That was a very great question. Unfortunately, Jonah had no answers for her.

But, as it happened, Rheadne nullified the need for answers when she kissed him again. That made the apprehension fall away.

"You're the Blue Aura, Jonah," she said once they parted. "You don't need to worry about anything. You just wait—we'll go to Wilkesville tomorrow night, drop this Deadfallen son of a bitch, and then, he can lead the Curaie to O'Shea. By the night's end, you'll be right here, celebrating the win with me."

Another kiss, and Jonah left. Once he was out of the tent, the apprehension returned. He just couldn't achieve peace about things, and he also felt disquiet about leaving Rheadne. Something was off.

Maybe he was overreacting. Maybe he still had Jessica's new vigilante mentality on his mind. Maybe he had nerves about having to work with Vera.

Or maybe those things were great distractions from the fear of the unknown.

The next night was there in the blink of an eye, and all parties met near the garage. A rather unpleasant surprise was that Jonathan needed to be a few minutes late for some reason, so he had assigned Trip to go over some things until he got there. Once everyone got over that, Trip dropped another unpleasant piece of information on them: Jonathan wanted them to drive to Wilkesville, not use the *Astralimes*.

"Why the hell do we have to drive?" demanded Hart, who, like his twin sister, Lia, was not pleased with that decision.

Jonah wasn't comfortable with it either, but if that's what Jonathan wanted, he'd have a good reason for it. But he didn't mind if Trip was an asshole to one of these Sanctum people. Indeed, his face frosted over as he considered the impertinent boy.

"Because the *Astralimes* are being monitored, boy," he answered. "Using them would place you at risk of engaging in danger before you're ready. If Harrill is alerted, he may leave town on the very *Astralimes* circuit you are so keen to employ usage of."

Logan openly turned to G.J. "What do you have to say about this, G.J.?"

"Jonathan is the one quarterbacking this, you little bitch," growled Trip. "So you better lock up that hole in your face, before I lock it for you."

Jonah almost smiled when Logan got rendered speechless. Rheadne flashed Trip a look of loathing, but Jonah had to disagree with her this time. Little punk deserved it, even if it did come from Trip.

"Wilkesville has about two thousand citizens," murmured Trip. "I think that we should start on the fringes of the four corners of town, and then work our way in from there."

"Bad plan," said Reena instantly. "It would have been great if he weren't a mobile criminal. I spoke to some of the spirits and spiritesses in that town, and found out that he is a creature of habit, believe it or not."

Trip's face was inscrutable. "You're half-smart, Katoa," he said. "I was gonna get to that. Now don't interrupt me again."

Reena's fingers tightened, but she let it go. She must have deemed trapping Harrill a more pressing matter than verbal sparring with Trip.

"I know that you guys in Sanctum have been prepping for this as well," continued Trip. "As Katoa so graciously informed us, Harrill is a creature of habit, which may expose a weakness. Lucky for them, which I guess is lucky for us all right now, Sanctum has an ethereal tracker. Rheadne, would you dazzle us with your gifts?"

"Could you be any more sarcastic, Rivers?" demanded Rheadne.

"You couldn't possibly imagine, woman," said Trip. "But, since we have a job to do, I'm afraid I don't have the time to show you. Now, kindly do what it is that you do."

He extended an interesting-looking map, which Rheadne snatched from his grasp. Jonah didn't know what she was supposed to do with that, but Rheadne spread it over the hood. They all saw that it was an extremely detailed map of Wilkesville. Rheadne placed her fingers on it, where they gleamed cerise. She scrunched up her face in concentration, and then nodded.

"Ethereal traces are the strongest in these four places," she announced, pointing them out. "An abandoned mill on Raynefield Road, just within town limits. They are present at another mill that survived the downsizings on Accel Lane. Also, they are at the only Wal-Mart in the town, and finally, a truck stop diner on Pender Road."

"Wonderful," said Trip. "I think that Jonah and Vera can take the truck stop diner."

Vera, who'd been taking most of the information in silence, finally engaged at that moment. Jonah glared at Trip. There was a savage grin on his face, which meant he knew. This was fun to him.

Rheadne's fingers tightened at her sides, but Terrence ventured out to attempt damage control.

"That's actually makes sense," he said to them all. "Trip's idea to split up the groups might hold weight. O'Shea knows who Jonah is, and is aware that he knows about the Crystal Diner. He might meet Harrill there for nostalgic reasons—who the hell knows? Jonah could—I don't know—kill the lights in the place, while Vera slows down the time in the event we might need to converge there, or something."

"Not to shoot you down, Terrence," said Vera, "but I'm not comfortable using my ethereality like that. That is one of the reasons why I was trained to keep the bulk of my Time Item ethereality from leaving the Astral and coming into my Earthplane experiences, recall that? It could get the best of me, especially if a situation gets too tense."

"That won't be a concern tonight, Vera." Jonathan appeared in their midst. "That was why I left Trip in charge, and went off-plane for a time. I needed to fashion something for you."

Jonathan extended a ring to her. Vera took it from him, looking both pleasantly surprised and puzzled.

"It's Jarelsien, like Reena's dampener," Jonathan explained. "I've placed a Protector's Proximity on it, which means that your ethereality will only function at a level that you can handle. It won't grow beyond your control."

"Well, ain't that sweet," said Rheadne under her breath.

Vera turned the ring over in her fingers. "How in the world—?"

"You forget that I was one of your Time Item tutors, Vera," said Jonathan, with a smile on his face that they hadn't seen much since Sanctum arrived. "Your skill and control are both growing, but that ring will keep things copacetic tonight."

Vera put Jonathan's gift on her right ring finger. Strangely, Jonah noticed that it looked impressive there. Even stranger, that fact made him slightly uncomfortable.

Jonathan's paternal demeanor dimmed once again as he turned to the Sanctum contingent. "In fairness, I would ask if there is anything else that you would wish to add."

"Nothing," said G.J., spreading his hands. "As Rivers has so eloquently put it, you are the quarterback."

"I assigned Jonah and Vera to the diner, Jonathan," said Trip. "I didn't think the entirety of the group needed to go to the place. Might be too conspicuous."

Jonathan raised an eyebrow, like he'd surmised that there might be more to Trip's decision that tactical planning, but he nodded. Jonah could have rolled his eyes. This was going to be just wonderful.

"You two had better hit the road," advised Jonathan. "I will designate everyone else, and then convene with the heralds."

"Take care of yourself, Jonah," said Rheadne. She didn't acknowledge Vera at all.

"You too," said Jonah. "All of you, actually."

Vera was already walking to Jonah's car before he'd left the group. He caught up with her and attempted to open her door, but she stopped him.

"I'm a big girl, Jonah," she snapped. "I don't need a goddamn thing from you."

Jonah's phone vibrated when Vera lowered herself in. He grabbed it with anxiety, hoping that it wasn't Jessica. But it was Terrence.

Talk to her, man, he'd texted. *You guys have been through too much for this bullshit.*

Jonah swallowed. Early Christmas miracles, huh? Fat chance of that. Once he got in, Vera frowned.

"Where is your G.P.S.?"

"Don't have one," said Jonah. "Hate those things."

"You don't have—?"

"Vera, you've been in my car before," said Jonah, who met her coldness. "Have you ever seen a G.P.S. in here?"

Vera turned her eyes forward. "Is it safe to assume that you already know where you're going, despite never having been there before?"

Jonah sighed. "Pender Road in Wilkesville is right off of I-40," he told her. "I passed that exit when I went to that new mall two counties over to get your *Wicked* stuff last Christmas."

Jonah had hoped to avoid having to go there, but if Vera was going to be like that, he had to shock her. And it worked. Her cold, doubtful mask slipped, and she was silent.

That silence, which was a relief and a drag, lasted the entire trip.

The truck stop looked exactly as Jonah expected. It appeared to sell everything from fishing rods, flannels that Spader would love, and enough bullets to make any Second Amendment supporter swoon. The diner, which was attached to the truck stop's side, looked slightly more reputable. Cars, trucks, and even a few motorcycles covered the graveled front.

Jonah parked in a space that proved to be a happy medium; it wasn't close enough to be in the bundle of vehicles, but it wasn't far away enough to stick out. He turned off the ignition, and prepared himself for potentially long, potentially boring wait. He couldn't expect conversation with Vera, so he pulled out his phone. Twenty minutes later, Vera broke the silence.

"The first half of your class is over, right?"

The question surprised him into alertness, but he matched her quiet voice. "Yes. It was over on the eleventh."

"Did you do well?" asked Vera.

"My last project before the Christmas break could have been better," said Jonah. "Ferrus saw fit to be a jackass; gave me a B-plus. Not that that is a problem, but I felt like I deserved a higher grade."

Very quietly, Vera chuckled. "You have him for the second half, too, right?"

"Yep," said Jonah, "and thinking of the second half of that class makes me miss Kendall's class that much more."

Vera nodded, and then there was more silence. Which Jonah broke.

"How have you been since—" Jonah stopped himself; if he finished the sentence that way, then even this paltry conversation would cease. "How have you been lately?"

Jonah could swear that Vera gleaned his near-mistake, but she decided to ignore the elephant in the room. Or was it the elephant in the car?

"I've been alright, actually," said Vera, and surprisingly, lightness had snuck into her voice. "I've actually re-established ties with some of my old acting friends. They thought that my house on Colerain Place got foreclosed. My friend Eden even thought I was an addict now, or something."

That actually surprised a full laugh out of Jonah. "Seriously? Just because you weren't at Colerain Place, you're an addict?"

"I know!" laughed Vera. "But I told them that I needed some time to reflect on things after a break-in. It was true enough, and they bought it. So all is well."

Jonah snorted. That story that Vera gave her friends was only a half-truth. She had indeed experienced a break-in, but the deed had been done by forces far sinister than burglars.

"Anyway, Eden and I wrote this play before I came to the estate," Vera went on. "We wrote it, and just stashed it. Eden believes that if it got up and running, it would take off like nobody's business. I do, too."

"Really?" said Jonah, interested. "What's the play's name?"

Vera gazed off, her mind now in her dreams. "Eden actually took the idea from a poem I wrote. It's called—"

Just that moment, a truck reversed and drove onto the road, temporarily illuminating the interior of Jonah's car. Jonah glanced out, recalling that they actually had a job to do, but saw nothing suspicious. Shrugging he turned back to Vera, but something was wrong. The way her jaw was set made it seem like she was in some sort of pain. Her eyes were on his face, but the gleam they'd had mere seconds ago was long gone.

"Vera, what's the matter?" said Jonah, concerned.

Vera shook her head, but it didn't look like it denoted that nothing was wrong. It seemed more like she shook it in disbelief.

"Vera, what is it?" Jonah tried again.

"How many times have you have had her in this car, Jonah?" she whispered.

"Huh?" said Jonah, and the word meant true confusion for once. "Her *who*?"

Vera's face hardened. "Rheadne, Jonah! Don't play stupid with me!"

"Rheadne?" Jonah looked at her, flabbergasted. What had brought this on? "She's never been in my car! Not ever!"

Vera swung out a hand so rapidly that Jonah expected a slap, but she plunged her hand into the darkness of the backseat. Seconds later, she yanked something into Jonah's line of sight.

Jonah tried to swallow, but his throat had the consistency of steel wool, or burnt toast. Crumpled in Vera's trembling fist was a brand new pink circle scarf.

"Vera, there is a perfectly good explanation for that—"

Jonah's phone rang. The sound was almost frightening, given the moment. Even Vera jumped. He put it on speaker with the one finger that still had feeling.

"Hello?"

"Jonah!" It was Reena. Her voice was as tense as his own. "Jonah, please tell me that you're at that diner!"

Alarm swooped into his head, and uncomfortably crowded itself between the dread and panic that was already there. "Of course. Where else would we be? What's wrong?"

"Jonah, he's there," said Reena.

"Excuse me?" demanded Jonah.

"Matt Harrill is in that diner!"

Jonah's eyebrows rose. Vera's anger faded.

"A-Are you sure?" she asked Reena. "How do you know?"

"Terrence and I found his hideout!" said Reena. "It's the mill on Raynefield Road!"

"How does that mean he is in the diner?"

"Shut up, and I'll tell you!" snapped Reena. "Harrill's been shackling spirits and spiritesses, like Creyton used to do. We've found them at the mill. They can't leave. But they were willing to tell us where he was so we could stop him."

Jonah glanced up at the diner, which didn't look so cozy now. "Can you help the spirits?"

"It'll take some time, but we can free them," said Reena. "But we don't want you guys there alone! We can't reach Alvin, Bobby, Trip, or Karin—"

"Trip might have something to do with that," said Jonah cynically.

"But we could reach Rheadne's crew," said Reena. "They were at the other mill. And the other Sanctum group—"

"We'll find a way to handle it," Jonah heard himself say. "Just get Terrence to call his dad. Tell him to rouse some contacts of his. It isn't like *we* can take him to The Plane with No Name."

Silence, then—

"Alright, Jonah," said Reena finally. "I'll go get Terrence; he's trying to calm the spirits. I'll text Rheadne to reach G.J. and the others. Just...just please be careful."

"We will, Reena," said Jonah. "You, too."

The call ended. Vera looked at Jonah.

"Do you have a plan?" she asked.

"I—"

"No, of course you don't," she snapped. "I got it, then."

"Wait, what?"

Vera pulled something out of her pocket and dabbed at her lips. Once she was satisfied, she pulled her blouse down so that her cleavage was much more visible, and also yanked the clamp out of her hair. It took the duration of all of those activities for Jonah to finally figure out what Vera was doing. Once realization hit him, horror did as well.

"No!" he cried. "Absolutely not, Vera! I won't let you!"

"You won't let me, Jonah?" Vera's look was scathing. "Last time I checked, my father was in Spirit."

Jonah wasn't even deterred. "Vera, no! You can't do this!"

"Watch me."

"Vera, this won't work!"

"Yes, it will!" snapped Vera. "Actress, remember!"

"Vera, that man is a Deadfallen disciple," said Jonah desperately.

"Is he really?" said Vera sarcastically. "And all this time, I thought we were dealing with butterflies and fairies!"

"Look, dammit!" said Jonah, who matched Vera once more. "Vera, please don't do this! This is not like you!"

"I know," said Vera instantly. "That's why it'll work. Just head to the back of the place, and wait for me."

She opened the car door.

"Vera!" Jonah grabbed for her, but very nearly got his fingers slammed into the car door.

Vera walked from the car, defiance in every step, but she slowed and looked less so as she entered the establishment.

Jonah couldn't believe it. He'd riled Jessica, and now she prowled the streets with a nine millimeter. Vera saw Rheadne's scarf, and suddenly she was playing honey-trap for a Deadfallen disciple.

Just how many women were going to do reckless things because of Jonah?

Then he recalled that Vera ordered him to the back of the diner.

Jonah rose from the car, making sure that his batons were well in reach. It wasn't difficult to get to the back of the diner, but Jonah hoped with everything in him that no one came out for garbage disposal or a smoke break. If they saw him, what was he going to say?

His thoughts went back to Vera. He already knew how she'd spot Harrill; Spectral Sight. As an Eleventh Percenter, he'd be the one with no spirits or spiritesses around him. But this plan was full of error. What if there were other citizens in Wilkesville who happened to be Eleventh Percenters and never knew? What if Harrill wasn't the only Deadfallen disciple in the place?

And the sixty-four-thousand-dollar question: What if Harrill discovered that Vera was an Eleventh Percenter before she saw him?

Those questions were unpleasant mental company. After almost twenty minutes of going out of his mind, Jonah was about to go into the place himself, consequences be damned. He should have forcibly restrained Vera in the damned car.

He reached for the back door, but it opened from the opposite side, and Vera burst out, breathing heavily and looking tense and poised.

"He's coming!" she breathed. "Get ready!"

Not a moment too soon. A man burst out of the back door, with the entirety of his attention on Vera.

"I was hopin' you didn't get too far ahead, darling—'"

Jonah whipped his batons out, and swung for the back of the man's head. Unfortunately, the man's reflexes were exceptional, and he caught Jonah's hand without even looking his way and flung him near Vera, who gave a little shriek and hopped out of Jonah's path.

Jonah whipped around, but saw that Harrill was ready. He had a meat hook clutched in his right hand, which gleamed a venomous green. One look at Jonah's blue-gleaming batons was all it took for Harrill's confusion to morph into rage.

"You bastards!"

He lunged at Vera with the meat hook, but Jonah swung his left baton with a plan to intercept. He'd hoped that Harrill's weapon would get caught up with his own, but Harrill surprised him again, and tossed the meat hook into the air before the two steels connected. Like a fool, Jonah glanced up at it, and what felt like a whip lashed across his chest, and he collided with a dumpster. Thankfully, he didn't get knocked off of his feet, but he was disoriented nonetheless.

Jonah saw the meat hook back in Harrill's hand, but saw no whip. It must have been an ethereality attack. But that information didn't help them now.

"What were you plannin'?" chuckled Harrill with no humor. "Did you think that you and sugar-bloomers over there could take me down? Ain't happenin', Blue Bell!"

Jonah swung again, but Harrill blocked it easily, and punched him in the mouth. The entire lower half of Jonah's face erupted with pain; it felt like the guy took his head off. Vera attempted something ethereal, but Harrill roughly knocked her away. She slammed against a dumpster, and slumped to the ground.

Jonah drilled Harrill in the back with a forearm, which propelled him forward a few inches. Harrill was barely scathed, grabbed Jonah at the wrists, and wrenched them, so that he'd drop his batons. That angered Jonah, and he head-butted Harrill. The man turned to spit blood out of his mouth, and Jonah took the opportunity to elbow him in the side of the neck. Harrill stumbled forward, but unfortunately, he ended up right at the spot where he dropped his meat hook. Harrill grabbed the thing, and swung it at Jonah with such viciousness that it was unreal. How in the hell could this evil bastard be a Green Aura?

Vera lunged forward, and wrapped her arms around Harrill's legs. Harrill laughed, but a flash of white later, his laugh turned into a howl.

Vera had extracted her knife while Harrill had been fighting Jonah, stabbed Harrill at the thigh, and drug the blade all the way down to his knee. He knocked her back, and raised the meat hook, but Jonah knocked it out of his hand and kicked it under the dumpster. Clutching his damaged leg with one hand, he raised his free one to perform another ethereal attack. Vera blinked blood out of her eyes, and flicked her wrist. Her fingertips gleamed white, and Harrill's action slowed to snail's pace. Vera's presence of mind gave Jonah a new vigor, and he manipulated the winds around him. He then pointed a sharp gust of winter air to Harrill's back, which shot him headfirst into the brick wall, where he slunk to the ground.

Finally, the man was done. Jonah and Vera had caught a break.

Jonah rolled his shoulders, and wiped blood from his mouth. That bastard loosened some of his teeth with that damned sucker punch. He was about to ask Vera how she felt when an older waitress kicked the door open with her foot due to the garbage bags in each hand. She gasped at the sight of all of them and dropped her burdens.

"Ma'am, it's okay," said Vera before Jonah could scramble. Her voice sounded harassed, and her already rapid breathing nursed it along. "This man couldn't take a hint. If this guy hadn't helped me, Lord knows what would have happened."

Jonah tried very hard to look the part of the gallant knight, and he had to admit Vera's torn shirt, blood at her forehead and nose, and wild hair made the story quite convincing.

The waitress's shock turned into a scowl as she looked over Harrill's unconscious form.

"Is that why you hurried away from him earlier?" she asked slowly.

"Yes, ma'am," said Vera, who didn't even waver.

The waitress shook her head, furious. "Men are such animals...no offense, sugar."

"None taken, ma'am," said Jonah quickly.

"Y'all want me to call the police?"

"Oh no," said Jonah. "Help is on the way, ma'am." It was true enough.

The waitress nodded, scowled at Harrill again, and went back into the diner, completely forgetting the bags she dropped.

"Damn," said Jonah suddenly. "Vera, she's going back in there to run her mouth! We don't need company of Tenths right now—"

"Have you forgotten that I'm the Time Item, Jonah," asked Vera with a grimace. "I slowed them down. By the time she starts gossiping, we'll be long gone."

"Nice," said Jonah, impressed. "But the other groups—"

"They'll all be here in five minutes," said Vera instantly.

"How can they all be here in five—? Oh."

Vera looked away from him.

"Well, are you alright at least?" he asked her.

"Still breathing," said Vera.

"You're bleeding, let me—"

He took a few steps forward, concerned, but Vera raised her hands.

"Don't even think about touching me, Jonah," she snarled. "Make no mistake. You're still on my shit list."

Jonah heaved a sigh. He hadn't even had Rheadne in his car! Why did he leave that damn scarf in there?

Suddenly, a small cabal of people convened on their location. Jonah wasn't even surprised that they'd used the *Astralimes*. The shit had already hit the fan.

Terrence and Reena both approached Jonah, but he mumbled that he was fine. Bobby and Alvin both looked relieved that they were okay, especially after they found out that they were the only ones near the Deadfallen disciple. Rheadne gave him a grin, but then smoothed over her features. Trip showed no emotion.

"Still physically alive," he said. "Oh well, no one's perfect."

"The hell with you too," responded Jonah.

"Were you able to free the spirits?" asked Vera.

Reena nodded. "They're fine. We told them to stay on the Astral Plane until further notice."

"And Dad got in contact with Patience," added Terrence. "Spectral Law Practitioners are on the way."

G.J. scoffed. "Rheadne, Hart, Logan, Lia…get on back to the camp. You too, Penny."

"Why?" frowned Rheadne.

"Not your concern," replied G.J. "Iuris, Cisor, Penny, and I will take care of this."

Jonah shot G.J. an incredulous look, but the uproar came from some of the others.

"We all had a part in this!" said Lia. "We helped!"

"You didn't do jack shit!" said Terrence. "Jonah and Vera took that guy down!"

"Just leave!" snarled Penelope at Lia. "Can't you just do what you're told? What would Mr. Kaine say?"

"You people are something else!" snapped Alvin. "*What would Kaine say?* The man isn't Jesus! Jonah and Vera caught Harrill, and you Sanctum guys handle it? Terrence has already told you that the S.P.G. is on the way—"

"WILL YOU ALL SHUT THE HELL UP!" shouted Trip. "You're all bitching like you got skipped on prom night! This is precisely why half you fools shouldn't even be here! Can we please take advantage of Rowe and this girl's lucky break and finish Jonathan's job, please?"

G.J. flashed Trip a murderous look, but then took several steps away from the group.

"Step away just in case I burst in flames, but I agree with Trip," said Reena. "We need to see this through. Now, Terrence, how far away did Mr. Decessio say the S.P.G. Practitioners—?"

She stopped speaking, but everyone knew why.

Laughter. Matt Harrill was laughing.

Everyone looked at him. Jonah, being the closest, heard it the clearest. He hadn't even realized that Harrill had regained consciousness. He braced himself, but there was no need. Harrill wasn't proving a threat. He hadn't even moved. He simply laughed.

"What's so funny?" Jonah demanded.

Very slowly, Harrill rose to a sitting position. His head bled from two points, his left eye was swollen, and his left leg was a mess, but his face showed nothing but mirth.

Jonah looked at Terrence and Reena, who were just as confused as he was. Vera forgot her anger at Jonah long enough to stare at the man in alarm. Rheadne still had her hand near her weapon, and Trip looked like he just wanted to know what the hell was going on. For once, there was no snapping between estate residents and Sanctum Arcist. They were equally puzzled.

"What's he laughing at?" asked G.J. some feet away. "Is he delirious?"

Jonah had to admit that the laughter was starting to cause him unease. He pulled out his batons, and knelt in front of Harrill. "What—is—so—funny?" he asked him again.

Harrill looked him in the eye. "Five…" he whispered, "four…"

Jonah backed away, but Harrill didn't stop.

"Three…two…one. *Per mortem, vitam.*"

Without warning, he tapped two of his fingers hard against his throat, and Jonah saw bruising that was already present there.

He felt an instant cold chill down his back; it was the darkest cold, identical to the cold that he felt from Creyton's cold fire in that dream—

G.J. took a sharp intake of breath, and everyone's focus shot to him. In complete shock, he looked down at the vivid scarlet that originated from the area of his heart, and worked its way down his jacket.

They were all horrified, but Jonah saw something that he hadn't noticed before.

A hooded figure, standing just behind G.J., wrenched a jagged knife from his back. As terrible as that was, it wasn't what made Jonah's blood run colder. It was the color that gleamed on the blade, which was evident even through the recent staining of blood.

It was auburn.

"No!" shouted Iuris. "NO! GET THEM!"

Cisor and Penelope rushed forward, but it was pointless. Like a magician's trick, a jagged stick appeared in the hooded figure's hand. A twig portal. The night's darkness seemed to wash over them, and soon just the hand holding the twig was visible. The hand snapped the twig in two, and then vanished.

Iuris, Cisor, Rheadne, and even Bobby, Alvin, and Reena crowded around G.J., who'd collapsed into Penelope's arms the minute she'd reached him. Those were the ones Jonah saw in his peripheral vision, anyway. He only had eyes for Matt Harrill.

"WHO WAS THAT?" he demanded, fear and desperation in his voice. "Was that Wyndam O'Shea? Tell me!"

Jonah knew that it almost sounded like supplication. He had to know if that was O'Shea.

"Use your brain, Blue Bell," whispered Harrill, glee in every part of his bloody face. "Who do you think it was?"

Jonah was about to grab and shake him, but Terrence pulled him away.

"Jonah, stop!" he cried.

"NO!" shouted Jonah, trying hard to break free. "I've got to know!"

"What do you expect to learn from him?" demanded Terrence, who tightened his grip. "And what did he mean when he asked you that question?"

Jonah deflated, and looked at Terrence hopelessly. "I don't know if you saw it, but the blade flashed auburn. I only know one Eleventh Percenter who has an auburn aura."

"Who?"

Jonah shook his head at this new nightmare. "Gabriel Kaine."

19

Old Lange Sign

Jonah wanted, with everything inside him, to be alone with Terrence and Reena so that they could talk things out. But, for the immediate future, that wasn't meant to be.

The rest of the night was a contradiction. A whirlwind that moved slowly. Patience and his associates arrived shortly after G.J. was attacked. They bound Harrill in fetters of ethereal steel and stood him up to use the *Astralimes* for The Plane with No Name. The bastard grinned the entire time; he even had the audacity to have a damned pep in his step (or as much of one as his bleeding leg allowed) as they disappeared.

Then there was the arduous task of moving G.J., who was somehow still physically alive. It was only a small comfort, though: one look at his bleach-white face told any rational person that he held on by fibers, maybe less. Iuris, Cisor, Penelope, and Rheadne used the *Astralimes* to move him, refusing the assistance of a protesting Jonah and Reena. Jonathan and Gamaliel, who had been notified by Trip and Karin, waited on the grounds. Reena wanted to summon the heralds that had been with them in Wilkesville to keep G.J.'s spirit in place if they could, and Jonathan was ready to summon Liz and any other Green Auras at his disposal, but Gamaliel shot that down.

"Your brat bastards are no more fit to be healers than you are to be Master of this House, Jonathan!" he snarled. "My son will go to the fort under the Old Lange Sign!"

Everyone stood around, and Jonah noticed that he, Terrence, and Reena were near Michael and Aloisa.

"Did he just say what I think he said?" demanded Terrence. "This is not the time to be thinking about New Year's Eve!"

"Not *Auld Lang Syne*," said Aloisa impatiently. "It's a healing haven of sorts where people at Sanctum who've been in fights with Spirit Reapers or other ethereal creatures can be healed discreetly and avoid the questions that the Tenths would pose. It's disguised as an abandoned warehouse under a very ancient banner that has the name Lange on it."

"Huh." Reena regarded them. "The Old Lange Sign."

But Jonah didn't care for name games. "Why do you two not look like you trust them?" he asked.

"No disrespect to the Greens we know and love," said Michael, lowering his voice, "but the Green Auras here at the estate are some of the best I've ever seen. Especially Elizabeth. I don't think that the medics under The Old Lange Sign are talented enough."

"I'd have to agree," said Aloisa. "Mr. Kaine never let it go after Jonathan undermined him." She made finger quotations around the word *undermined*. "His stubbornness is driving him to make do with potentially subpar Green Auras. Liz could probably make more headway in her sleep."

Liz wasn't too far away, restrained by Bobby and near tears in anguish.

"Let me help!" she cried, banging ineffectual fists against Bobby. "Don't let that senile old fool take him to The Old Lange Sign! Let me at least try!"

Cisor and some others had G.J. in between them on a makeshift gurney, and haughtily refused all assistance from the estate residents. Right after they spirited G.J. away, Gamaliel looked at the group at large.

"Iuris is in charge in my absence!" he shouted. "And Jonathan, when I return, we will have words."

"Of that, I am certain," sighed Jonathan.

They vanished. Liz roared in frustration.

"Why didn't you let me try? Why?" she hollered at Jonathan. "I would've done all that I could! I don't care if G.J. was an asshole jerk!"

"I know, Elizabeth," said Jonathan in a low voice. "I know. But Gamaliel had every right to do that."

"You pulled rank with Michael Pruitt—"

"That wasn't pulling rank, Elizabeth, it was honoring haven," said Jonathan. "And that was very different; Michael wasn't Gamaliel's son."

The word *son* jarred Jonah's memory. He looked over at Gamaliel's other offspring.

Gabriel stood apart from everyone. His hands were pocketed, and his face was emotionless. There wasn't anything there; no anger, no grief, nothing. He didn't even ask to go with them to The Old Lange Sign. He had simply stood there, quiet as a mouse and barely moving a muscle.

Jonathan looked at him, concerned. "Gabriel, I would never be so bold as to say that I completely understand, but if you need to talk, need to rest—"

"No." Gabriel's baritone voice was stoic. "Not necessary. Got some—got some stuff to do."

He turned and marched off. Jonah caught an odd look on his face as he turned. Had it been guilt? Shame?

Jonathan stared wordlessly after Gabriel, and then sighed again. "Jonah, Terrence, Reena," he said, "I am going to The Plane with No Name to personally question Matt Harrill. I want to speak with you three, along with Vera, when I return. I will also speak with Alvin, Titus, Karin, and Bobby, but at a later time. I should be gone about two days. The Plane with No Name exists outside of Earthplane time. I truly hope that you can get some rest after tonight's events."

He vanished. Reena instantly turned to Jonah.

"What aren't you tell me, Jonah?" she asked flat-out.

Jonah glanced at her dampener, brow furrowed, but she crossed her arms.

"It doesn't take essence reading," she grunted.

"Right," said Jonah. "Fine. But let's go to the studio. I'll be damned if I say anything out here."

"Jonah, are you sure?"

Reena looked at Jonah with such horror and disbelief that Jonah wanted to doubt his own suspicions. But the evidence that he'd seen with his own two eyes pointed defiantly in the other direction.

"I think so," said Jonah. "He told me, when he did that designation mess that he was an auburn aura."

"Gabriel..." Terrence shook his head. "I was actually starting to like him."

Reena absent-mindedly picked up a paintbrush and began to spin it. "I actually saw the auburn myself," she revealed. "It was like they tried to conceal it, but got a little sloppy."

"And the person was hooded, just like Inimicus was in Jonah's Spectral Event," added Terrence.

"Anybody could have been hooded on a December night when it's forty degrees, Terrence," said Reena.

"Just because a piece of evidence is obvious doesn't necessarily mean that you can rule it out," countered Terrence.

"If only I'd ever seen Gabriel fight," lamented Jonah. "That person who knifed G.J. moved like a true spirit. They almost had a dancer's grace. But Gabriel hasn't ever showcased any skills or talents."

"So what do we do now?" asked Terrence.

"I don't know," said Reena, who put down her brush with a little extra force. "It's still a long shot, see?"

"Reena, you were already doubting Gabriel—"

"True," Reena agreed, "but I saw an auburn aura and an auburn flash. I didn't see Gabriel. Just because I doubt him doesn't mean he's actually guilty. Many Eleventh Percenters have that aura color, Jonah. The only one that is unique is your own."

Jonah took a deep breath. Vintage Reena. Shoving a pin into his already shaky bubble. "Well if that's the case," he said steadily, "then our original plan has not changed. Watch Gabriel."

It was an interesting thing, but not a lot of estate residents were subdued by G.J.'s attack. No one was happy that it had happened, of course, but G.J. had made himself very unpopular over the past few months. Magdalena was particularly vocal about her desire for them all to vacate the premises.

"I mean, I'm just saying," she said in an innocent tone the next night, "after what happened, do you think Kaine will want to keep crashing here? I say disappear, and take your worshipers with you!"

Her words were actually met with some applause. Spader, Jonah saw, was appalled. Bobby and Alvin agreed with Magdalena, but were sorry that the man had been attacked. Jonah knew that the chance of Trip and Karin confiding their feelings was no chance at all, and Vera…well. Since she wasn't speaking to Jonah, he didn't know how she felt.

The next day, most talks focused on Christmas. Presents littered the underneath of the tree, and Jonah could see, just like last year, that his presents had no name tags, simply blue wrapping. It still seemed awkward. He took solace in the fact that it seemed that he'd be getting more presents this year; there were a great deal more blue boxes this time around. It was a bittersweet experience when he placed Vera's present under the tree, though.

As it turned out, Jonah wasn't the only one experiencing bittersweet feelings. Nella, who'd just gotten out of her high school for Christmas break, recounted an exciting opportunity.

"They've green-lit the nursing club's visit to Valentania York!" she told them.

"Wonderful!" said Douglas, who'd just come in from chopping wood with Benjamin and Malcolm. "What is Valentania York?"

Nella laid her head back on the sofa and sighed. "It's a holistic healing hospital right across the state line into South Carolina," she said. "You know how Liz actually wants her own practice to bring a personal touch back to it? I want a holistic practice. I want to help people fix themselves without excessive meds and all that. Valentania York is all about those practices. People are freed of cancer without using chemo, taught how to become fit without pills and nasty chemicals, get heart problems fixed without horse pills or surgery... they even have music therapy, which I adore. It's just wonderful. But I don't think we can go."

"Why not?" asked Maxine.

"It will be in early April, and it would require a few nights' stay," said Nella dully. "We have to come up with the money ourselves, so it's bakes sales, fundraisers, and all that stuff, but I don't know. It's almost January, and we don't have a lot of time."

"That's so unfair," said Akshara. "I mean; exactly how much do they expect a bunch of fifteen year-old girls to raise by the start of April?"

"It'd be easy," said Spader suddenly, "if you or your little friends knew how to gamble. I could give you some pointers—"

"Not now, not ever," said Liz. "And Spader, the next time you feel the need to give my sister spurious ideas about overnight prosperity, don't."

Spader shrugged indifferently. "I'm just saying. An honest life is boring."

"A fact that you are making very clear," said Jonah without thinking.

Spader and several others looked at him in surprise.

"What did you say to me?" he asked.

Jonah returned to the PS4. "Nothing, nothing."

Jonah filled Felix in on the events of December Eighteenth. Felix, too, was not sorry about G.J., but was interested in how they captured Harrill.

"You let Vera go in there alone?" he chided.

"Vera isn't some meek little girl, Felix," said Jonah, whose voice almost betrayed him. "When she puts her mind to something, she can be pretty relentless."

"Hmm," said Felix. "Maybe whatever you've done to make her jealous has also resulted in her becoming a stronger woman."

"Huh?" said Jonah.

Felix laughed, which was saying something. "Later, Jonah. I've got a Deadfallen disciple to interrogate."

The line went silent. Jonah stared at it, confused.

He'd also spoken to Bast in order to see if she'd found any interesting info on Gabriel. Bast hadn't gleaned much from her nightly rounds, but she had discovered something odd.

"*The last time I saw Gabriel Kaine, he was deep in conversation with a spiritess that I've never seen here before,*" she intimated to Jonah.

"Douglas said something similar not too long ago," said Jonah. "Did you catch what they were saying?"

Bast's yellow eyes blazed. "*He was very interested in how his father is taking G.J.'s critical status.*"

Jonah thought that was a tad bit odd. Why hadn't Gabriel just asked his *dad,* as opposed to some spiritess? He knew that his dad wasn't fond of him, but could those feelings be suspended at this particular time?

"Thanks, Bast," he said. He turned, but something splashed across his mind.

"*One more thing. There was something about a woman. Miss Seedie, it sounded like.*"

"Miss Seedie?" said Jonah with a shrug. "What would she matter? I wonder what she would have to do with all this."

"*She matters, Jonah,*" intimated Bast, "*because whoever she is, Gabriel is afraid of her.*"

Jonah gave Terrence and Reena the information right before their meeting with Jonathan in his study. Their Protector Guide had actually returned three nights later, instead of the two he said. Terrence snorted when he heard it, and Reena rolled her eyes.

"These people are clowns," she said. "Gabriel is afraid of a woman named Miss Seedie? He's more likely partaking in a certain seeded substance."

"I wouldn't dispute that at all," said Jonah, "but I'm confused as to why he is asking spirits and spiritesses about how his father is coping with G.J.'s attack. Wouldn't it be better to ask Gamaliel himself?"

"Doubt it," said Terrence, whose voice hardened. "I wonder if Gamaliel has ever spoken to Gabriel instead of *at* him. Don't take this the wrong way, but if Gabriel *did* stab G.J., can you blame him?"

"Yes," said Reena with conviction. "I would totally blame him."

Jonah and Terrence looked at her curiously, but she didn't look awkward or apprehensive.

"Look at my situation," she told them. "My mother said I was an abomination, I hate my sisters, and my stepfather didn't lift a finger to stop any of them driving me out. After all that, I still wouldn't kill any of them."

Terrence nodded shortly, as if he could understand her point. Jonah didn't know what to say. He didn't have it in him to murder family, but it wasn't like he'd have the chance. He didn't know where his mother was, and his father had been in Spirit for over a decade.

They reached Jonathan's study, where Vera was already seated. She nodded politely at Reena, and then totally disregarded Jonah and Terrence. Terrence looked at Jonah in confusion.

"The hell did *I* do?" he mumbled.

"Two things," Jonah mumbled back. "Have the audacity to be a man, and have the audacity to be my friend."

He looked at the odd assortment of items on Jonathan's desk, and noticed that the Vitasphera's interior was even darker than it had been before.

"Why is that happening?" Jonah asked. "Does it reflect the state of the realm or something?"

"Exactly," said Jonathan, who appeared right in his chair, no smile on his face this time. "The Vitasphera does just that, Jonah."

"Jonathan," said Terrence quickly, "I have to ask this before we start, because I've never known. Why do you have a necklace with the Vitasphera's Infinity emblem in it?"

At that, Jonathan allowed himself a small smile. "A mere trinket to represent my purpose," he said. "Now, let us discuss last night."

"Just us, sir?" said Vera. "What about everyone else?"

"You four were the ones who experienced calamity," said Jonathan. "Now, Terrence, Reena, tell me everything."

They recounted their story, which Jonah listened to with interest (given what happened to G.J., they hadn't really discussed much else). Jonathan listened with a quiet intensity, but spoke when Reena reached the shackled spirits.

"How long had they been shackled?" he asked her. "Did they say?"

"Four months, give or take," said Reena.

Jonathan looked away. "That means that Harrill hadn't been on the run, at least for a while. Did they tell you anything else?"

"Yes," said Terrence. "There was something about Harrill receiving messages via ethereal means from…from someone."

Jonah knew that he had almost slipped and said *Inimicus*. Jonathan caught the pause, but thankfully, Reena made the save.

"Someone is probably the only assumption we could make at this time, sir," she said. "The spirits and spiritesses probably weren't permitted to say names anyway, and even if they had been, they would have been too terrified to reveal anything beyond what they already had."

"That's true, Reena," said Jonathan, but Jonah could tell that Jonathan knew there was something more. Their mentor wasn't stupid. But he rolled with it nonetheless. "So that makes me wonder something: What exactly did you say to prompt them to reveal Harrill's whereabouts?"

"When they realized that we weren't Deadfallen disciples, it made them slightly less tight-lipped," answered Reena. "So they told us where he was. We contacted Jonah and Vera, hoping that a gut full of bad food would limit Harrill."

Jonah's mouth actually twitched as Jonathan turned to him and Vera. Reena was a health nut to the core, even going as far as to bank a capture's success on poor eating choices.

"So the story is now yours," he said to them. "How exactly did you get him alone?"

Vera licked her lips nervously. "Well, sir, I posed as a…a…"

Jonah knew why Vera had trouble finishing her sentence. Jonathan was a product of a vastly different era; one where forthright, bold women were not a dime a dozen. But the Protector Guide surprised them again.

"You posed as a slattern?" he asked her shrewdly. "A temptress?"

"Yes, sir." Vera actually blushed. "And that's how I lured him out back."

"He recovered from the trick very quickly," murmured Jonah. "But Vera got him distracted. She was brilliant."

Terrence openly snorted. Clearly, he didn't think much of Jonah's sycophantic praise. But Vera wasn't moved in the slightest.

Jonathan looked at her with awe and respect. "Titus revealed to me that you made it so they arrived on the scene with an eerie punctuality," he said. "So the Protector's Proximity was of some benefit, then?"

"Very much so, sir." Vera pulled the Jarelsien ring from a pocket and placed it on Jonathan's desk. "But if it's all the same to you, sir, I'd rather keep the higher levels of my ethereality on the Astral. Unless, of course, the situation demands otherwise."

Jonathan nodded, and turned back to Jonah, who volunteered the story.

"There was some bickering between all of us, and Harrill laughed," he began. "It was the damnedest thing. Then he did this countdown, said that Latin thing, and tapped his throat."

Jonah had actually tried to verbalize those Latin words, but Reena had been right; it wasn't possible. It seemed like his vocal chords would constrict on their own whenever he tried.

"So he said *Per mortem, vitam,* tapped his throat, and then another Deadfallen disciple ambushed G.J.," said Jonathan, his voice suddenly bitter. "Hooded, and face obscured, I'm sure. Did you make out anything at all?"

Jonah hesitated, and glanced at Terrence and Reena. They looked just as cautious as he felt. Vera, who wasn't in the know, raised her eyebrows in impatience. "The person tried to conceal the color of their aura, sir, but they failed," he revealed. "It was auburn."

"Auburn." Jonathan sat back slowly, a change in his expression that Jonah couldn't place. Was it comprehension? Disbelief? He truly did not know.

"Yes, sir," said Jonah. "I wanted to be sure, so I asked Harrill. I'd hoped that it was Wyndam O'Shea, but he told me to use my brain, and then asked me who I thought it was."

"And what is the answer to that question, Jonah?" asked Jonathan instantly. "Who do you think it was?"

Jonah took a deep breath. He should have known that all roads would lead to this, especially if they held nothing back from Jonathan. "Well, sir, the fact of the matter is that I've only met one auburn aura—"

"—and that would be Gabriel Kaine," finished Jonathan.

"Huh?" said Jonah, who then swore softly and gritted his teeth. Jonathan nodded.

"I thought so," he said.

Vera's mouth slowly fell open. "Gabriel? G.J.'s own *brother*? I can't believe he'd do that!"

This coming from a woman who got into a bloodbath with her own sister, thought Jonah, but he didn't say it. "How did you know, Jonathan? You supplied Gabriel's name without even thinking about it. Why?"

Jonathan rose and paced the length of one of the bookshelves. "Two reasons, Jonah," he said at last. "First, I've known Gabriel's aura color all along, because I know the aura of everyone who has ever traipsed these grounds. Second, when I interrogated Harrill once he was on The Plane with No Name, he, ever so slightly, alluded to Gabriel not only gravely attacking his older brother, but also being a *disciple* of a disciple."

"But sir," Reena blurted out, "I freely admit that Gabriel's actions are suspect; I've even wondered about his loyalties myself. But conversation about this has me feeling that he might be a long shot after all."

"Reena, you've said that already," said Terrence wearily. "But the evidence is *right* there in our faces—"

"Exactly," pounced Reena. "Right in our faces. Don't you remember what Reverend Abbot taught us about perfectly placed puzzle pieces?"

Jonah's eyes narrowed. That was a phrase that he'd committed to memory. Terrence had probably allowed it to ooze out of his ears the second it lost relevance. But Vera was in the dark.

"Please bring me up to speed," she asked them. "Reverend Abbott hasn't actually taught *me* anything."

Jonathan, who loved to see his students form answers on their own, motioned for Reena to continue.

"The reverend told us that phrase last spring during that 49er mess, Vera," she answered. "He said to be critical of answers that came in beautifully-wrapped boxes, because they were too obvious. He said that if the thought process was such that it took almost no thought at all, that's when you needed to be leery."

"Right," said Jonah. "But Reena, how is this a beautifully-wrapped box?"

"Jonah, we just touched on this before we got up here," said Reena. "Gabriel is a pariah in his own family. I don't know if Gamaliel hates him or simply treats him as a non-entity. G.J. is no better. Hell, none of those people are any better. It seems as though he has been reminded of his deficiencies his whole life. He's been compared to his older brother his whole life. You heard what Felix called them: The Heir Apparent and The Accident."

"Ouch," whispered Vera.

But Jonah was now with Reena's train of thought. Reluctantly. "All of his baggage makes him an obvious suspect," he said.

"But explain this, then," said Terrence. "If Gabriel is someone's patsy, if he is a Christmas present thrown to us from Wyndam O'Shea by way of Matt Harrill, then why does he do the nighttime strolls? The talks with unfamiliar spirits and spiritesses. The complete lack of emotion he showed when he found out his brother had a new hole to breathe out of, only he ain't breathing too well out of it."

"You all make good points," said Jonathan. "Gabriel does have motive, but he's far from the only auburn aura in existence. I will follow his moves. I will be on his case. I would do that anyway, seeing as how he's not thinking clearly at the moment. But at the same time, and despite the consequences, you apprehended Harrill, and that brings us one step closer to Wyndam O'Shea. Praise is in order, even under the circumstances. You may all go."

They all rose. Then Jonathan seemed struck by a sudden thought.

"Jonah," he said quietly, "Wyndam O'Shea has just lost one of his allies. It might serve to force his hand in some way, shape, or form. That said, check on Miss Hale."

Jonah sighed. "Yes, sir," he muttered. "I'm on it."

But Jonah, try as he might, could not get in contact with Jessica. It wasn't until Christmas Day itself that he made any contact at all, and that was with Ant.

"It's bad news, Jonah," Ant told him. "Jess is getting reckless; it's like that gun has made her crazy. She's doing all this stupid research, too."

"Research?" Jonah frowned, even though he was on the phone. "What the hell does that have to do with anything?"

"She's so focused on finding her stalker, Jonah," said Ant. "You gave her his name, and she has been searching for him ever since. For some reason, she's even bought an almanac to track down moon cycles. That mean anything to you?"

Jonah tightened his eyes, but didn't answer.

"I don't know what to do, Jonah," said Ant.

"You have to rein her in," said Jonah seriously. "I don't care how you do it; tell the Te—I mean, the police that she's exhibiting erratic behavior or something."

"She won't listen to me," said Ant hopelessly.

"Be a damn man, Ant!" snapped Jonah. "Turn on the charm! Offer her some foot rubs or spa treatments or something, I don't know! But get her away from that damned gun!"

He hung up the phone and tried to clear his head. It was Christmas, after all.

Terrence, along with his mom and Reena, whipped up an amazing Christmas dinner. Jonah finally got to meet Liz's mother and sisters, which was something that Nella had wanted to happen for a while (Their father was out of town on business, but would be back later in the day). Liz's mother, Patricia, was just as chipper as Liz and Nella, but she was four inches over six feet tall, which made conversing with her a bit emasculating (jokingly so). Sandrine, who was darker-featured and much more serene in temperament than her mother and younger sisters, was just as pleased to meet Jonah as he was to meet her. When he thought about it, Jonah had to realize that Bobby had really lucked out. His girlfriend's family was just as awesome as she was. How many couples could say that?

Christmas Day also brought Terrence's whole family again. Mrs. Decessio was in one of the best moods ever; she adored having all of her sons around. Terrence also proudly displayed the postcard that he'd received from his adoptive brother, the football legend Lloyd Aldercy.

Douglas spent most of the day trying to avoid his grandmother's criticisms, which Jonah could only laugh at when he caught glimpses, such as:

Mrs. Chandler: "I don't see why you have to keep a lamp on at night. That expends energy that you ought to conserve—"

Doug: "It's a personal choice, Grandma! You know that I'm not fond of the dark!"

Mrs. Chandler: "Why are you afraid of the dark, boy? Dark is what you get when you close your eyes! You afraid to go to sleep, too?"

Jonah had given Douglas flack in the past for his feelings toward his grandmother, but the exchange he'd just overheard started to make him believe that he was too harsh in his judgment.

Reena had gotten Jonah a leather-bound journal with some of the sturdiest pages he'd ever seen. He'd gotten her a Victoria's Secret gift card, which she looked at in horror.

"You might not be all that feminine," said Jonah, "but Kendall is. Besides—" He whipped a huge stack of painting canvases from behind his back, which prompted Reena to laugh and embrace him.

He got Terrence a set of cooking knives that were plain old steel, and an anthology of the Duke Blue Devils' championship basketball teams. Terrence returned the favor with a fiction genre manual and a new pouch for his reading glasses.

It was a simple enough matter for Jonah to look over and see if Vera had opened her present, especially with Reena chasing Sterling all over the family room for shouting, "Merry Christmas, Reenie!" at the top of his lungs. Vera tore it open, ran her fingers across the ebony cover, and closed her eyes. Then she looked in his direction, as if she sensed his eyes on her. He turned, and forcibly engaged Malcolm in conversation about his new woodworks.

Spader had let it slip—though how he knew was anyone's guess—that Iuris had ordered that no one in Sanctum's camp have any contact with the estate residents. Somehow, that didn't include Spader himself. Jonah knew for sure that Terrence had slipped hefty Christmas plates to Michael and Aloisa, with express instructions to tell no one where they got the food. He was sure that they wouldn't divulge, anyway; the food was too good to share.

When Jonah took out milk for the heralds, he took his chance to give Rheadne her present. The surprising thing was that she wasn't too keen to see him.

"Thank you," was her flat response. She didn't even look at the scarf. "Merry Christmas."

"That's it?" said Jonah, confused. He hadn't expected a present from her or anything, but this reception was daunting.

"What were you expecting, Jonah?" she asked him in a rather pointed manner. "To spend the night with me?"

"God, no!" said Jonah, shocked that the question was even raised. "Do you think I'm heartless? I know you guys are worried, and your focus is on G.J. I just wondered if you needed to talk, or—"

"Well, I don't," Rheadne interrupted. "It's not safe to talk, anyway. Good night."

That made Jonah a little puzzled. They'd had to take certain stealthy measures all those nights they'd had sex, and now it wasn't safe to simply converse?

Jonah could almost understand Rheadne's reticence. He usually wanted to be alone when he was stressed himself. But damn, such a reception was disturbing. Not to mention odd.

He hurried back to the estate, where the mood was much lighter.

12:06 AM

It had been the New Year for twenty-four hours and six minutes. Jonah, Terrence, and Reena spoke well into the night. The three of them were thankful to be in the minority of Eleventh Percenters who hadn't spent the whole day in a fog from a New Year's hangover. They were now on their way upstairs after laughing at Malcolm, who'd passed out at the kitchen table, and Bobby, who was carrying a slumbering Liz to her bed. The poor girl was out after *two* glasses of wine.

"She's learned her lesson," said Reena seriously.

"She only had two glasses!" said Jonah. "The girl is light for a lightweight! I could do better, and I hate alcohol!"

"Maybe I should see what my threshold is with drinking," said Terrence pensively. "See if I'm as lucky with it as food."

"You never know, man," said Jonah. "You guys did pretty well when I taught you how to do Mind Cages."

"Not a good plan," said Reena sleepily. "That's a different sequence of influences on your system—"

Reena's educational monologue was cut short by an almost primal cry that came from the family room. Malcolm shot up from the table, looking around wildly, while Bobby nearly dropped Liz, who hadn't stirred. Jonah was a different story. Every bit of his drowsiness faded. Terrence and Reena looked the same.

"You think I should—?" began Bobby, but Jonah shot him down.

"No," he said, "put Liz to bed! We'll see what's up!"

They reached the family room, where several people already stood, frozen in shock. Jonah's eyes widened.

It was Gamaliel.

He was on his knees, and gave no notice to the gathering audience around him. Jonah noticed that there was a scream in his eyes that was even more striking than the horrible cry they'd just heard.

"What is going on?" demanded Magdalena, who was one of the furthest away.

"He just came through the *Astralimes!*" said Ben-Israel, who seemed to have scrambled out of a recliner. "The old man almost face-planted!"

Gamaliel looked as if he didn't register any of this conversation. After a sequence of rasps, he raised his voice to a bellow that almost outstripped the earlier cry.

"JONATHAN!"

Everyone stood in awe. Maybe a little fear.

"JONATHAN!" the elderly Eleventh Percenter roared again.

Maxine, who'd flinched at the shouting, looked around in desperation. "Where is—?"

But then a dark silhouette appeared next to Gamaliel, and Jonathan was there.

"Gamaliel?" he said in alarm.

Gamaliel looked like a shattered man, a man who had seen one too many battles and decided that he'd seen too much. "IT'S ALL YOUR FAULT!"

"What are you—?"

"MY SON IS NO MORE!" Gamaliel shouted, his voice a troika of rage, disbelief, and despair. "NO MORE! AND YOU KILLED HIM!"

20

The Eris Effect

There was silence after Gamaliel's words, which spiraled horribly as the collective processed the news.

"Gamaliel," said Jonathan, who looked troubled at the news but befuddled by that last proclamation, "I give you my condolences for your loss, but I'm not sure that I follow—"

"Your plan." Gamaliel's voice achieved a power that his aged form no longer could. "I went along with your cock-and-bull plan, against my better judgment. I knew that nothing but misfortune could come of it!"

The front door banged open, and Iuris, Cisor, and Penelope spilled into it. Gabriel brought up the rear, but it seemed that he had come of his own accord and not as one of this pack.

"Mr. Kaine!" exclaimed Iuris. "We saw spirits moving about the yard in an uproar, saying that they followed you. What is wrong? Is it—?"

He put two and two together. Jonah almost felt sorry for him. Almost.

"No," he murmured, looking to the others that came with him. "*No.*"

Jonah looked at Gabriel, and distinctly saw something like a furtive guilt in his eyes. His mouth opened slightly, but then his expression shut down. Jonah felt another chill. Was the obvious suspect actually guilty this time? Was Gabriel guilty of fratricide?

"Pens," said Cisor in a hollow voice, "go alert the camp."

"Belay that, Penelope." Gamaliel rose, hatred in his gaze. "You will all hear me out before anyone spreads the word about my poor boy. It's entirely the fault of this undead vapor that my son is gone from me."

He pointed at Jonathan.

"Wait a second," began Malcolm heatedly, but Jonathan stopped him with a hand.

"He is speaking out of grief, anger, and despair," he told him. "Leave him be."

Jonah had clenched his fists. *Undead vapor?* Who the hell did he think he was?

"You are damned right I speak out of anger!" snarled Gamaliel. "G.J. is gone from us; your plan was a trap!"

"Wait, what?" said Cisor, glaring at Jonathan with suspicion. "What do you mean, sir?"

Gamaliel was so crazed that when he spoke, clumps of snuff flew out of his mouth. Many people near him shrank away. Reena looked as if she was fighting back a comment.

"The infallible Protector Guide here said the information on which he based this godforsaken adventure was his own," spat the old man. "That was a lie! The intel came from that mistake of nature, Felix Duscere!"

If Jonathan was still of the flesh, he probably would have paled at that moment. Jonathan closed his eyes.

"Duscere?" Penelope whispered to Jonathan. "The half-breed? Your big plan was from him?"

"Felix is a contributing member of society," snapped Jonathan, tired of the epithets. "He is not a half-breed. The information held weight, but anyone with even a partial brain would know that you'd have never entertained it—"

"That freak has hated me for years!" Gamaliel fired back. "He has had it in for me since before he debased himself with the contents of liquor bottles—"

"Because you gave his father a hard time!" Terrence blurted out, to everyone's surprise. "You rooted for Preston Duscere to fail just because he was a sazer! I pray that you aren't surprised that his son isn't really high on you!"

Gamaliel fixed Terrence with a glare so cold that it chilled the air. "Sazers are evil, boy," he rasped. "Born out of sin, and reared in disgrace. Their only redeeming quality is that one day, they pass into Spirit."

"Whoa," mouthed Jonah. That one was cold. Subarctic, even. And this man had the audacity to act like this after the passing of his son!

"Gamaliel, that is enough!" snapped Jonathan, whose composure had long since faded. "I was not honest with you, for reasons that I have already explained, and have no need to further clarify. You have my sincerest condolences for your loss, and I mean that from the bottom of my heart. I understand that you're upset, but I will not allow this hatemongering and finger-pointing in this residence. The blame of G.J.'s murder lay exclusively with the wielder of the blade that nicked his heart. And that was neither Felix, nor I."

"You have no heart, Jonathan," whispered Gamaliel, whose eyes never left Jonathan's face during that whole exchange. "You are but one rung above poltergeist; I don't give a damn what your title is. G.J. is gone, and it is your fault for being so trustworthy of subhuman creatures."

"Alright, you damned old fool," growled Jonah, who'd reached his boiling point. "Get the fuck out of here. Pull up your tents and bail hell on out! If you hate us so much, they why are your asses still here? You have my word as a gentleman that nobody here is stopping you."

"Mind your manners, Rowe," warned Iuris. "It's clear that Jonathan's standing, and your status as the Blue Aura, have given you a high opinion of yourself. But you're still just a bottom-feeding accountant. Make no mistake."

Jonah stepped forward, but Terrence and Reena pulled him back.

"And trust me," said Cisor, "we will leave when we are good and ready. Until then, be mindful of the granting of haven. We will most definitely use it until our business is done here."

"What is that business?" snapped Magdalena. "What is the point of your continued stay here?"

They ignored her, and focused only on Gamaliel, who had burst into angry tears. Near the door, the broken father launched into another tirade.

"Why my son!" he demanded. "It should have been you!" He pointed at Bobby. "Or you!" Maxine this time. "Or especially you!" he pointed at Douglas. "You stink of worthlessness!"

Douglas looked shocked and angry, but Jonah was more worried about Bobby. Liz was up in bed, and not down here to calm him.

Luckily, Jonathan barred Bobby's path before he'd even moved.

Gamaliel never ceased, and he stumbled near the threshold. Gabriel attempted to assist him, but Gamaliel leered at him.

"It should have been you, Gabriel," he cried out in rage and grief. "It should have been you!"

Gabriel's eyes widened in pain and shock, and Jonah feared for Gamaliel's physical life even further. He needed to stop saying things like that to his younger son. If Gabriel had actually killed G.J., Jonah had a feeling that he wouldn't balk at dropping his father, either.

Finally, they were gone, but Gamaliel's high-pitched exclamations were still audible. Everyone looked at Jonathan, whose gray eyes had the brilliance of laser beams.

"Carry on, people," he said through clenched teeth. "It's quite late, so your bodies will welcome the rest."

He vanished, but rest was the furthest thing from anyone's mind.

"Was that true?" asked Bobby. "Did Jonathan get that information from Felix?"

"Yes, he did," said Jonah. "God only knows how Kaine found out."

"But why did Jonathan need to lie?" asked Nella.

"You heard him, Nella," said Reena. "Kaine has a vitriolic hatred of sazers."

"So what if he was a sazer?" asked Maxine. "They're good at vanquishing vampires, aren't they?"

"There is more to them than just being vampire killers, Max," said Jonah sharply. "That's the main issue with close-minded Elevenths concerning sazers. They're good enough to *clean* the kingdom, but not good enough to *live* in said kingdom once it's clean. And Kaine out there? He wants the ethereal world to be sazer-free."

"Closed-minded elderly people are the bane of life, I swear," sneered Magdalena. "Seriously, the world would progress light years ahead if all the old, inflexible geezers would just pass into Spirit."

"Magdalena Cespedes!" said Reena, appalled. "Tell me that you didn't mean that!"

Magdalena hung her head. "No, I didn't," she mumbled. "It just had the right emphasis that I needed."

"Emphasis?" demanded Spader, coldness in his voice. "What if someone said those very words about your mom, Magdalena? Or your *abuela*?"

"First of all, keep your Spanish to yourself, Spader," snapped Magdalena. "I said inflexible; my mama and my *abuela* are progressive women. You don't have any right to call me out on anything, you tatty, pilfering bum."

Spader gritted his teeth, tossed an ace on the table, and left. His absence was practically ignored, as Maxine continued the conversation.

"The way that Kaine spoke to Jonathan! Blaming him for G.J.'s murder! Who does he think he is?"

"This conversation doesn't need us," mumbled Jonah, who tapped Terrence and Reena, but Reena had her eyes on Douglas. Jonah looked that way, and understood.

He quaked with fierce anger, and stood by the door like he wanted to kick it down.

"Can't say I blame him for being pissed," said Terrence. "He just got told that he stank of uselessness. His grandma probably hasn't even taken it there."

Thinking of family downing other family members jarred Jonah back to Gabriel, but he didn't say anything until they were all upstairs. "I'm sorry to beleaguer this point," he said, "but I'm convinced that Gabriel had something to do with G.J."

He told them about Gabriel's look of guilt and regret, then that impassive mask after Gamaliel's outburst.

Reena still looked undecided. "Jonah, that could very well have been the conflicting emotions he felt after losing his brother," she replied. "We just don't know if he's hurt anyone."

Terrence scoffed. "What changed exactly, Reena?" he asked. "You were the first one to doubt the guy all that time ago, and now you're determined to believe the best of him?"

"It's not that at all," said Reena. "I told you already that my stance changed when all roads began leading to him. Schemers that move in silence do not have blatant variables like Gabriel. The man's earned the right to be emotional right now. Yeah, he didn't exhibit much emotion, but between his brother's passing, his stupid father, and whoever the hell Miss Seedie is, the man's earned the right to *something*."

"I can't help but wonder," said Terrence, "how did Kaine find out it was Felix's plan?"

"Doesn't matter," said Jonah. "What matters is the fresh hell that has now been dumped on us."

"I don't think it's possible for you to be any more distracted than you are right now, Jonah Rowe."

Charlotte Daynard gave Jonah her trademark detached smile and a look of curiosity. He had a bunch of graded papers in his hands from Ferrus' class that he'd completely forgotten were there.

"I'm sorry, Miss Daynard," he said. "I just zoned out. What did you just ask me?"

"You young people and your inability to focus," sighed Miss Daynard. "I was asking if you had any worthwhile goals for this New Year."

Jonah pulled a face, but immediately smoothed it out. This year had already gotten off to an auspicious start, and school resuming wasn't even a relief after Jonah had seen his new semester's syllabus. Papers and exams would only serve to compound his already overflowing life even further. Yeah, he had goals. Surviving and keeping his head above water. Not that he would go into any of them with Miss Daynard. "I don't know if setting goals would be a worthwhile thing, Miss Daynard," he said. "Let's just say my goals would be…unrealistic."

Miss Daynard pushed her solitary grey hair behind her ear. "We all move through our lives so fast, Jonah," she said, with only the merest trace of inflection in her meditative voice. "I assure you, slowing down and taking things into perspective might work wonders for you. There are no unrealistic goals, just unrealistic approaches. This year could bring the end of unhealthy cycles and arrangements, as well as bring about welcome change for everyone. Especially for you."

Jonah was taken aback. That was a truly kind thing to say. And all this time, he'd written Charlotte Daynard off as some weird older lady who probably had more animal companionship than people. Though that could still be true, she still had nice and considerable side. "Thank you, Miss Daynard," he said. "I'm grateful for that. And I hope your New Year is full of great things as well."

She smiled. "It will be, Jonah," she said with conviction. "It will be."

The great thing about the new semester was that when it started, January was already almost over. So when February rolled in, Jonah had a decent routine again. His job at Two Cents was buzzing as it was the beginning of the new semester, and the funny stories were no different from last year. Remembering the promise he made to the spirit of Whit Turvinton's father, he did whatever he could to assist him, whether it was helping out with work, working one of the registers (which he loathed), or simply taking time out to converse. Jonah liked to think that his actions had benefit of some kind. Whit always seemed pleased and appreciative. But the consideration and kindness also had the unexpected side effect of making him even more attractive to Lola Barnhardt. She always found an excuse to compliment him or praise him, and always managed to make sure she was situated near him. Though Jonah didn't know how to repel her, he found himself wishing that *other* women he knew could be so receptive.

That situation was…unclear. Vera had made it obvious through in-difference and non-responsiveness that she wanted nothing to do with Jonah, which he had simply come to accept. He didn't like it, but it was what it was. What he couldn't accept, due to the fact that he could neither explain it nor understand it, was how Rheadne was acting to-ward him.

Since G.J.'s passing, she had been aloof and downright standoffish with him. He just didn't get it.

And he may as well be honest with himself. He missed the nights with her. It wasn't something that he lost sleep over or anything (though that was the case for a little while), but he missed her.

Initially, he thought that she and G.J. had had a thing, but Michael dashed that suspicion.

"G.J. was married to Mr. Kaine's cause," he told Jonah. "I assure you, that was not the case. But I'd better get back."

The fact that Michael and Aloisa had to hurry back before anyone realized that they'd had a conversation with an estate resident was ab-surd. It had been bad enough that Gamaliel had returned last Thanks-giving with a new bunch of lackeys, but since he'd lost his oldest son, he had practically cut off all contact with everyone in the estate. His people trained amongst themselves in their camp. The only one who had free reign was Spader, and Jonah couldn't fathom what he had to talk about with them. Bast had idly intimated that she'd seen Spader with Iuris and Cisor a great deal, speaking in hushed tones. She also said that Iuris and Cisor always seemed really pleased after those con-versations. He didn't know what to make of that, and when he told Terrence and Reena about it, they couldn't come up with clear opin-ions, either.

"Can't you use your essence reading?" Jonah asked Reena.

"Wouldn't do any good," Reena replied. "It wouldn't matter if I gleaned mischievousness and deviousness from Spader, because he al-ways gives off that vibe. He gambles, steals, and stashes away money. I wouldn't find anything that wasn't already obvious."

Jonah sat back and sighed. The woman had a point, as usual.

Trip, who trusted no one and trusted Sanctum Arcist less than that, surprised many people with sound experiments. When anyone asked what he was doing, he usually responded with a sneer or no response whatsoever. He sometimes recruited Karin, Markus, or Grayson to join him as well. Jonah remembered that Jonathan had Trip spying on the camp. He wondered what he'd gleaned, if anything. When he threw caution to the wind and questioned Grayson (who was much more approachable now than in the past), Grayson told him something very interesting.

"Trip is like a man possessed," he revealed. "It's almost like he's trying *too* hard. I've never seen him like this, and that's saying something. He must be on to something big."

Gamaliel's tirade after New Year's had left some lingering effects on certain residents. Bobby channeled his frustration in the weight room and on the road, usually dragging Alvin along. Maxine, who was another that Gamaliel told should have been in Spirit in G.J.'s stead, plunged herself into her Anime and Manga whenever her frustration got the best of her.

But Douglas was the worst by far.

Jonah had seen a marked change in Douglas' demeanor since that night. Sometimes he'd sit off in a corner, staring off into space, and then begin breathing heavily as though he'd been overcome with anger. He'd actually threatened to saw off Spader's head after witnessing him conversing with Penelope. That alone alarmed many people; Douglas would usually apologize with a red face if he ever said anything out of line. Not the case nowadays.

Jonah had an intense chess game with Douglas about two weeks into February. While he was still far from proficient, he had picked up a great many things. He tried his hardest to be strategic, and his improved skills had served him well. After a short time on thin ice, he saw an amazing opportunity.

"Uh, knight to king four," he said as he made the move.

Douglas' eyes widened, like he hadn't anticipated Jonah's making such a move. He picked up a chess piece and rolled it in his fingers, looking here and there on the ethereal steel chessboard. He seemed to be having a hard time, which made Jonah feel a flicker of excitement. This was the very first time that he'd ever gotten Douglas on the ropes...

Then without warning, Douglas roared and flung the chess piece with unusual force. It flew past several people and broke out a window.

"Douglas!" cried Jonah. "What the *hell*, man?"

Douglas ripped himself from the table, upending his chair in the process. He didn't answer, but Jonah caught disconnected words from him.

"Should have been me...damn old bastard fart...wasn't even my fault his brat got killed..."

His action left the previously lively room in silence. Terrence moved from his perch, and Reena dropped her sketch pad as they both went Jonah's way.

"What the hell was that about?" demanded Terrence. "Jonah, what did you do?"

"I didn't do a damned thing!" Jonah was instantly defensive. "I made what I thought was a decent move, and then Douglas threw a fit, and tossed a chess piece out of the window! He's lost his mind!"

"No, he hasn't," said Reena, eyes on the broken window. "He's had enough."

"Enough of what?" asked Jonah.

"Enough of the putdowns," answered Reena. "He puts on a brave face when his grandmother does it, but I bet he remembers every word, and it infuriates him. I think that that comment Kaine made about him the night G.J. passed into Spirit was the last straw."

Jonah thought on it. Douglas dealt with just as much criticism as anyone, but he let on like he took most of it in stride. Now he could see that that wasn't entirely accurate. It made him think about all the verbal abuse that Kaine regularly piled on Gabriel once more. One day soon, that crazy old man was going to be abrasive to the wrong person.

"That old man's got to go," he said flat-out. "He and all his buddies need to leave. They have no reason to still be here, anyway. Kaine's mouth is going to lead to a huge problem. He's already lost a son, but if he keeps on like this, it will only get worse. He reminds me of something Nana used to always say."

"What was that?" asked Reena.

Jonah took a deep breath. "She used to say that sometimes, crazy people can make even sane people act crazy."

February was now near its end, and Jonah looked forward to work. When he went in, Turvinton volunteered information about his wife and toddler. Surprisingly, the tangential information had a point after all.

"My wife and son have shown me that I have to move forward," he said.

Jonah's eyes didn't gleam, but all of his attention was on Turvinton now. "What do you mean?" was all he said.

"You may not have noticed, but I've been dealing with my father's death," he said. "Dad was my best friend. He was my whole world. Then he left—" he shook his head. "He died. And I wasn't doing too well. But I took a good look at my family, and realized that the best way to honor his memory is to be the best that I can be for Celia and Colton. So I'm taking conscious steps to move forward."

Jonah felt like a weight had been taken off of his shoulders. It wasn't a heavy one, but it was still a welcome change. Turvinton had come to the conclusion on his own, and was stronger for it. Indeed, when Jonah went into Spectral Sight later on, Turvinton's father's spirit stood nearby, speaking no words but looking very pleased. His composition had diluted somewhat, but Jonah wasn't dismayed. His boss had started healing, and it showed physically and spiritually.

Class went by without incident; Jonah didn't even fall asleep. The next assignment due in Ferrus' class was by far the easiest thing that Jonah had even seen, and he'd already made up in his mind that he was going to complete it before the next class, two weeks before the deadline.

Hands down, the uneventful days were the best.

He got home that night and saw movement in Sanctum's camp. Maybe they were training. He didn't care. Not his concern. Gabriel stood just inside the gate, with his head down, but Jonah didn't engage him in conversation. Gabriel would still be a questionable character tomorrow. He'd worry about him then.

He got out of his car and nearly slammed into Douglas.

"Sorry, Jonah," said Douglas idly.

"It's alright, Doug," said Jonah. "How're you—?"

He frowned at Douglas' appearance. He was not in his usual khakis, polo, or vest and bowties, but a white jogging suit and cross trainers. He looked so foreign in the getup that Jonah actually did a double-take to make sure that he had the right guy.

"I'm trying brisk walking," he explained. "Reena said that it helps with purging anger and negative thoughts."

"Ah." Jonah understood instantly. "Well, is it helping?"

"Nope," said Douglas.

Jonah almost laughed. "Doug, I hate them, too," he said. "Okay, not all of them. But I know what you're feeling."

"I don't like being angry, Jonah," said Douglas. "But just because I'm tired of my anger doesn't mean I don't still have it."

"I know what you mean," said Jonah. "But trust me, they aren't worth it. Not Old Dust, Mason, Cisor…none of them. Keep up your walking. It might even help you deal with…other stuff."

Jonah meant the remarks that Doug's grandmother always made when he said that, and he hoped that Douglas could see that. Douglas acknowledged it with a quick nod.

"Here's to hoping so," he told Jonah. "See you later."

Jonah clapped Douglas on the back, and headed inside.

Most of his friends had busied themselves with their usual pursuits, and Nella was telling Reena about how the fundraiser was going.

"It's not entirely fruitless," she said, trying hard to be upbeat. "We've gotten some funds, but it's a lot of stuff that we need money for."

"What exactly are you guys needing to cover?" asked Terrence.

"Room and board, food, gas…" the manufactured gleam in Nella's eyes dulled with every expense she named. "It's—it's a lot. But Valentania York is a big deal. It'd be worth its weight in gold."

Reena looked at Nella as though she respected her determination, but just couldn't see how they'd be successful. She didn't shoot her down, though. "I'll tell the folks at my job about your trip. Those folks love donating; makes them feel more virtuous than they actually are."

"I'll whip up some sweet confections for you, Nella," volunteered Terrence. "Can't go wrong with bake sales. The cheerleaders at my high schools always make stacks of cash from 'em."

Jonah felt like he ought to do something for Nella as well, but he couldn't think what. Maybe he could piggy back off of one of Terrence's or Reena's suggestions. The thought made him feel like he was contributing at least, and that was a very good feeling.

Dinner was yet another Every Man for Himself Night, and Jonah made do with leftover short ribs and mac and cheese. Once he'd eaten, he had no interest in lingering in the kitchen any longer than he had to, because Vera was there. He was about to explain to Terrence about the nice head start he'd planned for Ferrus' newest assignment when the strangest feeling washed over him. It was neither an intuition nor a premonition; it was cold hard fact.

A change had occurred. A change that was horribly wrong. Something had happened, and the consequences of it would be something that no one wanted to experience.

Jonah hoped that he was just being dramatic; hoped that he was overreacting. It wasn't like he was some clairsentient who could feel when things changed. But at the same time, Liz, who was in the process of tearing turkey meat, looked around wildly.

"Did you feel that?" she said in an uncertain tone to the room at large. "I just got, like, the strongest feeling of… of bad."

Jonah looked around. The confusion was shared by everyone. But in Reena's case, it wasn't confusion. It was fear.

"What is wrong with you, Reena?" asked Terrence before Jonah could. "Do you know what—?"

"I think it's called an Eris Effect," she breathed.

Jonah looked at her, his mind a composite of exasperation, admiration, and confusion. How the hell did she know these things? How did she keep them all straight in her mind?

"I read, Jonah," said Reena suddenly, a trace of irritation mixed with her fear.

"How many times do you have I to tell you not to read my essence, Reena?" said Jonah wearily. "But that's beside the point. What is an Eris Effect?"

"If what I read a while back is accurate, it's the feeling you get before an event that blights things," said Reena. "An event that has caused deviation from harmony—or the established harmony, anyway."

"And we would feel that why—?"

"We're ethereal humans, Jonah," said Reena. "Attunement is second nature, remember?"

"I know that, Reena," Jonah shot back. "I mean why would we be feeling blighting events?"

That very moment, a herald, bright brown and slightly heavier than Bast, entered through the flap in the kitchen door. His eyes were wide and his hair was on end. He stopped at the first Eleventh he saw—which was Alvin—and began to intimate thoughts. Alvin's eyes narrowed at first, but then widened so strikingly that Jonah thought that they'd pop out their sockets.

"Oh my God," he whispered, rising from his seat in horror. "OH MY GOD!"

"Alvin!" cried Bobby. "What did the herald intimate to you? What did he say?"

Alvin wrenched open the back door open with such force that some of the glass cracked, and flung himself into the night.

There was no hesitation as the entire group tore off after him. Jonah, Terrence, and Reena almost bowled over their own friends over to get to the forefront.

Not very far from the kitchen door, they found out what the herald intimated to Alvin.

Alvin stood frozen, mere feet away from two individuals, one kneeling and one prone.

It took awhile for Jonah, Terrence, and Reena to realize that they had achieved their goal of reaching the front. As a trio, they approached this odd scene, reaching Alvin first.

"Alvin, I want to know what that herald told you—" began Terrence shortly, but a look from Reena stopped him.

She seemed as entranced as Alvin as she pushed Jonah aside and went straight to the two figures on the ground.

Jonah followed her, tired of the dramatics, but Reena grabbed his arm.

"Jonah, no!" she hissed. "We'll only make matters worse!"

Jonah hadn't forgotten her vicious shove, and batted her hands away. When he reached the two figures on the ground, however, he saw what she meant.

The prone form choked and gurgled, while the ragged breaths decreased in quality as blood ran from the neck in such quantities that it reddened the yellowed winter grass. When Jonah saw the face, his own breath became ragged.

On the ground, his physical life fading with each spurt of scarlet, was Gamaliel Kaine.

He looked at Jonah with pure terror. He tried to say something, but it wasn't meant to be. Gamaliel's bloody hand slid from his neck as his head sank to the side. The silence left after his ragged breaths was deafening.

But it was pierced by a horrified voice.

"I didn't do it. I swear on all things ethereal. I didn't do it. It wasn't me."

The voice shocked Jonah for two reasons. One, because he didn't expect that voice, and two, because he instantly recognized it.

The voice belonged to the person kneeling next to Kaine, whom Jonah hadn't registered after he'd realized that it was Kaine on the ground. The person's hands and clothes were both covered with Kaine's blood.

It was Douglas.

21

Illuminations

Jonah stared at Douglas like he was an absolute stranger. Douglas stared right back, almost pleadingly as he did so.

"Jonah," he said anxiously, "it wasn't me. I just got here like five minutes ago. There was so much blood—I—I tried to help—"

"Douglas," interrupted Jonah, whose breath was shallow, "what the hell happened?"

"We need to discuss this anyplace but here," said Terrence. "We do not want to be found here! We need to go!"

He tried to wave away the curious crowd that had chased Alvin and the herald outside. If Jonah had been thinking straight, he would have realized that it wouldn't have been right to just abandon the scene, but his attempts to get an answer out of Douglas and Terrence's attempts to clear the crowd were noticed by Rheadne.

"There was an Eris Effect," she said loudly, "is that why you are all out here?"

Then her eyes fell upon Douglas and Kaine's body. Every particle of breath seemed to leave her body at the sight.

Jonah wished that Douglas hadn't tried to help. From a bystander's standpoint, he looked like a murderer. He was covered with enough blood to fill an old-school washbasin.

"I didn't do it," repeated Douglas yet again, but Rheadne hadn't moved.

"Rheadne, listen," said Jonah steadily, but she slowly raised her gaze, and once again, Jonah felt fear. The change in Rheadne's face was such that he thought she had experienced a walk-in. Seriously; he imagined that her spirit had suddenly been replaced by some vengeful, wrath-seeking force.

"What have you done?" was her wintry demand.

"We didn't do anything!" said Jonah. "Doug here says he found Kaine here, and I believe him—"

"MR. KAINE'S BEEN MURDERED!" Rheadne bellowed.

That was the moment that Reena rediscovered her voice. "Rheadne, you have to stop!" she yelled. "You don't understand; *we* don't understand—"

But it fell on deaf ears. Or maybe Rheadne simply didn't hear Reena over her own yelling.

"MR. KAINE'S BEEN MURDERED! THIS GRANNISON-MORRIS BASTARD KILLED HIM!"

"No!" said Douglas, who shot his eyes up to her. "I didn't! That's what I've been trying to—!"

Responders to Rheadne's words thundered across the grounds. Jonah heard exclamations from his friends in the crowd, heard Alvin shriek, "Where the hell is Jonathan?" and Terrence shout, "Alvin, pull yourself together! This shit just got worse!"

Sanctum Arcist had approached them so quickly that it was almost like they'd used the *Astralimes.* They were led by Iuris, Cisor, and Penelope. There were cries of shock and outrage, but Iuris' expression was that of a seething feral beast.

"What have you done?" he snarled. "What happened here?"

"That's what we were trying to tell Rheadne!" snapped Jonah. "There was the Eris thing, and a herald alerted us, and then we found Doug—"

"WHO'D JUST KILLED OUR TEACHER!" yelled Rheadne. "It's a good thing I was out here, or they'd have found a way to cover it up! I heard that one—" she jabbed a finger at Terrence— "telling them that they didn't want to be seen here! He was trying to get them to run!"

Terrence swore. "It wasn't like that! I just meant that this was serious and—"

"YOU'RE GODDAMNED RIGHT IT'S SERIOUS!" roared Penelope. "Mr. Kaine is on your ground, lying in his own blood, most of which is on this Chandler boy's clothes! If you want to be a savage, Chandler, get away from our leader's body. I'll give you a crash course that you will not enjoy—"

"To hell with that," growled Rheadne, who pulled something from her pocket that began to cackle dark pink, "I'm ripping the bastard's throat out."

"Wait, what?" Douglas scrambled to his feet. "I did not do this! I swear to God!"

"Swear to your ass for all I give a shit," snapped Cisor. "Rheadne, drop him!"

"WHOA WHOA WHOA!" Jonah jumped in front of Douglas. "You need to stop this! You have no idea what has happened! You're about to do this based on partial information!"

Jonah felt movement behind him, and realized that Reena, Terrence, a recovered Alvin, and Bobby had closed in around Douglas. Their other friends, who'd been some feet back during this time, moved forward.

Rheadne hesitated when Jonah jumped in front of Douglas, but Iuris pushed her aside, wielding a thin steel bar that gleamed with the color of his aura.

"Protect him if you wish," he whispered. "We'll just kill you all!"

"No you won't."

Jonathan appeared in front of Jonah, which stopped Iuris short. Jonathan looked emotionless. Calm. But his voice told a different story.

"Would you bring about carnage based only on what you've seen?" he demanded. "As an Eleventh Percenter, Mason, you should know how foolhardy that is. How many times have people been deceived by what they see?"

"Spare the floridity, spirit!" snarled Penelope. "What we see is out leader broken and finished, and your boy there covered in his blood!"

"I DIDN'T KILL KAINE!" Tears of anger and confusion ran down Douglas' face. "I didn't have that knife! I tried to help!"

"What knife?" demanded Penelope. "Where did you stash it?"

"I didn't stash it!" said Douglas. "It's not what you think! I didn't kill him!"

"That's like the umpteenth time you've said it," said Rheadne, her hard expression loosening enough for shrewdness. "Trying to reassure yourself? Trying to believe the lie?"

"He's telling the truth!" roared Jonah. "I can vouch for him! He was walking laps around the grounds for stress relief—"

"Right," said Cisor. "Because Mr. Kaine told him that he should be the one in Spirit and instead of G.J. He told the stumpy muscle head too, as well as Goggles back there."

"Motive," said Rheadne. "He was pissed about that since Mr. Kaine said it; I heard that he even chucked a chess piece out of a window the other night out of anger."

Jonah shut his eyes in frustration. Spader kept them well informed.

"Last time I checked," said Nella coldly, "chucking a chess piece out of a window wasn't the prerequisite for being a murderer!"

"How right you are, Chubby," said Iuris. "But what is about to happen isn't murder; it's vengeance! SANCTUM!"

Jonah and his friends were blinded by a dazzling of endowments as a weapon appeared in each and every Sanctum hand. Jonah heard more cries of alarm in his own crowd. Numbly, he wondered why they all happened to be endowed, but he couldn't devote much thought to that at the moment. Liz cried out, "No!" somewhere behind his back, but then something very unexpected happened.

Trip seemed to fall out of thin air. He drew back his hands, much like Reena did when she did her cold-spot tricks.

"Alright, you little fucks!" he snarled. "Through my ethereality, I can mimic the sound frequencies of amplified guitar riffs and the auditory disturbances of a Ghost Wave, not to mention vibrations of a dozen old-school boom boxes."

Some people looked confused. Others defiant.

"Let me break it down to the simplest common denominator, so that even the stupidest of you will understand," said Trip in a low, yet crystal-clear voice. "If I join my hands together, I will rupture your eardrums. I will make you see your lunch for a second time today. And oh yeah, some of you may be comatose for a while. Makes me no difference, but I just thought I'd inform you."

Iuris narrowed his eyes. "You're bluffing, Deadfallen spawn."

Trip's face didn't change. "Would you like to test me, pumpkin?"

A few people shrank away. Rheadne and Penelope looked at Trip's hands, alarmed. But for some strange reason, Iuris and Cisor looked neither alarmed nor afraid. They looked at each other and smiled.

"You know what this means, Jonathan," said Iuris. "Your sazer-perverted plans cost us G.J. Your boy there, Chandler, has just killed out leader, and you have refused to give him up. This only ends one way."

Jonah frowned. Behind him, Douglas said, "What does he mean?"

"War," grumbled Terrence, who looked at the residents of Sanctum Arcist with anger. "They are declaring war on us."

"Very good, Terrence," said Rheadne. "Know and understand that this could have been avoided. But that's all for shit now. Mr. Kaine will be avenged."

"If you think you can enact war on my lands, you will be sorry," said Jonathan calmly.

Iuris maintained that strange smile. "The benefits of haven are that we can wipe out all of you bastards and you couldn't touch us."

"You obviously fail to comprehend the finer points of haven," said Jonathan softly.

"We know what we need to know," said Penelope, who looked at Rheadne with newfound respect. "I knew you had it somewhere in you, girl."

Rheadne's eyes lowered to Gamaliel's body. "Loss brings out the worst in me. All my reason died with Mr. Kaine."

"Death isn't real, Rheadne," said Jonah at once.

She glared at him. "Whatever helps you sleep at night, Jonah," she said.

That dark, inhumane glare really affected Jonah. This was a woman with whom he had an easy friendship that became personal, and then physical. And now they were on opposing sides of a potential blood-bath. He didn't know what to feel. *How* to feel. But his personal feelings were hardly of any relevance at the moment.

Iuris and Cisor lifted Gamaliel's body and returned to their line, where they passed off the frail, physically lifeless burden to a grim-faced Sanctum man. Iuris then turned around to face Jonathan, Trip, Jonah, and everyone else.

"See you soon," he promised.

The Sanctum people began vanishing, their campsite right along with them.

* * *

If the Grannison-Morris Estate had been a normal place, Jonah would have described the family room as jam-packed. But this wasn't a normal dwelling place. Every single resident was in that room, comfortably placed.

But unfortunately, the comfort stopped there.

The faces were tense and fearful; Jonah could have given Reena a run for her money as an essence reader with the way he was gauging people's feelings at the moment. Maybe he was much more improved at it.

Or maybe those were his own feelings.

A momentary distraction was Nella, who had flat-out shot down Liz's request that she return home to their parents.

"Nella—"

"I won't!" snapped Nella. "I will not abandon my sister! Or any of my new friends!"

"Nellaina Sybil Manville—" began Liz authoritatively, but Nella waved a hand.

"Liz, that old trick doesn't even work when Mom pulls it," she told her. "I'm not leaving. Live with it."

She looked afraid, but her voice was set.

"Baby," said Bobby, pulling Liz away from her younger sister, "she is no more willing to leave than *you* are."

Liz scowled, but gave up.

Jonathan had insisted that Douglas shower and change clothes before anything else happened, and now he sat prime-placed on the center sofa. Douglas had his head in his hands, crying unabashedly, but Jonah knew that the tears had more to do with anguish than anything else.

"Jonathan," he kept saying, "you have to believe me. I'm innocent! But I can't let you guys go to—to war because of me. Let them take me. My grandmother always says that I don't have a brave bone in my body. Here's my chance to be brave."

"Douglas," said Jonathan, unimpressed, "it is not bravery to allow your physical life to go up in flames for something you didn't do. I know you're innocent, because I know *you*. As for your grandmother and all her remarks, well...Maudine's opinions are immaterial."

"With all due respect, Jonathan," said Trip, whose hands were suspended in mid-air along with Karin's and Markus', "if you are basing your belief in Chandler's innocence solely on faith—"

"Yes, Titus," said Jonathan sharply, "that is exactly what I'm doing. Now please stop speaking, do as I've requested of you, and listen." He turned to Reena, who knelt at the bloodstained clothing. "Do you have anything for us, Reena?"

Reena's eyes were tightly closed, her fingertips yellow with her endowment as she concentrated. She released a shuddering breath, and then her brow furrowed. "Doug is indeed innocent, Jonathan."

There were exhales of relief all around the room, but Jonah didn't share their comfort. As it turned out, Jonathan didn't, either. His eyes remained on Reena's befuddled face.

"But?" he asked.

Reena opened her eyes. "But Gamaliel's essence in his lifeblood has been...blocked," she said. "I swear, it feels like someone has put a brick wall up and is preventing my essence reading from reaching further depth. I've got nothing beyond Doug's innocence."

There was a look in Jonathan's eyes that Jonah didn't like. It looked as if he comprehended something that he wasn't willing to share.

"Jonah, you have been endowed," he said without warning, and Jonah reveled in the surge through his body. "Now, please assist me. Douglas, I need to know what you know."

Jonah understood. He needed to balance Douglas' hysteria. He set his mind to it, knowing that after the experience Doug had had, it wouldn't be an easy task.

Douglas swallowed hard, and dried his face. "Ever since that night after New Year's, I couldn't shake what Kaine told me," he began. "I'd never been so hurt and angry in my life. So I was walking laps to try to channel emotions. Then I ran into Jonah, who gave me some kind words—"

"That's true," said Jonah. "I can vouch for Doug, like I said."

"Thanks for that, Jonah," said Douglas. "But after that, I was walking again. I had half a mind to go up to Malcolm's woodshop and coax him into a chess game when Gamaliel appeared in front of me."

Jonathan's eyes narrowed. "Appeared? As in used the *Astralimes?*"

"No," said Douglas, "there was no wind. He just kind of faded into view."

"Okay," nodded Jonathan. "That means Auric shielding or a twig portal. What happened next?"

Douglas, at this point, seemed to be pleading with his eyes again. "Jonathan, I'm not crazy," he said. "I swear I'm not—"

"The swearing and prefacing are unnecessary, son," said Jonathan in a reassuring voice. "I am aware of both your innocence and your sanity. Now, tell me."

Douglas licked his lips. "Kaine appeared in front of me, holding this—really sharp knife," he said. "That thing looked almost a foot long. He wasn't the evil, condescending jackass that he usually was. He was scared. Scratch that; petrified is a better term. Jonathan, I have never seen someone that frightened in my life. He might have been wearing a bomb or something. He looked me right in my face and said, '*Don't make me do it. Don't make me. Please.*' But before I could figure out what he meant, he just—just rammed that blade into his neck."

There were gasps of horror all around. Terrence hung his head and muttered, "Jesus." Jonah winced, and Jonathan looked away, bitterness in his features.

"He did it himself," he said, "but he didn't want to?"

"No," insisted Douglas. "He didn't want to. He was horrified. The blood...Jonathan, it was like a burst mane. I tried to help him; tried to apply pressure. That's how his blood got all over me. Then there was this—this feeling that things were going to go a whole lot worse before they got better, if they even got better at all."

"The Eris Effect," murmured Jonathan. "Now close your eyes, Douglas. See if there is anything else in your mind that we may need to know."

Douglas did as he was told. Jonah fine-tuned his focus, and helped him balance as best he could. Then Douglas' eyes shot open. "Jonathan," he said, "I forgot. I should have told you right when I started. When Kaine held that knife, it was gray. That was his aura color, right? But when he dropped it, it vanished. Before it did though, it flashed another color."

Jonah felt a chill. He glanced at Terrence, whose expression was just the same. He couldn't catch Reena's eye, but he saw her tense.

"What was that color, son?" asked Jonathan.

Douglas swallowed. "It flashed auburn before it vanished."

"Damn!" shouted Jonah, bringing every eye to himself in the process. He looked around awkwardly. "Sorry, everyone. It's just that there is only one auburn that I know—"

"Damn right." Bobby jumped in unexpectedly. "The other Kaine boy. The freak show with the baritone voice."

"Gabriel?" Liz's eyes widened. "Wait...wait. Gabriel wasn't anywhere around last night!"

Jonah frowned. Liz was right. He'd only seen Gabriel just inside the gate, when he'd returned from LTSU. But when Gamaliel had been found, he was nowhere in sight. Had he struck again? The blade that had claimed G.J.'s physical life flashed auburn, too. Had Gabriel cracked after all the years of maltreatment? Or had Wyndam O'Shea found the perfect candidate to do some of his deeds?

But another thought came into his mind. This felt familiar, and he couldn't shake it. He had the wildest, most powerful feeling that something about this was familiar. Why was that?

"Did Gabriel do this?" asked Malcolm. "Was Doug in the wrong place at the wrong time?"

"Or the *right* time, if someone needed a reason to light a powder keg," said Bobby.

"Why would anyone go to such lengths as that?" said Magdalena. "It's no secret that Sanctum hates us, so who would pull the trigger, and actually give them an excuse?"

Now Reena actually did turn around and looked at Jonah and Terrence. They knew someone. Inimicus. Dammit, Wyndam O'Shea. Was this all his intricate plot? Creyton was nothing more than a trace in a cold fire now. Was O'Shea getting revenge for that or something?

"Jonathan," said Trip suddenly, "you should know that this just got kicked up a notch."

"What?" said Jonathan warily. "What do you mean?"

Trip raised his hands higher, and his fingertips gleamed a more brilliant red. "They just called in June Mylteer."

Jonathan rolled his eyes in disgust. Reena rose.

"June Mylteer?" she demanded. "*The* June Mylteer?"

"Since you already know who he is, Reena," said Trip coolly, "please allow me to resume my silence."

Reena's nostrils flared, but Jonah intercepted.

"I am so sick of being behind," he said, "but who is June Mylteer?"

"Child of a sazer father and Eleventh Percenter mother," said Jonathan. "He was practically raised at Sanctum Arcist."

"Why would a girl named June be such a problem?" asked Maxine.

"June is a man, Pearson," snapped Trip. "June is short for Junior. His given name is Abram Mylteer, Jr."

"Hey, Trip," said Jonah, "that silence thing? Stick with it. Give it your best shot. Now, why would Sanctum work with a known sazer?"

"He's not a sazer, Jonah," said Reena. "His dad is. He is simply an Eleventh Percenter, like his mother, Emily. That's one of the reasons Kaine was so high on him; he believed him blessed because he didn't get his father's sazer genes."

Jonah made a wry face. "Okay. So what's his deal?"

"Think of the mob," said Terrence. "Think of Sanctum Arcist as an ethereal Mafia—"

"That isn't hard," muttered Liz.

"—and June is like the wartime consigliere," finished Terrence. "A tactical savant and master strategist. You'd like him, Doug. He makes your chess strategies come to life."

"I don't like anything concerning Sanctum Arcist right now," grumbled Douglas.

Nella frowned for some reason. "I've seen those old movies," she said, "A consigliere is only worth anything if they have intimate knowledge of their enemy. Sanctum people only had access to lower-level bathrooms at the estate for the showers and what have you. They haven't seen much else; they don't know much else—"

"They have a source." Liz's eyes froze over. "A gossip girl who just happens to have man parts. What have you told them, Spader?"

Like predatory beasts, everyone tensed and turned to Spader, who started so hard that he fell off of his chair. He rose just as quickly as he had fallen, fear and shock on his scruffy face.

"But I didn't—"

"Royal, stop," said Jonathan in a quelling voice. "Just stop. I've known that they've been manipulating you ever since you showed an amenity to their way of handling their affairs. I simply believed that you'd eventually figure it out, given the questionable schemes you've been responsible for in the past. Am I correct in surmising that they promised you a place among them?"

Spader's eyes widened. He truly had no idea that he was being duped. Jonah would have felt sorry for him if he didn't hate him at the moment.

Douglas rose, leering at Spader. "You betrayed us?" he whispered. "You've been feeding them information on us all this time?"

"No!" shrieked Spader. "Just details about the estate! Iuris told me that they liked the place, since Sanctum is more like compound than a house setting—"

"WHAT NEXT?" shouted Douglas. "What are you going to say next? That you didn't know what they'd do with the information? You play people every day, Spader! How could you not know when it was happening to you? I thought we were friends, you bastard!"

He scrambled over the seat for Spader, with assault clearly his intention. Jonah thought it would be interesting to see such a vanilla guy go postal, but Jonathan rose.

"Stop," he told Douglas. "Royal was manipulated. He was not in control. The fact that he takes advantage of people does not make him immune to being taken advantage of himself."

"Man," said Terrence, "I hope I'm that forgiving when I'm in spirit form."

"But know this, Royal." Jonathan's voice was neither friendly nor understanding, despite what he'd just told Douglas. "You could have caused us a grievous setback had I not already known that you were being used. Since we have other concerns at the moment, your wrongdoing will be dealt with later. No one is going to work, school, or anywhere else this morning."

With a jolt, Jonah and many others looked beyond the windows and saw blood-red streams through the trees. They had literally been in the living room all night long, and almost no one had noticed.

"I will handle any excuses that you will need," Jonathan went on. "Have no worries in that regard—"

"Jonathan," Trip broke his silence yet again. "Knock knock."

Inimicus

An insistent rap on the door made them all jump. Jonah couldn't help but have a grudging respect for Trip's mastery of sound. But that was where it stopped.

Jonathan motioned to person nearest to the door—Spader—to open it.

A man of about thirty stood there, dressed in black and red. Jonah thought that his dark brown faux-hawk was tacky, but the expression was serious and determined.

"June," said Jonathan. "It's been a while. How is Emily, son?"

June didn't look as cold as most of the other Sanctum people, but the look in his eyes was something like disbelief. "She's gotten a hold of her cholesterol now," he answered. "A simple tonic from a Green Aura in Vero Beach. Now she can't go one day without telling everyone how she mastered it all on her own. Woman is something else—"

"Jonathan asked how your mama was doing, Mylteer," snapped Trip, "he didn't ask for a speech. Now skip to the end and tell us why Sanctum sent you here."

June's face hardened somewhat. "Good ol' T3," he mumbled. "Still got the heart of a broken brick. Fine. They want a conventional parley."

"What?" said Jonah. "Conve—with you?"

"Not me," said June. "I get sent to rogue situations because I can be dispassionate and detached."

"Your father's a sazer, June," muttered Reena. "One would have expected you to pick up a trick or two."

"But I feel this one," June admitted. "Jonathan, I've never liked you much, but I have more respect for you than a little bit, and my dad has always spoken highly of you. So the fact that one of your kids killed Mr. Kaine—"

"That is false, June," said Jonathan. "We've discovered new developments—"

"Save them for the meet," said June. "I am only the messenger. Right now Sanctum views you as rogue Elevenths. Iuris Mason's distinction, not mine. The meet is at 3:30 this afternoon, in the town square, near the Presbyterian Church. Mason has included himself in the reps, and he has chosen the ones that he wants to meet from your side."

"And who are they?" asked Jonathan, bored. "Do tell."

"There are Iuris' words, not mine," said June. "But he specifically said, and I quote, The Blue Beetle, The Food Network bitch, and Sodom and Gomorrah."

Jonah's blood began to boil. Blue Beetle? Food Network bitch? *Sodom and Gomorrah?* This was a serious matter; a potential war breakout was as serious as it was ever going to get. And they still saw fit to exhibit such immaturity?

Terrence breathed hard through his nostrils. Reena's form quivered with rage. Jonathan didn't look too hot, either, but when he spoke, his voice was neutral.

"Very well, June," he said. "Until next time."

June looked sincerely concerned. He didn't look like he was out for blood. "Jonathan," he said, "is it true? Did this boy, Douglas Chandler, kill my leader?"

Jonathan actually turned his back on June. "Would it change anything?"

"It would for me," said June.

That gave Jonathan pause. He turned back to June. "Douglas Chandler killed no one. He was in the wrong place at the wrong time, due to his desire to be a Good Samaritan. We know the truth, but we don't have any proof of it at the moment."

June released a breath, and Jonah could have sworn that a weight of stress lifted off of the man. He looked as if that was what he needed to hear. "Get proof, sir," he said, supplication in his voice. "I will do what I can to stall, delay, and redirect them."

He left. Bobby stared after him.

"Huh. So Kaine and his oldest son didn't manage to bite the heads off of everyone halfway decent at Sanctum? That's something."

"People rarely fit the boxes in which they're placed, Bobby," said Jonathan. "June's always been a good kid. Never really agreed with me, because my methods don't involve attack first, question later. But he's always been fair and decent. Now I need to find proof of Douglas' story."

Reena looked at Jonah, and nodded. The time had come. They had some time to do it, at least until 3:30.

"We'll help them out around here," said Terrence. "You take care of that, Jonathan. Food Network bitch... wow."

"Don't complain," snapped Reena. "I got Sodom and Gomorrah. I know exactly who said it. I will break that bitch, I swear to God."

Jonah walked straight up to Jonathan. "Let's talk, "he said bluntly.

"Talk, son," said Jonathan, who had just intimated something to Bast.

"Not here, sir," said Jonah. "It might be a lead on some proof."

Jonathan looked at him. "The den," he said.

They made the walk, and once there, Jonathan shut the door.

"What do you know, Jonah?" he asked.

Jonah ran his tongue across his teeth. "There is something that I should have told you a long time ago," he said. "It deals with someone labeled Inimicus. We think—well, I think—that Inimicus is Wyndam O'Shea, and also that Gabriel is working for him."

Jonathan looked pensive. "Inimicus," he said. "The Embedded Enemy. The one you miss when you never even knew they were there to miss in the first place."

Jonah nodded. He'd long since gotten over being stunned by the things that Jonathan knew. The man even knew the truth about Greek mythology, for God's sake.

"There is another side to that coin, Jonah," said Jonathan. "And that is Scius."

"True," said Jonah, "the obvious enemy. That was the 49er. He threw down the card before Trip buried him with the Ghost Wave last summer. The card burned the Scius illustration, and revealed Inimicus."

Jonathan sighed. "So Inimicus is in the game," he said. "Tell me, Jonah, did you get any inkling of O'Shea being Inimicus in your Spectral Event?"

Now that stunned Jonah. "You know about that?"

"I know the Protector Guide who did it," said Jonathan.

"Really?" said Jonah. "Because he told me that I'd forget his name. Can you tell me—?"

"Not important," said Jonathan.

"Right," said Jonah, instantly realizing that it *wasn't* important at this particular moment. "Well, when O'Shea massacred the Crystal Diner, it was a full moon. I saw him in the event, and then I saw him at Bobby's first football game. Both times he had a limp. He was talking to that cold fire, which was Creyton. A trace of his presence, anyway. But how is that?"

"A wonderful question, Jonah," said Jonathan. "So you believe that O'Shea is taking commands from the cold fire, is doling orders to other integrated Deadfallen, and pushed Gabriel into succumbing to his underlying rage and kill his father and brother? In essence, you believe that Inimicus has orchestrated this whole debacle, and that O'Shea is Inimicus?"

This was why Jonah loved this guy. He nodded and almost smiled. "Initially, I thought that O'Shea was trying to do what the 49er was doing last year. But now, I'm—I'm just not so sure."

Jonathan nodded. "It is a lot to prove, but none of it is impossible. I'm glad you told me this, Jonah."

"I got to ask, sir," said Jonah cautiously, "but what will you do with that info?"

Jonah managed a half-smile. "Matt Harrill may need another visit," he said. "Leave me now. And my very best wishes with the parley."

Jonah's eyes narrowed. "You believe that this will actually bear fruit, Jonathan?"

Jonathan's expression was neutral. "What are we without our hope, Jonah?"

3:30 P.M. was on them before they could blink. They'd spent the day trying to figure out ways to repel the impending attack, but they were at a loss. They were Elevenths with practice weapons who were about to be besieged by trained fighters fueled by the loss of their leader.

Prodigal—who'd use the *Astralimes* to the estate once he'd received a text from Terrence—offered to round up some friends from the sazer underground, but no one thought that was a great idea. The presence of more sazers would probably galvanize Sanctum even further.

Which meant that most everyone's hopes and terrors lay in the success of this parley.

Reena was completely at ease in the square; the cold was no problem for her. Jonah wasn't too troubled. Not with the weather, anyway. But Terrence was angry.

"Why did they want to have a conventional parley in this cold ass square?" he snapped. "Probably to mess with us with some more! We could have had it at the estate, seeing as how they know everything about the damn place."

"I can't believe Spader," grumbled Jonah. "To let those people turn him all about like that! How did just allow himself to be sucked in like that?"

Terrence snickered. Jonah looked at him, frowning.

"What was that?"

"Huh?" Terrence pulled Jonah's trademark slip-up right out of his book.

"You laughed at me, Terrence," said Jonah. "Why did you do that?"

Terrence sighed. "You were so mad about Spader, Jonah," he said. "But you don't seem to realize that you and Spader are in the same boat."

Jonah blinked. "Excuse me?"

"Of course you're blind to it," shrugged Terrence. "Having a fine-ass woman fucking your brains out will do that."

"What?"

"Oh, God," moaned Reena. "This is *not* the time for this."

"Seriously, Terrence?" said Jonah. "You knew all along?"

"One day," Terrence shook his head, "you guys will realize that I'm not as dumb as I look."

"I didn't—nobody said—"

Three people appeared in front of them, tossing twigs down at their feet: Penelope, Cisor, and, because of course, Rheadne. Penelope had actually had the audacity to get dolled up for this; she was attired in a plum-colored pantsuit, and had her dark-brown hair pulled back in a high bun. She looked like a damned school teacher about to supervise detention. Rheadne's eyes were still bloodshot, and she didn't look like she gave much thought to her appearance. Cisor, with his buzz-cut, glasses, and indifferent demeanor, looked as though he wanted this to be a formality. He looked like he wanted this to fail.

The three of them sat on a bench directly across from Jonah, Terrence, and Reena. Penelope broke in a cold smile.

"So June can relay a quality message," she murmured. "And your quickness on the uptake is remarkable!"

"It was low was what it was," grumbled Reena. "What if we sank to that level, huh? What if we had called you the Bitch, the Skank, and the Scarecrow?"

Rheadne rose, but Cisor placed a hand on her arm.

"Easy," he said. "This is a parley. Now, you three, this does not have to be long, or difficult. You want Sanctum to go away? You don't want us to beat the holy shit out of you? Then some teensy things that need to happen."

Jonah straightened. "As this is a highly volatile situation," he said, "I could do with a laugh. What are your demands?"

"Simple," said Cisor. "We want Douglas Chandler, unendowed and in ethereal chains, the current whereabouts of Felix Duscere, half of the ordinance in your armory, and your Vitasphera."

Jonah stared. And stared some more. The demands were so ridiculous; he had almost braced his ears to hear a laugh track. "Why do you want those things?"

"That's easy, too," said Penelope. "The first one is because Chandler will be drained of all of his lifeblood, just like he did to Mr. Kaine. Second, Duscere's been begging for a release from physical life since he came pissing out of his mother's womb, and now we have a reason to do it. Third, it's about time that your practice weapons be put to good use. And finally, Mr. Kaine was a million times more of a guide than your peace-pipe Casper. We will bury the Vitasphera with him. That's our price to leave you be."

"That's all well and good," said Terrence, "but there is just one problem: you're bat-shit crazy! Doug didn't do anything; Kaine was forced to kill himself! Felix would go into Red Rage and run roughshod all over your wannabe-warrior asses. We don't give a damn if that happens, to be honest. And Jonathan's Vitasphera is passed from *estate* guides. You want a trinket to throw in the ground with Kaine? The Bargain Mart's open till nine."

"You—!" roared Cisor, but Jonah forestalled him with a look of mock confusion.

"Easy," he said quietly, "this is a parley."

"This is serious." Clearly, Reena had had enough of the rigmarole. "What we need is time. We have information that may exonerate Douglas in your eyes and put your focus on the right enemy—"

"We're looking at the right enemy right now," said Rheadne.

"Kaine killed himself, but he truly didn't want to—"

"So he unwittingly killed himself with an invisible murder weapon?" said Rheadne in a voice weighed down by sarcasm. "While we're at it, did G.J. impale himself with an invisible blade, too?"

"You're not thinking straight, Rheadne!" spat Jonah. "If we could convene like adults, then Jonathan—"

"THAT IS YOUR PROBLEM, JONAH!" shouted Rheadne, finally rising from the bench. "Jonathan this, Jonathan that—my God, we should take one of the weapons in your armory and cut your head out of his ass! I've been listening to all of you since we got to that cursed place, and it seems like he gives you free rein to do whatever you want! You have no knowledge of discipline, structure, or obedience. Jonathan is bullshit. He is meaningless. The way you go on about him makes it real clear to us: You don't think of him as an authority figure. You think of him as an ace in the hole."

Jonah was stunned. He could have said anything; most of all the fact that what she'd just described was exactly how they'd treated Gamaliel

Kaine. But the conflicting emotions inside him choked out his ability to vocalize any words. Talk about backpedal; she'd gone from saying that he was powerful to accusing him of having his head lodged in a spirit's ass.

Now Penelope and Cisor were both looking at Rheadne with pride. "Welcome back, Cage!" said Cisor. "For a moment, we thought we'd lost you."

Rheadne shook her hair from her shoulders. "Distractions made me lose my way," she muttered. "I couldn't see past the worthless things that I wanted. But I'm back now."

Damn. Those words felt like acid across Jonah's insides.

Penelope joined Rheadne on her feet, and Cisor came smoothly to his own.

"You heard our piece," said Cisor. "Do you agree?"

Jonah pulled his gaze from Rheadne back to Cisor. Anger—that sweet, blessed emotion with which he was so familiar—began to erode the constrictions on his vocal chords. He rose. Terrence and Reena did the same. "I agree," his newly freed voice was a rasp, "that you can all go fuck yourselves."

"Seconded," said Reena.

"Thirded," said Terrence. "Wait, is Thirded a word?"

Cisor nodded, looking pleased with the outcome. "Tell Jonathan that what happens next is all your fault."

They lifted the twigs, and faded from sight. Terrence watched the twigs fall to the ground when they were no longer in use, and then smashed them with his boot.

"Dad always said using twigs as portals when there was a purer way to travel could always be tied to ill will," he said. "I'm starting to think that's true."

"True for some," corrected Reena.

Jonah looked at the ground. Reena placed a hand on his shoulder, which he didn't even have the will to shrug off.

"I'm sorry, Jonah," she said. "I assumed that you meant something to Rheadne. I never imagined that she'd call you as a worthless distraction."

Jonah remembered Terrence's revelation before Cisor, Rheadne, and Penelope showed up. He raised his eyes to Terrence, but before he could say anything, Terrence raised a hand.

"It's alright, man, I mean it." There was sincerity in his voice. "Rheadne went *way* down in my eyes when she left me to get eaten. What she just said about our friends and Jonathan sank her even lower." Then he grimaced. "But does she have to be so frickin' gorgeous, though?"

Jonah stared at nothing in particular. Reena rolled her eyes.

"Fetter your hormones, please," she told him. "We need to get back—"

"We're being watched," said Jonah suddenly.

Reena and Terrence looked around, wary and alert.

"Where?"

Jonah was running before he even realized it. He had been thinking about that word "distraction" before he was distracted by a random movement near the street.

A didn't turn out to be so random.

"Jonah, wait!" cried Reena, but Jonah ignored her.

The person froze in alarm when they realized that Jonah was racing straight for them, but then recovered and tried to flee. But it was pointless. Adrenaline made Jonah forget that he wasn't the best runner in the world.

He tackled the guy to the ground, and pinned him there. He couldn't make out his face, but then realized that when the man had fallen, his toboggan had shifted, which obscured his face. The man struggled, but Jonah pulled a baton free.

"You know who and what I am," he snarled. "One wrong move. Pull that thing off of your face."

Footsteps confirmed that Jonah's brother and sister were back with him. He didn't look at them. He paid them no attention. Resignedly, the figured grabbed the toboggan and tugged it off. It was Gabriel.

"What the—?" began Reena, but Jonah only felt rage. It was pure, like an undiscovered vein of oil that had impatiently waited to breach its confinements.

"Reena, give me your studio key," he threw at her, impatiently wagging his fingers in her direction.

In moments, the cold steel was in his palm, where it gleamed blue. He held it out to Gabriel.

"Hold the key," he ordered.

Gabriel looked at him, wide-eyed. "Jonah, I can explain—"

"HOLD THE DAMNED KEY!" shouted Jonah.

Gabriel took it, and the steel gleamed auburn. Jonah knew it would happen, but the triumph was still present.

"Thought you could get away with it, didn't you?" he asked him.

Gabriel frowned. "Get away with what?" he asked. "You knew my aura color already, Jonah. I told you it was auburn a long time ago—"

"You slipped up," interrupted Jonah. "Remember, Reena? Terrence? The momentary flash when G.J. got stabbed? It was sloppy, Gabe."

"What're you—?"

"And then you show absolutely no emotion, and said you had things to do. You wait for almost two months to pass, and then you jab a knife in your Daddy's throat. And Doug is your Lee Harvey Oswald. Did Wyndam O'Shea teach you that little trick, making the murder weapon vanish like that?"

Gabriel paled. "What's happened to Pop?" he demanded.

Terrence laughed coldly. "Drop the act, Kaine," he said. "I can call you Kaine, now that both Daddy and big bro are gone, and you're the only Kaine left."

Gabriel rose, a silent scream in his eyes. "My father is gone?" he whispered. "Pop—Pop is gone?"

"Why are you keeping up this pretense, Gabriel?" Jonah fired at him. "You know he is in Spirit! You put him there—!"

"Jonah." Reena sounded so stunned that Jonah looked in her direction. "It's not an act. He's not lying."

Jonah was about to shoot a retort her way, but then Reena raised her fist. Her dampener was there, and her hand was gloved. She had full range over Gabriel's essence.

What once was rage was now confusion. Jonah felt his own face go cold, and it had nothing to do with the winter. "How could you not know, Gabriel?" he asked. "Your father's been in Spirit for almost eighteen hours. Your buddies at Sanctum have declared war on the estate; we just had a parley—"

"The parley!" Terrence's exclamation was punctuated by his suspicious expression. "How were you in the dark when you sat there and watched that sorry excuse of a parley?"

Gabriel stared up at him, dry-eyed but woebegone. "I didn't know it was a parley," he whispered. "I happened across you guys and thought that a fight was about to break out."

Jonah raised his eyes to Reena, who nodded. So that was true, too. He couldn't take it anymore.

"Time out," he said loudly, "time out! I need a minute here. How could you not know about Gamaliel, Gabriel? Where have you been?"

Gabriel hung his head. "I twigged back to Florida to visit my mom," he said. "Wanted to give her whatever comfort I could for G.J., you know?"

"That's a lie," said Jonah. "I saw you last night."

"I saw you too," said Gabriel. "I twigged like five minutes after that. Spent some time with my mom, and then I twigged back about forty-five minutes ago."

This was all wrong. Gabriel hadn't done anything. To call this a mistake was so much of an understatement that it wasn't even funny.

Gabriel looked at them all. "My father is in Spirit?" he asked again.

Jonah felt terrible now. He had just told Gabriel horrible news in the worst possible fashion. "Yes."

Gabriel slumped against the wall of the general store. He buried his face into his hands for a few seconds, and then released a hard sigh. "I need a drink. Is there a bar—?"

"No," said Reena flatly. In a very uncharacteristic gesture, she grabbed Gabriel's hand. "You need food, not liquor. "We're going to eat, and then, Gabriel Kaine, you are going to tell us just what the hell is going on."

The Chuck Wagon was open, and largely empty. The owner was in a great mood. He even went as far as to tell them that if they liked the new meat loaf recipe, then their serving was on the house. Jonah, Terrence, and Gabriel took advantage of that, and the stuff was delicious. Reena ignored their protests of refusing free food, and chose a grilled chicken sandwich with no mayonnaise. The owner raised an eyebrow, muttered something about her being some type of bird, and brought out her order. For a while, they ate in silence. But after about half of their portions, they were done. Even Terrence, who usually had to be restrained from eating the plate itself. All their eyes were on Gabriel.

Reena waved the dampener in his face. "Are you going to make this tedious, Gabriel?"

Gabriel sighed. "No."

Jonah assumed that it was the truth, because Reena lowered the dampener back over her neck.

"We know that you didn't kill your father, because you didn't even know that he was in Spirit," she said. "But why the lack of emotion, Gabriel? You didn't shed a single tear when you lost your brother, and you aren't crying now."

"It's because you hated them, right?" said Jonah.

Gabriel shook his head. "I don't process grief like that," he explained. "I have never been one to bawl or weep when I was sad. They told me that I hardly ever cried as a baby. It's more...inward. Like ice in my insides. But I don't cry. Ever."

"But you did hate them, right?" said Terrence. "I mean, no one would blame you; your dad completely ignoring his youngest kid."

Gabriel's eyes contemplated his half-eaten meat loaf. "I'm not the youngest," he revealed. "I'm the middle child."

"Say what?" said Jonah.

"Pop was focused on his career," said Gabriel. "He didn't decide he wanted a family until much later in life. That's when he married my mom. He is—*was*— twenty-seven years her senior."

"Twenty-seven?" Terrence demanded.

"That isn't unprecedented," said Gabriel. "Anyway, G.J. came along, and he was everything that a son could be. So Mom and Pop wanted a perfect girl to along with their perfect boy. And they got her; Gabriella came along fifteen years later." He breathed through his nostrils. "Unfortunately, they got an unpleasant surprise two years before that, which was me."

Reena looked at him. "You have a sister?"

"Yes, Gabriella Nicole Anastasia Kaine." Gabriel said it in such an automatic tone that Jonah knew he must have said it a lot of times before.

"Why haven't we ever seen her?" asked Terrence.

"She is in undergrad at Florida State," said Gabriel. "And she is also Ungi—" he gritted his teeth. "She's a Tenth Percenter."

"What?" said Jonah, surprised. "Your baby sister is a Tenth?"

"Mom is, too," said Gabriel.

"But Gamaliel—"

"I don't think I was the first person in history to have a hypocrite for a parent," murmured Gabriel. "But anyway, you wanted to know who I am, Reena. There it is. Gabriel Metropolitan Kaine. The excess that slipped into the world between the son who was perfect because he was his dad incarnate, and the daughter who was perfect because she was a precious, delicate Tenth. I'm the middleman—or I used to be."

Terrence hung his head. "I have experience with feeling like excess," he said, "so I know what you mean."

Jonah had heard the bitterness in Gabriel's voice. "After what you just said, are you serious that you didn't hate them?"

"I loved my Pop," insisted Gabriel. "I worshiped him. G.J., too. I know that I was a mistake. I know that I was an accident. But I thought that if I tried really, really hard, they'd at least like me. I learned all of Pop's protocols. Even the ones I didn't agree with. Pop hated progression; he was old-school in every sense of the word. So I immersed myself in old stuff. Videotapes, voice recorders, vinyl records, old ethereal modalities and approaches—I even learned how to do complicated math in my head, just so I didn't need a calculator. I did all those things hoping they'd notice. I thought I'd make them proud. But I never did. *That's* what I hated."

Jonah looked at Terrence and Reena. All three of them had gone through things like this, but Gabriel...

"Where do you stand on Sanctum?" he asked him.

"I don't want to fight anyone," snapped Gabriel. "I didn't ever want to come to your estate, I *knew* their plan was bullshit—"

Gabriel froze. But Jonah, Terrence, and Reena all caught it.

"You knew *what* plan was bullshit?" demanded Jonah.

Once again, Gabriel's face went from red to white. He tried to leave the table. "I have to go—"

Reena clamped on his wrist, and Jonah saw him wince.

"God... *damn*, you're strong," he grimaced.

"This I know," said Reena. "Now sit back down, or I will break your wrist. And the other one, too. Then I'll break your jaw. And then I'll cap it all off by punting you in your fuckin' nuts."

"Good God, Reena," said Terrence. "Have you been practicing that threat?"

Gabriel's hand paled somewhat in Reena's grasp. Wincing, he lowered himself back down. "Alright, fine." His concession was reluctant, but he took Reena seriously. Any sane person would. "But I shouldn't even know. They don't want me anywhere near their plans. I shouldn't know. I want your word that you will keep me off The Plane with No Name."

"You don't get a damned thing until you tell us what's going on, Gabriel," said Jonah. "Now why did your dad show up, thirty deep, to our home?"

Gabriel looked at him, but said nothing. He looked like a caged, desperate beast. Terrence sat forward.

"Have you ever had both wrists and your jaw broken at the same time?" he asked. "Because I have."

"No, you haven't," said Gabriel.

"You got me there," admitted Terrence. "So do you want to be the first?"

Gabriel looked over at Reena's hands, and sighed. He looked like a man passing the point of no return, which Jonah really wanted him to do. They needed to know the truth. Finally, the truth.

"Pop is elderly now," said Gabriel at last. "Or he was, anyway. He was afraid of passing into Spirit. He didn't trust the safety of the ethereal world to its current representatives. Especially Jonathan. He felt that G.J. was well on his way, but he wasn't quite ready yet. He couldn't bring himself to pass the torch."

Jonah rolled his hand. "Go on."

Gabriel's face looked as though it'd finally break into tears. "Pop wanted to usurp Jonathan, and prolong his physical lifespan," he confessed.

Terrence blinked. Reena's mouth fell open, dumbfounded. Jonah felt the aged wooden table crack underneath his tightening fingers.

"So the Deadfallen activity in Florida—"

"—was true," said Gabriel. "We deal with stuff like that all the time. It was an excuse for haven."

"Which was needed why?" demanded Terrence.

"To get in with you guys," sighed Gabriel. "That first mission? Pop knew they were sazers because...because he put them up to it."

"What?" cried Jonah, Terrence, and Reena.

"I didn't do it," said Gabriel. "I tried to sabotage the plan. But that was a fail. G.J. nearly beat the shit out of me. But what we didn't know was that they were cannibals. Dad and G.J. set you guys up, but someone duped them, too."

"That's why you said that thing about a two-way betrayal," snarled Jonah. "You truly didn't know."

Gabriel shook his head. "I didn't want them to do it. They put me with Liz and Malcolm, and I tried as hard as I could to keep them safe. Luck was there."

Reena tightened her fists. "That explains why your father was so against the mission concerning Matt Harrill," she said. "Because it wasn't one that he orchestrated."

It seemed to Jonah that Gabriel was going through some internal healing. This bile must have been burning him from the inside out. Good for him, because Jonah was pissed. "Why didn't you tell Jonathan about this?" he demanded.

"I tried to stop it," said Gabriel. "I don't confront people until I have a plan. Surely, you can understand that."

Jonah rolled his eyes. Yeah, he could understand that. He was the same way.

"I wanted to approach him," continued Gabriel. "My dad, I mean. I wanted to approach him, reveal that I knew what his plan was. Maybe even get him to stop it. But then he said it should have been me instead of G.J., and I knew that I couldn't deter him."

Jonah looked at Terrence and Reena. Was Gabriel saying he thought he was saying? "Are you telling us that war was coming regardless?" he asked.

"You mean after Dad usurped Jonathan?" said Gabriel. "They didn't plan a war, Jonah. They planned a slaughter. It wasn't hard; they just needed the right motivation and they needed to keep hating you. That was why Pop switched out the first crew—"

"—because they started respecting us after Michael got healed," grumbled Jonah. "We assumed as much. So what was the motivation?"

"Gamaliel never got around to that motivation," said Reena. "But Gabriel, you keep saying they. You've said that more than once. Who, exactly, is *they*?"

Jonah froze. Terrence hadn't actually caught that, either.

Gabriel brought a hand to his temple. "Pop, G.J. Iuris, and Cisor," he said. "There are two that you haven't met; Mick August, and Anna Webb. Pop left them in charge of Sanctum while we were here in N.C."

"Penelope, too?" said Reena hopefully, but Gabriel shook his head.

"Penelope wasn't in that inner circle," he said. "They were close to offering her an invite, but it didn't happen before everything went to hell."

But Jonah didn't give a damn about Penelope. He eyed Gabriel sharply. "Was Rheadne in that circle?"

"No," said Gabriel. "She is just a believer. Easy to manipulate. They were all so easy to manipulate. But she wasn't in on it. It was just the ones I named. A clique within Sanctum Arcist. Pop called them The Network."

"Original," scoffed Reena.

Jonah was relieved, in spite of himself. He let the relief settle in him.

"I'm sorry, Gabe, but I gotta know," said Terrence, "how the hell do you know all this?"

Gabriel closed his eyes. "I've been recording them," he confessed. "It's an old tape recorder. G.J. would have checked if it was anything new, but he never checked the dusty, obsolete tape recorder that kept the table leveled. I told you that I have an affinity for old-school things, because of Pop. That's how I know all this, Terrence. But Reena, you're wrong."

"Wrong about what?" frowned Reena.

"Pop had motivation," said Gabriel. "He had the obvious one. The easiest."

"Which was?" asked Jonah.

"Y' know," said Gabriel. "The main one. I'm sure that it's crossed your mind from time to time since you met us, right?"

"I'm *sure* that we don't know what you're talking about," said Reena slowly.

Gabriel's face went blank. Then his eyes bulged. Jonah thought that they might pop out of their sockets, just like he did with Douglas earlier. "You don't know?" he whispered. "You're telling me that you don't know?"

"No," said Jonah, impatient, "but we'd like to!"

But Gabriel looked horrified. "You people really *are* innocent," he said. "None of you have hurt anyone. This has all been—"

"Gabriel," said Reena, "spit it out!"

"Pop was born at the Grannison-Morris estate," Gabriel revealed. "Jonathan never told you that?"

They all stared at him.

"WHAT!" they cried.

"Jonathan never told you?" Gabriel looked stupefied. "I—okay. Okay. Pop was born at the estate. His mom was an Eleventh Percenter who fled the Maritimes after some food shortage made a rough farm winter even worse than usual. Jonathan welcomed her; brought her to the Protector Guide in those days. She revealed that she was pregnant, and Pop showed up nine months later."

Jonah was rapt. Jonathan never ever spoke about his past.

"Pop idolized Jonathan," continued Gabriel. "He got his early ethereal training from him."

"Wow," said Jonah. "Gamaliel and Jonathan actually got along once?"

"Reminds you of Trip and Felix, no?" said Terrence. "What happened, Gabriel?"

"The Decimation happened," answered Gabriel. "Creyton came with all his hellfire and brimstone. Pop was pretty young at the time; I don't think he was even twelve at the time. Jonathan was protecting him; promised that he'd keep him safe. But when those Deadfallen disciples came looking for them, Pop panicked, which revealed their hiding place. He ran, but his actions got Jonathan killed. He's the reason that Jonathan lost his physical life that night."

Jonah looked down in shock. Not even Terrence or Reena, who'd known Jonathan longer than him, had known that. Bombshell? Understatement.

That was what Trip had been talking that night when Jonathan asked Trip to watch Sanctum, but aloud he said, "So that was why Jonathan lost his cool during that briefing in his study after Terrence had been abandoned."

Gabriel nodded. "Apparently, Pop was petrified when he found out Jonathan hadn't crossed on. So he trained and trained and trained. Became a famous Networker, and then mortified the Eleventh populace. That's the reason why he created Sanctum Arcist and made his little Network faction within it. Not just to give the Curaie the finger, but to also be prepared for Jonathan's vengeance. We were taught never to trust him, or any of you. And he was damned mortified when Jonathan found you a few years ago, Jonah. He would have killed to have been the mentor of the Blue Aura. But...obviously, that didn't happen. As such, he got even more rigorous with everyone. He couldn't fight anymore, of course, but he made sure that we could. He even had people scout your area here and there. Just to know the lay of land. Spirit and Spiritess count and all that."

Jonah closed his eyes. Now he knew why Rheadne was so far away from Florida the night he'd had his date with Vera. He supposed that he threw things off for her when she became attracted to him.

But even that was all to hell now.

"But Jonathan never went after him," said Reena rather jerkily. "Jonathan never went for revenge!"

"I know!" said Gabriel. "Many of us wondered why Jonathan had waited so long to come after Pop. Then some people started saying that maybe Jonathan hadn't done anything because he never planned to do anything. But if anyone said those things out loud, Pop would put them in sparring sessions with members of the Network. They'd get the piss beaten out of them—and that literally happened once or twice—and they never questioned Pop again. He was adamant that Jonathan would come and try for revenge. His paranoia broke him, and then he made G.J. a believer, Iuris, all the rest. My father planned to usurp Jonathan, and then slaughter you all. His old fear and concern would have been the motivation. But then—" Gabriel closed his eyes and swallowed, "but—then G.J. got killed. And now—now Pop is gone, too. And your friend Douglas looks like the murderer, you said. I guess the original motivation was no longer needed."

Jonah looked at Gabriel for several minutes. Then he looked at Terrence and Reena again. This was a lot to take in. "What the hell is your role in this, Gabriel?" he asked.

"I've been trying to help you people," said Gabriel. "I've been shoring up your defenses with any ethereality that I know. That's why I was at your gate all those nights. I've had conversations with some of your spirits as well as some of Sanctum's. I've convinced them to refuse endowments to anyone from Sanctum in the event that they were used for a siege on the estate. If I couldn't stop it, I could at least help."

Now Jonah didn't know what to say. They'd been so wrong about Gabriel. Reena had suspected him, but then said he became too obvious of a suspect when Jonah and Terrence began to doubt his motives. He'd been so focused on his notion of Gabe's hatred for his family.

"Did you guys really think that I'd kill my own father and brother?" asked Gabriel.

"We won't dwell on mistakes," said Terrence evasively. "But we should have listened to Reena—"

"Wait," said Reena suddenly, "wait, Gabriel. You said that your dad was going to usurp Jonathan to elongate his life. He had justified invading our home because of his decades-old mistake. Number one, usurping spirits is a dark ethereal maneuver. Two, why is he acting now, all of a sudden? What's changed?"

Gabriel swallowed. "Miss Seedie."

Jonah raised an eyebrow. Reena looked stunned. Terrence was the one who asked the question.

"Who is Miss Seedie?"

"I don't know." Gabriel sounded hopeless. "And I've tried so hard to find out. I've asked allies. Spirits and spiritesses. I even asked some of your cats when we got here. She just...showed up about two months before we came here. I started hearing her on the tapes before I saw her, so I assumed that she was a spiritess. But she is a real flesh and blood woman. Pop never told anyone about her. I only learned of her because of the tapes."

Jonah's eyes narrowed. "Really. Did he get this idea from her or something?"

"Yes," said Gabriel.

Okay. That wasn't expected.

"I thought she was a spiritess, but that got dashed," continued Gabriel.

"Now I'm afraid that she might be Deadfallen. And I can't find anything on her."

"How did that get dashed?" asked Jonah.

"I saw her one night," he said. "Pop hadn't closed the door to his study. He seemed... unfocused. And she was speaking so hypnotically."

Jonah's body went numb. What? "Tell me about her," he said shortly.

Gabriel was a little taken aback by Jonah's approach, but he went with it. "I only saw her once, mind you, so bear with me. I could better describe her voice—"

"Hypnotic," supplied Jonah. "Probably musical."

Gabriel frowned. "Yeah."

Jonah's jaw clenched. *No.*

"She was maybe 5'7" without heels," said Gabriel, eyes closed. "Not to sound creepy, but she was pretty for an older woman—"

"Did she look to be in her mid-forties?" asked Jonah warily.

"I think so," said Gabriel.

Once again. *No.*

"Jonah—" said Terrence, but Jonah raised a hand.

"Go on, Gabriel."

"Slightly tanned skin, like used to enjoy outside, but spends more time indoors nowadays," said Gabriel. "Dark brown hair—"

"—with a streak of white," finished Jonah, unnerved. "Is that right?"

Gabriel regarded him. "You know Miss Seedie, too?"

"Son of a bitch," said Jonah. He had to get up and move. Sitting stationary suddenly felt unnatural.

"Jonah, what the hell is wrong?" asked Reena.

Jonah didn't answer her. He looked down at Gabriel, who was still seated. Gabriel looked back at him, almost frightened. He had no idea. "Gabriel, you didn't find anything on her because Seedie's not her name," he told him.

Gabriel frowned. "What are you talking about?"

"Her name is not Miss Seedie," croaked Jonah, who was numb with disbelief. "Her name is Miss *C.D.* Charlotte Daynard. She's the departmental assistant at my school. The bitch was smiling in my face just yesterday."

Reena gaped. "There is a Deadfallen disciple posing as a Tenth at your school?"

"Yeah," said Jonah. "Wyndam O'Shea isn't Inimicus. She is."

"Inimicus?" asked Gabriel. "The Spectrology game?"

No one answered.

"Makes sense," said Terrence. "Someone you didn't know you didn't know was your enemy. O'Shea was a red herring."

"A murderous red herring," said Reena darkly.

"She would have access to my personal information," said Jonah in a hollow voice. "I've had conversations with her. She'd have seen my editorials, and known that I used to live and work up in the city. She probably sent Wyndam O'Shea after Mr. Langton and Jessica. She is probably the one who killed G.J. and Gamaliel. We need to go."

He got up from the table. Terrence and Reena joined him, but Gabriel remained seated. Jonah looked back at him.

"You too, man."

"No," said Gabriel. "I've answered all of your questions; told you more than I probably should have. But I'm not going to do anything to mar my Pop's legacy further—"

"You're going to help us," said Jonah slowly and clearly. "You're going to help us finally find Inimicus, and you will then reveal your Daddy's true plans, and stop this war. Or," Jonah looked away in a thoughtful sort of manner, "I can leave your wrists, jaw, and balls to Reena's mercy."

Gabriel looked Reena over, and made a split-second decision.

"I'm on my way," he said as he left his seat.

22

Journal of a United Front: Unanticipated Entry

They were at LTSU quicker than breathing; the *Astralimes* were a beautiful thing. Jonah was ready to barge right into the creative writing department, but Reena grabbed his arm.

"Jonah!" she hissed. "You can't just do it like that!"

"Daynard has ruined too much, Reena," growled Jonah. "She's Inimicus! I'm—!"

"Jonah, you have to wait." Reena barred his path. "What are you going to do? Burst in face-first, batons blazing through a building full of night school students and frazzled professors? That'll go over really well!"

Jonah gritted his teeth, and cooled it. Somewhat.

Gabriel looked over at Terrence curiously. "Does she—?"

"Yes," muttered Terrence. "Eternally."

Even though she was in earshot, Reena paid neither of them any attention. Her focus was entirely on Jonah. "Thank you," she said. "Now we are going to walk in there as four civilized adults. Hopefully, we can find Charlotte Daynard and corner her. We can summon Jonathan, who will summon the Networkers. Douglas will be cleared, and life goes on."

359

Jonah took a deep breath and released his grip on his batons, which slid back into his pockets. "Fine. Civilized it is."

The four of them entered the department, wary of everyone and everything. The strangest thing was that Jonah was familiar with this place. It was eight-thirty in the evening. The last class would be going on until a quarter to ten. Most of the classes and offices were locked. The nearest hall to them was pitch-black dark, save for the bright red **EXIT** sign at the far end, which sprayed waves of scarlet across the recently-mopped floor.

All was normal.

But normal felt wrong.

"Where is Daynard's office?" asked Reena.

"End of the hall," answered Jonah. "Last door on the left."

"Is she here late nights?" asked Gabriel.

"Usually," said Jonah. "She enjoys making her copies at night so she isn't bogged down the next morning."

"Alright," said Terrence, fired up. "Let's go bag this Deadfallen b—"

"Reena?" said a curious voice. "Jonah? Terrence?"

They all whipped around, startled. It was Kendall.

"Kendall!" said Reena in a voice that was way too boisterous. "Baby! Hi!"

"Were you looking for me?" asked Kendall.

"No!" said Reena. "I mean, yes! I mean—"

"What she means, Kendall," said Jonah hastily, "is that no, we weren't *all* looking for you. Just Reena was looking for you. *I* was looking for Miss Daynard."

Kendall snorted. "Well, Reena, you are in luck, because here I am," she said. "But you, Jonah, are out of luck. Charlotte resigned this afternoon."

Reena's eyes widened. Jonah crossed his arms.

"Are you serious?" he said, trying his damnedest to mask his suspicion.

"Hey, we were surprised too, my friend," said Kendall. "Especially Ferrus; he spent all semester buttering that woman up so she might become his personal assistant."

"Um, I realize that I am the stranger here," said Gabriel (Kendall, like they all had before, raised her eyebrows at his baritone voice), "but shouldn't university staff...don't you have a policy about putting a notice in before a resignation?"

"Yeah," said Kendall, "but I'm guessing that something came up in her life. All she said was that she was leaving for personal reasons."

Reasons which involve killing innocent Tenths and Elevenths, Jonah thought to himself.

"Personal reasons?" said Terrence. "Did she look sad or worried? Or nervous?"

"Nah," said Kendall. "She was her usual serene self. But she was sweet enough to give us all cards. Mine said that it was her—how did she put it—eternal privilege to have worked with me. Cheesy as hell I know, but hey, the gesture was there."

Something about that phrase stirred something in Jonah's mind, but he made no connections in his thoughts. Charlotte's resignation was so random an occurrence (or *not* random, rather) that it didn't allow much time for musings.

"But Jonah," said Kendall suddenly, "if it's important, I wouldn't be surprised if you caught Charlotte at home. She spent the whole day joking about how she had things to kill before hitting the road."

Jonah felt an icy chill down his spine. *Things to kill?* Of course, that sounded like banter to Kendall. But to them...

"Thank you so much, Kendall," he said to her with a smile and a nod. "I need to see her, but it's nothing life-altering or anything." Jonah would have to scold himself for lying later. "I hope that you have a safe night."

"Just wait a second," said Kendall, and Jonah braced himself for the inevitable questions. "Did you say that you needed to see me, Reena?"

"Oh yeah," said Reena hastily. "I just wanted to say I love you."

She walked into Kendall's personal space and kissed her. It took Kendall by surprise, but she responded in kind soon enough.

"Hot," commented Gabriel.

"Shut up, Kaine," mumbled Terrence. "We're trying to derail a war, remember?"

Jonah wasn't worried. Reena and Kendall weren't overly lovey-dovey and gushy, but they had no problem showing affection around people if they wished to. So in many ways, this really wasn't out of character. Now if only Reena would wrap it up.

They parted, and Kendall smirked at her. "Love you too, Reena. See you tomorrow?"

"Absolutely, baby."

Kendall nodded, and with a final smile and nod to Jonah and Terrence, she headed back into her office. Reena turned back to the three men, but she only had eyes for Jonah.

"Are we—?"

"Yeah, we're going to Daynard's house," said Jonah instantly. "Our weapons can flash there."

Terrence swore. "We should have asked Kendall for her address," he groused. "She probably could have told us in a second!"

"I already know Charlotte's address," said Jonah.

They all looked at him in surprise.

"You do?"

"Relax," mumbled Jonah. "It's nothing spectacular. It was on the directory last December, and I memorized it to send her a Christmas card. It was just random information at the time."

"Random, but it came in handy," said Gabriel. "You guys keep amazing me with your skills."

Jonah raised his eyebrows. "Know what would really be amazing?" he asked. "If we can put an end to this frickin' war before it starts."

Jonah remembered the address perfectly, and one *Astralimes* trip later, they were in front of Charlotte Daynard's house. It was a plain white two-story house. It was too pleasant a dwelling place to belong to such a duplicitous murderer.

"So this is where she lives," said Gabriel slowly. There was hardness in his eyes that hadn't been there before. "Inimicus, you said?"

Jonah took in the unimposing structure, wondering what lay inside. Yeah," he said at last. "Inimicus is... well, was Creyton's second, right-hand, or whatever you want to say. The embedded enemy. The one that you never saw coming in a million lifetimes."

"The one taking sick orders from a cold fire that contains a trace of Creyton's essence," said Terrence. "The one who sent O'Shea, probably on the orders of said cold fire, to waylay that diner."

"The one who loosed cannibal sazers on us and never intended to protect them," said Reena.

"The one who killed Pop and G.J.," grumbled Gabriel. "The one who put my father on this path that can now potentially lead to war."

Their reiterations of who Charlotte Daynard really was steeled Jonah's resolve. Initially, he had some serious reservations about breaking into her house. But now the decision couldn't have been clearer. Break into the house; find clues and possibly the bitch herself. B&E was a tool in the name of peace. At least in this particular instance.

"Here we go," he said.

They went to the door, and Jonah reached into Reena's hair, pulled a hairpin from it, and began to pick the lock. Gabriel looked impressed.

"Pop wouldn't have regarded you so spitefully if he knew you had a shady past," he remarked. "Were you a thief?"

"I don't have a shady past as a thief," spat Jonah. "I have a background losing keys."

The lock clicked. The way was clear.

They entered the house quietly and slowly, with Terrence shutting the door behind them. They each extracted their weapons, which served as flashlights for them all. When Jonah saw Gabriel's auburn-gleaming aura illuminate his mace-like weapon, guilt rippled across him again.

"That's another thing that made us suspect you, Gabriel," he told him. "Inimicus—Daynard—has an auburn-colored aura."

"All the more reasons to squash this bitch," murmured Gabriel.

"Daynard isn't here," announced Reena. "There are no sources of essence but ours, but there are still traces of her own essence in here." Reena shuddered. "Jonah, she is definitely a Deadfallen disciple. Her essence is one of the vilest, cruelest I've ever felt. I wish I could have been with you one of those days you went up your school. I could have read her while she was masquerading as a departmental assistant."

Jonah sighed. Just then, Terrence stumbled and they heard papers fall to the ground.

"Sorry," he muttered. "We need a full light. I can't make out stuff."

"We can't turn on the lights, Terrence," said Jonah. "We're burglars, remember?"

"Oh yeah."

"What did you just drop, anyway?"

Terrence lowered his hands low to the floor so as to use his endowment to illuminate the objects. He snorted. "Generic cards," he answered. "Looks like they ain't been here too long. Funny how she saw fit to kiss everyone's ass, saying all that crap about being Privileged Eternal or Eternally Privileged or whatever—"

Jonah's head whipped Terrence's way. "What did you just say?"

Terrence looked at Jonah in surprise. "What?"

"That thing you just said," said Jonah. "What was it?"

"Oh, the Eternally Privileged thing?" scoffed Terrence. "It was that thing that Kendall said Daynard wrote in the card she gave her."

"Yeah, I got that," said Jonah, "but that's not the way you said it at first."

Terrence rolled his eyes. "I screwed it up, Jonah," he said exasperatedly, "you don't have to bring light to it—"

"Will you just say it the way you did at first, please?" snapped Jonah.

Terrence sighed. "I said, Privileged Eternal."

Jonah could have dropped his baton. He hadn't been crazy. When Kendall had told them what Charlotte's card had said, a prickle of recognition had sparked in his mind. He hadn't recognized it at first because he hadn't heard it before.

He'd read it before. In a text message.

Oh, this was bad. This was *very* bad.

"Terrence, Reena, Gabriel," he said, throat dry as hell, "don't touch anything. We're are in the wrong place."

"What are you saying, Jonah?" asked Reena. "This woman is Inimicus, and finding her will clear Douglas and avert war."

"Yes," Jonah agreed, "all true, all true. But we are in the wrong place because I know why Charlotte isn't here."

"Where is she?" demanded Gabriel, his tone more vengeful than curious.

Jonah felt a flicker of panic. "One minute."

He pulled his phone from his pocket and dialed a number that he never thought he would.

It rang. And rang. And rang.

"Damn it," said Jonah, who ignored the puzzled look that everyone gave him, "pick up!"

"*This is Jessica Hale. Leave me a message and I'll get to it when I get to it.*"

Despite his panic, Jonah frowned. What kind of a voicemail message was that? "Jessica!" he said after the beep. "It's Jonah! Wyndam O'Shea is not the one you need to worry about! It was all a trick! The real problem is a woman named Charlotte Daynard, and I think she's coming for you! If you get this message, do *not* go home by yourself!"

He ended that call and immediately began to dial a new one. It was about that time that he saw the comprehension in Reena's eyes.

"Jessica?" she said, fearful. "How do you know, Jonah?"

"How do you know?" asked Terrence.

"Who the hell is Jessica?" asked Gabriel.

Jonah didn't answer any of them. His new call picked up on the first ring.

"Hello?"

"Ant!" Jonah practically shouted.

"Rowe? What—?"

"Have you heard from Jessica?" Jonah demanded. "Is she with you?"

There was a silence after the question that Jonah didn't like.

"I...I haven't seen Jess since yesterday, Jonah," said Ant. "She said she needed some time to relax and be by herself, just to clear her thoughts."

Jonah tightly closed his eyes. "Have you spoken to her, at least?"

"No, Jonah, I haven't," said Ant, sounding concerned now. "I wanted to, but when she told me to leave her alone and let her relax, I just couldn't disobey. It was like I felt the need to listen to her."

Now Jonah gritted his teeth. "Ant, meet me at Jessica's house," he said shortly. "I won't be alone, so don't be surprised."

"Jonah, should I be worried?"

"Just meet us there!" Jonah hung up the phone, angry. "Such a weak *bitch* of a man!" he snapped. "Does he have to cater to her every whim?"

"Jonah, talk to us!" ordered Reena. "We're trying to stop a war here, remember?"

"Charlotte Daynard is going to finish off Jessica," plunged Jonah. "I think she might consider her a loose end."

They all stared at him.

"I ask you again, Jonah," said Reena. "How do you know?"

"The thing that Kendall said about the Thank-You cards," said Jonah. "She said that Charlotte wrote that it was her eternal privilege to have worked with them. I didn't make the connection until Terrence misspoke, and said, Privileged Eternal. Privileged Eternal was the signature on Jessica's text messages. Why would Charlotte say that? How would she even know about those words if she hadn't been keeping tabs on Jessica?"

"My God," Reena whispered. "And Kendall said that Charlotte told them all that she had things to kill before she moved on."

"Things to kill," grumbled Terrence. "The nerve of that—"

"Don't even say it, man," said Jonah. "No word you say would be venomous enough."

Gabriel moved forward. "I really hate to break this to you guys," he said delicately, "but if we go to this Jessica's house, it will be our third unauthorized *Atralimes* trip."

"I know," sighed Jonah. "But this is wartime, so-called, I'm going to go by that old mantra."

"What old mantra?" asked Terrence.

Jonah readied himself for the *Astralimes*. "All is fair in love and war."

Of course, Reena remained the level-headed one. Before they took the two steps, she suggested that they choose a spot maybe a half block or so away so as not to alarm Ant or any neighbors with their sudden appearance. They did what she asked, and stepped behind a maple tree that towered over a home with a **FOR SALE** sign on it. From the very start, there was a bad omen.

"Jonah," said Terrence, "I went into Spectral Sight as soon we got here. There isn't a single spirit or spiritess around."

Jonah, who'd been about to go into Spectral Sight himself, really didn't want to hear that news. It meant that it was almost a foregone conclusion that some sort of ethereal hell had broken loose.

"Look there!" whispered Gabriel. "Car just pulled near that house. Is that the man you're waiting for?"

It was. Jonah imagined that Ant would be on edge right about now, so they couldn't very well walk up to him like a huge gang-up.

"Try not to look imposing, please," he told everyone.

They walked up to Ant's car. Terrence, Reena, and Gabriel fell back a little because Jonah was the only one who wasn't a stranger. Jonah knocked on Ant's window, and unsurprisingly, he jumped. Upon seeing who it was, however, he deflated a bit and opened the door.

"Rowe!" he said tersely. "What's going on? Why did you want me to meet you here?"

"Because we need your help, Ant," said Jonah. "My group of friends and me."

Ant glanced at Terrence, Reena, and Gabriel, gave a shaky kind of nod, and turned back to Jonah.

"Did you try to call Jessica on the way here, Ant?" asked Jonah.

"Is Jess okay?" Ant answered Jonah's question with a question. "I can't lose her, Jonah. I can't."

"Ant—"

"I know that you can't understand why I'm in love with her, but I know that I can make her happy if she just allows me to."

"Ant, we—"

"Can you help her? Can you end this whole—?"

"Shut up, Ant!" snapped Jonah. "We won't know anything at all until you unlock her door!"

"Shouldn't we call the police?" asked Ant.

"They wouldn't be any good," said Terrence. "I'm afraid you're going to have to trust us, bro."

Jonah knew that Ant wouldn't be any trouble. His blind servitude to Jessica saw to that. But Jonah didn't want anything to happen to Jessica, if only for Ant's sake. The man would probably never stop grieving.

The quintet gathered at the door, quiet but focused. Ant reached it first, and went to work the key in the lock.

The door was already ajar.

Jonah's eyebrows rose. He glanced at his friends. They all came to a silent agreement. Then he turned back to Ant. "Um, Ant? You are, um, going to see something weird. Just—just don't panic. We're on your side. No questions asked, okay?"

Ant's fearful eyes were still on the door. "Yeah, okay."

They pulled out their weapons, and their aura colors gleamed. Ant's eyes widened, but Jonah shook his head.

"No questions asked," he repeated.

Ant remained silent. Jonah could tell that it took some effort. The man pushed the door open, but Jonah put a hand in his way.

"Let me," he told him.

Jonah stepped in front of him. Terrence, Reena, and Gabriel were as poised and ready as they'd ever be. Together, they walked into Jessica's house. Jonah flicked the light switch, but nothing happened. No matter. He focused, and the lights popped on.

He wished they hadn't.

Jessica's living room was a crime scene.

Every item she owned seemed to be smashed, overturned, or up-ended. Reena took a sharp intake of breath. Terrence muttered, "Oh, man." But Gabriel moved to a bamboo plant that lay across dark laundry.

"Guys," he said solemnly, "this is India Drew."

Jonah looked at the laundry again, and saw that it was not laundry. It was a body.

It was a woman, who had maybe been in her mid-thirties, but had star-white hair and vivid blue eye shadow. There was a bullet wound in her chest.

"Jessica actually got one," said Terrence. "I ain't a fan of guns, but if one was turned on a Deadfallen disciple—"

"Where is she?" demanded Ant, who hadn't even seemed alarmed at the corpse. "Where is Jess?"

Terrence left them and moved near the stairs. Once he reached that destination, he released a ragged breath.

"I think that the story continues upstairs," he announced.

"Why's that?" asked Jonah.

"Look here."

Terrence pointed. There was a trail of blood leading up Jessica's staircase. It was asymmetrical, but unmistakably led a grisly trail.

"It must have started here," hypothesized Reena, who turned her back on India Drew. "They didn't anticipate that a Tenth would ever be pushed to the brink and fight like a cornered beast."

"Given the blood trail, they must have tried to corner her upstairs," said Gamaliel.

"But then…" Ant's voice was quiet at first, and then it elevated. "Jessica! JESSICA! Maybe she's not dead!"

He bowled Jonah over to get past him and scrambled up the blood-lined stairs.

"ANT!" shouted Jonah, attempting to regain his balance. "DUMB-ASS, WAIT!"

Pure adrenaline steadied him, and he ascended the steps without waiting for his friends. He reached the second floor and nearly tripped over someone else. With a jolt, he realized that the body was that of none other than Wyndam O'Shea. Jonah paused only for a second, and then hurried on. He could deal with him lying there on the floor, in his own blood. As insane as it was, he had been a red herring. Screw him at the moment.

Jonah didn't know his way around Jessica's house, but it wasn't large. He saw where her bedroom was situated, but not because of process of elimination.

It was because someone else had been cut down by Jessica's gun.

Charlotte Daynard.

Now Jonah had to pause and marshal his thoughts. He had to clear his head, if only marginally so. But it was not that simple.

His insides writhed. There was wide range of emotions in his head that he didn't understand. He'd seen corpses before. He'd dealt with the loss of physical life before. He truly believed the notion that Jonathan preached about life never ending.

But that was ethereal logic. And this wasn't ethereal violence. A different set of rules applied there, for the most part.

This wasn't ethereal. It was a shooting. A firearms massacre. This was the type of thing that made him avoid the nightly news, because gunshot incidents seemed to take up most of each news report. Had this been ethereal violence, he might have been able to compartmentalize that. But these were physical lives, horrible though they were, who'd been extinguished by a gun-toting, frightened, and desperate woman. Charlotte, Wyndam, and India may have been dangerous Deadfallen disciples. Hell, Charlotte had been Inimicus. But none of that mattered once they stared down the barrel of a nine millimeter.

A sob caught Jonah's attention. It was Ant. He moved forward, steeling himself as he walked past Charlotte's bullet-pierced form.

He stepped into Jessica's bedroom, swearing that it felt like something shifted. He needed to focus, and used his own ethereality to balance his nerves. Nothing had shifted. He needed to get his head in the game.

He paused only to register that this dark bedroom seemed rather large, but his eyes then fell upon a shocking sight.

Inches away from Ant's sobbing form lay Jessica Hale, spread-eagled and eyes closed, with an empty gun mere feet from her hand.

23

The River, The Turn, The High Card

Ant wept uncontrollably. Jonah hurried to his side.

"She's dead, Jonah," said Ant haggardly. "She's dead!"

Jonah felt numbness that he couldn't explain. Jessica lay there, which meant that he'd failed to save her from the world she'd gotten sucked into thanks to him. He should have felt guilt. He should have felt anger at himself, but all he felt was numbness.

He gritted his teeth. Fine. He wasn't feeling anything right now? Because of weakness? Then that weakness would just have to be strength.

"No, Anthony," he grumbled, not even using the guy's nickname. "Jessica's not gone. I won't let that happen." He then raised his voice as high as he could, though his eyes remained on Jessica. "Guys! Charlotte Daynard's been killed! We're up here in the bedroom!"

He touched Jessica's chest and torso. He felt no blood, no holes. So whatever the issue was had to be internal.

"We need to be careful, man," Jonah told Ant. "She night have a back, neck, or head injury."

It was time for instincts to take control. He was no medic, and the furthest thing from a Green Aura, but he was the Blue Aura, damn it. Balance was his zone. He focused on Jessica, hoping that his ethereality would wash over her and bring balance to whatever was causing this non-responsiveness. Tricks like these had gotten simpler the more experienced and stronger he became as an Eleventh Percenter. So here was to hoping that luck was on his side.

Miraculously, Jonah noticed something. Jessica hadn't been seriously injured at all. He thought he could put the pieces together himself. When the Deadfallen disciples broke in to her house and sent her completely over the edge, she'd reacted with animal instinct. But it probably went without saying that she was horrified after seeing what she had done (Jonah had to believe that even a bitch like Jessica had to feel something amiss after shooting people). Every emotion that had been imprisoned inside her came unchained all at once, and she must have fainted and hit her head on the floor.

An emotion cracked through the numbness inside Jonah. Relief.

"She's not gone, Ant," he said in a much lighter tone. "She fainted. Banged her head."

Ant looked at him, daring to hope. "She's alive?"

"Yes," insisted Jonah, placing two fingers at her throat, which confirmed his words. "She has a pulse."

"Thank God," Ant whispered as he grabbed Jessica's shoulders and shook her. "Jess? Jess!"

Jessica slowly opened her eyes (Jonah thought Ant might do a little dance because he was so relieved). They were slightly red and clouded, but Jonah attributed that to her recent head bump. "Wh—What?" she whispered. "What's going on?"

"It's alright, baby!" said Ant jubilantly. "It's over! It's finally over!" He turned to Jonah. "Where are your buddies?"

Now Jonah frowned. That was a very good question. He glanced at the hallway. It was dark again; had he lost his hold on the lights when he'd placed all of his focus on Jessica? "I need to—"

"No, please don't leave, Rowe," said Ant. "We've got to help her! She's shot people—killed them. How will we get her out of this?"

It was at that moment that Jessica realized that she and Ant weren't alone.

"Rowe?" she whispered. "I thought I told you not to come into my house again."

"Well after you didn't pick up your phone, I had no choice," said Jonah, who wasn't angry with Jessica for the first time ever. "I was trying to warn you. What do you remember?"

Jessica's bloodshot eyes rolled onto Jonah. "It's—It's a blur." Her voice had slightly risen above the whisper now. "I was having a stiff drink to calm me down, and three people broke in with knives glowing like Christmas, but I was ready. I just started shooting—I had no choice. Are they dead?"

"Um," said Jonah evasively, as he hated that word nowadays, "they aren't with us anymore, no."

Jessica tried and failed to focus her gaze on the men next to her. "I had no choice," she repeated. "I'm not a bad person."

Jonah wrestled with himself concerning that one, but switched gears. "Let's not dwell on stuff, Jess. Let's raise you up against the wall here. Be careful, Ant; I think she has a concussion."

They methodically lifted Jessica to a sitting position. Ant tried to lower himself next to her, but Jessica pushed him away.

"Back up," she murmured.

"But I was just—"

"Seriously, Tony," said Jessica, "back up, and give me some room. My head is killing me."

Jonah swallowed. It seemed that Jessica was almost back to her old self. But he chose not to react to it. Jonathan's words about not letting personal feelings cloud the heart swirled about his head again. He rose, almost angry with Terrence, Reena, and Gabriel. He, Ant, and Jessica could have been eaten alive by now.

He walked to the bedroom door, and willed the lights back on.

It didn't happen.

Frowning, he focused his ethereality once more. No effect. That was odd. The hall was dark; he couldn't even see Charlotte's and Wyndam's bodies anymore.

Were Terrence, Reena, and Gabriel down there in that dark? Why hadn't they shouted when the lights went out?

"What's the matter, Rowe?" said Jessica.

Jonah glanced back at her, annoyed that Ant had actually done what she's said and backed off. Weak little wimp. "I had some friends with me," he muttered. "They should have been up here by now."

Jessica's placid face showed irritation. "You—you brought strangers into my house?"

"Get over yourself, Jessica." Jonah was not willing to do this. "The man who stalked you is gone. The woman he was working for? You shot her, too. Plus, another one of their stupid buddies. We just helped you out. Can you give me the benefit of the doubt just once?"

"No," said Jessica stubbornly. She probably would have snapped had she not been so groggy. "You should sit down so we can discuss the finer points of respect."

Jonah took his attention off of the dark hallway and glared at Jessica. "Because you recently hit your head, I'm going to pretend I didn't—"

"I'm not asking you, Rowe," said Jessica. "I'm telling you. *Sit down.*"

"You're cra—"

But then, Jonah's body froze. He couldn't explain it. It was like his free will had been snatched away, and a foreign agent invaded his body. Completely against his will, he seated himself in a nearby rocking chair. Jessica licked her lips.

"Now, was that so hard?" she asked.

She rose with an eerie fluidity and grace that one wouldn't expect of a recently concussed person. Jonah couldn't even move a finger. It was like his every muscle was restricted by invisible bonds.

"What's going on?" he spat.

Jessica calmly reached into her pocket and pulled out a cigarette, which she lit and brought to her mouth. The pull she took from it that was almost sensual in its deliberateness, and she closed her eyes and exhaled in complete bliss. Jonah looked at her in alarm and confusion. "God, that is good." Her voice was clear and strong. "It's been so long…"

Suddenly, her eyes shot open, and she looked at Jonah. She completely ignored Ant, who hadn't moved or spoken. Through Jonah's attempts to regain control of his body, he noticed that her eyes weren't cloudy or red anymore.

"You asked me what is going on," said Jessica. "Well, it's a neat little gift of mine called Clepovoluntas. C.P.V. for short. I can steal people's wills, and magnify them into an all encompassing control device."

"What?" said Jonah, but Jessica wasn't done.

"And those idiots you were looking for aren't here," she told him. "We left them back at my house when you crossed that Threshold of Death."

"Threshold of—?" Jonah's eyes bulged. "No. Oh God, NO!"

Jessica's eyes gleamed. "Yes, Jonah."

With her free hand, she pulled down the collar of her turtleneck. There was a bruise at her pulse. She then rapped the bruise with the two fingers that held her cigarette, which made the light at the end of it zoom like a firefly, and said four words that she couldn't have said any more clearly if she tried.

"*Per mortem, vitam.*"

The room melted. The image literally faded away. It went from a heavily feminine bedroom to a widely shaped den with outdated, dusty furniture that lined the northern wall. Jonah was absolutely horrified, and Ant didn't have a clue in the world what was going on, but Jessica simply took another pull from her cigarette before she tossed it into the fireplace. The thing erupted into a cold fire. The icy blast washed over them like spray from a chilled river.

This whole time, Jonah had been praying that this was a bad dream. But the waves of cold from that fire confirmed that that prayer wouldn't be answered.

"You—you can't be," he croaked. "You can't be an Eleventh Percenter."

Jessica's expression twitched. She was suddenly furious. "I am not just an Eleventh Percenter," she hissed. "I am *Deadfallen*."

She held something in Jonah's line of sight. It was the final piece of his nightmare.

The Inimicus card.

"Your search is finally over, Jonah," whispered Jessica. "Now you know, you dumb son of a bitch."

24

Ghost Story

Jonah's mind was reeling. He didn't know what to do. Hell, he couldn't actually do anything. He couldn't move.

This was a blade that cut on two levels. The first level was the fact that he couldn't move anything but his mouth, head, and eyes. The second level was the fact that he and Ant were in mortal danger, and there wasn't anything that he could do about it.

He was trying to break through the control that Jessica had over him with his balancing ethereality, but it was useless. This was one of the most powerful things he'd ever experienced.

"Jess?"And finally broke his silence. "What is this, baby? Why can't I move?"

"Because I don't want you to," snapped Jessica. "Now shut up, before I order you to."

The man was terrified; Jonah could see it. He wasn't doing much better, but at least he knew what Jessica was talking about. Some of it.

"Why, Jessica?" he demanded. "Why are you doing this? Hell, what are you doing? Where are we?"

Jessica pointed two fingers at the base of the fireplace. An indentation began to gouge itself where she pointed. She moved her finger along, lengthening the indentation without a word to either of them. Jessica was more focused on this unusual activity than Jonah had ever seen her at Essa, Langton, and Bane. When she finished (Jonah wasn't sure where she ended it, as he could only turn his head so much), she finally answered.

"We are where life went to hell for the Transcendent's chosen," she said. "Why I do it is because it is my task to right the wrongs of the traitor." She went out of their sight, but came back into view with what looked to be a neat bundle of clothes. "And what I am doing? You will see soon enough, Rowe."

"I don't know what you mean, Jessica," said Jonah.

Jessica walked up to where Ant stood, grabbed his shirt, and literally ripped it from his body. Ant winced; Jessica's fingernails pierced his flesh when she did that.

"Yeah you do, Rowe," she told him. "You were the start of all this."

Jonah frowned. "You mean when I killed Creyton?"

Jessica looked at Jonah with such concentrated rage that it was scary. "You didn't kill the Transcendent," she spat. "You got lucky."

Jonah's eyes narrowed, but Jessica was looking at Ant again. "Put these on," she commanded, thrusting the clothes into his hands. "Do it now."

She flicked some fingers, which unrestricted Ant's movements just enough for him to put on the black shirt, vest, and long coat that she gave him. Jonah had to keep talking. This C.P.V., or whatever Jessica had called it, was likely to drive him insane.

"What are you doing, Jessica?" he repeated. "Some sort of sick role-playing?"

Jessica moved up to Ant and buttoned up the shirt to his throat. She then fixed the coat's collar. "You're just begging me to shut you up, too, aren't you, Rowe?" she said. "Save your questions. It's not like they're mine to answer."

"Why Langton, Jessica?" snarled Jonah. "That idiot man would have done anything for you. Wasn't that the whole point of you prancing around, looking like the poster woman for the Corporate Sluts of America?"

Jessica was in Jonah's face so quickly that he'd have started if he could move. "I was never a slut, Jonah," she snarled. "I was in control the entire time. Sluts need validation. I validated men. I gave them a reason to live, far more than their lackluster girlfriends and wives, anyway. That fat bastard wished that he could just *touch* me... that's how smitten he was. Why did I kill him? Because I was tired of leading him on. It made me sick to my stomach, having to smile in his face every day. Now, I don't have to anymore."

Ant gasped in horror at Jessica's confession. He, like everyone else, thought that Langton had passed because of poor health. He looked at Jessica as though he didn't know her. Which was actually the truth.

"Tell me, Jessica," said Jonah, hoping to get her mask to slip, and maybe regain control of his body, "were you still um...validating men after you yoked Ant into a relationship?"

"Yep," answered Jessica. "Women, too."

Jonah's eyes widened. He didn't expect her to just come right out and admit it, especially with her boyfriend inches away from her.

Jessica grinned. "Were you expecting to get me to crack, Rowe?" she asked. "Expecting to break me? Won't happen. I'm not ashamed of anything I've ever done, whether it was with my body, my mind, or my ethereality. I have always used my assets. They just stretched further than the ones you always thought."

Jonah narrowed his eyes at her, not even hiding his disdain. Jessica's upper lip curled somewhat at his gaze.

"Get off your judgmental high horse," she grumbled. "Like my mom used to say, it's nothing that men haven't been doing forever."

"And like my grandmother used to say," countered Jonah, "if they all jumped off a cliff, would you do it, too?"

Before Jessica could respond, Jonah felt another negative wave wash over him. Once again, he felt wrongness, foreboding, and the feeling that life was about to go wrong in the absolute worst way possible.

He saw that Ant sensed it as well. But Jessica just laughed. The jarring thing was that it wasn't evil, maniacal laughter that one would expect from a murderer. It was the same appalling, girlish giggle that she'd always done.

"You feel that, baby?" she said to Ant. "That was called an Eris Effect."

Jonah's mouth fell open. It did not go unnoticed.

"Yes, Jonah, I know what an Eris Effect is," she said. "I am an Eleventh Percenter, after all. Did you think I was stupid, too?"

Jonah wanted very much to say yes, but he didn't know what Jessica would do in response. So he swallowed the retort.

"Good boy." Jessica seemed to know that Jonah had just showed restraint with his words. "Because I'll fill you in on why that Eris Effect just occurred. It means that June Mylteer's plan to deter and delay Sanctum has failed. They've betrayed him, and have bucked his counsel. There will be war, and the fun thing about it? Your friends at that damned estate don't even know that Sanctum is playing dirty. Jonathan is expecting a later siege. Nope. It's happening tonight."

Jonah couldn't even register the fact that Jessica knew who June Mylteer, Sanctum Arcist, and Jonathan were. He barely registered the fact that the bitch was not only an Eleventh Percenter, but Inimicus. But none of that mattered at this second. Those Sanctum bastards disregarded their consigliere and planned to sneak attack the estate?

"Jessica, you have to stop this," he said. "Innocent people will lose their physical lives—"

"They will *die.*" Jessica rolled her eyes. "You dilettantes and your *life never ends* bullshit. It was pretty classic when I had to act like I didn't know what you meant those times you slipped up and used ethereal jargon."

"Jessica, Creyton is gone!" Jonah roared. "That is damned *vapor* in that fire! It's nothing! He can't do anything for you! Douse that crap and let us go!"

Jessica smiled. "My Transcendent is gone. Jonah, do you think I'm in this for *me*?"

She removed that corked vial of lifeblood samples that Jonah remembered from the Spectral Event. The 49er's lifeblood samples. What the hell?

Jessica let the vial fall to the ground, and it smashed there. But, like a sentient mass, the lifeblood slithered into the indentation that she made in the floor. Jonah followed the path she made with it, and saw that it ringed Ant. Unbridled horror gripped him.

"NO!" he shouted. "Jessica, this won't work! For the love of—!"

"You men are such bitches," chided Jessica. "Just accept that his is happening, Rowe. And yes, it *will* work."

It was at that moment that Ant realized that whatever Jessica was doing didn't bode well for him. He was so petrified that he began to cry.

"Jess, just let me go," he pleaded. "I don't care that you cheated on me, and I will never repeat what I heard here! I swear! I'll move away! I'll vanish!"

Jessica rolled her eyes. Ant probably hadn't seen true evil in his life. Not the type of evil that was purely merciless, pitiless, and remorseless. It made Jonah sick to his stomach, but it made Ant sob even more bitterly.

"Jess, please, I love—"

"SHUT UP!" bellowed Jessica, and Ant was finally struck dumb, like she'd threatened to do before. "Damn!"

She pulled a knife from her pocket, which gleamed with her aura color—auburn. Just the sight of it made Jonah's chest hurt.

"You set war events in motion," he said. "You were the one that killed Gamaliel Kaine and G.J."

"Mmm hmm," said Jessica. "And it was fun, Jonah. Now, shut up."

The smile faded from Jessica's face, and she refocused on her activities. Jonah knew that he'd lost her again. She was so powerful. The damned C.P.V. was unbreakable. But he couldn't stop. His mouth was all he had left.

"Jessica, this will not work," he attempted. "Countless physical lives could be lost!"

Jessica ignored him as she raised her knife over the lifeblood on the floor. Her hand was wrapped around the blade.

"JESSICA! Anthony Noble loves you! He is—!"

"He is the means to an end that he was always meant to be," Jessica snapped. Then, with her entire being focused on the knife in her hand, she muttered an eerie sequence of words: "In Lifeblood, in spirit, in victory, and in harmony, Astral and Physical Converge. Sovereign Transcendent, Rise Anew."

She made a fist around the blade, crying out as she did so. The scarlet pooled at the base of her wrist, and then droplets detached and fell, joining the lifeblood on the ground.

"NO!" shrieked Jonah, who tried in vain to move.

It took that lifeblood a millennium to fall, but when it did, hell broke loose.

The fire blazed so harshly and brightly that Jonah could see his breath in the room. It left the fireplace, followed the blood trail like it was gasoline, and connected with Ant. He screamed in the most dreadful agony fathomable; Jonah would never forget those screams. The cold fire began to consume Ant's flesh, but not the clothing. The poor man screamed, shrieked, and bellowed. His sounds were so sick and grisly that Jonah prayed that it would stop, if only for Ant's sake—

The fire completed its work. Anthony Noble was gone, and all that was left was a face-down, clothed skeleton. Jonah blinked at it, his horror absolute.

But it wasn't over. Even though the cold fire had followed the trail of lifeblood, the lifeblood remained after the fires had ceased. Then, he lifeblood began to move, as if buffeted by wind. Wails came from it, even more terrible than the ones that Ant had just loosed seconds before. The skeleton, which hung limp in the clothing, began to tremble. A portion of essence rose from the lifeblood moat, and hit the clothed skeleton. Jonah's eyes widened in shock as the essence seemed to give the skeleton a transparent exterior, like plastic or rubber. A second essence hit the skeleton, which provided even further substance. More essences detached themselves from the lifeblood and made contact with the bones, followed by even more. Finally, Jessica began to tremble, and made a sound like she'd been hit with a jolt of electricity. A portion of her essence left her through the bloody wound on her hand, and collided with the form on the ground, which collapsed once more.

Silence. Deafening silence.

Then, still face-down, the form began to move. First, the left hand propped itself against the floor, and then the right one. Weight being fully based, the figure hoisted himself up to his knees, where he rose his head and looked at Jonah.

A hodgepodge of emotions warred in Jonah as he stared into the face of the predator that was the apex of the Deadfallen. The Transcendent, the monster, the antithesis of life itself.

The face of Creyton. Returned from the grave.

"Hello, Jonah," he whispered. "I told you that I'd find a way."

25

Praeterletum

Jonah was scared. He knew that it wasn't tough, or badass to admit that, but he didn't care. He was scared out of his mind. This was nightmarishly wrong. This was the sickest ghost story on earth.

Creyton rose to his feet and took a few tentative steps, but got the hang of it in no time. He looked over his arms and hands, and then cracked his knuckles and neck muscles. It was clear that he planned to take his time reveling in this moment.

Jessica was very disoriented from what she had just done, but when she raised her head and saw Creyton, she completely forgot all about her sluggishness and wound, and broke out into a blissful smile. The smile was indulgent, greedy, and accomplished, much like a kid who was happy with getting away with doing something terrible.

"Transcendent," she breathed. "My spirit and life are yours."

Creyton regarded her. "Inimicus. Your faithfulness is a blessing. Sacrificing a portion of your lifeblood and essence. I am grateful."

"You knew that you could trust me from the moment you granted me discipleship, Transcendent," said Jessica.

"You honor me with your words," said Creyton, and Jonah heard that note of a threat, that unspoken guarantee that anything other than complete servitude would carry grievous consequences. "Do you wish me to fix your hand?"

Jonah winced when he saw Jessica's wound. She attempted to treat the injury with negligence, but it was clear as day that it pained her greatly.

"I'm Inimicus, my Transcendent," she told him. "Heal me. It is an honor of the highest order to keep my body perfect and impeccable for your service."

Jonah stared. Hadn't this bitch just been going on and on about being in control? Besides all that, that last part sounded horrible; was he reading too much into it?

But he couldn't think about that right now. It was unimportant compared to what he was facing. If he could just *move...*

Creyton grabbed Jessica's damaged hand, and it began to steam like a tea kettle. Seconds later, her hand was unblemished once more.

"You showed restraint, just as I asked," said Creyton once he'd dropped Jessica's hand. "For a moment, you very nearly faltered. That cannot happen again, Inimicus. Do you understand me?"

"Wholeheartedly, Transcendent," murmured Jessica. "Wholeheartedly."

"How are you back?" roared Jonah, who couldn't hold back anymore. "How is this possible?"

"All in good time, Jonah," said Creyton, whose eyes were still on Jessica. "At this moment, I await the return of all my disciples."

Footsteps around Jonah alerted him to other presences, and he involuntarily attempted to turn. It wasn't possible to get a good look. Creyton laughed.

"Grant him partial range of motion, Inimicus," he ordered.

Jessica made a lazy motion with her hand, and Jonah's upper body was free. It was such a relief to have control over something, but it was a small comfort, given the fact that his lower body was still bound. He looked around and saw India Drew, Wyndam O'Shea, and Charlotte Daynard. So they hadn't been killed. That had been an illusion, too. They were joined by a half-dozen other people, all of whom knelt in Creyton's presence.

"Transcendent," they all said in unison. "*Per mortem, vitam.*"

"Rise, my disciples," said Creyton. "The core of my regime. How wonderful it is to see you again. And what of the others, Charlotte?"

Strangely, Charlotte sniffed the air. "All of our integrated brothers and sisters are here, my Transcendent," she said in that meditative voice that now made Jonah nauseous. "Just like the old days, they are all in their designated places, and eagerly await your words when you are done with us."

Despite the fear, Jonah narrowed his eyes. Creyton's own disciples didn't all know each other. They had to wait in separate rooms, for Creyton to address them independently of the others. In addition to all the dark, terrible things that he'd done, he also micromanaged.

"Thank you, Charlotte," said Creyton, who turned to Jonah. "I believe that you are familiar with some of my Deadfallen, Jonah? Charlotte here tells me it was quite entertaining to befriend you."

"That bitch wasn't my friend," snarled Jonah. "Now tell me how—"

Creyton slapped Jonah so hard across his face, his neck popped. He slunk back into the chair.

"You are in no position to insult or command anyone here, boy." Creyton's voice was clipped and low. "Now, show some respect. What would your dear Nana say? I told you that I would answer your question in due time. But I believe introductions—official introductions, I mean—are in order."

He walked to Charlotte. "Charlotte Daynard. Departmental assistant, taxidermist, debutante…and one of the most efficient killers I have ever taught. And, oh yes—not Inimicus."

They shared a laugh. Jonah took a leveling breath, still seething from Creyton's hit.

"Wyndam O'Shea," continued Creyton, once he'd reached the rusty-haired, twisted-faced lunatic. "He, too, is a superb killer. But at the full moon, he can turn death into an art form reserved only for the elite of the elite. Again, not Inimicus, though you wanted him to be so badly."

"He might not be Inimicus," grumbled Jonah, "but he still massacred an entire diner—"

"He did not," spat Creyton. "And if you interrupt me again, boy, I will extract your windpipe, and watch it burn in cold fire."

The mental picture made Jonah grimace.

"The one responsible for the Crystal Diner, Jonah," said Creyton slowly, "is the woman you hated. The woman for whom your enmity was so strong when you were colleagues. And, most importantly, the woman who led you directly into my clutches. My dear Inimicus."

The disciples in the room laughed, and applauded. Jessica gave Jonah a wintry smirk.

"Jessica Hale," said Creyton. "Powerful, dangerous, and so very gifted. When I discovered her, she was a broken girl. No guidance, no direction, and no purpose. I showed her who she was, and made her who she is now. I made everything that you see here, Jonah."

Jonah couldn't believe what Creyton had just revealed to him. "Jessica was the one who massacred that diner? There is no way!"

"I'd advise you not to underestimate me, Rowe." Jessica looked at her auburn-gleaming blade and grinned. "I knew that you had a Spectral Event that night. The funny thing was that you actually saw me go into the damned place. But since I told Wyndam O'Shea to misdirect your focus, you paid no attention. You were so busy being focused on the rusty-haired guy with the limp. You didn't even notice the wet-haired, blonde woman in the back."

Jonah grimaced and closed his eyes. He *had* seen Jessica in the Spectral Event! She was the blonde woman, with the rain-soaked hair. He hadn't seen her face, and paid her no attention, because he was focused on Wyndam O'Shea. Damn, was he stupid.

"Transcendent," said Jessica, "before you regale Rowe with your story, I implore you to purge us of these commonplace distinctions. Purge us of this masquerade of having to act as though we are Ungifted, or too asinine to embrace our superiority."

Creyton's eyes narrowed, but it wasn't in suspicion. He enjoyed being back. He'd give them a treat, right here and now. But Jonah knew a thing or two about bullies. Soon enough, the bloom would be off of the rose. The hell-raiser would re-emerge shortly thereafter.

"Draw your weapons," ordered Creyton.

Every disciple did so, and each regarded the color of their aura with hatred and scorn. Every aura color one cared to name was present here—red, green, white, orange, yellow, purple, gray, purple, brown—all of them. It was so jarring for Jonah to realize the wonderful spectrum of colors that he'd seen so many times at the estate were also the aura colors of evil people. It just wasn't right.

Creyton regarded the colors with condescension. "These shades indicate the trappings of the unworthy," he grumbled. "Variety leads to confusion, which leads to disorder. You, my disciples, made the intelligent choice to advance past the peons, the Ungifteds, and the so-called heroes. You chose to transcend. So I grant you the blessing. *Per mortem, vitam.*"

"*Per mortem, vitam,*" they repeated.

All the colors faded to black. Every single one. In normal circles, such a cascade of dark would have been viewed as depressing, but this particular crew was ecstatic. Rambunctious, even. Jonah hated them all. Anger was the only emotion that offset the fear. Felix told him that a long time ago, but the difference between then and now was inconceivable.

"Now, Jonah," said Creyton, and Jonah could see that the tyrant was already breaking through, "you questioned how I am back."

"I killed you!" snapped Jonah. "I beat you!"

Creyton grabbed him by the collar and yanked him from the chair. It was a shocking thing, because Jonah figured that since he couldn't move, he'd be stuck to the chair. Not the case. "Is that what you believe?" he rasped. "Has Jonathan fostered that belief with philosophical, florid filth? Very well. Let's see then."

He threw Jonah back down into the chair.

"Free him, Inimicus," Creyton commanded.

Jessica flicked her hand, and Jonah was in control of his body once again.

"Take out your batons, Rowe," Creyton ordered.

Leery, Jonah removed them from his pockets. The blue gleam wasn't inspiring at the moment, because it was surrounded by so much darkness. Literally.

And of course, Creyton.

"Charlotte, your shawl," said Creyton.

The item was in his hand almost before he'd finishing speaking. Creyton blindfolded himself with it, turned his back on Jonah, and raised his hands.

"I have handicapped myself, Rowe," he said. "Two ways, no less. I want you to kill me. Since you have beaten me before, do so again."

Jonah stared at him. What was this? Was he serious?

"Do it, Jonah," said Creyton, more insistently.

Jonah hesitated. This was a trick. He'd be impaled from fifteen different angles...

"DO IT, YOU UNWORTHY LITTLE SHIT!" shouted Creyton.

Jonah roared, and swung. Creyton reached behind his head, and caught Jonah's right arm before his baton connected with the back of the man's skull. He elbowed Jonah with that same arm, which made him stagger away. Although still blindfolded, Creyton reached out, grabbed Jonah, and snatched him back in range. He struck him with a flurry of hits in his face, chest, and abdomen; Jonah got hit seven times before he could even catch his breath. To top it all off, Creyton ripped Jonah's left baton (which he'd managed not to drop) away from him, and crowned him in the head with it. The force slammed him back down in the chair so hard that he almost knocked it backward.

Jonah clutched both hands to the side of his head, teeth clenched. The punches didn't feel wonderful, but the head strike was the killer. It felt like his skull had been splintered at the point of impact.

Creyton pulled Charlotte's shawl from his eyes, and tossed it back to her. With murderous eyes on Jonah, he chucked the batons painfully into his lap.

"See?" he spat. "You did not beat me. You were in the right place at the luckiest time. Now focus, or you will miss the story that you so desperately desire. Inimicus, if you please."

Through the haze of pain, Jonah heard Jessica emphatically command, "STAY!" as though he were a dog, which elicited laughter from the other Deadfallen disciples. The rage at that leveled his pain somewhat, but not by much. He raised blurry eyes to Creyton.

"You thought you were better than me, Rowe," said Creyton. "Thought you were a more powerful Eleventh Percenter. Thought you were destined to be the victor, because you have the notion that right is on your side." He shook his head. "No. On all counts. When I told you that you'd gotten lucky in S.T.R., it wasn't sour grapes. It was fact. You didn't kill me. *I* killed me. My own creations—the daggers that I made from the vapor—killed me. But I didn't cross over to the Other Side. And the daggers ought to have done that. Why didn't I cross on? I'll tell you."

Jonah watched Creyton walk away from him, and face the cold-burning fire. Every face in the room was on him, like a favored teacher who'd just returned from sabbatical.

"When you thought that you'd vanquished me, I simply went to the Astral Plane, but in that deadened spirit form that the unworthy have tricked yourselves into believing is still life," he grumbled. "But I'd be remiss if I said that it didn't have its advantages. A perfect example of that was the fact that, while in that form, time is even more farcical than it is on Earthplane. I spent the equivalent of twenty Earthplane years figuring out why I was still here, and not on the Other Side. I discovered that it was for two reasons. The first one, at least in part, was me. My prolonged lifespan created certain unprecedented conditions that would not allow me to be extinguished. The second, which was equally as important, was the Lifeblood Loophole."

Creyton paused, and focused on the fire. He seemed to have a vain streak in his storytelling abilities, and reveled in having a riveted, engaged crowd. Jonah would have admired the trait in anyone else, but in Creyton, it was just as vile as everything else.

"The Lifeblood Loophole is extremely ancient Spiritual Law," continued Creyton. So ancient, in fact, that it is completely overlooked by those imbeciles in the Phasmastis Curiae. What it entails is that if an Eleventh Percenter succumbs to his own weapons in ethereal combat, his vanquishing is exclusive to the physical body. The spirit is not forced to the Other Side."

Jonah stared at him, stunned, but Creyton had only just begun.

"That part was lovely, but the next part is where *I* come in," he told Jonah. "During my research on the Astral Plane, I discovered that if one's spirit can procure fifty samples of lifeblood, then the blood that was spilled by my own weapons is not only nullified, but can open the door to a second life."

The Deadfallen disciples were just as engrossed as Jonah was, but for vastly different reasons.

"The Spectral piece was done, at least for the most part," said Creyton. "And I needed to keep tabs on you, Rowe. I didn't give a damn about you before; you were beneath me, and not worth my time. But then you had to meddle into my affairs. Therefore, you got my undivided attention. And that, Rowe," Creyton clicked his tongue, "that is a dangerous thing."

Jonah's mind went back to the first time that he'd ever met Creyton. He had been trapped and immobile that time as well. He'd always thought that Creyton froze him in time because he might have actually posed a threat. But the brief assault that occurred mere minutes ago dashed any hopes of that.

"Alas, that is beside the point," said Creyton. "The Spectral piece was done, which left the lifeblood piece. So, through spiritual and mental means, I linked with a disciple well-equipped to track blood. The 49er."

Creyton's mouth twitched. Rage rippled across the group. The 49er's name was a hated one among the Deadfallen. No surprise there.

"I took up residence in the essence and form of that ignorant Eleventh Percenter, Aaron Miles," said Creyton. "The 49er assisted me when I twigged out of the Astral Plane, and simply called myself Roger. I caught a break with *Time Games* and the Time Item, but of course, you thwarted me, Rowe. You destroyed that shell, but my essence remained, just as before. So if going back in time to reverse your activities was out, the plan with the lifeblood samples could resume. I moved on to leave the 49er to it."

It was at that point that Creyton's voice, already cold, cooled even further. Some of the Deadfallen noticed this, and stepped away from him.

"But that lifeblood-looting, self-serving, backstabbing fool went into business for himself," he whispered. "He marred and perverted a perfect plan. Titus Rivers the Third did him a favor when he made his location unstable, but when he is found, he will be sorry. He will be lucky if I don't *eat* his heart, as opposed to staking it."

Jonah couldn't believe it. He had been right. He and Jonathan had been right. There had been a plan in place before the 49er decided to take it over. The original plan had been to resurrect Creyton. Something that shouldn't have been possible.

"The nocturnal bastard did get one thing right, though," conceded Creyton. "As Scius, he was to alert Inimicus if he were ever in danger of failing. Well, the minute he dared defy me, and deviate from my plan, he was destined to fail. So he tossed down the card, which alerted Inimicus when it became clear that his own plan would come to naught. The saving grace of the entire situation is that once Inimicus was in play, I had a disciple that I knew would never fail me. I needed to be careful, very careful indeed. Inimicus is my most sacred prize. My embedded weapon. The fabrics had to be woven seamlessly. And that required Inimicus' history with the Ethereal World's so-called savior, Jonah Rowe."

The Deadfallen disciples in the room laughed; Charlotte was actually in tears. Jonah looked over at Jessica, who seemed to almost be salivating in preparation of Creyton's reaching her part in the story. The murderous bastard had been contemplating the fire again, but he turned his back to it.

"This is the part of the story where I have to reveal the glitch," said Creyton. "Jonah and Inimicus share a mutually vitriolic hatred for one another. They would rather bury the other one alive than lend a helping hand. So how then could their lives intersect in the manner most beneficial to my cause? By exploiting infallible Rowe here's weakness."

Jonah looked at Creyton. His head was much clearer, though it still ached. What did Creyton mean when he said weakness?

"Now, my disciples, you are well aware that I have an astute talent for discovering the weaknesses of others." Creyton was a master at this. He roped the Deadfallen in like the criers of old. "And as I amassed my arsenal and prepared my re-entry into the physical, I discovered Jonah Rowe's weakness."

He knelt in front of Jonah. Jonah didn't like the amount of discomfort that his dark eyes boring into him created. He felt like he ought to show at least a modicum of strength when faced with this killing psychopath. It was a challenge.

"You want to know your weakness, Rowe?" Creyton whispered. "Do you want me to divulge the truths that you don't even tell yourself? The truths that you don't tell that Time Item twit, Vera? Or the far more beautiful one that you dally about with in the night, Rheadne?"

Jonah felt his face heat, and he swallowed. Creyton raised his voice so as to continue addressing his crowd.

"Rowe lost his grandmother, Doreen, in 2002," he announced, which earned a flurry of mock pity from the Deadfallen disciples. "Her death has colored his very existence; greatly altered his life. So much so that he developed a phobia of not being where he is needed the most."

Jonah gaped. Creyton had figured that out? Jonah had never told anyone that; he'd never been able to properly verbalize it! How did Creyton discover that?

Creyton grinned when he saw the horrified look on Jonah's face. "I'm right, and you know it, boy," he whispered. "But just wait. It gets even better."

Jonah, still dumbfounded, watched as Creyton pulled a chess piece out of his pocket.

"Enter Wyndam O'Shea, who is in character as a stalker to Inimicus," he told them all. "Inimicus' situation earns Jonah's interest, because she feared for her life, with O'Shea lurking in the moonlight. Her idiot boyfriend tries and fails at gallantry at every pass. Jonah learns of the full issue, and then makes the O'Shea connection with the diner, because he believed that O'Shea did it. Inimicus sweetens the pot by purchasing a starter pistol and using Auric Shielding to make it appear as a nine-millimeter. And Jonah is now hooked. Because he has to be there. He can't abandon a person that has come under his care. We had him."

Jonah hung his head in shame. How could he have been so gullible? He had believed that he could save everyone. Believed that he could rescue Jessica. He wouldn't have been able to stay away. And he'd had no idea that they were banking on that fact.

"The final piece may very well have been the most fun," said Creyton. "That was Gamaliel Kaine, the grizzled, ethereal veteran who ran afoul of the Phasmastis Curaie, and created an entire army of misguided lambs, just because he cowered in fear of Jonathan."

Something sparked in Jonah's memory. Something from the Spectral Event. Inimicus—Jessica—intimated to Creyton's presence in the fire that the lambs had begun to implement their plans. She had been referring to Sanctum. He almost missed Creyton's next words.

"Getting all roads to lead to my resurrection was a simple matter of playing on everyone fears." Creyton cracked his muscles, like he was readying himself for a fight. "Give a few simple promises to cannibal sazers in exchange for ethereal meat, and they will do anything, absolutely anything...like staging Eighth Chapter crimes with others among my disciples to make Sanctum Arcist sweat a little."

Jonah's eyes narrowed. No. There was no way.

"Like attack a debutante, and have Gamaliel fend them off as best he could, and then have that debutante be so grateful that she decided to keep him company, give him sweet words, and plant seeds...seeds that would guarantee that he'd believe beyond a shadow of a doubt that he could extend his physical life, if only he enacted revenge on Jonathan, who would have done the same eventually. Jonathan would have never done so, of course. But it was a cute seed to plant in the old fool's head."

Jonah shook his head, feeling a numbness that had nothing to do with his current immobility. "It was you from the jump. You got Jessica to put this whole mess in motion from the very start."

"Very good, Rowe," said Creyton, "but Inimicus was not alone. Charlotte—sweet Miss Seedie—got Gamaliel Kaine hooked into it, much like yourself later on. Your conjoined missions were fun—I grant you that—but plans really ramped up when Gamaliel Jr. was an unfortunate victim of Jonathan's plan, hatched upon Felix's information."

"Jessica did that," grumbled Jonah. "She was the one with the auburn aura we saw."

"Glad you saw that, Rowe, because you were supposed to," said Creyton. "It worked out so beautifully—the way you were so quick to suspect Gabriel. Not that I blame you, because it was the perfect notion. The slighted son finally snapped, and punished the father and brother that ignored him. But the control lay with us all along."

"Control..." Jonah turned vicious eyes on Jessica. "Doug said that Gamaliel told him not to make him kill himself before he stabbed himself with that knife. You meant for him to run into Douglas."

"Not particularly," shrugged Jessica. "Any of you fools would have sufficed for the scheme to work. But damn, if it wasn't fun to watch you guys at each other's throats!"

Jonah felt lead within his body. This whole thing led back to Creyton. This was worse than blocking paths, or whatever else. Everything that had happened was part of an elaborate plan. Now, Sanctum Arcist and the Grannison-Morris estate were about to go to war.

"If it's any consolation, Jonah, Kaine and his Network were going to betray you anyway," said Creyton. "It had been in his head for years, but he just didn't know how to go about it. I just nursed it along, and worked things to my advantage. And Gabriel was an amazing way to hide Inimicus. Wyndam and Charlotte were as well. Inimicus couldn't be revealed until the moment was perfect. And that had to be at the moment where her lapdog and her blue knight were in the same place."

Jonah shook his head. "But India... Charlotte... Wyndam... the bodies. They were shot—"

"You only saw what Auric Shielding allowed you to see, Jonah," said Creyton.

"Why did you have to kill them?" Jonah had to ask. "Gamaliel, G.J... I mean, if you were going to start a war, why not watch them fall then?"

Creyton snorted. "How considerate of you, Rowe," he said. "But they were merely ingredients for war. Even Langton's death was a great element. It hooked you even further into my goals. On top of that, they served as forty-seven, forty-eight, forty-nine..."

For some reason, Jessica smirked. Creyton looked her way.

"And fifty," he finished. "The Lifeblood Loophole. I have achieved what no one could achieve. Praeterletum. Back from the dead. Not as a wraith. Not as a walking corpse, nor as a revenant. But very much alive. True transcendence. Sanctum will descend upon that infernal estate, and burn it down. When the smoke has cleared, what's left of both parties will be trodden underfoot. The true predators will take their place in the food chain once again."

Jonah couldn't swallow anymore. "And your plan for me?"

Creyton's humorous façade faded. Jonah saw it in his eyes. "You will atone for your sins, Rowe. The worst wrong in the history of the ethereal world has been partially righted, with my resurrection. It shall be complete with your death."

Jonah's mouth twisted. "So you want me to fight you?"

The Deadfallen disciple's laughter was even louder this time.

"I'm not going to fight you, Rowe," snapped Creyton. "You've proven that that would be futile. Let me show you what Praeterletum has done for me."

He grabbed Jonah's hand, and thrust a baton into it, so that it gleamed with the blue of his aura. Creyton then bent nearer to Jonah, so that the tip of the baton touched where his heart was. Direct contact.

There was no effect whatsoever. Creyton hadn't even flinched.

"You see?" Creyton tossed the baton back on Jonah's lap. "Futile. And have you noticed? No electricity here, Jonah. There will be no light-show miracles for you this time, boy. You are dead. But before I kill you, I have one final blessing to grant. Go ahead, Inimicus."

Savage bliss illuminated Jessica's face. "I thank you, Transcendent."

Creyton took a step back. Jessica pulled a length of something from inside her shirt, and methodically wrapped her right hand with it. Jonah saw it momentarily flash auburn before it went jet black. What kind of ethereal steel was that?

"Remember what I told you, Rowe?" she said quietly. "That day you walked out of Essa, Langton, and Bane? I told you that you would never be noteworthy. I told you that all your grand plans would fail. And look at you now. My affirmation is true."

Jonah looked at the duplicitous skank. God, she'd played the hell out of him. Even her ethereal power fit her. Total control, with someone backing her every move. Opportunist to the end.

"Let me reveal something else to you," continued Jessica. "The moment I found out that you were an Eleventh Percenter, I couldn't do anything myself, as my Transcendent had us in Integrated status. But I still wanted you very dead."

"That so?" grunted Jonah. "Then why didn't you do something about it?"

"I tried, Rowe," replied Jessica. "Who do you think sent those minions, Howard and Walt, after you that night you passed by my favorite club?"

The wave of shock that hit Jonah was almost as debilitating as Jessica's ethereality. Howard and Walt had said that it had been because of a link he'd made when he'd thought of his grandmother, but now he knew that it had been more than that. He struggled against her control, infuriated. Jessica watched him with a sick, twisted pleasure on her face.

"Thought you should know that before you die," she whispered.

"Mother—!"

"Uh-uh." Jessica clamped the bottom of Jonah's mouth, forcing him into silence. "I'm not finished. I would have murdered you in your sleep after your lucky break with my Transcendent, but he came into my dreams, and told me to wait. He told me that one way or the other, he was on the path back from beyond the grave. He promised me personal time with you before he crushed you, once and for all. That time is now."

"Rot in—"

Jonah couldn't finish. Jessica struck him, hard, across the face with the fist wrapped in that mystery material. Jonah felt the skin on his jaw part. It hurt and stung, but Jonah made no sound. Not for Jessica.

Jessica straddled him, exhaled, and then punched him again. There was a coppery taste on his tongue after that one. A third punch. He almost didn't feel it. A fourth, and then a fifth. Jonah had never experienced it before, but he was pretty sure that Jessica had just broken his jaw. His head slowly went back on the seat, and he was vaguely aware of the laughter all around him. But Jessica grabbed his damaged face and forced it up so that he could look her in the eye.

"That was for every time you called me a bitch," she growled.

Jonah blinked a few times to bring her face into focus. His speech was altered on account of his broken jaw, but the defiance could be sensed a mile away. "You think it was just five times, *bitch*?"

Jessica looked deranged, and drew back once more, but Creyton raised a hand and her fist froze.

"Enough, my dear," he said calmly. "Your personal time is at an end."

But Jonah wasn't paying any attention. Because a miracle had happened. In her rage, Jessica's mask had finally slipped. He was free. With his body free, a new sense of purpose engulfed him.

He wasn't losing his physical life here. It wouldn't happen. He had to escape, and stop the war. His friends would not go up in smoke like that. And Sanctum Arcist— probably the largest contingent of douche bags he'd ever met—didn't deserve it, either. Jonah saw one chance. One. It didn't require skill, or timing. It required luck.

And a sacrifice.

But Jonah couldn't think. He just had to do.

Creyton had pushed Jessica back to her spot, and they were exchanging silent words. Jonah inched his glove from his pocket—it was tricky and time-consuming with all the eyes on him—and used it to curl his hand around both batons without them flashing blue. *Turn around, Creyton... Turn around, you bastard...*

Creyton turned, and Jonah shot up from the chair. He flung both batons at the man's face. Creyton lazily swatted them aside, but Jonah knew that would happen. He just needed the momentary distraction for the next part.

He bolted for the window, grabbed a stunned Wyndam O'Shea, and threw himself through the glass, with the Deadfallen disciple positioned beneath him. They hit the ground hard, and though Jonah felt the impact, it wasn't as bad as O'Shea, who got all of the breath knocked out of him. Jonah pulled himself up, kicked O'Shea in the face for good measure (there was no way the man could be a threat after a fall like that, but Jonah took no chances), and fled. He had to get away from Creyton. The last thing he needed was for that bastard to freeze time.

Jonah heard the screams and roars of not only Creyton and the Deadfallen disciples that were in the room with him, but also those of the Deadfallen disciples that had been in the other rooms awaiting Creyton's counsel. They were coming, and he knew it. He raced toward the woods, not even aware of where he was. He heard doors get broken off of their hinges, and heard windows destroyed. He made the mistake of glancing back, and tripped over a stump. He fell to the ground, with the wounded side of his face hitting the dirt. The loosened soil aggravated the open wound, but the passing wind soothed it somewhat. But that was only a negligent comfort. Jonah had lost so much ground when he'd tripped, and he knew that he wouldn't get another chance to escape—the Deadfallen disciples were gaining with every step—

Jonah held up his hands, as though that would help him.

And something strange happened.

His hands flashed blue, and the wind in front of him became visible to the naked eye, like he'd consciously made it so. Then, it lowered into the earth where the Deadfallen disciples were gaining ground, and exploded.

The air that had lowered into the ground literally exploded.

Every Deadfallen disciple got caught up in Jonah's radius. Earth, debris, and people flew through the air, and landed in awkward, painful positions all over the property.

Jonah looked at his hands. How in the hell had he just done that? He'd never done ethereality like it. Not in training, not by accident, not even when Felix had pushed him past his boundaries.

But he'd done it tonight. And the wild, crazy maneuver had just saved his physical life.

Jonah heard a howl of agony, and recognized Jessica instantly. Apparently, she had been thrown into the air like everyone else, but landed even more awkwardly than everyone else. She now writhed on the ground as she clutched her right arm. If Jonah had been thinking straight, he'd have been thankful to have hurt her. She'd broken his jaw, after all.

But then something caught Jonah's attention from the other side of the wasteland he'd just crated.

Creyton stared at him from afar.

He hadn't been caught up in that blast (which sucked), but the emotions on the bastard's face were a mosaic of things: fury, confusion, and something like…shock?

Yeah, he was stunned. He had no idea how Jonah had done what he had done, either. Hell, neither did Jonah. It was a mystery to both of them.

But Jonah couldn't think about that right now. He still had to get away, plus, there was still a war to stop.

He turned his back on Creyton and the chaos, and used the *Astralimes* to escape.

26

Blessed are the...

Jonah used the *Astralimes* to reach a drug store on Main Street in Rome, having filed away that strange ethereality. He knew he had to stop the war, but that would require speaking. That was a very tricky thing now that Jessica had bashed his jaw. The pain was terrible, he could already feel swelling, and his teeth weren't aligning the way they usually did. He needed to take something. Liz would be pissed about it if she ever found out that he used it, but he needed something.

Jonah looked around the drugstore with ease. Had he still been in the city, this sort of subterfuge would never have worked, but in a quiet town like Rome, all the stores closed at around eight or nine at night. That was great for him right now.

He grabbed the most powerful painkillers that he could find, downed three, and stuffed some more in his pocket. He hoped that it would kick in soon. If *only* Liz were here with her concoctions.

The box of painkillers that Jonah ripped open read $7.49. He tossed a ten-dollar bill next to the torn box, and stepped through the *Astralimes* again.

The whole thing almost came to a screeching halt as soon Jonah stepped on the estate's grounds. The resulting wind that followed the ethereal travel caught the attention of two people who were with Sanctum Arcist. Jonah hurriedly lowered himself behind some hedges as one of them turned.

"That was a strong gust of wind," said a suspicious voice that Jonah recognized. It was Vaughn, the idiot that Bobby slammed through a bench during the first conjoined training. "Someone may have just used the *Astralimes.*"

"It wasn't the *Astralimes,*" hissed a voice that Jonah recognized as Aloisa's, "it was your damn conscience! This is horribly wrong, Vaughn. We are making a mistake!"

Huh. So not everyone believed the story of Gamaliel's murder. Aloisa was still their friend. Relieving and refreshing.

"They have no one to blame but themselves, Aloisa," Vaughn shot back. "They didn't turn over the bastard who killed Mr. Kaine, so now they all burn."

"What if there was a misunderstanding?" persisted Aloisa. "What if we're after the wrong people? What if—?"

"Just shut up, Aloisa, "snapped Vaughn. "They signed their warrant. Now roll with it, and wait for the signal, or I might just let slip that you're a traitor."

Jonah was angered by the way Vaughn threatened Aloisa, but he was also distracted. *Signal?*

Then, he remembered what Jessica said. Sanctum had disregarded June Mylteer's counsel and jumped the gun, so they could attack the estate early. But he never imagined they'd be in place so fast. Vaughn and Aloisa were far from alone. Jonah sensed presences all around the estate. He didn't know how he knew, but the outer edges of the woods were bulging with people, all waiting for some signal. Jessica had been right about that too; they weren't going to be upfront about it. They were going to stab them in the back, pillagers-in-the-night style.

Reflexively, Jonah reached for his batons, but then remembered that he'd sacrificed them to escape Creyton and the Deadfallen disciples. He was unarmed.

Wait. No he wasn't.

He looked at his fingertips, and remembered one of his first experiences with Rheadne. Long before he was a "distraction."

May as well turn a negative into a positive.

He focused his ethereality into his fingers until he felt them sting, and lunged. The second his fingers made contact with Vaughn's and Aloisa's backs, they crumpled. He'd endowment-tased them. He regretted doing it to Aloisa, but he knew it'd have been fishy if her associate was out cold while she remained unharmed. He tried to mutter an apology to her limp form, but his jaw wouldn't cooperate. It was too damn sore.

Jonah filed the pain away as best he could, and ran like he was racing against time –a notion that he didn't even want to entertain again. He banged through the front door just as heard a cry of outrage from the woods. A trembling, green-gleaming knife was at his neck, but the owner lowered it just as quickly.

"Jonah!" cried Liz. "Thank—"

Then she got a good look at his face.

"GOD!" she screamed. "What have you *been* through?"

Terrence and Reena were at his side in seconds, speaking words that were incoherent because they spoke over each other.

"Jonah, we didn't know what the hell happened—"

"You went up them damn stairs, and then we got knocked back here, it was the damndest thing—"

"We tried to tell Jonathan, but he wouldn't let us leave—"

They tried to push him down to a chair, but he steeled his hold, and resisted them.

"No," he mumbled. "Jonathan!"

Jonathan was at his side, as were so many others, and Jonah didn't like it. They didn't understand.

"I—!" Jonah had to stop. His jaw was killing him. The painkiller's effect on his injury was moving at the pace of snail snot.

"Elizabeth!" said Jonathan loudly.

"Right!" said Liz. She fumbled at her pants pocket, yanked out a vial of clear liquid, and pressed it into Jonah's hands. "Here, Jonah! It will fix your jaw enough to talk!"

Jonah tossed it back, and most of it got into his mouth. The pain dulled to a tolerable level, which was great. But the relief was fleeting.

"Now Jonah, son—" began Jonathan, but Jonah shook his head.

"Jonathan, Creyton is back from the grave," he croaked.

Jonathan's eyes widened. "*What did you say?*"

"But that ain't all, man," Jonah rushed out. "Sanctum is coming! They didn't listen to Mylteer; they're out there right now! But they've been played. All of us have been played."

With a look of rage, Jonathan rose and threw open the front door. Everyone followed him out, but he didn't notice.

Sanctum was very near the estate now, approaching with the ferocity of a lynch mob. The multitude of aura-powered weapons almost illuminated the night sky, and the shouts were feral. But Jonathan faced the oncoming Elevenths and calmly raised his hand.

"TITUS!" he roared.

"Right here, Jonathan!" said Trip's voice from somewhere.

The man willed himself into view and raised his hand like Jonathan had. His fingers gleamed with the red of his aura at the same time Jonathan's gleamed gold, and then what sounded like the bass from an old-school boom box flew out in visible waves over the people from Sanctum. Every endowment was gone; Jonah saw the aura colors fade from every weapon. Some people lost their balances, some people ran into each other, some people clamped their ears and screamed, and others fell to their knees and vomited. The estate residents, completely unaffected, looked on in awe. Trip looked at them with merciless glee.

"You feel that, assholes?" he demanded. "That's your brain all twisted around. You can't carry a spiritual endowment without a functioning equilibrium! As a matter of fact, you can't do *anything* except whine, moan, and heave out your guts."

"Now hear me, Sanctum Arcist." Jonathan looked and sounded angrier than Jonah and his friends had ever known, and the fact that his voice was so calm made it even scarier. "What you have attempted to do was vile, disgraceful, reckless, and stupid. But I am not without mercy. Which is a very good thing, for *you* all. Iuris Mason and Knoaxx Cisor, get up. Now."

Giving Jonathan the most undiluted looks of loathing on earth, both men struggled to their feet.

"Focus on me, and it won't be so bad," ordered Jonathan. "What Titus has done can easily be reversed. It just so happens that we need to talk. I have become privy to some very disturbing news. News that affects us all. Jonah needs to speak, and we all need to listen. Give me your solemn oath, right this second, that you will not attempt any further treachery while Jonah speaks his piece. Because if you try anything else, what you're experiencing right now will be bliss compared to what I do next."

Jonah regarded his mentor, as did all of the other estate residents. He knew that protecting the residents at the estate was always Jonathan's top priority, but he'd never seen him in a state of anger so fierce that people cowered in fear of him. Who knew that within the riddle-quoting sage-like spirit lay such an edge and temper?

Iuris tried to say something, but the effort was just too much, so he nodded. Jonathan looked over at Cisor, who dipped his head once. The Protector Guide stepped back.

"Titus, if you please."

Trip looked extremely reluctant to reverse the process, but he flicked his fingers and the waves above the Sanctum Arcist people dissipated. They began to pull themselves together, though their spiritual endowments remained absent, which was evidenced by the fact that the weapons they lifted from the ground remained unremarkable.

"No," ordered Jonathan. "The weapons stay on the ground. Or Trip's auditory disruptor waves go back in the air once again."

All hands left the weapons, and the people who'd picked weapons up dropped them without hesitation. Iuris looked at Jonathan with incredulity and rage.

"You son of a bitch," he growled. "You violated haven!"

"Actually, I didn't," said Jonathan. "Haven stipulates that I grant parties complete autonomy whilst on my grounds, so long as they comply with my protocols. If, by chance, a party protected under haven performs untoward gestures, such as declaring war, then they make their protection null and void, and are completely at the mercy of the granter of haven. Mark my words, boy, there was no way that any battle plan against me or my charges would have been successful. But now it is time for you to shut your mouth. Jonah needs to speak." He turned to Jonah, and when he spoke again, his voice was much kinder. "Son, tell them the bombshell you gave me moments ago."

Jonah walked to a center point of sorts that put him between the estate residents and the members of Sanctum Arcist. He was aware of all the eyes that burned his form against the winter night. And he took a deep breath.

"Creyton is back."

He was met with stark silence. Eyes widened, but not a single word was heard.

"B—But Creyton is gone," said Michael Pruitt. "You were the one that killed him."

Jonah looked down. "I thought I had, but he's back. He made this huge plan, took advantage of something called a Lifeblood Loophole or whatever it was, and carried it out. Jonathan, you and I were right when we thought that there was another plan in place before the 49er took the thing over for himself. The plan was to resurrect Creyton. The 49er failed him when he betrayed him, so he used his embedded enemy, Inimicus."

"Jonah, I'm not liking how you said that," said Terrence. "It sounds like you know something new. Inimicus was Charlotte Daynard, right? And Wyndam O'Shea was the red herring, yeah?"

Jonah would have gritted his teeth if his jaw worked properly. "No, Terrence," he told his best friend. "Charlotte is in the core of the Dead-fallen, and she never got shot by the way, but she wasn't Inimicus. Jessica Hale is Inimicus."

Jonathan closed his eyes. Jonah caught glimpses of his friends, who looked stunned. Vera was wide-eyed, just like Liz, Malcolm, and Bobby.

"No." Reena shook her head. "The woman you hated from your old job? The one who was being stalked and bought the gun, and—?"

"Stop, Reena," said Jonah wearily. It filled him with such pain and anger to hear the crap all over again. "Just stop. It was all a lie. Jessica and Wyndam O'Shea were working together, for God's sake."

More questions came, but Jonathan raised his hand.

"Jonah, these piece-nil fill ins will only lead to further confusion," he said. "Try this instead. Close your eyes, take a deep breath, as though you were activating Spectral Sight, and tell us everything."

Jonah did as he was told, spun his mind back to the beginning, and launched into it all. He told them how the whole nightmare began with the 49er's hijacking of Creyton's original plan. He told them about the Spectral Event, and how it wasn't Wyndam O'Shea who massacred the diner, but Jessica Hale. He told them about how the cannibal sazers had been promised meat if they staged incidents with Deadfallen disciples near Sanctum Arcist outside Fort Lauderdale, which would put them on edge. He told them about how Creyton had ordered Jessica to betray both the sazers and the mismatched Elevenths at the same time, and how Jessica laid the false trail of being stalked, knowing that Nelson would tell him, which would get him on the hook. He told them about how the second conjoined mission had evolved into a trap when Matt Harrill alerted Jessica to his location, where she killed G.J., and then used her C.P.V. power to make Gamaliel kill himself in Douglas Chandler's presence.

"You *see?*" snarled Douglas to the Sanctum group. "I told you that I didn't kill Gamaliel Kaine! He was begging me not to make him—"

"Doug, son," said Reverend Abbott, whom Jonah hadn't actually realized was there until he said something, "your innocence has long since been established. Let this boy continue."

With a nod of gratitude, Jonah did just that. He told them about the trick he'd fallen for, and how Jessica had pretended to be grievously injured and creating a façade to make them think that she'd killed three people in self-defense. He told them what happened after he'd crossed the Threshold of Death, and as much of Creyton's monologue as he could recall (which, strangely, was nearly all of it). He told them of Creyton's achieving Praeterletum, and that was around the time that his jaw started aggravating him again. He drank some more of Liz's tonic, and then continued.

"…then he gave Jessica permission to beat my head in, but she got a little too zealous and accidentally relinquished her power over me. I threw away my batons, used O'Shea to break my fall out of the window, and ran. I did that—that weird wind -in-earth thing, and ran."

Jonathan looked at Jonah. The gaze was questionable, but Jonah didn't know what to make of it. He didn't even know what to make of what he had done to escape. It still didn't make sense.

"That sounded like some very powerful ethereality you performed, Jonah," was what he said. "I must say I'm thankful that it saved your life."

Jonah didn't know how to respond, so he simply nodded. Terrence unashamedly turned to Malcolm.

"What does Praeterletum mean?" he asked him.

Malcolm swallowed. "Beyond Death, more or less," he answered. "Creyton is the first Eleventh Percenter to—and I say this for lack of better terms—to come back from the dead."

"But that can't be!" Penelope sounded nothing at all like her usual self. "It's a known fact that when a spirit departs from a body and passes into the next life, it cannot re-enter it!"

"He didn't re-enter his body," said Jonah. "He used that sick procedure to burn away everything that was Anthony Noble, and took over *his* body. Haven't you been listening to me?"

It was at that point that Jonathan did something strange. He looked over at Trip, who raised his eyebrows. Jonathan responded to the expression with a slight shake of the head. He then looked at Jonah with narrow eyes. "Jonah, please tell us exactly how you learned that Charlotte Daynard had laid a trap to further divert you from the true Inimicus."

Jonah wondered about Jonathan's odd exchange with Trip, but refocused. He'd left that part out deliberately. The same fiery emotions that gave him the strength to escape earlier flared up once more. "We have an Inimicus of our own, Jonathan," he said. "Well, Sanctum does."

The opposing group looked up at him in surprise, but now Terrence and Reena joined him in the center of everyone.

"Clarify that statement, Rowe," snapped Penelope. "Who among us would dare go into an enterprise that could lead to such ruin?"

Jonah's face was so sore, even with Liz's tonic, and his loquaciousness hadn't helped matters. Reena clapped his shoulder and took over.

"The Network," she said.

Jonah saw Iuris and Cisor pale. He thought he saw two figures attempt to shrink away, but Jonathan cleared his throat.

"Mick? Anna?" he called. "Would you care to tell us just where you're going?"

The other two people abandoned all pretense and tried to flee, but the group closed in on them, with Michael pushing Mick forward and another guy pushing Anna forward. Jonah took in a quick visual of these two people that he hadn't yet seen: Mick was a deeply-tanned guy with brown hair, and Anna was a fair-skinned woman with pitch-black hair that was clearly a dye job. Whatever. But Terrence glanced at their hands and pulled a face.

"Ah," he said with mock interest, "so you're a married couple."

"Engaged," corrected Rheadne without looking at Terrence. "What is going on? Who is this Network?"

Terrence laughed. He actually doubled over. "Can't believe you didn't know, Rheadne! Your Lord and Master created a clique within you guys that he trusted to do things that he knew the rest of you weren't willing to do."

The injustice of it allowed Jonah to once again ignore his ailments. "Not just you, Rheadne, but all of you need to listen to me," he told the Sanctum people. "This war that we almost had? It was indeed fostered by Creyton. But Gamaliel Kaine was always going to betray us, because of the beef with Jonathan."

Remarks of confusion rang from both camps, but Jonathan's eyes flickered.

"Allow me to take over now, kids," he said. "Everyone, Gamaliel was still afraid of me. After all these years, he still thought that I'd avenge my passing, which occurred due to his blunder."

Rheadne looked as though she'd lost feeling in her body. "But he told us that you were biding time," she murmured. "He always said that vigilance was paramount, especially after he'd gotten on in years."

"I *said* that Jonathan didn't strike me as a wrathful being!" snapped Michael. "June Mylteer said the same thing!"

"But you didn't forgive him." Cisor broke his tense silence at last. "I remember that day in your study!"

"I forgave Gamaliel, boy," said Jonathan. "Did the anger remain? Yes. I had a plan, and it would have worked, but Gamaliel's fear betrayed our whereabouts to the enemy. Yes, his abandonment infuriated me, and that fury carried over into spirithood. But I never entertained the thought of vengeance." He turned to Jonah, Terrence, and Reena. "I already know that Gamaliel brought his kids here because he planned to create a conflict that would end with his usurping my spirit, so as to elongate his lifespan," he revealed. "But I am now aware that Creyton's scheming and machinations were the reason he thought that he could do such a thing. But Gamaliel and his Network had plans to betray us either way."

Jonah looked at him, stunned. "How did you know that stuff, sir?"

Jonathan sniffed. "I had an eye—or perhaps I should say ears—on Sanctum from the minute they got here," he revealed. "Titus has kept me well-informed, and a lot of things I surmised on my own. Creyton's machinations were unknown to me, as well as Sanctum's plan to ignore Mylteer's counsel, and attempt to attack us in the night. I knew that Gamaliel wanted to burn this place down and usurp my spirit. But be aware that there was no way I'd get usurped, and there was no way this estate would get burned down, even if your sneak attack had come to fruition."

Now the Sanctum people looked horrified, and Jonah didn't blame them. Many scathing eyes turned to the four remaining members of the Network.

"That boy over there," Aloisa pointed at Spader. "Was he your source of the estate's weak points? You were never going to invite him into Sanctum, were you?"

The four remaining members of the Network said nothing. It wasn't necessary. Mason looked ready to chew bricks.

"Jonah," said Jonathan, "as I said, the Creyton element was pretty much new to me. These four—and G.J., of course—would follow any order given to them. But was Gamaliel working of his own volition?"

Jonah took a deep breath. It would have been too easy to say yes. Too easy. But just the thought of hiding it made him feel guilty. "Only partially, sir," he admitted. "He did want you gone, but he just wanted to vanquish you at first. The idea that he needed to usurp you, and lengthen his life came from Charlotte Daynard. She staged a phony rescue when Gamaliel saved her from a sazer or something, and then masqueraded around him calling herself Ms. Seedie. She was the one who drilled it into his head, convinced him that he needed to usurp you. That part was her. All a part of Creyton's big plan from the very start."

The Sanctum people looked deflated and stunned. Rheadne actually buried her face into her hands, and muttered, "My God."

Anna and Mick looked tense as hell. Cisor was awash with false calm. But Iuris was damn near irascible.

"This is why Mr. Kaine chose us!" he shouted to his Sanctum comrades. "None of you could have ever done what was necessary! And how did you," he turned his glare to Jonah, "become so informed? Even *we* didn't know about this Seedie woman. We know how Jonathan knows everything; the Deadfallen spawn over there kept him informed."

"Refer to me by that way again, Mason, and I will be your goddamned end of days," growled Trip.

Jonah ignored Trip's threat, since it wasn't aimed at him, for once, and was more than prepared to answer Mason's question, but the need to do so was nullified when a deep, unsteady voice said, "Me."

It was Gabriel. He appeared from nowhere and tossed down a twig, which he crunched under his foot.

"It took a while to get here," he explained. "When Jonah went into that bedroom, Terrence, Reena, and I got all thrown back or whatever. I wound up back in Florida. It was kind of disorienting, and I had to rest up. That's why I didn't use the *Astralimes,* Jonathan. I just didn't have the energy to focus."

"I understand, son," said Jonathan. "And I thank you for destroying that twig. We can't have loose ones around anymore, seeing as how Creyton has returned from the grave."

"Wait, what?" Gabriel's fatigued face shifted in seconds.

"It was you?" rasped Iuris. "You betrayed your own family? You duplicitous bastard!"

"My father betrayed the family by making this little clique in our midst," Gabriel fired back. He didn't look fully recovered from the revelation of Creyton's return, but Iuris' words must have been an infuriating distraction. "I know everything. I've got audio of every terrible thing you guys have done, even before my father was manipulated into wanting to usurp Jonathan's spirit." He showed them a box of old-school cassette tapes. "I knew about Miss Seedie. And I knew about your plans. But you didn't know that Pop got manipulated, too."

"That's entrapment!" said Anna in an annoyingly nasal voice.

"Look up that word, Anna," snapped Gabriel. "Actually, it's nothing of the kind. I didn't trick you guys into doing anything. You provided everything yourselves. I kept it a secret for so long because I didn't want to besmirch my father and brother's names. But since you're scheming played a part in almost starting a damn war, I had to prioritize."

Cisor looked at him in shock. "You want to take over Sanctum now, is that right?" The man didn't even try to conceal his doubt and disbelief. "You are the forgotten son of Gamaliel Kaine! No one will follow you!"

Rheadne wiped furious tears from her face, and walked to Gabriel. "I will."

"Me too," said Michael.

"Same," said Aloisa.

"Me too," said Vaughn, after a brief struggle with himself.

Many Sanctum people still didn't look too trusting of the estate residents, but it was nothing at all compared to the way they regarded the treacherous quadrangle of Iuris, Cisor, Anna, and Mick. A bunch of them murmured that they would support Gabriel, and all of them backed away from the foursome, which made them look more isolated than ever.

"You've done the right thing, Gabriel," said Jonathan. "But I cannot imagine how difficult it was."

"It is torture," admitted Gabriel. "It's hell, more accurately."

"I know, son," said Jonathan, with a hand on Gabriel's shoulder. "But eventually, the feeling of venom in your system will pass. I can assure you of that."

Jonah looked at Terrence, who mouthed, "*These people are messed up!*" and then at Reena, who was about to shake her head before her eyes widened in horror.

"JONATHAN!" she shouted.

Jonah wheeled around. Iuris had yanked a knife from the ground, and charged at Jonathan once he'd turned his back to him. He would never get there in time; not even Reena would be fast enough—

But their attempts were unnecessary.

Just when Iuris was seconds away from vanquishing Jonathan, the Protector Guide whipped around and caught the blade. He literally blocked the attack by grabbing the blade. Lifeblood dripped from the cut it made (Jonah still marveled at the fact that spirits still bled), but Jonathan was otherwise unharmed. Everyone who witnessed it looked shocked, but none more so than Iuris. The rage in Jonathan's eyes made Jonah step back. He'd be damned if he got caught up in a warpath.

"You continue to test me, boy," Jonathan whispered. "You cannot seem to realize that I can kill you if I so desired. But I'm not going to. I would never demean myself by lowering to such a cowardly act."

"Suck it, spirit," growled Iuris.

Faster than blinking, Jonathan lowered his lifeblood-covered hand from the knife blade to Iuris' wrist, and squeezed. It snapped like dry wood. Iuris roared as he dropped the knife, and clutched his injury. But the man still had the audacity to be defiant. Jonah shook his head. Some people just never learned. Should Jonathan have broken his face instead?

"What do you want me to do?" he whispered. "Apologize? Kneel?"

"No," saidd Jonathan. "I don't want you to kneel. I want you to stand. Tall, strong, and resolute. I want you to be a man, for the first time in your life. Because if you are anything less—if you show any weakness at all—then I assure you, Iuris Mason, that you will be fodder on The Plane with No Name."

Jonathan blinked, and spectral fetters bound Iuris', Cisor's, Mick's, and Anna's hands. They were even shackled to each other.

"That is where I'm taking you personally," Jonathan added.

Anna whimpered. Jonathan clucked his tongue.

"I just said strength is what you need, Anna," he reminded her.

It was at this moment that some of the doubting eyes on Jonathan began to change into ones of respect. Or fear. One could hardly tell.

"I am re-issuing the blessing of haven to you," said Jonathan to Sanctum's group at large. "Rest, and don't a single one of you even think about leaving. There are more things that need to be said. To my own students, I will be back in two days and seventeen hours. I know that is an oddly specific amount of time, but please do not ask me why. The trek to The Plane with No Name is a tricky one when you've got prisoners in tow. When I return, we will all discuss Creyton being physically alive—*again*—and what that will mean for all of our futures. Cassius, I want you to preside over Family Court to deal with Spader. Fairly, objectively—you are aware of what to do."

"Yes, sir," said Reverend Abbott.

"Leave Jonah alone tonight," Jonathan continued to everyone else. "I'm sure he'll be much more sociable later on, but let him rest. Rest yourselves while you're at it. That includes you, too, Terrence and

Reena." Finally, Jonathan looked at Jonah. It seemed that all of his negative emotions faded. He looked so sympathetic and paternal that it was almost hard to believe that he had just snapped someone's wrist. "Jonah, we will speak further when I return, but what I will say to you right now is this: If you ever, *ever* had any doubts about your worth as a man, a friend, and Eleventh Percenter—*anything*—let your performance tonight serve as a testament to how rare and invaluable you are to us. Peace and blessings."

Jonah had no words for that, so he just nodded. Jonathan nodded back, and he and his four prisoners vanished.

The groups began to disperse. Liz walked to Jonah and grabbed his hand. Jonah didn't even feel awkward; he knew she simply wanted to treat him more thoroughly. Reena put a hand on Jonah's shoulder, but then they were all distracted by a wintry voice that rose above all the muttering.

"That's it?"

It was Penelope. Everyone looked at her with confusion.

"That's it?" she repeated. "Jonathan speaks his piece, and you just blindly follow like slaves?"

"Look who's talking," murmured Terrence.

"Nels, let's just go," said Rheadne, who grabbed Penelope's wrist, but she wrenched it out of reach.

"No! These assholes are happy to see us like this! They're pleased that we've been turned inside out!"

Reena let go of Jonah's shoulder.

"Reena, let her run her mouth," hissed Liz, but Reena ignored her.

"You know what, Pulchrum?" she said to her face. "Were it not for us *assholes*, you would probably be bleeding on this lawn, with a javelin through your right eye. We've saved everyone and now we have a common enemy. You've survived. You've got a strange, strange way of showing gratitude."

She turned away, but Penelope glared at her still.

"You would know all about strange, wouldn't you, Sodom and Gomorrah—"

Reena whirled around and uppercut her. Penelope flew through the air, and actually lost one of her shoes as she landed in a heap on the ground. Reena spat at her feet.

"Told you I'd get you back, bitch," she grumbled.

"Hell yeah!" screeched Terrence. "First round, knockout, bi—!" Then he saw Reverend Abbott's stern eyes on him. "Sorry, Reverend. Mama taught me better than that. Piping down, now."

Jonah didn't even bother with Terrence's words. He looked at the people of Sanctum Arcist. What a drastic transformation they'd undergone over the course of this. They were all so confident, so strong in their convictions, so fiercely loyal to their leader. Now they were a deflated, confused, leaderless group who didn't know what to do. It was a sad thing to behold. It made him think of what Rheadne told him that night in her tent. Now her words had come to life.

"Wolves without an Alpha," he mumbled.

"What was that, Jonah?" asked Reena.

"Nothing, Reena." Jonah turned and allowed Liz to take his hand again. "Nothing."

* * *

"Liz."

Liz wouldn't meet Jonah's eyes. Not even when she properly set his jaw, attended to the knot on his head, or dabbed at the wounds that Jessica's punches made on his face with some tonic that smelled like Pine-Sol. The wound had begun to close, and things began to mend. But she wouldn't meet his eyes.

"Liz."

She turned away and reached for her satchel of vials. "I'm sorry you had to take Tenth painkillers," she said in an oddly formal voice. "I have the materials here that would have eliminated the need. But you're well on your way now."

"Liz, you—"

"Your jaw is fixed," Liz went on, "and you won't have the headache anymore. You had a mild concussion, but I've handled that for you, too.

You just need to stay awake for a bit. Don't do anything to strenuous with your face for a little while, either—"

"Elizabeth!" Jonah whipped her around and grabbed her shoulder. "It's fine! You've saved me in more ways than one tonight. Now what is wrong with you?"

Liz couldn't take it anymore. The damn burst, and she was sobbing. "Jonah, you'd have never gotten away if it weren't for one tiny thing, and I don't know how to feel about that," she got out. "I—you are my big brother, one of my dearest friends. And if you hadn't escaped—if Creyton had gotten you—"

Jonah wrapped her in a tight embrace. "But he didn't," he told her. "I'm good, Liz."

Jonah was anything but, but Liz needed to hear it. Bobby walked into the infirmary and saw them. Thankfully, he understood and wasn't suspicious. Jonah met his gaze.

"*You'll handle it?*" he mouthed.

"*Yeah,*" Bobby mouthed back. "*I got it.*"

He detached himself from Liz, thanked her again, and left the infirmary. Reena and Terrence were waiting.

"I just wanted to say goodnight, and try to balance your dreams," said Reena hastily. "That was it, I swear."

"I'm gonna make the biggest breakfast for you tomorrow morning, man," said Terrence. "A pound of bacon, a loaf of toast, the works—"

"Will you come on?" said Reena, annoyed. She pulled Terrence, who put up a bit of a fight.

"Want some banana pancakes, Jonah?" he persisted. "Spanish omelet?"

"If you don't come on," snapped Reena, who finally succeeded in pulling Terrence with an ungracious yank.

Jonah adored his brother and sister. But he was ready to put this night behind him.

If that were possible.

He reached his bedroom door, pushing his emotions as far down as they would go. He hoped that sleep would be tolerable.

But his bedroom was already occupied.

Vera was seated on his bed. She had the same look that Liz had had on her face; like she couldn't decide whether to be relieved at his survival, or terrified about his near miss. She looked as though she'd been crying at some point as well, but unlike Liz, she'd gotten herself under control.

"Vera?" Jonah was a little more than surprised by her presence. He hadn't been one of her favorite people lately. "What are you doing here?"

"Whatever I want, Jonah," murmured Vera, but there was no heat in her voice. "I'm a big girl, remember?"

When they made eye contact, then it finally hit Jonah. He'd been unfair to Vera.

No, she was not his girlfriend, so technically speaking, he didn't owe her anything.

But they didn't live in a technical world. He had been unfair to her.

Jonah had always hated the men who disrespected women, and then realized what they had done after the fact. And then he'd turned around and done the same damned thing. This was just great.

"Vera, I—"

"Don't, Jonah." The edge was back in Vera's voice. "Seriously, do not. It isn't necessary, and at this point, wouldn't help a damn thing."

Jonah fell silent, for a moment, but he couldn't leave well enough alone. "You don't have to be here if you don't want to," he said.

Vera focused on him, in a way that only she could. "If this is where you'll be, then this is where I'll be," she told him.

She turned on his bed, and invited him to lie across her lap. Jonah cautiously complied, and Vera began to rub the back of his head, carefully avoiding the bandages that Liz had placed at his temple, and on his face. Jonah knew that he should just relax, but he ventured once more.

"Are we—is all forgiven?" he asked her. "What does this mean?"

Vera's inhaled through her nostrils, and closed her eyes. "It means lie here, shut up, and just *be* here with me," she told him. "We don't have to talk. Let's just...be."

"I can do that," said Jonah.

So there they sat, in silence. Vera used one hand to rub Jonah's head, and the other was draped across his chest. It was the hand that he always held—sometimes accidentally, and sometimes on purpose. Experimentally, he inched his fingers nearer, so as to lock them with Vera's. She didn't object.

Jonah closed his eyes, and allowed true relief to wash over him. Reena had said that it would take a miracle. While he wished that it hadn't been Creyton's resurrection, he still found solace in being back in Vera's good graces.

27

Family Court

Gamaliel Kaine, Sr. Gamaliel Kaine, Jr. Anders Langton Anthony George Noble

The four names were displayed on four glossy teak place markers in the cemetery near the Glade. Jonah looked at them solemnly. Reena placed a hand on his shoulder, but said nothing. Terrence tried very hard to mask his confusion, but eventually lost the battle.

"Jonah," he said, "you *hated* Langton and the Ant guy! And everyone here hated Kaine and G.J. Why does it bother you so much? I mean, it's screwed up the way things went down, but let's face facts. None of them were decent people."

Jonah sighed, his eyes never leaving the markers. "They meant something to somebody," he said quietly. "They were all someone's father, someone's brother, and someone's son. Jonathan says that all life happens for a reason, and I believe him. They were torn away from their physical lives for no other cause than evil. No, they didn't have any redeeming qualities, but it still doesn't change the fact that they were worth something to someone."

"Well said, Jonah," said Reena. "Very well said."

Terrence looked mutinous, but sighed. "It's a pretty cool display," he remarked. "How did Malcolm score the teak?"

"Didn't ask," said Jonah. "Didn't matter."

Terrence nodded. "Do you want to talk about it?"

Jonah knew what he meant, but shook his head. "No point till Jonathan comes back and we have our big discussion."

Terrence nodded again, looking at the place markers. "I would salute and tell them rest tranquilly and all that," he said, "but... yeah."

Jonah and Reena didn't respond. They felt the same way.

Jonah straightened. "No point staying here anymore," he said to his friends. "We are due in court soon."

Jonah figured that this whole Family Court thing would be an informal façade where Spader got rebuked, proverbially slapped on the wrist, and sent along.

Nope.

The setting was a beautiful library off the hall where Jonathan's study was located. Every estate resident fit comfortably in there, and this was not being treated as a laughing matter. Everyone was dressed casually. Reverend Abbott wasn't wearing his pastoral robe, but his stark-white shirt, black tie, matching suspenders, and slate-grey slacks almost made Jonah want to gear up for a sermon.

Spader sat in the center of the group, and looked very uncomfortable in a red shirt and black slacks. He still had the black and blond-spiked hair, and he hadn't shaved. Jonah thought the whole get up could have been done better, but shrugged. Spader could have been a Ralph Lauren model and still be contemplated as scornfully as he was now.

As Jonah, Terrence, and Reena took their seats, Jonah surveyed his friends. Many people looked angry and displeased with Spader, but he could feel that all of their minds were on the same thing. It was the elephant in the room; the subject that no one wanted to breach yet wanted to discuss. Jonah himself wondered what Creyton was doing now; what fresh hell he had planned for the Earth and Astral Planes. He still couldn't believe that the man had come back from the grave. He was the first Eleventh Percenter to ever have done that. And his entire attention was on Jonah?

And Jessica. She had played Jonah so well. He'd always prided himself on seeing through the bullshit, but he had dropped the ball *spectac-*

ularly with her. He'd always hated Jessica; viewed her as a solipsistic, conniving, self-serving slut. But he never *imagined* that she was an Eleventh Percenter, let alone Inimicus. He remembered how Malcolm had described Inimicus when they'd discussed the matter: Inimicus was more complicated than just the devil you didn't know. It was the devil you *didn't* know you didn't know. The one you wouldn't see coming in a million lifetimes.

Damn if Malcolm hadn't been on the money with that one.

"Order," said Reverend Abbott in his all-encompassing voice. "Family Court will now commence. For those of you who are not familiar with the concept, Family Court is a process that the Protector Guides can employ in the event that a resident has engaged in activities that threaten the physical lives of an entire dwelling place, which in this case, is the estate. In many ways, Jonathan is allowed to police the estate as he sees fit, since the Spirit Guides trust his counsel and fair dealings. We will do Family Court as though he were here. As this is not traditional Tenth Law, or even Eleventh Law for that matter, there are no lawyers, no jury. Simply us. I listen to arguments from people who have already been chosen to speak, and then a decision is made on how to proceed, which I can either approve or deny. Royal will comply with the decision that we make once arguments are concluded. Failure to comply will get the matter bumped up to a hearing with the Phasmastis Curaie. And I assure you, son, that that will be a much harder process. Do you understand?"

Spader looked like a frightened lamb in the midst of deliberately starved lions. Which come to think of it, was exactly what he was. He nodded. "Yeah."

"Pardon me?" said Reverend Abbott, who narrowed his eyes.

"Yes, sir," murmured Spader.

"Very well," said Reverend Abbott. "Now, we hear the viewpoints of your peers."

The chosen residents pulled no punches, though a few tried to be objective. Several people spoke, but a few stuck out amongst the group.

Douglas: "Spader wanted to defect to Sanctum Arcist, and allowed himself to be seduced by promise of a place there. In my personal opinion, someone blind, deaf, and dumb could have seen through the ruse with no issue. The fact that Spader has gamed innumerable people over the years and didn't realize it when it happened to him makes this situation even worse. It's almost like he wanted to branch out with his gambling and start gambling *lives*."

Magdalena: "Spader was quick to defend those idiots the second they got out of line. Forget the fact that they promised him a place; it was like he was already one of them in action and spirit! He disregarded the people that knew him all for so-called greener pastures. He was the only one they allowed in their camp after old man Kaine distanced them from us! Since he acted like he was one of them, then I say treat him as such."

Malcolm: "I've known Royal since he was twelve years old, and during those years, he has shown himself to be a capable and sharp young man. The argument of what he is can go on for a good while, but the thing that we can all agree on is that he is not stupid. He is an intelligent person who made a stupid choice. I feel that this should be a lesson, not a crucifixion."

Jonah was fascinated that Malcolm had spoken so much at once, but in his attempt to be fair, he had inadvertently handed Liz bullets, which she shot with such unbridled zeal that he was surprised that she wasn't salivating as she spoke.

Liz: "Malcolm, my sister will be sixteen on May 14th, which is a very impressionable age. But even midway through adolescence, Nella wouldn't have exposed people she calls her friends to such potential carnage! We could have experienced butchery of unknown proportions because of Spader's stupid choice, and that's exactly what Creyton would have wanted! I would have been suspicious the second those people asked me about parts of my home that weren't fortified! Malcolm, you know that I'm with you on many things, but I refuse to excuse Spader because he is young. If young people can be lauded for doing great things, then they can be punished for doing terrible things."

The situation was compounded even further by Trip. Even though he'd played a huge hand in protecting everyone, he still hadn't changed one iota in personality. His brief, simple statement was evidence of that.

Trip: "Fuck the little bastard. Throw the book at him, and since we're in a library, that could be literal if you choose to make it so."

Reverend Abbott rolled his eyes. "Thank you, Titus," he said. "That was quite insightful. As a matter of fact, it was a little too insightful for me to entertain. Therefore, it's stricken from the record."

Trip sneered as usual, but that didn't alarm Reverend Abbott in the slightest.

"Do you have anything to add, Robert?" he asked Bobby.

Bobby swallowed. At the estate, Bobby could have been considered the closest thing that Spader had to a friend, which was laughably ironic considering that he was dating the woman that Spader wanted so badly. He glanced at Liz, whose upper lip twitched as she hatefully regarded Spader. "Funny thing," he said slowly, "but I don't think my opinion would weigh either side."

Jonah snorted. If he had defended Spader, he'd have incurred Liz's wrath. So he remained neutral. Smart man.

"What I would like to hear, though," Bobby went on, "is Spader's piece."

Spader blinked. Bobby looked at him pointedly.

"They're killing you, man," he said. "Jonathan said that this had to be objective. That can't happen if you sit there like a knot on a log, not saying anything."

Spader swallowed massively. "I don't know what to say, Bobby," he muttered. "I fu—sorry, Reverend—messed up. I thought they liked me, and appreciated my input. That was refreshing. But I got screwed. I was blind, just like Doug said. Do what you gotta do."

Jonah's eyes widened. Why was Spader allowing himself to be devoured like this? It was almost as if he didn't care. Was he that depressed that Iuris and Cisor screwed him? He couldn't be this indifferent.

Bobby looked frustrated, but sat down. Reverend Abbott gave him a curious look (probably because he knew why he withheld his opinion), but sighed.

"Suggestions for disciplinary actions?" he asked.

"Banishment," said Magdalena without hesitation. "Send him home to his parents and siblings."

"Ethereal boot camp with the Spectral Law trainees," said Douglas.

"Two weeks on The Plane with No Name," said Benjamin.

"Two months in the sazer underground," said Alvin.

"A part-time gig scrubbing toilets at my high schools," said Terrence.

"How about banish him, send him to the sazer underground, do the S.P.G. boot camp, the two weeks on The Plane with No Name, and conclude with the toilets?" suggested Liz.

Jonah stood up. He couldn't take it anymore. This was had long surpassed vicious. His friends didn't realize how blinded by anger they were.

Reverend Abbott raised an eyebrow. "Jonah?"

"Reverend, I need to say something, but I realize that you're the one in power here," said Jonah. "For that reason, may I approach you, and run something by you, please?"

Reverend Abbott nodded, and beckoned him forward. Jonah ignored the eyes on him, because they didn't matter. When he reached Reverend Abbott, he leaned in and went over what he wanted him to approve. Reverend Abbott listened with rapt attention, and was receptive to Jonah's plan.

"I will allow you to proceed, Jonah," he said. "You have the green light to address everyone."

"Thank you, sir," said Jonah.

He turned to face his fellow residents, and cracked his neck muscles. "Guys, listen to yourselves. My goal is not to anger anyone here, but I really want to know whether or not you guys hear yourselves right now? None of those punishments will work! Creyton has returned from the grave. Do you get that? He did a leap-frog from Spirit. That was supposed to be impossible. There is no telling what he and his damn disciples are about to put the ethereal world through. And you want to throw one of our residents out in the cold?"

The reminder of Creyton's return gave some people pause. Some of the angry faces went a little slack. But Jonah continued.

"It would be a different thing if Spader *wanted* to leave; that'd be another matter altogether," he said. "But you guys are talking about the banishment and grievous punishment of an eighteen-year old Eleventh into an ethereal world that is now littered with Deadfallen disciples? No. I wouldn't suggest that be done to you, and I don't think we should do it to Spader. I personally say that he stays, where we can help him. Where we can help each other."

The only ones that looked angry were Trip, Karin, and Markus. But what else was new? Jonah had reached everyone one else. Even Liz looked a little sheepish now. But she was quicker to recover than the others were.

"Jonah, *something* has got to be done," she insisted. "He can't just go scot-free. His mistakes almost unleashed hell on us."

"Very true, Liz," said Jonah, "but I've got a plan that I've just discussed with Reverend Abbott here, and he's fine with me throwing it out to you guys. It's a solution, not a punishment."

The residents looked around in surprise. Jonah glanced back at Reverend Abbott, who mouthed, "*Go on. You have my approval.*"

"Alright, here goes." Jonah looked at Spader, whose face was a mask of false calm. "I'm not an expert, but I've watched more TV than I care to admit. There is a common theme in certain shows and movies. When a guilty party is about to get what's coming to him or her, they grab a stash of money, and blaze right before the hammer is dropped."

Spader's mouth opened slightly. It was the first emotion he'd shown through his mask.

"Spader is a compulsive gambler," continued Jonah, "but remarkably, his schemes usually work. I am not dumb enough to believe that

Spader hasn't been stashing money since at least his early adolescence. Am I right, Spader?"

Spader's face was an emotionless mask again. Jonah shook his head. This little bum was employing a poker face. No problem.

"Reena, would you help me, please?" asked Jonah.

"My pleasure, Jonah." Reena grinned, and pulled off her dampener.

Jonah grinned himself, and turned back to Spader. "How much have you stashed, Spader?" he asked. "Five thousand?"

Spader said nothing.

"Ten thousand?"

Nothing. Jonah felt his eyebrows rise.

"Fifteen thousand?" he asked. "Twenty thousand?"

Spader remained poker-faced, but Reena perked up.

"Ding!" she announced. "Somewhere thereabouts. He tried to keep it from me by leveling out his emotions, but they have nothing to do with his essence."

Spader rolled his eyes, and swore under his breath. Surprise rippled through the group, and Jonah was no different.

"Twenty thousand dollars?" he exclaimed. "Spader, what have you been doing? You are eighteen years old! You're a hustler! You don't have a business!"

"That's the beauty of it," muttered Spader. "Who needs a business to make money? Getting money's easy for me."

Jonah briefly wondered how his late adolescence would have been if he'd had twenty thousand dollars at that time. But he filed those thoughts away. "I'm glad that you think getting money is easy, Spader, because you'll need that gift later on."

"How you figure?" frowned Spader.

Jonah grinned. "You're going to fund Nella's group's trip to Valentania York."

"What?" said Nella, eyes wide.

"*What?*" said Spader, eyes wide.

"You heard me, Spader," said Jonah.

Spader looked calculating. "So, what? You want me to supplement the funds they've raised? That's nothing. Whatever. I could do that in my sleep."

"Uh-uh." Jonah shook his head. "You're funding the whole thing."

Residents snickered. Spader abandoned his new poker face.

"Say what!"

"The whole thing," repeated Jonah. "Food, room and board, trans—the whole nine yards."

"How many girls are in Nella's club?" cried Spader.

"Fourteen!" answered Nella. "Plus our teachers and chaperones!"

"But they've raised funds on their own!" protested Spader.

"It can stay in their treasury," said Jonah. "Or they can get souvenirs with some of it when they get there. I don't care. And since you won't possibly spend all of your stash on the trip, whatever you have left can go to—somebody help me out here—"

"The Brown Bag food clinic up in town," suggested Douglas. "My cousins and I volunteer there sometimes, and they always need money for food. They're in need of some financial sustenance right now, as a matter of fact."

Jonah smirked. "How does that sound to all of you guys?"

"I'm good with it," murmured Douglas.

"I suppose that's fair," muttered Magdalena.

"Cool on my end," said Malcolm.

"Fairer than anything *I* had in mind," grunted Liz.

Jonah nodded, and returned his gaze to Spader. "It's on you now, man."

Spader looked as though he'd swallowed a bottle of turpentine. "You're talking about wiping out my entire stash, Jonah," he whispered.

"Just like your actions almost wiped out physical lives, Spader," countered Jonah. "This arrangement won't be as costly as that. No more runaway stash, man. You're one of us, like it or not. Like I said, I just ran it by Reverend Abbott, and he is cool with it. You can take our deal, or take your chances with the Curaie."

Spader took several deliberate breaths. "Fine," he said through clenched teeth.

Nella cheered in utter delight. "This is amazing!" she squealed. "Valentania York! I have to call Kayla! Marybeth! Elisa—"

"Nellaina!" hissed Liz.

Nella paused, remembering that she was in a serious situation. "Sorry," she blushed. "I'm... gonna sit down now."

Reverend Abbott smiled. "Very well," he said. "Fair and objective, just like Jonathan desired. Family Court is adjourned."

Jonathan returned at almost the exact time that he said he would, and he immediately gathered Sanctum Arcist and the estate residents in the courtyard for one final time, as the Sanctum contingent would return to Florida once he was done. When they'd all convened, Jonah noticed that a few of Sanctum's people sat among the residents. Michael and Aloisa preferred the estate residents' company, and Rheadne sat rather neutrally. Penelope and many others remained segregated. Jonah laughed when he saw Penelope wearing a hood and sunglasses, because he knew exactly why. Reena's uppercut had broken her jaw, swollen an eye shut, and, inexplicably, mildly lacerated her tongue. Jonah was also now well aware of the damages that facial punches could do, but he'd gotten punched five times in the face with a fist encased in endowment-powered wrapping. Penelope got hit once. Lightweight.

Granted, Reena was significantly stronger than she looked. But Penelope was still a lightweight.

Jonathan gave Bast and Laura some instructions, and both of them scampered off. He then put a hand to his temple, looking troubled as could be. Jonah couldn't help but notice that even though Jonathan was a spirit, there were moments where he looked physically alive. Even as a spectral life form, there were times when he was the most human of them all.

"I remember when Gamaliel was a boy of eight, and used to follow me everywhere I went," he said in a solemn voice. "One day, I was instructing him on the finer points of Auric shielding, and he asked me quite out of the blue how he could be a good man when he grew up. I told him that all he had had to do was stay on the right track. He asked me, 'How will I know which track is the right track?" and I told him, 'You'll always know the right track, because that will be the one with all the obstacles.' " He raised his eyes from the ground and surveyed the group. "I told you all that because we will all be facing obstacles now that Creyton has achieved Praeterletum. He slung-shot himself from the afterlife itself, and usurped an innocent man's spirit and body to fashion a new form for himself. His desire and need for minions is gone, and he has re-activated every integrated Deadfallen disciple he has at his command. There is no way to know what his plans are yet, or what his return from the grave has done to the natural order of the ethereal world. But I say to you, even with all of these obstacles, we are on the right track."

Jonah frowned, looking at Terrence and Reena. Some of the others looked around in puzzlement as well.

"Creyton sought to destroy us," he said. "He orchestrated his elaborate plan, and from an untrained eye's glance, one would think that his end goal was merely to return from the grave. He is the first Eleventh Percenter to have ever done so, after all. But his end goal was multilayered. Not only was it his resurrection, it was also our annihilation of each other, so that he and his disciples could reap our spirits. Why did he want to do that? It's hilariously simple. Because we are a threat."

Those words got a lot of people's attention. Jonathan moved closer to them. His troubled expression gave way to determination.

"Your very existence is a vital threat to Creyton's occupation in the ethereal world," he insisted. "He wanted us to destroy each other for that reason. He cut open old wounds; he even created new ones in the process. But his grand plan failed. And that lets me know that we have right on our side. But by no means is that enough. The new question is this. What will you do now?"

Jonathan's expression looked close to supplicating to Jonah. It was in that moment that he realized just how uncharted these waters were. It filled him with a fear of the unknown.

Again.

"Gamaliel was a powerful, influential Eleventh Percenter," said Jonathan. "He was a dear friend of mine for such an infuriatingly short period of time. I freely admit that the anger I had for the damage he wrought hadn't abated. But I never entertained the notion of revenge. Gamaliel allowed an unfounded paranoia to completely ruin him. The time that he spent plotting demises was time that he could have spent enjoying his family or appreciating elderly life with well-deserved rest. But his fears and paranoia allowed one of Creyton's disciples to convince him to commence a course of events that not only destroyed him, but also his oldest son."

Jonah saw some people tear up. Some of Sanctum's people tried the whole hardened and emotionless thing, but they failed. Gabriel shared no tears of course, but he looked so lost and woebegone that Jonah felt like he ought to buck his natural reactions and let the tears fall just this once.

"I did not say that to criminalize Gamaliel, because that helps nothing at this point," said Jonathan. "I said it to show you that life is a gift. One of the truest blessings in this world. An even greater gift is the fact that you have the free will to live your life as you see fit. Now that Creyton has returned, will you live your life in fear, or will you take a stand? And more importantly, would you allow yourselves to stand together?"

Those words jolted people. They looked among themselves: the family unit that was now slightly augmented with new friends and the defiantly segregated mass, bent on harboring archaic hostilities. Jonah thought that Jonathan's wish would take an act of divine intervention. But the Protector Guide looked more hopeful than the rest of them.

"This isn't a matter of possible, it's a matter of necessary," he said. "Many of the beliefs that we hold concerning each other have been given to you. Taught to you. Fed to you. Your ability to make your own choices has been compromised for too long. This can change. It *has* to change. Creyton banked on our misguided differences to destroy us. If that had happened, he would have blighted innumerable lives without lifting one finger."

The plea in Jonathan's eyes was now absolute. There was no mistaking it even if one tried.

"It is not my way to quote religious doctrine," he said, "because I believe wholeheartedly that paths of faith are best navigated alone, remaining a personal thing. But just this once, I will quote the book of First Peter, Chapter Three, Verse Eight: *Finally, be ye all of one mind, having compassion for one another, love as brethren, be sympathetic, be courteous.* Let that sink in. It is not a coincidence that Jonah escaped. It is not coincidence that the truth of everything is out now. It is not coincidence that Gabriel did everything in his power to stop his father's and brother's plans. We are all still here. Creyton was thwarted, and speaking as a former ally of his, he will not suffer that lightly. We survive only if we are a unit. Divided, we surely fall victim to the purest, most undiluted evil in existence. All I ask is that you allow rationale to prevail. Because if rationale prevails, so, too, shall we. Sanctum, safe travels. I will say until we meet again, because I have no interest in goodbyes."

They all rose. Several Sanctum people returned to the campsites in silence, while others stayed behind to say parting words to the estate residents. Jonah had half a mind to converse with Jonathan about other matters when someone tapped his shoulder.

It was Rheadne.

"Terrence, I think that Vaughn had some interest in your pecan waffle recipe," said Reena.

"Reena, anybody can put pecans in a waffle mix—oh." He got the point. "Oh. Right."

They walked off, leaving Jonah and Rheadne alone. After several awkward moments, Rheadne broke the silence.

"I really fucked up, didn't I?"

"Oh yeah," Jonah agreed. "No need to sugar-coat it."

Rheadne rolled her eyes, but she seemed angrier and more frustrated with herself than anything. "Would it mean anything if I apologized?"

The speech that Jonathan had just given them splashed across Jonah's mind as he considered the question. "I suppose so," he said finally. It was something, at the very least.

"Maybe we can try this again someday," said Rheadne.

Jonah looked at her. "Maybe."

She narrowed her eyes. "Are you just saying that to placate me?"

"No, Rheadne, I'm not," said Jonah, and he meant it. "In light of recent events, I have learned never to say never. But I know that at this moment in time, you, me, Gabriel—all of us have a lot of soul-searching to do before anybody can consider attachments."

Rheadne's face relaxed. "There is more truth in that than a little," she said. "It's been an interesting experience getting to know you, Jonah. All things considered. For the record, I don't regret a single second of our time together."

"I don't, either, Rheadne," said Jonah. "I regret the fallout."

Rheadne nodded, and kissed Jonah. The contact was nothing major or ostentatious. It just was what it was. Then, she left for the campsite to gather her belongings. Jonah saw Vera, who scornfully watched Rheadne's every step. He hoped that she realized that he'd done nothing to initiate that kiss, but when she glanced at him, there was no coldness or anger in her features. Good news.

"You alright?" asked Terrence.

Jonah turned around, and his eyebrows rose. "How did you—?"

"I was able to shake Reena off because Jonathan had to talk to her about something," said Terrence. "But seriously—are you alright?"

Jonah sighed. "That might be a bit broad," he replied, "but some things are looking up."

Terrence shook his head. "Still a fine-ass woman, though."

"A misguided, misinformed, in-need-of-clarity fine-ass woman," said Jonah.

"Semantics," dismissed Terrence. "But now she's gonna go back to Sanctum, where she'll probably link up with Gabriel—"

"I wouldn't be so sure," said that deep voice, and they turned to see Gabriel behind them.

"Why do you say that, Gabe?" said Terrence.

"I just lost my dad and oldest brother," said Gabriel. "I got responsibilities to Mom and Gabby. And the Curaie's going to have Sanctum under investigation and scrutiny for...who knows how long. None of us know what's going to happen. Suffice it to say, I've got a lot of things to sift through before I could ever try to give proper attention to a woman."

Jonah hated it, but he pitied Gabriel. The look on Terrence's face showed that he did as well. His father and older brother were gone, which had to have hit him hard, and that was compounded by the fact that he still had to deal with the emotions that he had concerning the years of maltreatment and neglect from them. And they guy was still so young. "Gabe, I think you'll come out of this stronger than before. Losing family is rough. I won't deny that. But you have to make your own decisions now. You can't waste any more time in your life wondering what your father or G.J. would have done. You can't live for anyone. Not Sanctum, not even your mother and Gabrielle. Just you."

Gabriel lowered his head. "You say that like it's an easy thing."

"Look, man," Jonah was just a little worked up now, "I was your age not *too* long ago. I didn't have as much sense as I thought I had back then, but I had more sense than people gave me credit for. The same is true of you. You've just never had the chance to showcase it. Now is that time. You've got a great head on your shoulders, man. You'll be great."

Terrence nodded, impressed. Jonah mouthed, "*Shut up.*"

Gabriel managed a small smile. He had a long road ahead, but Jonah truly believed that he'd come out better on the other end.

"This is for you."

Gabriel handed Jonah some type of paper wrapping. Curious, Jonah tore it open, and his eyes widened. They were his batons.

"Are you kidding me right now?" he exclaimed. "How did you get them?"

"Well, Creyton and the Deadfallen disciples had to clear out of that house once you'd escaped," said Gabriel. "When Jonathan told me that you had sacrificed your batons, I went to the place that matched the description you gave him. Pop may have ignored me, but that didn't stop me from picking up his evidence-retrieving skills."

Jonah just regarded them with awe. It felt good to have them back. They felt like extensions of his hands. "I can't thank you en—"

"Don't even worry about thanking me." Gabriel looked adamant on the matter. "Consider it atonement for the fallacies of my family. That's all we'll say about it, deal?"

He turned, took three steps, but then whirled around like he'd forgotten something.

"Pop was wrong about you," he said.

"I'm sorry?" said Jonah, puzzled.

"He said that your skill and worth would always be in question because Jonathan was the one that found you, not him," said Gabriel. "But seeing some of the things you've done…Jonathan clearly is doing something right here."

Jonah had no words for that, but Gabriel wasn't expecting a response. He simply gave a two-fingered salute and left.

Reena rejoined them, looking strangely nervous.

"What's up with you?" asked Terrence.

"I—I'll tell you later," said Reena with a steadying breath. "Let's just see these guys off right now, okay?"

Terrence would have probably prodded (and Jonah would have helped him do so), but at that moment, they overheard Michael Pruitt conversing with Spader.

"I truly don't want to go back to Sanctum," the guy was saying. "You guys have it together here."

Spader sort of shrugged. "Well, you guys have to rebuild and all, you know?" he said. "I guess that you can only go forward with new approaches and all that. You, Aloisa, Rheadne, Gabriel—you can help the rebuilding effort. That requires being there."

"You're not coming with us?" asked Michael. "You would be more than welcome to do it now; no invites under false pretenses, or anyone using you. I don't doubt that we could use your help bouncing back from this mess."

"Nah," Spader shook his head. "You've got a decent group already. My zone is right here."

Michael nodded. "Worth a shot. Hopefully, we'll see you again soon."

He shook hands all around with Spader, Jonah, Terrence, and Reena, and then joined Aloisa in taking down their tents. Jonah looked at Spader with surprise, but it was Terrence who spoke.

"That was cool stuff, Spader," he remarked. "There is hope for you yet."

Spader rolled his eyes. "I'm touched," he muttered. "Now if you'll excuse me, I have to get my hair trimmed, and change into more casual clothes."

"What for?" asked Jonah.

"For all intents and purposes, you." Spader shook his head again. "Since I've bankrupted myself, the man that runs the Brown Bag food clinic invited me to dinner with his family. And that ain't all. Tomorrow, Nella's club is treating me to a dinner that they made for me. I'm their guest of honor. The cover story is that, after years of poor choices, I'm bettering myself by giving back. So, you've made me a damn hero, Jonah. Thank you, oh so very much."

"There is honor in helping others, Spader," said Reena emphatically.

Spader regarded Reena with irritation. "I gave away every cent I had, and in return, I get two free meals, one cooked by a bunch of giggly girls. That's a great honor, Reena. Hooray."

Jonathan allowed everyone to have the next few days free of anything ethereal. Sanctum had been successfully seen off, with Jonathan telling them they were welcome back at any time, and to contact him if they needed anything. About a week after they'd left. Jonah, Terrence, and Reena were summoned to Jonathan's study. Jonah and Terrence had no idea what to expect, but Reena looked nervous all over again.

"Felix is with us," said Jonathan before anything else was said. "I told him that he would just have to cut back on his vampire hunting duties, and deal with Spirit Reapers for the foreseeable future. He grumbled, but that's immaterial; he's onboard. Prodigal is onboard, too. I've even gotten June Mylteer on our side."

"How did you manage that?" asked Jonah. "He actually admitted to disliking you."

"It turns out that he dislikes Creyton and the Deadfallen disciples more," replied Jonathan. "But that isn't the point of this meeting." He turned to Reena. "Reena, have you given thought to how to handle the task I've given you?"

Reena's hands were actually trembling. "Yes, sir. I—I have dinner plans, and I'm doing it tonight."

"Very well," nodded Jonathan. "You may go ready yourself."

Reena rose, and Jonah couldn't bear the suspense any longer.

"What is going on?" he asked.

Reena faced him and Terrence. There was a fear in her eyes that Jonah had never seen there. It even outstripped the fear she had when she'd seen the Haunts that time. "This is the night that I tell Kendall everything," she said. "The truth. About me, about you—all of us."

"What!" Jonah couldn't believe his ears. "Why?"

"Because if we are going to protect Kendall, or at least help in that regard, she can no longer be blind," replied Jonathan. "It would lead to awkward situations if she remained in the dark. She could have anonymous guards near her and think of them as people who wish her harm."

"I was already trying to figure out how to tell her," managed Reena, "but not because Creyton returned from the grave."

"But Jonathan," Terrence's voice was desperate for Reena's sake, "they got a great thing going! They've even crossed the whole *I love you* mountain and all that. This is a huge risk."

"It is, Terrence," concurred Jonathan. "But a love that risks nothing is nothing." He looked at Reena with concern in his eyes. Even though this was necessary, he wasn't heartless. "Good night, Reena, and good luck."

Reena nodded, steeled herself, and left. Jonathan focused on Terrence.

"Your mother came close to losing three of her sons," he said. "Alvin, Bobby, and you. When she was informed of Creyton's resurrection and what could have happened, she was understandably distraught. She wants the men in her family around her for more than a weekend. You might want to contact Lloyd as well, Terrence. Take time with your family. Keep your connections strong, and you shall be strong as well."

Terrence looked as though he hadn't fully realized the effect that things would have on his family. Jonathan's words hit him hard. "Mama, Dad...of course, sir. I'll get right to it."

He left, too. Jonathan then turned those piercing eyes on Jonah. He felt like he was going to be asked to bear his soul or something.

"Jonah, I cannot tell you how proud I am of you," began Jonathan. "You were outmatched, injured, and cornered. Yet when you made the decision that your physical life would not end in that accursed place...when you made up your mind to tell the truth and quell the potential war—you did not fall victim to Creyton's schemes. I applaud you, and I thank you."

"You thank me?" stared Jonah. "For what?"

Jonathan looked down at the Vitasphera, which had gotten even darker, and sighed. "You must remember, Jonah. I have seen true war on these lands. True carnage, true devastation. So many physical lives lost...and Creyton there, with his earliest disciples. It is something I wish to never see again. Trip and I had a hand in its prevention, but you revealed the full truth. For putting everything out there, and ending the threat of war with Sanctum Arcist completely, I thank you."

Jonah sat in silence for a few seconds before murmuring, "You're welcome, sir."

Jonathan rose. "Jonah, there is nothing that I can tell you that will change the fact that Creyton—*Thaine*—is back in this world," he said. "It has never happened before. This is truly unknown territory."

Jonah had already gone through this fifty times in his head. Deliberating about the days ahead would not help anything at all. He was going to tell Jonathan as much, but Jonathan continued speaking.

"You don't have to tell me that you've gone over it innumerable times in your head. I will tell you that you needn't worry. You are not isolated, alone, or any of the things that hampered you when you first encountered Creyton. You have grown much since then."

Jonah raised an eyebrow. "But I was already a man when you met me, Jonathan."

"You can be grown and still be a baby in many respects, son," smiled Jonathan. "Trust me on that. Now, there is one thing that I want you to do for me."

Jonah waited.

"When does your semester end?"

That wasn't the question that Jonah expected at all. "Um, May 8th."

"On the last day of your class, I want you to hit the road," said Jonathan.

Jonah frowned. "You want me to leave?"

"For the summer," nodded Jonathan. "A road trip befitting a college student."

"May I ask why?"

"Because I know how you feel," said Jonathan. "Your mind is teeming with racing thoughts, panicked emotions, justifications, and griefs. It would do you no good to be around people in that state, trying hard to fight through it while putting on a brave face for those around you."

Jonah said nothing. Jonathan hit the nail right on the head.

"So you will have the time to yourself," said Jonathan. "See some things, offset those thoughts. And you can return here anew, ready to take the next steps."

"Um," Jonah still didn't get something, "aren't you worried about Creyton going for me while I'm on the road?"

"Not at all," said Jonathan. "You set him back a mighty long way by escaping, Jonah. Creyton considers himself an artist, son. He considers his carnage in terms of masterpieces. Going for you now, so soon after you fouled up his *brilliant* plan, would be tantamount to a crayon and pastel throwaway to him. He won't come for you just yet. Trust me. I know Thaine well."

It was an interesting thing. Jonathan had worded the situation so well that Jonah's mindset went from resistance to the idea to it being one of the most important things he needed to do. How did Jonathan do that?

"I've got no problem with that, sir," he said.

* * *

The period between that night and the eighth of May was far from a smooth one.

Kendall hadn't taken the truth well. According to Reena, she'd left that dinner confused, frightened, and angry. She wouldn't return Reena's calls, nor would she even speak to Jonah when she saw him at LTSU. That wore on Jonah a little bit for two reasons. The first one was the fact that he'd always considered Kendall to be a cool person, who became a friend through her relationship with Reena. The second was the fact that he was burned out on women ignoring him. Reena was understandably distraught, and Jonah and Terrence kept their distance from her. Last thing they wanted was to be attacked because she didn't feel like being cheered up. Jonah felt a little annoyed at Jonathan (since it was his bright idea for Reena to reveal everything to Kendall), but the deed couldn't be undone.

Then, one Saturday near the end of March, Kendall pulled up at the estate as Jonah and Terrence were chopping wood to store in the woodshed, so that it could dry all year long. She looked at them, but wasn't up to a greeting.

"Is Reena here right now?" she asked.

"Yeah," said Jonah, "she's—"

"If she's here, then I know where she'll be," interrupted Kendall, not even breaking stride.

Jonah and Terrence looked at each other, but said nothing. What could they say?

They saw Reena the next morning, in far greater spirits than she'd been in the past few weeks. But she said nothing to them. Half the day passed before they confronted her.

"Did you and Kendall get to talk?" Jonah asked her.

"Yes," Reena replied.

"And?"

"All is well," said Reena.

Jonah and Terrence stared at her. "Go on."

Reena snorted. "I've gone as far as I'm willing to go. You want to go to lunch at the Chuck Wagon? I wouldn't mind a cheesesteaks, provided the bun is whole grain."

"Say what?" said Terrence, gaping at her. "A cheesesteak, Reena?"

Reena shrugged. "It's the weekend," she said. "Treat day, no?"

Jonah could have laughed. It was that type of party, huh? Well, so long as she was back on the same page with Kendall.

The next time Jonah saw Kendall (she'd left the estate while he was still asleep that past weekend) was at Two Cents, when she personally sought him out, requested privacy, and apologized to him for how she'd acted.

"You have to understand that I've never heard anything like what Reena told me, Jonah," she said. "It's straight off of *Supernatural*, or something. I needed time to think. Work it around in my head. It was just…unexpected. I didn't know how to react, but I probably could have done a better job than I did. But it did make one thing make sense."

"What was that?" asked Jonah.

"The way you guys reacted at Thanksgiving dinner, when I brought up Sanctum Arcist and sazers," said Kendall.

They shared a laugh over that, but then Kendall sobered somewhat.

"There are many things that I still don't understand," she admitted. "But you guys are awesome, and Reena has been nothing but wonderful to me since the moment we got together. I didn't want to throw that away. This Eleventh Percent thing is just another aspect that I'll love about her."

When Jonah recounted that story to Terrence, he just shook his head.

"You know, one day soon, I'll do awesome things like you and Reena," he said, "and then women will notice me."

"Now, Terrence," began Jonah, fearing a Rheadne flare-up on the horizon, but Terrence stopped him.

"Hey, I'm fine with it, truly," he told him. "Gives me something to aspire to. But you get to go to bed at night knowing that from a culinary standpoint, you can't touch me."

"I'll give you that," muttered Jonah. It was true, after all.

Spader had begun the unenviable task of regaining what little respect that he had around the estate prior to his blunder with Sanctum. It was not going well. The only people who bothered with him outside of Jonah, Terrence, and Reena were Alvin and Bobby, and Alvin only dealt with him because he wanted to learn how to play bridge. In Nella's eyes, Spader was a bit of a hero, if only a bit. She and her nursing club had returned from Valentania York full of wonder, thrills, and ideas, and she regaled them all. Spader returned to his disassembled lock whenever she brought it up, though.

"I funded it," he muttered to a laughing Bobby. "My investment in the subject ended there."

Jonah avoided thoughts of Creyton as much as he could, which was difficult when he was at school because he had to pass by the office which used to be Charlotte Daynard's. It sucked, because thoughts of Charlotte led not only to thoughts of Creyton, but thoughts of Jessica. He hated that woman almost as much as he feared Creyton. He found himself wanting a one on one with her, which was saying something. His grandmother had always stressed that laying violent hands on a woman was abhorrent, but she'd never met Jessica. He was certain that if she had, she would have gone across her face with her cane.

Before Jonah knew it, the semester was over, and it was time for his summer trip. He'd passed Ferrus' class with an A-minus, which was picture frame-worthy. He promised Jonathan (and himself) that he would do his best not to think of Creyton, Jessica, the other Dead-fallen disciples...any of it. When they reared themselves again, that would be the time to focus on them.

But not on this trip.

"Any idea where you're going?" asked Reena as Jonah dropped his bags in his car.

"A couple places," said Jonah. "Wilmington, Wrightsville Beach, Rhodanthe, Emerald Isle... maybe even North Myrtle Beach. Places where I'll hear ocean waves and not crickets."

"Don't get too comfortable out there in the Outer Banks," said Terrence seriously.

Jonah chortled. "This is home, Terrence. You know that."

"Drive safely, Jonah," said Reena.

"And avoid trouble," said Terrence, "unless it's fun."

Jonah laughed, bade goodbye to his brother and sister, and then got in his car and drove off. Part of him wished that he could have seen Vera before he left, but she was out of town with Liz and Nella. Ah, well. He'd have to text her or something.

It was when he stopped at the gas station to fill up his tank that he noticed something.

There was a flash card on the floor of the passenger side. It must have been on the seat when he'd driven from the estate. It read:

Jonah,
Stay out of trouble. Please. If danger rears itself, just walk in the other direction. Or drive or run. Whatever you need to do. Have fun and clear your head, since that's what you're supposed to be doing anyway.
Come back to m all of us soon.
Vera

Jonah looked at the scratched out *m,* and smiled. That was definitely something to keep his mind off of Creyton.

He filled up his gas tank, got in the car, and placed the flash card in the glove compartment. Then he buckled in and took the nearest exit for I-40 East.

About the Author

T.H. Morris was born in Colerain, North Carolina in 1984, and has been writing in some way, shape, or form ever since he was able to hold a pen or pencil. He relocated to Greensboro, North Carolina in 2002 for undergraduate education.

He is an avid reader, mainly in the genre of science fiction and fantasy, along with the occasional mystery or thriller. He is also a gamer and loves to exercise, Netflix binge, and meet new people. He began to write *The 11th Percent* series in 2011, and published book 1, *The 11th Percent*, in 2014, followed by book 2, *Item and Time*, in May of 2015, and book 3, *Lifeblood*, in November of 2015.

He now resides in Denver, Colorado, with his wife, Candace.

Connect Online!

Twitter: [@terrick_j](https://twitter.com/)
Email: Terrick.Heckstall@gmail.com
Author Page: www.facebook.com/authorthmorris
Website: 11thpercentseries.weebly.com

By T.H. Morris

The 11th Percent (The 11th Percent Series, Book 1)
Item and Time (The 11th Percent Series, Book 2)
Lifeblood (The 11th Percent Series, Book 3)

Coming Soon
Lifeblood (The 11th Percent Series, Book 3)
Grave Endowments (with Cynthia D. Witherspoon)